RIVER ROAD

The Beginning

by

Terry Bressler

ISBN-10: 0615653278
EAN-13: 9780615653273

Edited by Barbara Kalender Bressler
Skyline Publishing

This book is dedicated to
The Wine lovers of the World
Let's make a toast

"To life and to the beauty of life"®

THE BEGINNING

I never expected a second chance, but there I was flying up the Hudson River compliments of the Trans-el Recruiting Agency who recruited me for a position with the Sterling Chemical and Dye Company of New York. This company is owned by the Gruel International Wine Company and I was hoping to become their new CEO.

It had been five years since the terrorist attack on the World Trade Center and twenty-five years since I was last here.

While growing up in New York, I did not quite appreciate the beauty and majesty of all these incredibly tall buildings, but as I flew over them, I was overwhelmed thinking that all of this was created by man.

Let me introduce myself. My name is Ron Slater, a forty eight year old, washed up executive in the United States sinking textile industry. If I sound mad, it is because I am, somewhat.

What I did not know was that I was about to be given another chance. A completely new life was about to unfold before me. When I left this city twenty-five years ago, I never expected to return in this manner.

My prospective new employer, Seth Gruel, is the president and founder of the Sterling Chemical and Dye Co. He was looking to hire me and was willing to pay big bucks for my services and technical expertise. Mr. Gruel also arranged for a short helicopter ride up the Hudson River to reacquaint me with the area.

It was a beautiful clear day. The water looked so clean and refreshing, not as I had remembered it. As we descended slightly, I felt as if I could reach down and touch the tops of the small white sailboats as they raced beneath me. Flying further North I could see the span of the George Washington Bridge and was amazed at how majestic it looked.

As we approached the Jersey side of the river, the pilot called out, "Look down, do you see that tan brick building? That's where you'll be living."

The building stood by itself on the west bank of the Hudson River. The pilot maneuvered the helicopter and flew around the building as if he were a kid riding a bicycle. As we continued flying around the building, I was able to see the tennis courts and swimming pool that were adjacent to the main building. Then I noticed a small red brick building along side of the parking garage that did not fit in with the rest of the landscape. I could not take my eyes off a thick brown haze that hovered over the roof of this small building. Suddenly I had an eerie feeling as if something was reaching out to me.

The pilot then shouted out, "It's time to return."

Looking down at my watch, I realized that it was almost five-thirty. My dinner appointment with Mr. Gruel was for eight o'clock at a restaurant called Joseph's. I was told that Joseph's was a trendy, upscale Baltic restaurant and a favorite of Mr. Gruel.

As we approached the heliport at West Thirty-Sixth Street, I was beginning to feel the pressure of our first meeting, wondering what Mr. Gruel would be expecting of me.

Before leaving the helicopter, I turned to the pilot and thanked him for the tour. As I walked down the small flight of stairs to the tarmac there was a limo waiting for me.

The driver's door opened and a rather small muscular man wearing the same thick framed sunglasses as the pilot stepped out.

"That's strange," I thought.

"I'm Pauly," the driver said, "Mr. Gruel sent me to take you to the hotel." He then opened the rear door allowing me to get in.

After I made myself comfortable, Pauly slowly walked around to the driver's side of the limo and slid in behind the wheel. I asked him which way we are going. There seemed to be some hesitation in his voice when he said, without turning his head, "Up town."

Since Pauly appeared to be a very quiet person, I tried to create some basic conversation with him, but it was difficult to get any verbal response.

Pauly was about five feet five inches tall and must have weighed at least 225 lbs of solid muscle. His hair was graying but well groomed and he appeared to be in his fifties.

As we turned onto the West Side Highway, going north, I noticed many changes in the city since I left.

Pauly then pulled off the highway and drove across Fifty-Ninth Street, made a right turn onto Fifth Avenue and stopped in front of the Plaza Hotel. I was very impressed by Mr. Gruel's show of comfort and dollars.

Pauly opened his door, stepped out, walked around the limo and opened my door. As I got out, greeting me was a very tall and muscular African American bellman who was wearing a burgundy uniform and a pair of the same thick framed tortoise shell sunglasses similar to Pauly's.

"Welcome to the Plaza," the bellman said. Pauly took my luggage out of the trunk and placed it on the sidewalk. The bellman turned to Pauly, thanked him and picked up my luggage with very little effort. I followed him as he walked up the stairs through the front doors. It was strange how fast the bellman walked through the lobby past the registration desk and onto a waiting elevator while all along I was being greeted by the hotel staff who knew my last name. "Welcome to the Plaza, Mr. Slater," each one said as I past by.

When we entered the elevator, the doors closed behind us. The bellman then called aloud, "Twenty-first floor." He never put my luggage down or made small talk. When the elevator stopped and the doors opened, he turned and told me to follow him.

We walked down a long corridor that had burgundy and gold wallpaper on one side and a heavy dark oak mosaic wood paneling on the other. There were miniature crystal sconces hanging several feet apart from each other creating a soft mystical light.

When we reached my room, the bellman put my luggage down and took out a passkey that slid into the lock and opened the door. He allowed me to walk past him into an extremely spacious suite of rooms decorated in an early eighteenth century motif.

The bellman brought my luggage in and began to unpack my things. I walked towards the burgundy velvet covered windows. As I opened the draperies, I could see that I was directly overlooking Central Park. I just stood there looking out of the window when the bellman called out to me, "The bar in the parlor is filled with wine, dial 2301 at any time for my service." I reached into my pocket to offer the bellman a tip. He said that it would not be necessary and walked out closing the door behind him.

I just stood there taking this all in. I turned towards the window again and stared at the view. That's when I realized how late it was. I didn't want to keep Mr. Gruel waiting, so I quickly changed into a suit and felt rushed as I left to go down to the lobby.

As I approached the elevator, the doors opened. I walked in and without pressing any buttons, the elevator started moving. It passed all the floors and stopped at the lobby.

Walking through the lobby, I was again greeted by several bellmen, one after the other saying, "Have a good evening Mr. Slater," until I reached the front doors.

As I rushed down the front steps, I could see Pauly leaning against the limo waiting for me. He did not look too happy as I asked him; "Were you waiting long?" he just stared and said, "You're late." He opened the rear door allowing me to slide in and then closed the door behind me rather hard. He walked around to the driver's side and slid behind the wheel.

Soon we found ourselves sitting in heavy traffic. I tried to break the silence, "So Pauly, what is Mr. Gruel like?" With that, Pauly stopped the limo, turned his head and gave me an incredibly long stare and a half smile that was unforgettable. Never uttering a word, he turned back around and continued to drive to the restaurant.

"What's wrong with this guy?" I thought.

It seemed as if the ride took forever, but it only took about ten minutes. We pulled up in front of Joseph's and Pauly jumped out of the driver's side and walked swiftly around the front of the limo to open my door. As I got out, Pauly just gave me that same stare with a silly smirk on his face as if he were trying to tell me something that I should have already known.

I entered the restaurant and was immediately greeted by the maitre d', a stocky man with a thick European accent. "My name is Joseph," he said, "please follow me Mr. Slater, Mr. Gruel is waiting for you."

As we walked through the dining room, I had an unnatural feeling of entering a time warp. As I glanced around the crowded restaurant, I noticed that the draperies were that same burgundy color and made from the same velvet fabric that was in my hotel room. There were also many types of battle flags with various types of life like battle armor hanging on the wall. They appeared to be from the seventeenth century.

The room was filled with cigar smoke and it looked as if all the patrons were all drinking the same vintage red wine as a musician played classical music on an old piano.

We continued to walk through the restaurant that had burgundy and gold Florentine wallpaper on all the walls. There were also three very large crystal chandeliers hanging from the ceiling in the center of the main dining room.

As we approached a private dining area, a rather tall-distinguished looking man stood up. His hair was combed straight back with touches of grey on each side and he was wearing a black silk business suit with a burgundy tie that stood out against his white shirt. Putting out his hand, he introduced himself, "I'm Seth Gruel, and you must be Ron Slater. I am so glad you were able to join us this evening."

"Thank you Mr. Gruel, I'm glad to be here," I replied.

"Please call me Seth."

"I would prefer that you call me Ron, as well," I told him.

Seth then introduced me to his two lady friends, Denise and Heidi, who were joining us for dinner.

Taking a deep breath, I sat down but could not help but notice how beautiful these two women were.

5

Denise was wearing a seductive low cut burgundy satin top with a black satin ribbon around her neck and she had long dark brown hair that fell to her waist. Her dark brown eyes and her deep red lipstick made her features stand out that much more.

Heidi, who had shorter light brown hair, was wearing a very low cut burgundy sequin top that showed a lot of cleavage and she seemed to derive pleasure in showing it off.

After a few minutes of small talk, the maitre d' brought a bottle of red wine to our table. I did not recognize the gold label on the bottle or the town that it came from.

As the maitre d' walked around the table he was very careful, making sure not to spill any of the wine as he poured it into each of our glasses.

Seth stood up and made a toast, "To life and to the beauty of life." He then turned to me saying, "I hope you don't mind but I took the liberty of ordering for you."

The waiters continued to bring a variety of delicacies to our table that I had never eaten or even seen before.

Seth then stood up and started serving everyone by placing a little from each dish on each of our plates. I had not eaten since early that morning and I was ravenous. Forgetting my table manners, I immediately picked up my knife and fork then quickly placed them back on the table and waited for the others to start eating. Once I began, there was no stopping me.

I looked up and realized that Seth and the two women were not eating. It seemed as if they were just going through the motions and moved their food around their plates. This struck me as odd. As soon as I put my fork down the waiter came back to our table and took away all the food.

Seth asked me if I enjoyed my dinner as he opened another bottle of that same wine. After more conversation and a third bottle of wine, Seth said, "You must be tired after such a long day and we have a lot to discuss in my office tomorrow."

Standing up, Seth began to walk away from the table and we all followed him towards the front door. As we walked past the maitre d', he shook Seth's hand and thanked him for his generosity and they began to talk.

The two women and I waited outside. Seth approached us; I shook his hand thanking him and the two women for a wonderful dinner.

Turning towards the street, I could see Pauly with the rear door open leaning against the side of the limo. Just as I approached the limo and was about to climb into the back seat, Denise slid in from behind me. "Excuse me," she whispered as she began to make herself comfortable. "Hope you don't mind, I need a ride."

I realized how attractive she was; especially when I noticed that her already short skirt was pulled up to the middle of her thighs. It was difficult for me to take my eyes off them.

"Actually, I'm just going for the ride," she said. Pauly closed the door on my side as Denise took out a bottle of the same wine we had at Joseph's, along with two wine glasses from a small cooler that was attached to the back of the front seat. "Would you care to join me?" she asked. I agreed as she poured the wine into my glass. As if on queue, a dark glass divider slid up, separating the front seat from the back.

Pauly began to drive slowly through Central Park. I was not sure what to expect when Denise pushed a button on her side and soft music began to play. She kept staring into my eyes leaving me with the feeling that she was reading my mind. Denise then touched her glass to mine making the same toast that Seth made earlier, "To life and to the beauty of life."

After Denise took a sip of wine from her glass, she placed it into a glass holder, then taking the glass out of my hand she began drinking from it then placed it into another holder on top of the cooler. I was at a loss for words, I tried to speak, but could not. She turned towards me telling me to relax as she leaned over and gave me a light kiss on my lips and then my neck. She then began to open a button on her blouse and said, "Can you help me with the rest?" As I leaned over her, looking into her eyes, I could not help but put my lips on hers kissing her gently. As we kissed I could feel one of her hands loosening my tie and her other hand on my belt buckle as she pulled down the zipper on my pants. I felt a rush going throughout my body. I continued to open her blouse and fondle her breasts as she began to kiss me repeatedly. Denise gently pushed me back on the seat. As she leaned over me, she began to make passionate love to me. It was one of the best experiences I ever had.

It seemed as if hours had passed when I began to feel the limo slowing down. As I looked out the window, I could see we were in front of the Plaza. I quickly pulled up my pants when Denise said, "It's time to go now." I asked her if I could see her again. She just smiled as Pauly opened my door.

I smiled back at her as I walked up the Plaza steps.

The next day I woke up early with the anticipation of my first business meeting with Seth.

As I rushed down the front steps of the Plaza, I could see Pauly leaning against the limo parked out front. "Good morning, beautiful day," I said. Pauly did not answer me; he just opened the rear door allowing me to get in, and then walked around to the driver's side sliding his muscular body behind the steering wheel. He told me that we should be at Seth's office in 15 minutes. We turned on to Sixth Avenue and were moving very slowly in traffic when Pauly turned on the disc player. Music that did not sound familiar came through the rear speakers. When he turned the volume up everything outside the limo appeared so surreal, I thought I was having an outer body experience. In those few minutes that the music was playing, I seemed to have lost all sense of time and urgency.

Pauly then turned off the music as we stopped in front of a magnificent tall glass office building.

Looking at my watch, I could see that only fifteen minutes had passed, but it seemed like much longer.

I got out of the limo and saw Pauly, with a smirk on his face uttering the words, "Twenty-first floor." He continued to smirk as I turned and walked towards the front doors.

When I walked into the building, all I could see were glass and tall trees surrounding me in the lobby. All the security guards were dressed in gold jackets with burgundy color trousers and the same gold trim that the bellman in the Plaza wore, and they were all wearing the same tortoise shell rimmed sunglasses.

One of the doormen came directly over to me, "You must be Mr. Slater, please follow me." He then led me to a side elevator. I checked my watch again to make sure that I was on time. It was eight fifty-five and I had five minutes to spare.

I walked into the elevator, turned towards the elevator doors and noticed that the doorman had disappeared. The doors began to close and I could not find any buttons to press. The elevator began to move as the lights dimmed. The same music that I heard in the limo began to play. I again, had that feeling of a loss of time. This felt very strange.

When the elevator doors opened, I got out and checked my watch. It was now eight fifty eight.

Looking down the hall, I realized that this was not your average reception area. As I walked towards the reception desk, I noticed that one wall was covered with a garish smoked mirror, while on the opposite wall there was the same Florentine wallpaper that I saw in Joseph's Restaurant the night before. The carpet was a burgundy color, with a touch of gold running through it. The lighting was not your usual office lighting either. There were crystal chandeliers with bulbs in the shape of a teardrop.

No one was sitting behind the oversized reception desk. There were no papers on it, just a black telephone. I heard a door open and a young woman appeared in the doorway. All I could see was her silhouette against a bright light shining from behind. She began walking towards me and I could see her long brown hair combed to one side and her tight black form fitting dress that came up to the middle of her thighs. That's when I realized it was Denise. I was quite surprised to see her again. She introduced herself as Mr. Gruel's personal assistant. Speaking in a very soft voice she said, "I'll tell Mr. Gruel you have arrived. Can I offer you a cup of coffee?" I responded, "Dark, one sugar." She smiled and slowly walked away.

As I stood there watching her walk away I thought, "This could be the right job for me."

Moments later, Seth came out from behind a large heavy oak door. He was wearing a dark velvet burgundy smoking jacket with a gold embroidered crest on the pocket and a gold ascot around his neck. With his six-foot frame and his graying hair, he looked very distinguished and overpowering.

He asked me to join him in his office and asked Denise to bring in my coffee. He was very polite and personable. "Why don't you pull up a chair and make yourself comfortable," he said in a low but authoritative voice.

"I hope you enjoyed yourself last evening." I told him that the entire day was much more than I had expected, including the hotel accommodations. As Seth continued to talk, I looked around the room at the dark paneled oak walls and desk and the burgundy draperies that covered the windows. This was becoming all too familiar.

Seth told me that the reason he picked me for this position was because I had a thorough background in textiles and dying.

"I see you've been in this industry for more than twenty-five years with a specialty in the area of chemicals and dying. I also read that in all those years you held only two positions, leaving both with impressive records."

"I know that you are divorced with two children, do you get to see them?" Seth inquired. "My children are grown and live apart from each other and me, so I don't see them as much as I'd like," I replied.

"I'm looking to build a future with you and Sterling Chemical," I said, when Seth interrupted me, "I like to hear the word future; life itself is based on the future."

Seth questioned me about my roll with Sterling. I was very honest in expressing my feelings and told him that the reason I became recently unemployed was that, I believe, the U.S. textile manufacturing industry was sold out by NAFTA and the Clinton administration. This would eventually cause the economy to head into a deep recession and immediate changes must be made very soon if Sterling Chemical was to remain in business.

Seth appeared puzzled as I explained that he would have to close several of his plants immediately if Sterling Chemical was to remain profitable. I also told him my feelings about how the Clinton and Bush administrations sold out the U.S. textile industry and the United States manufacturing sector to China and Mexico, with his free trade status to countries where workers make less than fifty cents and hour. The American public ate it up until their jobs were threatened. The U.S. will be paying the price for that some day.

Seth, realizing that I was getting carried away, suddenly interrupted me, stood up, put out his hand and said, "I know I picked the right person for this position, I would like you to be Sterling's new CEO, so let's drink to the future."

Seth shook my hand vigorously, and then pressed the intercom button paging Denise, "Come into my office and bring with you my favorite wine and three glasses. Seth then asked if he could be excused for a few minutes to make an important call, "I'll be right back", he said.

After Seth left the room, I stood up and began to roam around the office. I walked over to the window, opened the draperies slightly and realized that I could not see the street or the adjoining buildings. There was nothing but dark clouds and a thick fog in front of me. Suddenly I heard the door open from behind and I immediately pulled the draperies closed and turned around. It was Denise holding the same familiar wine bottle with the gold label and two wine glasses. "Where is Mr. Gruel?" I asked. She replied in her soft voice, "Seth asked to be excused for a while, something urgent came up. He suggested that I stay with you until he returns."

As Denise started pouring the wine into the two wine glasses, I could not take my eyes off her. She raised her glass making a toast wishing me a long life. We clicked our glasses together, not taking our eyes off each other. I could also feel the intensity of her stare when I asked her, "Am I doing something wrong?" Not answering she took the wine glass out of my hand and placed it on the desk. We both hesitated for a moment trying to anticipate each other's next move, not saying a word, both trying to sense what was about to happen. I gently put my hands on her arms pulling her towards me, embracing her, kissing her passionately as I held on to her. I could feel my pulse beating fast as I slipped one hand under her dress while pulling down the zipper with the other. I realized that she was not wearing a bra when I felt the firmness of her breasts against my chest. She began to take off my tie and unbutton my shirt. As our bodies embraced I felt the warmth of her body against mine. She began to bite down hard on my neck, then my chest. I kept her body tight against mine as we slid to the floor engulfed in a sea of passion as she continued to make love to me.

A few moments later, Denise stood up holding on to me, and then began to dress. She excused herself and left the room.

I could not wrap my head around what had just happened.

I quickly dressed and then Seth entered the office. "Please accept my apologies for leaving you so long, I hope Denise was hospitable while I was gone. By the way, I took the liberty of bringing your luggage here. Pauly has it in the limo downstairs. He will drive you to your new living quarters in Edgewater, New Jersey, just over the George Washington Bridge. I am sure you will find it to your liking."

I thanked Seth for his trust in me and shook his hand one more time. Seth put his hand on my shoulder as he walked me to his office door, "I know you will be extremely reproductive in our company." I knew Seth meant to say productive.

As I left Seth's office, I noticed Denise sitting behind her desk. She stood up, putting out her hand, saying in her soft voice, "We will be seeing each other again soon." I turned and gave her a smile as I began to walk down the hall towards the elevator.

There were no buttons to push but the doors opened. When I stepped into the elevator, the doors closed quietly behind me. I did not feel the elevator move but I sensed that it was. I did not hear any music and the ceiling lights were much brighter, as if they were throwing off rays.

"Looks like this will be quite an adventure," I thought.

THE RIDE TO RIVER ROAD

As I left the building I did not notice the doorman, but Pauly was there leaning against his limo that was parked against the curb. As I approached the limo, Pauly opened the rear door allowing me to enter, and then closed the door behind me without saying a word. I watched him walk slowly around the limo and slip behind the steering wheel.

As we began to drive, I asked him which route he intended to take to Edgewater. He turned his head slightly towards me with that same smirk on his face and continued to drive.

I began to relax and could hear the same soft music that I had heard earlier coming through the rear speakers. It sounded so heavenly, and I had a feeling of confidence, something that I had not felt in a long time.

Even though I could feel the limo moving, everything I saw through the window seemed to be moving at a much slower pace. .

I just sat back and enjoyed a euphoric feeling while still trying to take in all the events that were happening to me. All I could do was just enjoy this motionless feeling of everything around me being so peaceful and complete. However, I could not get myself to believe that this was how the future was going to be.

I tried looking out the side windows but everything seemed so hazy and foggy. I could feel my eyelids getting heavy. I tried not to fall asleep but I just could not stay awake.

When I woke up it seemed as if I had been sleeping for hours but it was only about thirty minutes. I then felt a series of bumps beneath me. I opened my eyes and realized that we were now driving on the Jersey side of the Hudson River going north on River road.

The haze and fog had given way to beautiful tall buildings and I could now see the New York Skyline. Driving further north I could see the same group of sailboats that I had seen from the helicopter the previous day.

Pauly suddenly made a sharp right turn and without saying a word, pointed to the spacious tall building that I had flown over the day before. We slowed down and approached a small security guard house. A guard in a gold jacket wearing bronze framed tortoise shell sunglasses approached the limo. As soon as he recognized Pauly, he waived us on past a sign that read "Hudson Waters".

We drove a short distance around to the front of the building. The grounds were well kept and you could see the landscapers working as uniformed security guards walked by. We passed the pool area and the tennis courts. Then I could see that isolated building that was spewing smoke.

Pauly stopped in front of the lobby and a doorman immediately came out from behind the automatic sliding doors wearing the same burgundy uniform and tortoise shell rimmed sunglasses as did the doormen I encountered in New York City.

Pauly pushed a release button on the dashboard that opened the trunk, and then sliding himself out from behind the steering wheel, walked around the limo to open my door, as if in rhythm. When I got out I was greeted by another doorman, "Welcome to Hudson Waters Mr. Slater, my name is Ralph. I hope you had a relaxing trip. If I can be of any service to you please do not hesitate to call me at anytime."

As I turned to thank Pauly, he was already pulling away from the curb and the bellman was loading my luggage onto the luggage cart.

Ralph then suggested that I follow him through two automatic sets of sliding glass doors.

I could see that the lobby was quite lavish with exceptionally high ceilings. That same gold Florentine patterned wallpaper covered the walls.

As we walked through the lobby, I stopped for a moment as Ralph pointed out a rather large waiting area that decorated with two over sized upholstered sofas and several oversized upholstered chairs covered in the same burgundy and gold colors that were in Seth's office. Two steps led to a side staircase that led to a second floor balcony. Hanging from the ceiling down to just above a large glass table in front of the sofa, was a large crystal chandelier. On a high wall behind one of the sofas was a large painting of a very distinguished looking man wearing a black tuxedo standing in front of a medieval castle and looking across a large field of grape vines, encased in a heavy antique picture frame.

As I continued to follow Ralph, we stopped at the front desk where Ralph introduced me to Sal, the concierge of the building. He stood up and said, "If there is anything you need at any time, Mr. Slater, please do not hesitate to call me, the entire staff welcomes you to Hudson Waters."

As Ralph turned towards the elevators, I said, "Where to now Ralph?"

He replied, "Twenty-First floor, the penthouse."

He pushed a button on the far left and the doors opened immediately. I walked into the elevator with Ralph right behind me, and noticed that the floor was a thick burgundy carpet that had a gold crest resembling the letter G in the center.

The elevator was voice activated and Ralph spoke very softly, "Twenty-First floor." I felt no movement but within moments the doors opened and Ralph turned to me, "Please follow me, Mr. Slater." What I saw next was unbelievable.

THE PENTHOUSE PARTY

I walked out of the elevator and was astonished to find myself standing in my new penthouse apartment. All I could see were ceiling to floor windows.

I walked onto the large wrap around terrace that went from the north side of the building to the south side. The view was spectacular and I was beginning to feel high, as if I had been drinking. The sky was extremely clear and there was a sweet fragrance in the air. As I walked around the terrace, I could see the Verrazano-Narrows Bridge and the Statue of Liberty on the south side and could practically put my hand out and touch the George Washington Bridge on the north side. I felt as high as the Empire State Building as I watched the same white sailboats below me that now looked liked toys from this distance. I could also see the other bridges that connected Manhattan to the other boroughs; it was a view to behold.

Then for no known reason I began to feel like a man who had extraordinary powers, not corporate powers, but strange powers. I never had such a feeling of supremacy and calm before.

I walked in from the terrace to view the rest of the apartment. I have never lived anywhere like this before. There was a round fireplace surrounded by odd shaped rocks that stood off the center of the living room with a low hanging overhead hearth held up by four heavy chains. To the left of the fireplace, set into the wall, was a huge tropical fish tank. As I walked closer to this wall of water, I could not get over these magnificent fish, in many shapes and colors. It was amazing to watch them as they moved so gently between tropical plants and various shaped rock formations.

Suddenly, I heard Ralph's voice calling, "Mr. Slater, I would like to show you the rest of the apartment before it gets too late. Remember,

Mr. Gruel is throwing a dinner party in your honor tonight and I would like you to get settled before he and his guests arrive."

Ralph offered me a wine glass and left the room. He then returned with a bottle of wine with the same gold label on it, just like all the other wine bottles.

As I drank the wine, I found myself getting very drowsy. I walked into the TV room with the glass in one hand and the bottle of wine in the other. I sat down on a reclining chair and soon felt myself dozing off.

When I opened my eyes again, I was lying on a bed in a different room. My head felt heavy and my thoughts were very hazy. As I tried to open my eyes, I could hear soft music coming from the living room. I just lay there for a moment and then sat up on the edge of the bed trying to focus, when I noticed that I was wearing a completely different outfit from the one I was wearing earlier.

I walked to the window and pulled the draperies open. The day had turned into a very clear night. As I stared out the window, I could see all the bright lights shinning from across the river and a very low but bright full moon.

I heard the bedroom door open. When I turned around, I saw the silhouette of a very petite woman standing in the doorway holding a bottle of wine and two wine glasses.

As she stepped into the room, I knew that it was Denise. Only Denise could walk into a room like that. Without saying a word, she began to pour the wine. With the glasses full, Denise carefully picked them up and took a few steps towards me as I stood by the window. I turned to face her, she then handed me a glass and made a toast "To life and to the beauty life." We both took a sip of wine from our glasses, not saying a word. She took the wine glass from my hand and placed it on the windowsill, then placed her two hands on my arms pulling me closer to her, pressing her lips against mine. Then kissing me on my lips and my neck, she fell to her knees, pulling me closer to her as passion, again, overtook her.

Afterwards, Denise dressed and gave me a smile as she walked out of the room.

I then found myself standing next to the bed pondering what had just happened, again, asking myself, why me?

I thought that Seth and the other guests would be wondering what was keeping me so I hurriedly dressed.

When I entered the living room Seth immediately came over to me, shook my hand, then asked, "Does this apartment meet your needs?"

I assured him, "This apartment, and the last few days more than met my needs and my highest expectations."

Seth placed his arm around my shoulder and brought me over to meet the rest of his guests calling out, "Everyone, let me introduce you to our new CEO, Ron Slater."

"Ron, this is Gary Wolfen, our chief financial officer." Gary shook my hand and wished me luck. Seth continued to introduce me, "This is John Saber, our production manager, Henry Radcliff, our Southwest Distributor, over here meet Richard Sozich, our national sales manager, Jan Nelson, who is head of our customer service department, Bob Stillwell, our plant manager. This is Doc Langer, our Vice President, and last of all, my oldest friend, Captain Ulrich, who is in charge of all our ships."

After shaking their hands, Seth walked me to the other side of the room where he raised his wine glass and in a very loud voice began to make a toast by saying, "Hi everyone, I hope you are all having a good time."

"I think we have a very good team here," Seth continued, still holding his glass high. "Before we start drinking and loosening up with each other, I would like to propose a toast to Ron Slater for making the right choice by joining our company and to the undying future of Sterling Chemical. Let me not forget our eternal lives together, and to life and to the beauty of life."

As everyone held up their glass to toast, I gazed around the room. Heidi, who I had met the night before, was mingling with Denise and other guests.

Denise, with a full glass of wine in her hand, walked over to me as if nothing happened earlier and handed me her glass. What I did notice was that everyone in the room was drinking Seth's favorite wine and there was no other liquor, or food, for that matter. I also noticed that no one in the room appeared to look over forty years old, except for Seth and me.

As I was being introduced to the guests, the men would give me a hug, then kiss me on both cheeks, as if I was a member of the Mafia, while the women would bow their heads, and kiss the back of my hand as if I was their new ruler.

As the night wore on I noticed that one guest at a time would quietly walk out of the living room and go onto the terrace with a glass of wine in their hand. They would then face the full moon, bow their heads for a moment, as if in prayer, then come back inside.

The general conversation of the evening was not about the company, politics or sports; it was about life and the future of their lives together as a group, not a company.

I approached Seth and asked him why no one was discussing company business. He said, "Tonight is a night for celebration, walk with me onto the terrace and let us enjoy this moment together, looking at the moon."

We both stepped onto the terrace. The full moon was directly over the small brick building that adjoined the tennis courts. Thick brown smoke emerged from the roof, clouding the clear sky. It appeared as if the moon was inhaling this brown smoke.

Suddenly, Seth bowed his head as if in a moment of silent prayer. I could hear soft piano music coming from the living room. I turned to see who was playing but there was no piano, it seemed so surreal. Just then, a flock of Black Birds flew in front of us and the smoke stopped. The moon continued to move off to the right of the building as the birds flew away.

Seth turned to go back inside the living room still holding his glass of wine. As I followed him, I noticed that all the guests were gone, and no one said good night to us.

"I will see you in the morning, we have a lot to discuss," Seth said, as he walked into the elevator.

Ralph came in the living room holding a glass of wine. "I thought you would like some before you retire for the evening." I thanked him and took the wine with me into the bedroom.

The bedroom was exceptionally large with ceiling to floor windows and a sliding glass door alongside the windows that led onto a separate terrace. Heavy crushed velvet burgundy draperies covered the windows that could be opened or closed by the touch of a button. The carpet was a thick deep burgundy color that extended into the bathroom. Hanging over both sides of the bed were several gold and silver figurines that looked like antiques. The bed was very large and covered in the same heavy fabric that covered the windows, except it had a large gold embroidered crest that was the shape of the letter G in the center. A large gold figurine that was the image of the moon was on the wall above the headboard.

I lay in bed drinking the wine and as it made me drowsy I began to wonder, "What did all this burgundy, gold and tortoise shell framed sunglasses represent and why was Denise, who I just met the other day, being so friendly?"

THE PENTHOUSE

The next morning an alarm clock that was on the night table next to my bed awakened me. It was set for six a.m. I woke up ready to do my regular half hour workout before leaving for the plant, on this, my first day.

At seven a.m., the phone rang. I grabbed the receiver fast, anxious to find out whom was calling so early in the morning. It was Sal from the front desk, "Mr. Gruel called earlier this morning and left a message explaining that he would meet you later this evening and that it would not be necessary for you to be at the plant today. He suggested that you stay around the building."

Disappointed, I said, "Thanks," and hung up the phone.

Now that I was wide-awake, I decided to have breakfast, by myself, on the terrace, catch up on some local news, and explore the building.

I thought I would get myself acquainted with my new apartment first. As I walked around, I counted three additional bedrooms, each one having its own private bathroom which included a marble Jacuzzi and a shower. All the bathrooms had side doors that led into a central hallway, that led into a large workout room filled with all sorts of exercise equipment, and a redwood steam sauna that had two levels of benches. There was an oversized Jacuzzi and shower next to the sauna.

Once outside the workout room I continued down the main hallway and came upon a wine room. This room was temperature controlled, plus there was a combination lock embedded into a very large sliding glass door. I peered through the door trying to get a better look, but all I could see were racks of red wine from the ceiling to the floor. All of the bottles had the same Gold label on them.

"Seth must have gotten a really great buy," I thought.

Then I walked out onto the eastside of the main terrace thinking I could get some early morning sun. It was a beautiful clear morning and I could begin to feel the warmth from the sun as it came across the terrace. I noticed that one of the guests from last nights party left a wine bottle on the floor. As I leaned over to pick it up, the wine bottle exploded and totally disintegrated in front of my eyes. I bent over looking for glass fragments of the bottle, but I couldn't find any. I walked back inside, bewildered and confused, thinking, "No one would believe this."

I called Sal at the main desk and told him that I was on my way down, "Please send the elevator up to the twenty-first floor," I requested.

As I stepped in front of the elevator, the door opened immediately. I went inside, turned around and noticed that there were no buttons to push. Then I remembered that it was voice activated. "Lobby", I said. I felt a slight jolt and it began to move.

When I reached the lobby, I saw Sal standing behind the concierge desk talking to a young woman. As I approached the desk, I could see that she was in her mid thirties, very tan, wearing a short summer dress and tortoise shell framed sunglasses. She was very attractive so I just stood there looking at her. She turned towards me and asked my name. "Ron, Ron Slater" I replied.

"My name's Ellen, do you live in the building?" She asked.

"I just moved in, do you?"

"Yes, on the eighth floor, what floor are you on?" she asked.

"The penthouse," I answered.

"I would like to come up and visit some time," Ellen said as she walked into the elevator. I answered in a loud voice as the elevator door closed, "Some day soon, I hope."

I turned to Sal, "Good morning, I understand that I am supposed to stay around the building today. What do you recommend I do?"

"You can take a walk on River Road and then spend the rest of the afternoon by the pool," he suggested.

"A walk would be good," I thought.

THE FIRST MORNING

I went outside and found myself facing the same brick building Seth was praying towards last night. It was isolated from the main building and still had brown smoke spewing out from the top that was drifting into the clear blue sky. I just stood there for a while, looking at it, then decided to take a walk north on River Road.

As I walked past the guardhouse, the guard leaned out from the open window and waved to me, "Enjoy your walk, Mr. Slater."

I walked towards the George Washington Bridge and went through the Fort Lee Park, then took a short rest.

As I sat there high above the bridge, I was able to look across the span that leads to the Bronx. I began to think of my youth and the fun times I had growing up in the Bronx playing baseball and football. I even went fishing under that bridge. That was a great time in my life.

After a while, I decided to walk down River Road in the opposite direction to look into some stores. I was crossing the street just past Hudson Waters when I noticed some people walking towards me wearing the same tortoise shell framed sunglasses that were worn by the doormen, the security guards and that woman, Ellen, who I had met at the concierge desk earlier. I did not give too much thought to it as I walked into a small cigar store; I thought I would treat myself to a good cigar that I would smoke in celebration of my new position.

A short man came out from behind a closed curtain and asked if he could help me. I asked him if he sold Cuban cigars. "Yes I do," he answered, "follow me."

We walked into a smoking room where I noticed a large gold figurine that looked like the moon hanging on the wall. The man bowed his head slightly and muttered a few words to himself as we passed it.

After making my selection of cigars, I followed him to the front of the store.

"I just moved in across the street to Hudson Waters," I told him. He hesitated for a moment and then said, "It's a beautiful day, so these cigars are on the house."

I thanked him as he followed me outside the store after placing the same tortoise shell framed sunglasses over his eyes.

A MEETING AT THE POOL

When I entered the grounds of the building, I noticed that strange brick building still had brown smoke spewing out from the top. It made me nervous just looking at it.

I continued to walk towards the pool hoping to smoke my cigar and relax for a while. As I walked through the pool gate, there was a lifeguard sitting under an umbrella wearing the same type of sunglasses that I was beginning to see everywhere. "Welcome, Mr. Slater, can I bring you a lounge chair?" I thanked her and began walking away when I heard someone call me from across the pool. "Ron, Ron, sit over here." As I looked across the pool, I saw that it was Ellen lying on a lounge chair.

I walked towards Ellen while noticing how oddly shaped the pool was. It looked more like a pond. There was a narrow walkway around it made from Colorado stones imbedded into concrete. The air had a sweet smell created by the exotic flowers along side of the walkway amidst odd shaped rocks.

As I walked up to Ellen, she stood up. Her beauty amazed me. That golden brown tan that I saw earlier covered her entire body. It was easy to see that she took good care of herself; especially in that scanty gold bikini she was wearing. Her hair flowed down her back and she was wearing the same tortoise shell framed sunglasses that everyone else seemed to be wearing.

She stretched out her hand and asked, "Would you care to join me?"

"I would, and I have all afternoon free," I replied.

She gave me a big smile as we both lay down on our lounge chairs.

I took this opportunity to ask her questions about things that seemed quite irregular to me.

"It seems that you are wearing the latest fashion in sunglasses," I said. She avoided answering. "I like them, I was told they are made from bone and are very fashionable," was all she said.

"Tell me about the building," I asked.

She went on to tell me that she has been living here for a little over two years and hardly speaks to anybody. "Seth Gruel owns this building and brought me here from Florida," she said. "We met in a lounge one evening and when I told him the type of work I was doing, he offered me a job at twice the salary I was making and flew me up north, all expenses paid, including my apartment."

As we continued to talk, she told me something very disturbing.

"When I leave for work in the evening people are first coming to the pool. They stay by the pool until the early morning hours drinking wine, and then disappear before sunrise."

"What kind of work do you do?" I asked.

There was a slight hesitation in her voice, "I am a research chemist associated with St. Joseph's Hospital in Clifton.

"What type of research are you involved with?" I inquired.

"I specialize in the research of rare blood types and blood disorders. When the board of directors of this building read my application, they immediately approved it without an interview."

Ellen looked at her watch, and then looked up at me with a big smile, "I don't have to be at the lab until later this evening. Would you like to join me upstairs for a drink?"

"Why not, that's the best offer I've had all day".

We stood up and Ellen took my hand. We began walking together towards the building when she whispered, "I feel as if I have known you for a long time." I told her that I feel the same way.

As we passed the front desk, we saw Ralph and Sal.

Ralph asked us if there was anything he could do for us. We just smiled at him and kept on walking.

The elevator door opened just as we reached it. We got in and held hands as the door closed. Ellen turned to me and gave me an unexpected kiss on the lips. "I'm glad I met you," she whispered softly.

"I'm glad too," I told her.

When we reached Ellen's floor she grabbed my hand as assurance that I was getting off the elevator with her. She held onto my hand as we walked towards her apartment. She suddenly turned and gave me a long passionate kiss. Then Ellen opened her apartment door without using a key. When I asked her about that, she said, "No one living in this building has keys to their apartment, Seth wants it that way."

I realized that I did not get any keys to my apartment. I thought they would be waiting for me at the front desk when I returned from my walk.

"Please come in," she coaxed.

As I followed her through the open door, Ellen turned towards me and gave me another rather long passionate kiss while reaching to close the door at the same time. I could sense her longing as she continued to hold on to me, kissing me.

She then let go telling me that she wanted to change out of her bathing suit. As she turned to go to her bedroom, she pointed to a wine cabinet in the living room and told me to open a bottle and make myself comfortable.

When I opened the wine cabinet, all I could find were the same bottles of wine with the same gold label. "What is going on with this wine?" I wondered.

As I walked around, I could see that Ellen had a well-decorated apartment with many pictures on the walls. There was a portrait of Seth hanging above a sofa, which struck me as kind of strange. Against the opposite wall was another sofa covered with many fancy pillows and a large picture of a castle hanging above it.

Ellen's apartment was very large. It had an open dining room and a large glass dining table that stood in the center of the room with six silk burgundy and gold striped chairs around it and a chandelier similar to the one that was in Joseph's restaurant, only smaller, hanging above the center.

When I walked into the living room, I could see the terrace. I opened the sliding glass door and walked out onto the terrace that was facing south. I could not help but notice that strange, isolated building again.

I was still on the terrace when I heard Ellen calling me from her bedroom, "Pour the wine, I'll be right out."

I walked into her small kitchen and found a corkscrew bottle opener in one of the drawers.

When Ellen came back into the living room, she was wearing a sheer negligee. It was obvious that she was intentionally showing off her body. She was so beautiful that when I looked up at her, the corkscrew slipped from my hand cutting my finger. My finger began to bleed, and when Ellen saw the blood, she immediately put my finger into her mouth and began to suck on it until the bleeding stopped. "Does that feel better?" she asked.

"Much better thank you," I replied.

She then untied the belt on her robe exposing her slender body. As she began to kiss me, I fell backwards onto the couch with her on top of me. We lay there for a while making love and continued to enjoy the passion that we felt, throughout the rest of the afternoon.

Ellen stood up and began pouring more wine in our glasses, then explained, "This wine is very special and I only share it with special people on special occasions such as this."

"I consider myself very lucky," I told her.

Ellen then walked over to another large enclosed wall closet and opened the door. Inside were bottles of the same wine with the same gold label. I just stood there staring at the bottles when a slight chill ran through my body. I asked her, "How did you get all of this wine?"

"When I moved into this apartment all these wine bottles were here, and whenever I leave an empty bottle of wine around, the bottle is always replaced by another."

We continued drinking wine when Ellen walked over to the CD player, put on some soft music, and turned up the volume. I could not believe what I was hearing. I heard this same music in the back of the limo. I also heard it in the elevator in Seth's office building.

"Where did you buy this CD?" I inquired. She said someone at the pool gave it to her soon after she moved into the building. "Whenever I listen to this music I get in a mood," she said, as she turned towards me and slipped out of her robe again. All I could do was stand there as she walked slowly towards me, filling me with new excitement.

She took the glass from my hand and placed our glasses on the cock-tail table in front of the sofa. As she leaned over me she kissed and bit my neck. I could hear her breathing harder as the music seemed to be getting louder. She would stop for a moment only to sip wine from a glass we were now sharing.

The more wine she would drink, the more intense she would become.

She kissed with her eyes open; they appeared hypnotic, as if she wanted to devour me. All of a sudden, I felt a sting and then warmth running down my neck when I realized that she had bitten me. I raised my hand to my neck to stop the bleeding. Ellen apologized as she stood up and went for a towel.

I raised myself up and looked at the clock that was sitting on a side table. I was thinking that we were on the sofa for almost two hours. I was amazed to see that I was so wrong. Actually, it had been many hours. I never had an experience like this before, and I did not want it to end.

When Ellen came back, we both sat on the couch as she gently applied a warm towel to my neck. I was so relaxed that I must have fallen asleep.

When I opened my eyes, Ellen was gone and it was dark outside. I began to dress and then walked around her apartment when I saw a note on the dining room table.

"Great time, we must get together again, Ellen."

I left Ellen's apartment, took the elevator up to my apartment, and went directly to my bedroom. My body felt drained. I looked at the clock; it read 6:00 A.M. The sun was beginning to rise and I knew that if I were to lie down and fall asleep, the rest of the day would be shot. I decided to go into the sauna and then shower to try to wake up. It helped somewhat.

Suddenly the phone rang. It was Sal calling to tell me that Mr. Gruel left a message saying that Pauly would pick me up at eight-thirty this morning and that I should wait for him in front of the building.

I was somewhat nervous, fearing that I might be too tired to conduct myself properly.

As I dressed, I kept looking at the clock. I knew I had plenty of time. I was very hungry; I did not have any dinner last night, so I opened the refrigerator hoping that I could find something to eat. I could not believe what I saw. Everything you would need, and then some, was in there. Seth thought of everything.

The phone rang again just as I was about to make myself a cup of coffee and a fast breakfast. It was Sal, "Pauly arrived early and wants you to come down right now."

I immediately put on my jacket and walked towards the elevator while putting on my tie. When I arrived in the lobby, I could see Pauly impatiently leaning against the limo. When he saw me coming, he opened the rear door.

"Good morning" I said. He just gave me his usual stare, not saying a word.

"Where are we going?" I asked. "We are going to Mr. Gruel's office" he replied.

"What did I do wrong now?" I wondered.

There was no music playing, which gave me time to think. I tried to replay the last two days in my mind, but I was too nervous to concentrate. I just sat back and closed my eyes. I must have fallen asleep because the next thing I knew, I was in front of Seth's office building.

Pauly opened my door, looked at me and did not say a word.

Walking through the front doors of the building, I was greeted by the same guard that I met the other day, wearing the same uniform and the same tortoise shell framed sunglasses.

"Come with me Mr. Slater, Mr. Gruel is waiting for you."

I was even more nervous as I stepped into the elevator. I could feel the elevator moving but this time there was no music playing.

When the doors opened I stepped out hoping to see Denise's friendly face, but she was not there. I stood there for a few moments, then Seth's office door opened and he walked out.

"Good morning" I said, putting out my hand. Instead of shaking my hand, Seth put his arm around my shoulders and directed me in to his office.

"Have a seat," he said. I pulled up a chair in front of his desk as he said, "I hope you have been sleeping well?"

"Very well, thank you, is anything wrong"? I asked.

"Actually no, I brought you to my office to see for myself how you are adjusting. Have you met any people in the building?"

"I met a very nice young lady, her name is Ellen. We sat by the pool for awhile, and then she invited me up to her apartment for some wine," I told him.

"That is very good," Seth said. "How are you enjoying the wine? This is a special vintage that I brought back from Europe many years ago. This is all I drink."

"Where is Denise?" I asked. "She is preparing a light breakfast for us and should be back in a few minutes."

"When do I start working at the plant?" I asked.

"There were some delays at the plant and I would prefer for you to stay around the apartment building until the problem is solved," he told me.

"Can I be of some help?"

"The best thing for you to do at this time is to do nothing."

Then I heard the door open from behind, I turned to see Denise pushing a small breakfast cart into the office. I felt relieved to see her. "Do you need some help?" I asked. "Not now, perhaps a little later," she said, as she left the office. I wondered what she meant by that remark.

Seth continued to talk about the problems at the plant but nothing seemed to make sense. The more I questioned him about the problems, the more evasive his answers were.

Denise came back into the office and told Seth that there was a very important phone call for him in the other office. Seth excused himself and left.

I was very hungry now, so I pulled the cart closer to me. I asked Denise to join me, but she declined saying she was not hungry. She poured me some coffee then sat across from me.

33

I asked her how long she has been working for Seth. "For many years," she replied. "How serious is the problem at the plant?" She appeared reluctant to answer then said, looking away, "Many lives depend upon this plant."

That struck me as very strange.

Denise then answered a ringing phone, listened for a minute, and then hung up. She told me that Seth had to leave and Pauly will take me back to the apartment.

Before I left I told Denise that I thought she was hiding something from me.

"I will talk to you later, this is not the place," she said, holding the office door open for me as I left.

I sensed that something was very wrong, almost sinister.

I rode the elevator down to the main floor and noticed that there were no guards around.

I began to walk rapidly out of the building when I saw Pauly waiting for me with his usual, fed up, look. He hurried me into the limo, dashed around to the driver's seat and sped away. I asked him, "Is there a problem that I should be aware of?" He just gave me his usual stare.

We headed up the Westside highway towards the George Washington Bridge. I could see my apartment building as we crossed over the bridge as well as the brown haze that was lingering over the far side of the building.

When we approached the other side of the bridge, Pauly drove directly down River Road towards the building, speeding past the guardhouse.

He got out, but by the time he came around to open my door, I had already let myself out. He slammed the door behind me and was already driving away as I reached the front doors.

I was very anxious to get up to my apartment. As soon as I opened the door I walked straight to the terrace so I could take a better look at the building below me. There was an excessive amount of this strange brown smoke coming from the top of this building filling the sky. I had no idea what was happening inside.

As I walked into the bedroom to take off my suit, the phone rang. It was Denise asking me if I was all right. "I am fine, but what is going on?"

"Stay in your apartment and I will call you later," she said.

I hung up the phone and it rang again. This time it was Ellen. "I'm just resting in my apartment, would you like to come down?" she asked.

"I'll be down in a few minutes," I told her.

I walked into the living room and stared at the oversized fish tank, it seemed to relax me. I just stood there for a while trying to make sense out of what was going on around me.

I decided to go down to Ellen's apartment. The door was unlocked so I just let myself in. She was waiting for me on the couch wearing that same sheer robe with the belt untied. She looked beautiful just lying there.

She asked me if I would like to join her in a glass of wine. I poured wine into two glasses. She then clicked our glasses together and made a toast, "To life, and to the beauty of life." That struck me as strange; she used the same toast Seth used.

We made small talk for a while as I tried to contain myself from attempting to make love to her. What I really wanted was to find out what was going on in this building and why there was so much brown smoke coming from the top of the building across the street, and why was everyone so interested in the *beauty of life*. All Ellen would tell me was that they are having some serious problems with the heating system.

That was odd; it was the middle of July.

I tried to get more details out of Ellen, but to no avail. I sat with her for a few more minutes, and then politely excused myself. "I'm expecting an important call upstairs; I'll call you later or tomorrow."

Picking myself up from the couch, I gave Ellen a kiss and let myself out of her apartment. She appeared disappointed that I could not stay any longer.

THE LABORATORY

When I entered the elevator, I noticed a yellow button on the wall panel that was blinking on and off. I pressed the button out of curiosity. I soon realized that I made a serious mistake.

Four walls made of heavy steel slid down around me covering the door, the panels and the emergency exit. The elevator began moving downward and kept moving down for about two minutes when it came to a sudden stop. I stood there with my heart pounding waiting to see what would happen next. The steel panel covering the elevator door slid open. After much consideration, I decided to cautiously step out of the elevator.

As I looked around, it appeared to me as if I was in an old mineshaft. I began to walk slowly; everything looked hazy. Torches lit the entire tunnel, and there was a very strong, but sweet, smell lingering in the air.

I was careful following a narrow path, trying not to make any noise, when I came upon a thick wooden door. I heard some strange noises coming from the other side, so I placed my ear against the door. It sounded like a broken steam pipe hissing. I was too curious to turn back now, so I opened the door slowly, not knowing what to expect. I found myself looking at a modern, well-equipped laboratory. I was baffled. "Why was this here, underground?"

I had worked in a laboratory while in College and recognized some of the lab equipment. There were Petri dishes and cell culture plates and plenty of empty bottles. I also noticed extracting purification kits used for blood testing, many shake flasks and filter tips. If I remember correctly these items were also used to eliminate blood contamination. "What does blood contamination have to do with textile dying?" I wondered.

I could not comprehend why all this was here and exactly what they were being used for.

As I continued to walk further into the laboratory, I saw a slightly opened door on the far side of the room. As I peaked through, I could see a large group of people, sitting on chairs, facing each other. I recognized many of the faces from the party the other evening, including Heidi. There were guards from Seth's office building, the man from the cigar store, even Joseph, the maitre d' from the restaurant, plus other people that I had seen around the building.

They were each holding a glass of wine, and each one was wearing a dark burgundy robe decorated with gold trimming. I could also see a large figure of the moon hanging from the back of the podium.

Then I heard a side door open and stepping out through the door was a very large figure in a hooded dark burgundy cape holding up two bottles of that same wine, but the bottles were much larger. The figure stepped onto the podium facing the figurine and bowed his head as if in prayer. Then the figure turned slowly facing everyone and removed his hood. I just stood there in disbelief. It was Seth.

Everyone stood up facing Seth, then bowed his or her head three times. Seth raised the two bottles of wine, turned towards the gold figurine of the moon, and bowed his head again. He then turned back to everyone holding up the two bottles making a toast, "To life and to the beauty of life." He then told everyone, "Let us now bow our heads and pray."

At that point I decided to back out of the room before I was discovered. I walked very quietly through the laboratory door.

A rush of adrenalin raced through my body as I then bolted for the elevator. Once inside the elevator, heavy perspiration began to run down my face as the door closed behind me and the side panels slid down covering the walls and the buttons. I began to panic as I called out, "Penthouse, penthouse," but I felt no upward motion. I looked up at the ceiling and continued to call out in a louder voice, "Penthouse, penthouse." I then felt the elevator begin to rise from under my feet. I stood there frozen in a corner, hoping that I would not be discovered by any security cameras.

The elevator continued to rise as the side panels slid up. Then suddenly the elevator came to a stop and the door opened.

I was relieved but still breathing heavy as I entered my apartment. I needed a drink but all I could find were bottles of that same wine, so I took a bottle with me to the terrace to try to calm down. I placed the bottle on a small glass table that was facing the sun. I then went back in to get a bottle opener and a glass. When I returned to the terrace, the bottle appeared to have exploded. I just watched in disbelief as the bottle disintegrated right in front of my eyes.

Then I heard the front door open and was surprised to see that it was Denise.

When she saw me, she came running over, hugged me and asked, "Are you alright? I was worried about you."

"Come on the terrace with me, I would like to show you something?" I demanded. She hesitated, then put her hand in her handbag and took out a pair of tortoise shell framed sunglasses and put them on before going out.

I asked her to sit down by the glass table while I go inside to get a bottle of wine for us. She stood up saying, "I am not very thirsty now."

I said, "I am thirsty and would like a glass of wine, I'll be right back."

I did not tell her what I just witnessed because I wanted her to see it first hand.

I rushed inside to get another bottle of wine when I heard Denise's footsteps behind me. When I turned around, she was standing right there. She pushed herself against me, placing her arms around my neck, pressing her lips to mine. I pulled away telling her that I had a very hectic afternoon and I would like to get some fresh air. Denise appeared reluctant, and then said, "Why don't we drink the wine inside." I told her that I would prefer to sit outside and get some sun."

I could see in her face that she was nervous, "Is there was anything wrong? Or is there something you would like to tell me?" I asked.

"Ron, she said, "Why don't we sit on the couch inside so we can talk for awhile?" I reluctantly agreed as I picked up the two glasses and went inside. We sat down on the couch next to each other.

Denise just kept staring at me. She did not say much as I began to question her. I first asked her what she knew about the laboratory under the building. She looked surprised then asked, "How did you find out about that?" I told her it was purely by accident and I continued to tell her what I saw.

She looked at me in a very strange manner, staring straight into my eyes with a great deal of intensity. When I turned away she leaned over me and started kissing me, then suddenly, I felt her biting my neck. I could feel her trying to read my mind as warm blood began to run down my neck and onto my shoulder. My reaction was swift as I pushed her off me. "What's wrong with you, what are you doing?" I yelled.

She tried to lean over me again but I wouldn't have it. I pushed her away again and tried to control her, but she was very strong. She had a crazed look on her face as I managed to hold her down.

Suddenly, Denise just passed out on the couch with her eyes wide open, staring at me with a crazed look on her face. As she lay there, I could not take my eyes off her because of her beauty. I could not believe what was happening.

I continued sitting beside her for about an hour, when she turned her head and tried to sit up. "What happened?" she asked. I tried to explain as she asked me for a glass of wine. She trembled as she held onto the glass I handed her with two hands.

After I poured the wine into her glass, she lifted it to her lips and sat back on the couch. Then Denise began to speak, "I have something to tell you that you that must believe, but first you must pour me another glass of wine."

As I poured Denise another glass of wine, I sensed something was very wrong. "What is going on, what did I get myself onto?" I asked.

"You must leave this building before it is too late, but first I will explain everything to you."

Denise began speaking in a very soft voice. "Before I start you must tell me about Ellen."

I told Denise how we met at the pool the other day and that she invited me to her apartment. "Did anything happen between you?" she asked inquisitively.

"Ellen tried to seduce me but I was not in the mood so I came back to my apartment."

"Is that all?" Denise asked.

I looked straight into her eyes, "I am telling you everything. Ellen showed me her wine cabinet filled with the same wine that everyone is drinking everywhere. She wanted me to drink with her; instead I went back to my apartment."

I think Denise believed me because she began to calm down.

"First, she said, you must know that every word I tell you is true and you must not interrupt me.

"I agree," I said, as I poured her more wine.

HISTORY PART ONE

Denise began to speak....

"This story begins with Seth's father, Dr. Fredric Gruel, who lived for over 250 years in the Romanian city of Transylvania. He comes to me and speaks to me every night as if he were still alive," she added.

The year was 1808 and there was a lot of fighting going on among the Baltic countries. It seemed that every city in Romania had an army. The city with the largest army at that time was Transylvania. Seth's father, Fredric, was a well-established doctor and wealthy landowner who had two older brothers. The middle brother was Ludwig Von Gruel, a ruthless killer, who led his armies throughout Russia. The oldest and most famous brother was Count Vladimir Gruel. People in Transylvania did not speak of him. They feared him because he was a ruthless warmonger who led his army throughout the Baltic's, charging into towns killing the men, raping, and killing the women. After their killing frenzy, the Count would allow his men to celebrate their victories by drinking the blood of their victims while dancing around large wooden stakes in the ground and set them on fire.

Everyone feared the Count except Fredric who wanted peace, but was too weak to fight his older brothers.

Fredric had the same powers as his brothers but he tried hard to curb his lust and desires. He was more educated and worldly than his siblings who could not agree with him on anything. The three brothers were many years apart and did not care for one another.

Count Vladimir Gruel, the elder brother, was jealous of his younger and more popular brother Fredric who was a well-respected doctor and scientist and an advisor to the King of Romania and many other aristocrats throughout Europe.

43

The Count suspected that Fredric was about to turn him over to the authorities so he had him exiled to England instead of killing him. Because the aristocratic community feared the count, they would not come to Fredric's aide.

Fredric's success and wealth came from his land that produced an abundance of grapes from his vineyards. Fredric made wine that he sold and shipped throughout Europe. This gave him much wealth and access to other countries.

Fredric, who could not prevent this forced exile from Transylvania by his older brother, decided to willingly leave his homeland for England and arrived in London several weeks later.

FREDRIC IN LONDON

Fredric, who was in his early thirties, was a tall, handsome man who wore his long dark brown hair straight back in a ponytail, as was the style of the day. He had a flair for fashion and always wore a black velvet jacket with a white ruffled shirt and a white or gold ascot and high black boots. He was single and sought after by many women or their mothers hoping to introduce him to their daughters.

Of his many friends and business associates in London, Fredric was most impressed with Count Lexer, who attained much of his wealth as a distributor of Fredric's wine. It was at a ball given by Count Lexer that Fredric's life was about to change.

As Fredric's carriage pulled up in front of Count Lexer's estate, he noticed a beautiful young woman walking up the steps with an elderly gentleman by her side. He could not take his eyes off her. He called out to his driver to stop as she disappeared into the mansion. Fredric opened the door and jumped from the carriage. He ran up the steps to try to catch another glimpse of this beautiful young woman. To his misfortune, she disappeared among the many guests that were attending the ball.

Upon entering the mansion, two servants greeted Fredric who took his hat, cape and walking stick. He was amazed by the magnificent size and décor of the main hall. In the center of the hall hung a huge crystal chandelier with paintings of nude men and women on the ceiling above it. Gold and white striped wallpaper covered the walls with candles burning in crystal sconces giving a warm glow to the room.

A servant escorted him past a large spiral staircase, then through two very large carved wooden doors. Upon entering a larger room where there were many other guests in attendance, another servant called out "Count Lexer welcomes Dr. Fredric Gruel of Transylvania."

Upon hearing Fredric's name, Count Lexer walked over, placed his hand on Fredric's shoulder, and thanked him for attending. "Thank you for inviting me," Fredric replied. The Count, still holding on to Fredric's shoulder handed him a glass of champagne that he took from a gold tray offered by a servant. Let us make a toast, he said "To life and to the beauty of life, and also to a long friendship." Fredric then raised his glass again making another toast "and to the beauty of a young lady who is attending this party." Count Lexer asked, "Which one, there are so many?" Fredric's eyes searched the ballroom, and then he saw her. She looked like a princess. She was wearing a low cut, silver embroidered ball gown with diamonds around her neck that framed her lovely young face.

"Who is that young lady standing across the floor next to the tall man with the mustache?" Fredric asked. "Her name is Leona; she is the daughter of Dr. Stroud, the Doctor to the Queen," Count Lexer replied. "Please excuse me," Fredric said, as he started walking across the dance floor amidst couples dancing around him.

Fredric approached Leona and asked, "May I have the next dance?" She hesitated before answering, "I'm afraid I do not know you, sir." She took out a dance card filled with names from a small purse hanging from her arm. "This is a list of the gentlemen who are ahead of you; you will simply have to wait." Fredric looked into Leona's eyes then introduced himself, "My name is Dr. Fredric Gruel of Transylvania." Leona continued to stare into Fredric's eyes then took out her list again and turned to the gentlemen waiting to dance with her. "Would you all mind waiting just a little while longer?" Fredric stood fast, looking at the other men, as he took Leona's arm, proceeded to walk, with her, onto the dance floor, and waited for the musicians to start playing again.

When he put his arm around her slender waist, Fredric realized that this beautiful young woman, with her long brown hair flowing down to her waist, seemed to have captured his heart. He could see only her deep brown eyes as the orchestra began to play and they moved gracefully around the dance floor. It seemed as though they were standing still and the ballroom was moving around them.

They danced to the music while staring into each other's eyes when suddenly Fredric was overcome by a feeling that he could spend the rest of his life with her. The faster the orchestra played, the faster they turned together as they held tightly on to one another.

They were a beautiful couple as they danced around the ballroom floor.

When the music stopped, they just stood there gazing into each other's eyes as if there were no one else in the room but them.

As they walked off the dance floor, Fredric stopped for a moment, turned to Leona and asked her if he could see her again. She gave him a big smile, "Can you come to my home tomorrow evening?"

"I will see you then," Fredric replied, as he walked Leona back to her friends.

Fredric said his goodbyes and left the party wondering how he could keep Leona from finding out that he was part of a family of vampires and the younger brother of the villain, Count Vladimir Gruel.

The next evening, as promised, Fredric went to Leona's house where she lived with her father, a well-respected doctor. Her mother had passed away when Leona was a child and she was completely devoted to her father.

Fredric arrived just after sunset in his black, horse drawn carriage adorned with the Gruel family crest engraved on the outer sides of both doors.

When the carriage came to a stop in front of Leona's house, the coachman climbed down, opened Fredric's door and placed a stool in front of the door, allowing him to step down.

Fredric walked slowly towards the front doors of the house. Even though there were kerosene lit lamps he was not able to see much except for the red brick facing and the three marble steps leading up to the front doors.

He looked around for a moment then began to knock on the door. When the door opened an elderly servant, wearing a black tuxedo greeted him. "You must be Dr. Gruel, please come in. Miss Leona is waiting for you."

As Fredric stepped through the front doors, he saw the lavishness of this grand house. The servant took his hat, cape and walking stick and disappeared into the next room. Upon returning, he asked Fredric to follow him into the study where Leona was waiting with her father.

As he followed the servant, he saw more of the luxury that Leona was accustomed to.

The servant opened a large pair of oak doors that led to the study and announced Fredric's arrival. Leona and her father were seated with their backs to the door and facing a large stone fireplace that was burning brightly. They both stood up at the same time turning towards Fredric. Leona took a few steps towards him extending her hand. Fredric then bowed gently kissing the back of her hand while lifting his eyes, not able to take them off her.

He then heard a mild but intentional cough coming from Leona's father. "I do not mean to interrupt, but I am Leona's father, Dr. Stroud." Fredric put his hand out to shake his, "I am Dr. Fredric Gruel," He said. "By any chance are you related to Count Vladimir Gruel of Transylvania?" the doctor asked. Fredric answered with a firm, "Yes I am. He is my older brother."

Dr. Stroud began to relay stories of his brother's ruthlessness that have traveled across Europe and England, not really knowing if they were true.

The doctor wanted to know more about Fredric's background. He offered Fredric a glass of Port hoping to engage him in a conversation regarding his family. Fredric accepted his offer and raised his glass making a toast, "To life and to the beauty of life."

"That is a very nice toast. Let us sit by the fire where it is warm," Dr. Stroud suggested.

I understand that you are a doctor, what specialty of medicine do you practice?"

"I do not have a practice; I do research in the field of Hemophilia and also specialize in the research of rare plants. I also own several thousand acres of land on which I grow wine grapes and I export my wine throughout Europe. I would like to send you a case of my best wine, if you would allow me to?" Fredric offered. "I will be looking forward to receiving it, thank you," The doctor replied, and then added, "It is getting late and I am tired. If you will excuse me, I would like to retire for the evening. I hope to continue this conversation with you in the near future," He said to Fredric, and then turned to Leona, "Please excuse me my dear, do not stay up too late, I will see you in the morning."

Dr Stroud stood up, gave Leona a kiss on her cheek, and then left the study closing the doors behind him.

Fredric and Leona were now alone for the first time. As if on command, they both stood up facing each other and were not able to take their eyes off one another. There was no exchange of words, when suddenly; Fredric tossed his glass into the fireplace causing the flames to rise. He then placed his hands on Leona's shoulders pulling her towards him while at the same time staring into her eyes with great intensity. Leona could not say a word; she could only follow Fredric's telepathic commands.

Fredric had a deep feeling of passion and longing going throughout his body. Still looking into Leona's eyes he gently put his hands on her shoulders slowly pulling her dress down revealing her breasts. All Leona could do was to keep staring into Fredric's eyes as he took a step back to admire the beauty of her body and her long light brown hair resting over her perfect, firm breasts.

Fredric just stood there staring at Leona, not saying a word. He took a step towards her as they both stared into each other's eyes. He leaned closer to her placing his hand under her chin kissing her gently on her lips and then pulled her dress up over her body until it rested on her shoulders again.

He knew he would now have to hold back the passion that was building inside of him. Fredric had also made up his mind that he wanted to spend the rest of his life with her.

"I would like to see you forever and ever," Fredric said longingly. "Forever is a very long time," Leona replied with a smile. Fredric began to walk towards the study doors, and then stopped briefly to tell Leona that he would like to call on her again, very soon.

As Fredric passed through the study doors, the elderly servant gave him back his cape, hat and walking stick. He nodded to the servant as he opened the front door allowing him to leave.

THE PUB

Fredric's driver climbed down from his coach and opened the door when he saw Fredric approaching. Upon entering the carriage Fredric told the driver, "Take me to the city, to the bistro." Fredric was feeling good but his meeting with Leona left him longing for female company.

The road became winding as they approached the outskirts of the city. "Whoa," the coachman yelled to the horses as he pulled back on the reins. The carriage pulled up in front of a pub that Fredric never patronized. As he stepped down from the carriage and walked towards the pub, he told his driver to pick him up one half hour before sunrise.

The pub was very dark with air filled with heavy smoke and smelling like stale, foul beer. As Fredric entered, he hesitated and looked around as if he were a lion in the jungle looking for his next prey. He noticed that the room was filled with a rowdy group of men and women singing, drinking and smoking. He stood there for a while when a barmaid approached him and asked, "Would you be needing a table, sir?" He nodded and followed her to an empty table next to a roaring fireplace. "Are you hungry or would you like something to drink," she asked. "I'll just have a drink. Why don't you join me? Bring a bottle of your best champagne with two glasses."

As the barmaid walked away, she stopped, turned her head and gave him a flirtatious smile. She walked past another barmaid who muttered, in her thick cockney accent, "What is such an aristocratic gentleman doing in a place like this?"

Fredric could not help but notice how pretty the barmaid looked in her low cut checkered blouse that revealed her cleavage and her long skirt that was pulled up on one side and tucked into her waist showing off her long slim legs. Fredric kept looking at her as she walked through the crowded floor towards the bar.

A few minutes later, she returned with an open bottle of champagne and two glasses. She placed them on the table then pulled over a chair and sat down across from Fredric. "What is your name? Fredric asked of this cockney barmaid. "Molly," she replied. "Do you like working here?" he asked. "I do and I make good tips working here by being nice to gentlemen like you." Fredric looked into her eyes and proposed a toast "To life and to the beauty of life."

As they drank together, Molly became very loud and silly. "Another bottle of champagne," Fredric demanded. When Molly stood up to go to the bar she had to hold on to the back of her chair for a brief moment to steady herself.

When she returned to the table, Fredric suggested they take the bottle upstairs so they can spend some quiet time together. "I have a nice room upstairs," she said in a slurred voice.

Fredric stood up, put some money on the table, and then followed Molly through the thinning crowd up a broken wooden stairway that was along side of the bar.

When they reached the top of the stairway, Fredric looked down at everyone and just shook his head, then followed Molly to her room. He stayed close to her as she opened the door and entered a very small, shabby room. There was a broken dresser to the left of the door with a ceramic basin on it filled with water. A wrinkled bedspread covered a very large bed that leaned against the wall next to a small nightstand. There were candles burning, giving off a strong odor of wax but not much light.

Molly closed the door behind Fredric and proceeded to tell him how handsome he was. He smiled at her while looking deep into her eyes. Fredric then placed his hands on her shoulders drawing her close to him while pulling her blouse down revealing her round full breasts. Fredric leaned over Molly kissing her on her lips and then her neck while continuing to undress her. He began to unbutton is pants while still staring into Molly's eyes then placed one hand behind her legs picking her up and placing her gently on the bed. She seemed impressed with his strength and at the same time bewildered. Molly did not say a word as she continued to stare into Fredric's eyes as he moved on top of her.

Fredric continued to stare into Molly's eyes as his facial expression slowly changed. The whites of his eyes turned blood red and his two eye teeth began to protrude downward. He leaned over Molly placing his body over hers, kissing her passionately, as she tried to scream out. Because of Fredric's size and strength, she began gasping for air and could not remove herself from beneath him. He was afraid someone would hear her screams so he placed one hand over her mouth and nose while holding her down with the other and then bit into her neck. She tried to escape but could not. He turned her head to bite down on her neck again as she struggled for a few more moments, then there was no more movement, just blood running down the side of her neck onto the pillow.

Fredric lay on top of Molly for a short while longer. He then stood up thinking, as he looked at her lifeless body sprawled across the bed that someone might wonder where she was. All he could think of now was how fast he could get out of the pub.

Fredric bolted from the room leaving the door open and raced towards the stairs. When one of the barmaids walked past the open door, she noticed Molly's nude body lying across the bed, and began to scream. When the male patrons heard the screams, they tried to stop Fredric as he leaped down the stairs. The men made a desperate attempt to hold him down but Fredric was much too strong for them as he picked up and flung each one across the smoke filled room, breaking the back of one and the arm of another Fredric was able to escape by crashing through the front doors.

When he spotted his coach Fredric began to scream at the coach-man, "Ride fast." He caught up with the coach and jumped into the back seat still screaming, "Ride fast, don't stop, the sun will rise soon."

As the coach sped away, he looked through the rear window and watched as the men who gave chase after him became small specs in the distance.

As the coach picked up speed, Fredric sat back and thought about the brutal act he had just committed. For the first time in his life, Fredric was scared. He began to cry out loud realizing that he could have committed this same act of brutality on his new love, Leona. He also knew that this loss of self-control and lust for blood could not continue. He placed both of his hands over his face and continued to cry, making strange howling noises.

Finally, the coach approached Fredric's house and began to slow down. Fredric jumped from the coach and ran up the front steps just as the sun was slowly rising. He walked through the front door, grabbed a bottle of wine from the top of a table in the foyer and quickly dashed up the stairs to his bedroom.

There was one window in the bedroom covered with a heavy dark velvet drapery. He instinctively ran over to the window and closed the drapes just in time. He opened the bottle of wine and poured it into a glass that he kept on the night table next to his bed and began to drink the entire bottle while still pondering the heinous act he had committed before falling into a restless sleep.

FREDRIC'S RETURN TO TRANSYLVANIA

Fredric awoke the next evening and began to pace around the bedroom. He was very concerned that there would be a repeat of what had happened the previous night. He sat on the edge of his bed trying to figure out what to do, when he suddenly realized that in his haste to leave Transylvania, several weeks earlier, he did not take the medicines on which he was experimenting. Perhaps one of these might have prevented the murder and help keep his need for human blood under control. It was then that he decided to return to Transylvania as soon as possible so he could continue his research and develop some medication that would stop this horrible dependence and thirst for human blood.

Fredric was falling in love with Leona. He had to see her again and perhaps convince her to go with him back to Transylvania.

That evening he had his coachman take him to Leona's house.

Fredric was quite nervous when he knocked on her front door. There was no answer. He knew he was not expected; perhaps Leona saw him from her bedroom window and told her servant not to answer. He knocked harder. Finally, the servant asked from behind the closed door, "Who is it?"

"Dr. Gruel, I have come to see Miss Leona." The servant opened the door slightly and asked, "Is Miss Leona expecting you?"

"No. but I must speak to her," Fredric said in a firm voice. "Come in, but you must wait here," the servant said.

Fredric was very anxious to see Leona, but it was her father, Dr. Stroud, in his gold silk bathrobe, who was walking towards him. "Why are you here so late?" he asked. "I must talk to Leona, it is very important that I talk with her tonight," Fredric insisted. The doctor told Fredric to follow him into the study and then closed the door behind them.

Dr. Stroud told him in a strong voice. "I think it would be in everyone's best interest if you do not call on Leona again." Fredric appeared very distraught as the doctor explained that he had checked into his past only to find out what kind of a merciless killer his brother, Count Vladimir Gruel, actually was and Fredric was of the same blood.

Fredric tried, in vein, to explain to Dr Stroud that he was nothing like his brother. This was a problem that he had to live with all his life and he refuses to be blamed for his brother's wrong doings.

"I have come here to ask for Leona's hand in marriage and tell her that I must go back to Transylvania for a few weeks so I can continue my research and I want her to come with me. I love her very much and you must believe me when I tell you that I will cherish and protect her and not let anything happen to her."

Dr. Stroud did not appear to be receptive to what Fredric had to say. He began to pace the floor and puff on an unlit pipe.

"Under no circumstances will I give my blessing for my daughter to go with you to Transylvania." Then, abruptly, with no more conversation, the doctor put his hand on Fredric's shoulder and told him that it was getting late and Leona had already retired for the evening. He assured him that he would discuss everything with her in the morning, as he walked him towards the front door. "I will explain to her that you are asking for her hand in marriage, but I want you to know that I am against this and Leona must think very carefully before she makes a decision."

When they reached the front door, Dr. Stroud opened it. Fredric extended his hand to the doctor and told him he would be back in several weeks and that he appreciated his understanding. The doctor then closed the door behind him.

Fredric entered his awaiting coach and called out to the driver, "Take me home, directly home."

Fredric arranged to leave for Transylvania by steamer the next evening. The first stop was to be in France, then he would be transported by train to Germany then take another train through the mountains of Romania to Transylvania.

After the steamer trip, and then several days of sleeping on the train in a room with no windows only a bed, a chair and two candelabras that created a misty light and no human blood to sustain him, Fredric was very weak. His one comfort was a box of Transylvanian earth that lay on the floor next to his bed. His servant, Joseph had given it to him before he left for England.

The train came to an abrupt stop as it reached the station.

A short time later, his servant awakened Fredric, "There is a young woman waiting outside to see you. Shall I bring her in?" he whispered. As he tried to sit up, Fredric realized just how weak he was. "Give me a few minutes to get myself ready then bring her in." he answered.

The servant left to fetch the woman. When he returned he knocked on the door, opened it and allowed the woman to pass in front of him, then closed the door behind her.

There stood a young woman in a heavy blue coat with a small grey hat resting on an angle on top of her strawberry blonde hair.

Looking her over, then staring straight into her eyes, Fredric asked her why she was on the train. "This is how I earn my living" she replied. Fredric inquired as to her name and age. "Catherine and I am 19 years old," she answered meekly. He then asked her to remove her coat while continuing to stare into her eyes. She opened her coat allowing it to drop to the floor.

Fredric began to unbutton her white ruffled blouse as she stood there not saying a word. Then he unbuttoned her skirt and removed her undergarments, leaving her naked. "How much will you pay me?" she asked. "Do not speak now," Fredric whispered, staring at her naked body. She took a step back falling onto the bed as Fredric stood over her, slowly unbuttoning his trousers. He then lay on top of her as the whites of his eyes began to turn to a deep red. He began to kiss her as she tried to move out from under him. He held her down with one hand and placed the other hand over her mouth and nose as his eyeteeth began to protrude downwards. She tried hard to push him off her, but he was to over powering.

Fredric bit into her neck taking her life until her body went limp and blood was running down her neck onto the bed. Her eyes remained wide open looking up at the ceiling as he removed himself off her then stood up.

Fredric quickly dressed himself, grabbed his things and rushed out of the cabin leaving his box of earth behind and this poor young woman sprawled across the bed. He then leaped off the train just as it began to leave the station.

Fredric decided not to allow himself to think of why he committed this heinous act again. He merely comforted himself by believing that he will discover a cure for what he could not control.

FREDRIC EXPERIMENTS

Even though there was a full moon, it was very dark outside the train station. There was a heavy mist lingering above the ground making it more difficult to see.

Fredric was impatiently waiting for his coach to arrive when he spotted a light coming towards him. As it came closer, he was able to recognize that it was his coachman Pulaski. "I am sorry master, I could not find you in this mist," he apologized.

Fredric held the lantern and followed the coachman, who was carrying his luggage down a narrow dirt path, to where the coach was waiting. Fatigued and anxious, he climbed into the coach and told the driver to take him directly to his castle.

After climbing on top of the coach, Pulaski picked up the reins and yelled to the lead horses, "Move out, move out". The black feathered plume on top of the horse's mane began to blow in the wind as they moved in unison into a fast gallop. They moved through a series of winding turns and narrow dirt roads as if they knew every turn and patch in the road.

As he sat in the coach Fredric's mind began to wander back to the recent incident on the train. "How horrible it was to have to kill in order to sustain oneself," he thought.

After a long uncomfortable ride, Pulaski pulled back hard on the reins causing the horses to slow down almost to a walk as the carriage crossed over a narrow mote that led up to the front doors of Fredric's castle.

Pulaski jumped off the driver's seat and opened the coach door. Fredric was so weak that he had to hold on to both sides of the coach as he stepped out into the chilly night air.

There was a mist hovering over the damp earth as Fredric walked up to the castle doors.

Pulaski had to force open the heavy wooden front door. It squeaked as he finally pushed it open. The castle was very dark and damp and there was a thick musty odor in the air. Fredric held a handkerchief over his nose and mouth as he began to cough.

Pulaski then left to tend to the horses leaving Fredric alone in the dark foyer. Just then, his much-loved servant, Joseph entered the front hall apologizing, "I was not expecting you, master, I did not hear from you regarding your return. Stay here and I will light the candles so you can see your way up to your bedroom."

Joseph began lighting the candles enabling Fredric to see that the castle was not properly attended to while he was away.

The castle halls were made of thick grey blocks of stone that went all around the interior and up a stone stairway near the back hall that led to the upstairs bedrooms. Mounted on both sides of the wall and up the staircase were gold sconces. There were several fabric paintings held up by swords representing several hundred years of the Gruel family history, but there was one in particular that was hanging by the front stairway that Fredric always stopped to look at. It was a large portrait of Fredric himself standing on a hill overlooking his vineyards.

As Joseph continued to light the candles, Fredric stood there looking at his portrait remembering when he was a very young boy. He was happy then, life was simple. There were many servants in the castle and all the rooms were bright. His parents always gave splendid parties and the guests would dance under the large chandeliers that lit up the main hallway. All Fredric could do now was stand there in total silence, think of the past, and wonder if Leona could accept the kind of life that he leads now.

Fredric was getting very tired as he ascended the stairs to his large, but sparsely furnished bedroom. There was a large wooden, burl-finished bed with four engraved corner posts. Covering the bed was a dark burgundy velvet bedspread that had the family crest embroidered in the center. The bed was in a far corner away from the window. Fredric did not like to sleep on a pillow so the bed stood perfectly flat with a large gold figurine of the moon hanging on the wall above the headboard.

Before retiring, Fredric walked to the window, pulled the drapery open, and bowed his head until the moon faded behind the clouds. He then closed the drapery and lay down on the bed falling into a deep sleep.

When he awoke the next evening, he felt very weak and depressed. He could only think of what he had experienced with Leona. He was truly in love with her and it was beginning to wear on his mind. He knew that if he ever wanted to be with her, he must develop a cure for this insidious disease. There must be something that would prevent this horrible craving for human blood.

Several days went by as Fredric began to calculate, in his mind, how he was going to proceed with his experiments.

He read the journals of Sir William Harvey who was an English Physician noted for discovering how blood circulates throughout the human body.

Fredric believed that blood was the river of life for every human being. He also knew that if he was to remain immortal, he had to develop a special blood transfusion device that would transfer a blood substitute into his system without upsetting the basic element of his immortal life, and his existing blood cells.

Now he was ready to work in his laboratory in the basement of the castle. There he could read his medical journals and restore his medical instruments that would allow him to continue his work.

First, he scrubbed down the worktable and benches then he washed the walls, then the floors. Fredric had no help; he was simply driven by his own desire to succeed.

Fredric knew that he must create a method of blood doping that would increase the number of red blood cells in his body allowing him to improve and sustain his body while weaning himself off the desire for human blood.

Over the next several weeks, Fredric would pace the laboratory floor and throw objects in fits of rage. He could not yet achieve his goals. His mind would wander and his thoughts would always be of Leona. "Is she waiting for me? Has she forgotten about me? Has she begun to see another man?" He had no one to talk to so he began to talk aloud to himself only to cry out that much more.

Fredric's desire for human blood was starting to grow again. In the past, whenever he had a thirst for human blood, his servant Joseph, being a vampire himself, would find a way to provide it for him. Fredric never asked him where he attained the blood. He felt assured that he would do the same this time.

However, one evening while working in the laboratory, the thirst for blood began to overtake him and he could not control himself any longer. He could not wait for Joseph to provide him with the needed blood. He called out to Joseph, "Call Pulaski right away and have him bring the coach around to the front."

"At once master," Joseph replied.

Fredric took off his white laboratory coat and replaced it with his formal black velvet jacket and cape. He then grabbed his walking stick, dashed up the stairs and rushed out the front door.

There was a full moon and Fredric could feel the power of the moon drawing on him as he entered the back of the coach. He called to Pulaski, "Take me to the village."

As the coach moved swiftly along the winding roads towards the village, Fredric started to develop a feeling of hopelessness. He knew what he had to do in order to keep sustaining himself.

As the coach approached the small village of Krimsky, Fredric called out to Pulaski, "Slow down, turn in towards the back streets." He did not want any of the town's people to recognize his coach.

As the coachman carefully steered the coach through the back streets, they came upon four women standing together. "Stop," Fredric called out to Pulaski. As the coach came to a halt, Fredric leaned out of the window asking them, in a very pleasant voice, "Would one of you young ladies like to take a ride with me?" The four young women began to whisper among themselves before one of them stepped forward and accepted the offer.

Fredric opened the door and put out his hand to help her to step in. She sat down along side of him while the other ladies began to giggle.

Fredric called out to Pulaski to proceed slowly.

As the coach pulled away, Fredric took out a blanket from beneath the seat, "This will keep you warm," he said as he laid the blanket across her lap.

As she took off her hat, Fredric noticed how young she was. "What is your name?" Fredric asked of the young woman. "My friends call me Tina."

"Do you always get into coaches with strangers?" he asked. "Every so often," she replied.

As they talked, Fredric noticed how her long blond hair rested gently on her shoulders and the amount of makeup she wore was in strong contrast to her light blue eyes and fair skin.

They continued to talk as the coach moved slowly through the village. The more Tina looked into his eyes; his desire for her blood became stronger.

"How old are you?" Fredric asked of this poor soul. Thoughts of Leona crept into his mind when she answered, "Nineteen."

Tina then leaned across her seat and placed her hand on his inner thigh. She began to kiss Fredric on his neck, then his ear. Fredric placed his hand on her breast at the same time Tina unbuttoned her red coat and then her dress. He stared into her eyes as he slipped his hand under her garments.

Fredric was becoming confused with emotion, not wanting to hurt Tina and thoughts of Leona kept entering his mind. He placed his hand on Tina's neck pulling her closer to him. At the same time he felt himself losing control and he began to turn into the vampire he really was. Fredric could see the fright in her eyes as he began to turn into this malicious monster. The whites of his eyes turned to a blood red as his eye teeth began to protrude downward. She tried to push him away as she gasped for air but he held on to her neck tightly until she stopped moaning.

When Fredric realized that she was no longer breathing, he leaned over her, biting down on her neck draining the warm blood from her body. He became crazed in his frenzy for her blood.

After satisfying himself, he pushed Tina's still body away from him. Her eyes remained open, staring at him as if asking, "Why did you do this to me?"

The first thought that came into his mind was his obsession with Leona. He placed his hands over his face and began to cry out, "Why, why?"

He then called to Pulaski to drive towards the castle.

Fredric was not able to take his eyes off Tina's still body leaning against the back seat. He called out to Pulaski, "Pull off the road."

When the coach came to a stop, he opened the door and gently removed Tina's body and carried her into the woods to a small clearing. He placed her body on the ground and began to put leaves and branches on top of her. Tina's eyes continued to look up at him until she was fully covered.

Fredric, beside himself in his anguish, stood up and walked back to the coach with his head down. Before entering the coach, he turned towards the direction of the poor girl's dead body and bowed his head in prayer, asking for forgiveness for the crime he had just committed. He entered the coach and called out to Pulaski, "Take me home."

Arriving back at the castle, Fredric immediately ran down the stone stairway to the laboratory. He had to continue working and he would not leave the castle again without discovering a true blood substitute.

Fredric began experimenting by mixing his blood with the blood of small, warm-blooded animals and injecting it into himself. His biggest fear was that one of these animals was contaminated with a disease and he would become infected with a disease that could affect his body or mind or both. He experimented using a variety of plants, and insects hoping to find the illusive blood substitute.

Fredric knew that time was running out. Leona would surely forget about him if much more time went by.

One evening, while the moon was full, Fredric decided to take a walk through his vineyards. He began thinking of the different ways his wine would ferment but not turn sour and lose its glucose consistency. As he continued walking, the somber expression on his face changed to joy for the first time in many weeks. This might also work with blood, he thought. Elated, he began to run back to the castle. In his haste, Fredric did not notice the under brush that was growing from between the grapevines causing him to loose his footing several times and fall. He was so excited about his new idea that he picked himself up and continued to run until he reached the castle where he leaped down the stairs and began working on his new idea.

Fredric began the experiment by using a fermented mix made up of his wine grapes with a small percentage of alcohol and then mixing in his own blood cells with the fermented wine grape mixture. He believed that if he could keep this new discovery at the same temperature as his body for a period of two weeks, this blood substitute would stabilize. He would then be able to drink this new blood as a substitute for the human blood he always killed for.

Fredric endured a tormenting two weeks. Finally, the time had come for him to test his new blood mixture. He poured it into a glass and began to drink with such excitement that it spilled down his chin and on to his shirt.

He took empty wine bottles from his wine cellar and filled them with his newfound liquid, life-giving substitute.

Fredric continued to produce the new wine and would drink up to four bottles each night.

He knew that he must now test himself to be sure that it worked. He called out to Joseph to summon Pulaski to bring the coach around to the front of the castle. Fredric, wearing his black suit and cape, waited for his coach knowing that this evening would be the most important one of his life. He then jumped into the coach as he called out to Pulaski, "Take me to the village, quickly."

As the coach drove off, Fredric knew that he was about to test the future of his life. The coachman kept yelling out to the horses, "Faster, faster," as he whipped them with the reins. Fredric had to hold on to the sides of the coach as it reeled from side to side.

As the coach drove on, he was able to see the spot in the woods where he placed the body of the prostitute Tina. "Hurry up, your driving to slow," Fredric called out.

The coach approached the outskirts of the village. "Make sure you take the back streets," he yelled.

As the coach went through the narrow, back streets, Fredric noticed two women standing in the doorway of an old building. He called to Pulaski to pull off to the side of the road and wait for him.

He stepped out of the coach and proceeded to walk down the narrow, poorly lit, cobblestone street towards the two young women.

One of the women called out, "Can I be of some service to you, sir?" Fredric looked at her for a moment then said, "Maybe, I am looking for an hour of relaxation." The two women whispered to each other then one of them said, "I can give you some of that, sir." Fredric walked back to the coach with the young woman walking closely behind, then opened the door of the coach and held out his hand to help her enter. She hesitated for a moment saying, "My friend disappeared a while back, how do I know I can trust you?"

"I am a nobleman who will pay you well," Fredric said as he used his hypnotic powers while gazing into her eyes.

She entered the coach and sat down next to him as he closed the door behind her. "Drive on," Fredric called to Pulaski knowing that he knew exactly where to go.

As the coach moved forward, Fredric placed his hand under her chin, carefully untied a black ribbon and removed her hat. "What is your name and how old are you?" he asked. "My name is Lottie and I am eighteen, but I will be nineteen in two weeks," she replied in a soft voice. He kept staring into her eyes as he gently ran his fingers through her long thick red hair. She continued looking into his eyes and asked, "How can I please you, sir?" He did not answer; he just continued to look into her eyes as she began to unbutton her coat, then her blouse.

As Fredric placed his hands over her small breasts, he began to feel a new urge rushing throughout his body. This was something that he had never felt before. It was a true desire to make love to a woman without the urge to kill her for her blood. At that moment, Fredric was overwhelmed with the knowledge that he was capable of making love without the desire to kill.

Fredric gently lifted Lottie's head, gave her a kiss on her far head, and thanked her for her time. "I am not finished sir," the young woman insisted. "I am," he replied, "I am completely satisfied." Fredric called out to Pulaski, "Drive back to the village."

"I am very sorry that I was not able to satisfy you, sir," Lottie said shyly. Fredric reached into his purse, took out some money and placed it in her hand.

As the coach came to a stop he opened the door and helped Lottie pass by him as he held her hand. When she stepped out of the coach, she turned and gave him a smile. "Have a long life and enjoy the beauty of life," Fredric wished her as he watched her walk down a dark narrow street and disappear into the night.

"Pulaski, take me back to the castle" Fredric contentedly called out.

Arriving back at the castle, Fredric immediately ran down to the laboratory and began to celebrate the first day of his new life. He paced around the laboratory with new excitement knowing that he could go back to London to see Leona again and ask for her hand in marriage.

Fredric opened several bottles of his new wine, gulping them down one after the other. He was not able to quench his thirst until he finally passed out.

He must have been asleep for several hours when he suddenly woke up thinking that everything was just a dream. He slowly looked around at the mess he made in the laboratory and all at once he began to remember everything that had occurred. It was true, after all his hard work; Fredric actually did find a blood substitute that worked.

Now he knew that he had to return to London immediately to try to convince Leona to marry him.

It was still early in the evening so Fredric sent his coachman to the home of Dr. Rolf Luden, a close boyhood friend and confidant, to ask him to come to the castle.

Dr. Luden was the only person who knew that his older brother, Count Gruel, had turned Fredric into a vampire when he was a young boy.

Like Fredric, Dr. Luden was a well-known doctor to the elite and wealthy people of Transylvania and he also had his own vineyards but he was not a vampire.

Several hours later, the doctor arrived at the castle. Fredric met him at the front door and escorted him downstairs to the laboratory.

Dr. Luden was a tall, handsome man with a full head of wavy, dark brown hair and a well-trimmed beard. Upon entering the laboratory, Fredric sat him down and explained to him about his experiments and his new blood substitute.

Dr. Luden was extremely pleased for his dear friend as he shouted out excitedly, "We must share a bottle of your new discovery together." Fredric then told him that he had never tried this on a mortal before. "Then we must get drunk together," his friend, insisted.

Fredric began to pour the wine without any hesitation and both of them started to drink. "This wine seems to taste a lot sweeter and has a deeper color than your other wines, why is that?" Rolf asked. "This wine is made from my blood," Fredric answered. After hearing that, Rolf spit out the wine and started to retch, "How could you?" he asked. Fredric laughed while he gave his friend a glass of water. It took a few minutes for Rolf to feel better.

"Sit down, my friend; I have some very important news to discuss with you." Fredric went on to tell him that he had always been his closest and dearest friend. "You know what I am and my new discovery could possibly turn my dead life around and make me near normal, but I cannot live in Transylvania any longer, I must leave." Rolf looked at him oddly, "Where will you go, where will you live? What about the vineyards, who will take care of them?"

"When I was in London I met a young lady, her name is Leona and I am deeply in love with her. I want to marry her but she has no idea that I am a vampire. She thinks I am just a doctor doing research and that is why I came back to Transylvania. When I go back to London I intend to take many barrels filled with my new wine with me, but I need someone to oversee my vineyards while I am gone. The vineyards will be my only lifeline. Rolf, can you do this enormous favor for me? I have no one else to ask."

Rolf just sat there for a few moments with his head bent over and his hands covering his face, not saying a word. He raised his head slowly, "This is such a surprise, but you are my best friend and I cannot say no to you. I will help you any way I can." Fredric walked over to Rolf, as he stood up, shook his hand and gave him a big hug.

Fredric then suggested that they celebrate together by opening a bottle of wine. Rolf gave Fredric a strange look and said, "I'd rather not." Fredric laughed and said, "Wine from my regular stock." They then toasted each other with a glass of vintage wine.

FREDRIC GOES BACK FOR LEONA

Fredric knew that he needed a trustworthy sea captain to attain a ship and crew for his long arduous trip to London. Rolf will make all the arrangements for me. He had, after all, said he would do anything he could to help me, Fredric thought to himself.

The next day, Rolf set out to find a sea captain after Pulaski delivered the request to him. Rolf visited local pubs to put out the word.

After several days of anxiously waiting, there came a knock at the door. Dr. Luden's servant opened the front door to find a scruffy looking, unshaven old codger wearing a torn black coat with a black woolen hat pulled over his ears and most of his head. "I'm looking for a Dr. Luden, is he here?" the old man asked, "Whom shall I say is calling?" the servant responded. "Tell him Captain Ulrich." The servant told him to wait while he called the doctor.

"There is a strange looking gentleman at the front door looking for you, sir," the servant advised the doctor. Rolf instructed his servant to let him in and wait with him.

The doctor came into the front parlor and asked the man how he could help him. "My name is Captain Victor Ulrich; I was told that you are looking for a ship and crew that would take you to England." The doctor told him that he was, and asked if he could arrange it. "When do you want to leave?" the captain asked. "As soon as possible, but I will not be taking the trip. It is for a very dear friend of mine who is ill," the doctor disclosed.

"Any special cargo involved?" the captain asked. "Yes, there will be barrels of wine and some furniture, and also, my friend must have a room where there is no sunlight. He must also be able to walk around the ship at night. He is not a well man and is not to be disturbed, that is a must. Do you understand?"

"Yes," the captain replied, "I understand."

The doctor advised the captain that he would pay him half when he gets back to him with the name and location of the ship and his friend will pay him the other half when he arrives in London.

The captain assured the doctor that he would be back in three days with all the arrangements made.

Three days later, Captain Ulrich returned to Dr. Luden's house to finalize the preparations. It was agreed that all the barrels of wine and the furniture would be loaded on the ship during the day and Dr. Gruel would board the ship at night.

The next day Rolf went to Fredric's house to explain all the arrangements. Fredric was extremely thankful for what his friend had done for him. "Rolf, I do not know if I will ever come back to Transylvania, so I have made arrangements for you to become a partner with me in my export business," Fredric happily advised him. Rolf gave Fredric a hug, "I wish you well, my friend. I hope you know what you are doing."

Rolf left the castle leaving Fredric and Joseph alone. "Let us go into the library," Fredric suggested, giving him the opportunity to tell Joseph that he had made the decision not to take him along on his journey.

"Joseph, you have been like a father to me all these years, but I do not know what the future has in store for me. I need someone to take care of the castle while I am away and help Rolf with the vineyards. I hope you understand."

Joseph was upset and disappointed.

He told Fredric to sit down as he spoke in a low but firm voice.

"Fredric, there is something I should have told you many years ago, but I was afraid." Joseph began to speak with some hesitancy in his voice, "Fredric, Count Gruel is not your older brother, he is your father."

"What are you saying? That can't be true." Fredric shot back. He then picked Joseph up with very little effort, and was about to hurl him across the room. Joseph pleaded. "Put me down, please Fredric put me down, you're hurting me." Fredric put the screaming man down and started to pace around the library. "What was I thinking", he thought. "How could I ever hurt my devoted servant and friend?"

Joseph was a dedicated servant to the Gruel family. The short, stocky, well-educated man had been with the family for many years before Fredric was born. Joseph helped raise Fredric after his mother died when he was a young boy. Joseph educated Fredric and it was Joseph, a vampire himself, who tended to Fredric when Count Gruel turned him into a vampire while he was asleep in his bed.

"I do not believe you, Fredric said, "You are just saying this because you are not coming with me to England."

"Let me explain, when your mother and Count Gruel were young they were very much in love. The castle was alive with activity back then. It was a happy place. Then the unthinkable happened. One evening when the count arrived home from one of his campaigns, after being away for several months, he appeared frail and tired. Your mother took the count upstairs to their bedroom and began to help him undress only to discover two small punctures on the side of his neck. When she asked him what these puncture marks were from, he told her that he was attacked and bitten by a vampire bat several weeks earlier and that he felt a change going throughout his body ever since. You were just a young boy and had no idea what had happened.

As the weeks went by the count could not see in daylight and the sun caused his bones to become brittle and his body become somewhat disfigured. He had also lost his appetite for food.

One evening, when the count was down in his laboratory, your mother walked in on him and watched, in horror, as your father drank the blood of a rat.

The count and your mother could never sleep together after that.

A short time later a Small Pox epidemic broke out in the village and your mother, unfortunately, came down with the disease and died several weeks later.

The count felt that the devil himself had taken over his soul. Now the count only had hatred and revenge in his heart and he became the loathsome man that he is today.

The reason he turned you into a vampire was because he did not want the burden of taking care of a child. He thought that you would be able to take care of yourself if you were a vampire, and so he left me alone with you; I was to be your servant and caretaker. I am sorry that I had to tell you this now, but it is the truth and it had to be told."

Fredric looked straight into Joseph's eyes with sadness and told him, "You did the right thing by telling me. I am sorry that I have to leave you now, but it is getting late and I must go."

Fredric was walking towards the front door when Joseph called out to him, "Wait, master, wait, I have something for you." He handed Fredric a burgundy and gold box that contained more earth from Transylvania. "Because you left the sacred box of earth on the train, I am giving you another. Keep this with you always. It will give you comfort and keep you safe throughout eternity."

The coach was waiting for Fredric when he left the castle to begin the long journey back to London. He was aware that the trip to the seaport would take several hours and he must get there before the next sunrise.

The long drive to the seaport gave Fredric plenty of time to think about what Joseph had told him.

The story of his childhood seemed to make sense, but how was he to know for sure?

Fredric arrived at a hotel in the fishing village early the next morning, just before sunrise and went straight to his room. He made sure the draperies were closed tight so as not to allow any sunlight in. Then he went to sleep.

That evening there was a knock at the door. "Who is it, Fredric asked, "Dr Gruel, I am Captain Ulrich. All of your possessions have been brought on the ship and we are just waiting for you."

"I am ready to leave" Fredric responded.

He then followed the captain through the poorly lit, narrow streets until they came to the boarding plank that led up to the ship.

As they walked up the plank to the deck, Fredric could not stop looking at the three tall masts and the crew that were waiting for the captain's orders to set sail. It was then that Fredric realized that he would be the only passenger on this small ship.

The captain decided to take Fredric to his cabin before they set sail. Fredric followed him down a flight of stairs near the bow of the ship that led to a small cabin. Upon opening the door, a strong musty smell from damp rotting wood emanated into the hall. Inside the cabin was a small table and chair in a corner with an unlit candle on top and two unlit lanterns. One hung from a center beam and the other was on a small night table that stood along side of a narrow bed. As requested, the window was heavily boarded up to prevent sunlight from coming through. "I'm sorry but this is the best cabin we have," The captain explained. Fredric did not reply realizing the futility of the situation. He merely advised that captain that he must leave four bottles of his wine in front of his cabin door every evening after the sun sets.

The trip was to take three weeks, so Fredric settled in for a long monotonous journey.

Every evening Fredric would put on his burgundy velvet robe and open the cabin door where the four bottles of wine would be waiting. He would take in the bottles and immediately pour wine into a glass and make his toast, "To life and to the beauty of life." After drinking all the wine he would go up onto the deck and stare at the moon, not conversing with any of the crewmen.

After the first week of watching the same routine, some members of the crew were beginning to get suspicious of Fredric. "What was so special about this wine?" they wondered.

One night they conspired to wait until daybreak when Fredric was not on deck, and go down to the hull where the barrels of wine were being stored. They took one of the barrels and brought it up to their quarters thinking that Fredric would not miss it. They opened it and started drinking the wine by pouring it in a metal cup and passing it around.

It did not take long before each of the crew felt the effects of the wine going throughout their bodies. "There are so many barrels of wine,

I am sure this Dr. Gruel won't miss another barrel," one of them said. They laughed as they brought up another barrel, then another.

Not only were they getting drunk and losing control of themselves, but after several days, most of the crew became ill and began to lose their day vision.

The captain did not know what was going on and he could not understand why these men could not work during the day, only at night, after the sun went down.

Fredric also began to notice something strange. Each evening, as he would walk the deck, more of the crew would be topside with him.

A few more days went by when Fredric decided to go below the deck to where his barrels of wine were being stored. Upon entering the bottom hull, he was overcome by the heavy, musty air as he tried to feel his way around in the dark. He thought he heard some strange sounds coming from within the walls of the ship so he immediately used his powers to illuminate the hull that then took on a deep red glow. Suddenly hundreds of rats began to scatter around him and their sounds became louder and louder. This did not intimidate Fredric and he walked over to the wine barrels and counted them, only to find that several of them were missing.

Fredric became enraged as he leaped back up the stairs where he confronted the crew. "Why did you take my wine?" he screamed. "Don't you believe in sharing?" one of the crew shouted back.

Two of the crewmen rushed Fredric, grabbing him by his arms trying to tie him to the mast. Fredric became completely uncontrollable as the whites of his eyes turned to deep red and he broke loose from their grip. He began to hurl them, one by one, as each one tried rushing him again. He picked up a wooden beam and threw it through the stomach of one of the men. The blood began to gush out of the crewman's mouth. Fredric then picked up another with one hand and swung him into the mast breaking his neck. As two more crewmen rushed at him, he grabbed a rope from the mast and tied it around their necks hoisting them up the mast with one hand until they stopped kicking and screaming. It was all over in a matter of minutes.

The remaining crew stepped aside, in fear, as Fredric ran past them to go down to the captain's quarters.

Fredric began banging on the captain's door. Just as the captain opened the door, Fredric grabbed him by his nightshirt and pulled him out into the hall. He picked him up by his shoulders, held him up in the air, and continued to shake him, at the same time yelling, "What have you done with my wine?"

Fredric then dropped the captain to the floor. He suddenly realized that the crewmen were turning into vampires. Fredric was overwhelmed by the enormity of the changes that were taking place in the crew.

He also realized that he now had powers that he had never dreamed could be possible.

Fredric slowly walked back up the stairs to the deck that leads to his cabin. A full moon was coming out from behind some thick clouds and it appeared very low and bright, then he noticed the strangest thing. All the remaining crewmen were lined up on the bow of the ship facing the moon with their heads bowed. Fredric thought it was a trick and the men were going to rush him again, but instead, as he approached the stairway, the crewmen began to slowly walk towards him. Fredric stopped, not knowing what to expect. He turned towards them and looked directly at them when they all began to line up behind one another and face Fredric.

Astonishingly, one by one, each man took Fredric's hand, bowed his head, kissed the ring on Fredric's right hand and called him master.

When the last crewman bowed his head and kissed his ring, Fredric turned and walked to his cabin in disbelief. He sat down on the chair next to the table and opened a bottle of wine while thoughts of the recent events flooded his mind.

Fredric concluded that when a mortal drinks his wine continuously, over a short period of time, their blood cells will be replaced by new cells that were created by Fredric and therefore transform them into a partial vampire.

Fredric did not understand the total magnitude of what he had created, but the more thought he gave to it, the more he realized that he had created the beginning of a new life form with him as their leader and master.

After another week at sea, the ship finally docked in London. Before Fredric left the ship, he grabbed Captain Ulrich by the throat, *you had better not touch my wine or you will be swimming with the fish, do you understand?*

"Yes, I do," the terrified captain replied.

"I will make arrangements to remove the wine barrels from the ship," Fredric explained to the captain.

He then turned to the crew, "I have left several barrels of the wine for you in the hull. Drink the wine slowly; it will have to last until I can bring you some more."

Fredric then walked down the plank to his waiting carriage and told the coachman to take him home.

BACK IN LONDON

It was nearly four months since Fredric left London. He did not receive any letters from Leona in all that time and he was very anxious to see her, but he knew that he would have to wait one more evening before that could happen.

The ship arrived very early in the morning.

When Fredric walked down the plank he could see his coachman anxiously waiting for him.

He entered the coach just as the sun was beginning to rise, then he yelled out to the coachman, "Hurry up, hurry up, you must go fast." After a few kilometers, the coach arrived at his house.

Fredric opened the coach door, ran up the front steps and then opened the front door. He leaped up the entire flight of stairs to the second floor and immediately went to his bedroom and closed the partially opened draperies to block out any light from coming through.

Before Fredric got into bed he took out the small burgundy and gold box from his pocket that Joseph had given him before he left Transylvania and spread out some of the earth on the floor under his bed. Now he could go to sleep feeling protected.

Upon awakening the next evening, Fredric rose slowly and sat on the edge of his bed. He thought about his future with great anticipation. He could not wait to see Leona again.

Fredric dressed and walked onto the second floor balcony and into an adjoining room where his coachman had left several bottles of his new wine. He immediately opened and drank from two bottles. He then went to the main floor foyer where there were two more bottles of wine and a glass sitting on a table waiting for him. He poured himself another glass then walked outside to face the moon. Fredric held up the glass of wine and made his toast, "To life and to the beauty of life."

The coachman was already standing by the side of the coach when Fredric opened the front door, leaped down the front steps and got in. He shouted to the coachman "Take me to Dr Stroud's house."

The ride seemed endless, but when the coach pulled up in front of Dr. Stroud's house, Fredric immediately jumped out before the coach could come to a complete stop.

Fredric hesitated for a moment, regained his composure, then opened the front gate and slowly walked up the front steps and began knocking on the door. Soon a servant opened the door, "Can I help you?" he asked.

"Yes you can, do you remember me?" he asked. "I am Dr. Gruel, I am here to see Dr. Stroud."

"Is he expecting you?" asked the servant. "No, but I am sure he will see me," Fredric insisted. "Come in, but you must wait here, the doctor is in his study. I will go and announce you." The servant began to walk towards the study when he suddenly paused and turned towards Fredric to reassure himself that he was still standing by the front door.

The servant knocked on the study door, then opened it. The doctor was reading by the fireplace, "What is it?" he asked. "There is a Dr. Gruel waiting for you by the front door."

"Bring him in," the doctor responded.

Fredric followed the servant to the study. When he entered he saw Dr. Stroud standing in front of the fireplace wearing his gold silk robe and holding his hand carved pipe. "Dr. Gruel, what brings you here this evening?" he asked. Fredric nervously said, "Sir, I am here to ask you for Leona's hand in marriage."

Dr. Stroud, looking directly at Fredric asked him, "What makes you think that after all this time Leona has any interest in even seeing you?" Fredric tried to explain, "But I sent several letters weeks ago explaining that my research was taking much longer than I had anticipated and I would have to stay in Transylvania so I could finish my experiments. Sir, please believe me, my intentions are honorable and my love for your daughter runs deep within me. All I could think of while I was away was Leona. Could you please tell her that I am here?"

Dr. Stroud took a couple of steps towards Fredric, placed a hand on his shoulder and explained that Leona has been seeing another man. "You cannot blame her, she is young and beautiful and full of life and she did not hear from you at all," he explained. It was as if you had vanished."

Fredric pleaded with the Doctor to let him see her again so he could explain. When Fredric realized that he was begging, he quickly regained his composure.

"Let me think about the situation for awhile and I will get back to you in a few days," Dr. Stroud said calmly.

Fredric had never been refused anything before and it was hard for him to show restraint, but he knew he must be respectful, so he politely thanked the doctor for speaking to him at such a late hour.

The doctor walked Fredric to the front door and the servant handed him back his cape and hat. He had never felt so rejected. He climbed into his coach and told the driver to drive to the city.

It was getting late as the coach arrived in the city. "Stop in front of that pub," Fredric shouted to the driver. When the coach stopped, Fredric let himself out. He walked into the crowded, smoke filled pub and sat down at an empty table. The patrons were singing and dancing in the middle of the small dance floor. Their gaiety made him feel even more miserable.

After a short wait, a pretty barmaid approached Fredric and asked if he would like a glass of ale. He stared into her eyes as he said, "I want you with a pitcher of ale." The barmaid began to laugh out loud as she retorted, "The ale is cheap, but I am not." He grabbed her wrist while staring into her eyes blocking out the loud noise that was filling his head. He released her after telling her to find a room upstairs and bring back a pitcher of ale. She nodded that she would obey his wishes and left.

As Fredric sat by himself, it was hard for him not to think about Dr. Stroud's refusing to let him see Leona.

Fredric had briefly forgotten about the barmaid when she suddenly reappeared and told him to follow her upstairs. Visibly upset, he stood up and followed the barmaid up a staircase to a narrow hallway lit by a few candles. She then attempted to open a door that was falling off its hinges. Fredric told her to step aside as he pushed the door open with one hand.

Fredric followed the barmaid into this small smelly room that looked like it had never been cleaned. The barmaid walked around the bed that was practically against the door and placed the pitcher of ale on a small wobbly night table.

Fredric stood behind her, as there was little room to stand between the bed and the door.

As he closed the door, the woman asked, "What is your pleasure tonight?" Fredric could not control himself as he quickly turned and faced her with the whites of his eyes turning to a blood red. He placed both of his hands tightly around her throat. She began to gasp for air as he pushed her onto the bed. He then lay on top of her doing as he pleased. She tried to fight back but she was loosing consciousness. Her eyes remained open as her arms slowly dropped to her sides.

Fredric stood up, looked into the poor woman's open eyes, and then realized that had no desire for her blood.

He straightened himself up, gave her one more glance, then opened the door and quickly left. He walked down the stairs through the front door of the pub to where his coachman was waiting.

As Fredric entered the coach, he told the coachman to take him home.

During the ride home Fredric became filled with self-hatred, *"How could I have done this?* I killed this poor woman because I was thinking of Leona being with another man and I took out my frustrations on this poor barmaid."

When the coach pulled up in front of Fredric's house, he did not wait for the coachman to open the door; Fredric just let himself out and walked up the stairs.

Upon entering, he went directly to the wine cellar, pulled a few bottles of wine off the shelf, and took them up to his bedroom.

He immediately started to drink while pacing the floor trying to control the rage that had welled up inside of him. He knocked over a lamp and kicked a footstool.

The wine began to take its effect and calmed him down. Fredric then started drinking from a third bottle that made him extremely tired. He climbed onto his bed and fell into a deep sleep.

The next evening loud knocking on the front door awakened him, but he was so tired from the previous evening that he could hardly move. The knocks became louder and louder, so he reluctantly picked himself up, got out of bed and leaped from the balcony to the first floor where he composed himself before opening the door.

Much to his surprise, there stood Leona.

Fredric froze for a moment, staring at her, not saying a word. Leona was also staring at him not saying a word. Fredric was feeling pain and joy at the same time as he backed into the foyer not taking his eyes off her. Leona followed him into the foyer as the door closed behind them.

Once inside, Leona walked up to Fredric, placed her arms around his neck, hugged him tightly and gave him a long passionate kiss.

Fredric asked her how she knew he was home. "My father told me that you came to our house last night, I am so sorry that he did not wake me," she apologized. Fredric, taking Leona's arms from around his neck, stepped back just so he could take another look at her. Then he explained how he missed her and craved for her while he was away. "I sent you letters telling you about my research and how much I missed you, but I did not hear from you." He tried to explain but Leona interrupted him saying, "I missed you so much, I was so worried when I did not hear from you for weeks. When my father confessed to me that you had come to our home and that he had held on to your letters, I was furious.

I want to marry you, Fredric. I love you and I want to marry you."

At that moment, Fredric felt an eternal craving for life that he had never felt before.

He gently picked Leona up and carried her up the stairs as if she was weightless. She put her arms around his neck and tightly held on to him.

Fredric carried her to the master bedroom and placed her on his bed. As she lay there, he began to disrobe, anxious to see if Leona would object. She did not; she just lay there watching as he dropped his clothes to the floor. Leona then moved to one side allowing him more than enough room to join her.

Fredric lay down next to Leona and began to fondle her and kiss her passionately. He told her how much he missed her and loved her. Leona responded the same way.

Fredric then began to unbutton Leona's satin blue dress and there was no hesitation from her as she lay there helping him take it off.

Fredric leaned on his side so he could stare at Leona's beautiful, delicate body with its lovely curves as they continued to fondle each other. He continued to tell Leona how much he loved her while he slowly moved on top of her, not being able to control himself any longer, as they became one.

They lay in each other's arms for a long while, still lost in the exquisite sweetness of what they had shared, when Fredric said, "It is getting very late Leona your father will be worried. Get dressed and I will have my coachman take you home."

Leona appeared giddy with excitement as she told Fredric how happy she was and asked him when he will come to her house to talk to her father. "I will be there first thing tomorrow evening. I will never leave you again," he promised.

Fredric called out to his servant, "Have my coach brought around to the front of the house." He then walked Leona down stairs towards the front door.

The two lovers embraced once again before saying good-bye.

Fredric watched her as she ran to the coach and climb in. She leaned out of the window and waved as he followed the coach with his eyes until he could no longer see it.

Fredric returned to the house, went directly to the wine cellar, and removed several bottles of wine to bring with him to the study. He was troubled about Leona not knowing he was a vampire. After consuming two of the bottles, he decided to bring the other two upstairs to his bedroom.

He sat down on the edge of his bed and drank the rest of the wine with no desire to do anything more.

PROBLEMS WITH LEONA'S FATHER

The next evening, as promised, Fredric went to Leona's house to meet with her father and try to convince him to allow him to marry her.

As the coach pulled up in front of Leona's house, Fredric leaped out with great excitement while it was still moving. He ran up the steps to the front door, and knocked repeatedly until the servant opened the door.

Fredric immediately stepped in, not allowing the servant to close the door on him. "Please tell Dr. Stroud that Dr. Gruel is here," he said. The servant, taken by surprise, told him to wait right there while he would go and tell the doctor.

It was easy to see that the doctor was in his study by the direction in which the servant walked.

Fredric impatiently waited by the door for the servant to return. After waiting a few minutes longer, the servant returned only to tell Fredric that the doctor could not be disturbed at this time. Fredric became enraged. He walked past the servant and straight into the doctor's study.

The doctor was sitting in front of the fireplace with his back to the door and did not see Fredric enter. When the doctor turned around he saw Fredric standing there, he stood up and said in a loud voice, "I did not invite you in, what are you doing here?"

"I have come here one last time to ask for your permission to marry Leona."

"I will never allow you to marry my daughter, do you understand?" the doctor angrily shouted at Fredric.

Fredric, enraged by the doctor's attitude, closed the study door behind him and walked up to the doctor. He placed his right hand on Dr. Stroud's shoulder applying pressure while staring directly into the doctor's eyes. Dr. Stroud tried hard to release Fredric's hand but

Fredric was too overpowering for him as he slowly slumped into his chair. Fredric kept applying pressure to the doctor's shoulder until he was unconscious, then he let go and began feeling for the doctor's pulse. There was none.

Fredric composed himself and then opened the study door and called for the servant, "Get help, get help, the doctor had a heart attack, he needs help."

The servant ran out the front door for help just as Leona came running down the stairs after hearing the commotion. "Fredric, what happened? What are you doing? Where is my father?" She demanded. Fredric tried to restrain her from entering the study until another doctor could arrive.

Shortly after, the servant returned with an elderly gentleman wearing a night cap and a long striped night shirt under his coat. "I am Dr. Kravet, a friend of the family, he told Fredric, and I live a few doors away."

Then the elderly doctor, with a distraught look on his face, asked Leona, "Where is your father?" Weeping uncontrollably, Leona pointed to the study.

The doctor walked into the study to see Dr. Stroud slumped over in his chair. He felt for a pulse, but it was too late.

He turned to Leona and told her, "I am sorry to tell you my dear, but your father has died." Leona continued to cry as she tried reaching over the doctor to touch her father. Fredric put his arm around her in an effort to console her.

Dr. Kravet looked up at Fredric and asked, "Who are you?" Fredric explained that he was there to ask Dr. Stroud for Leona's hand in marriage. The doctor then turned to Leona, "Is this true?"

"Yes, it is true," she answered.

"Did you see what happened?" Dr. Kravet inquired of Fredric. "Yes, I was with the doctor when he suddenly grabbed his shoulder and slumped over in his chair without saying a word. I thought he was having a hear attack, so I ran to tell the servant to get help."

Dr. Kravet walked into the next room where the servant was waiting and told him to go for the police. The servant put on his coat and left knowing that this was the right thing to do.

The doctor then told Leona, "Let me take you up to your room and give you a sedative, it will calm you." "I am afraid to be alone right now. Can you or Fredric stay with me?" Leona asked. "I will stay with you until you fall asleep," Fredric said as he put his arm around her waist and led her upstairs.

Dr. Kravet gave Leona a kiss on the cheek telling her, "I will be right here if you need me."

Fredric walked Leona up to her room, "Maybe the thought of losing you was too much for your father to bear. He was just putting out his hand to congratulate me when he slumped over. I helped him into his chair, but I think his heart gave out from the excitement. I am so sorry Leona."

Leona lay down on her bed, then closed her eyes as she continued to weep. Fredric sat by her side until she fell asleep and then quietly backed out of the room.

By the time Fredric came down stairs, two police inspectors had arrived and were speaking to Dr. Kravet.

The doctor introduced Fredric to the Chief Inspector, "This is Chief Inspector Michaels."

"Inspector, this is Dr. Fredric Gruel. He was with Dr. Stroud when he died."

The Inspector began to question Fredric, "You do not sound like you are from around here." Fredric advised him that he recently arrived from Transylvania. "And what kind of a doctor are you?" The inspector inquired. "I am involved in research. The study of blood," Fredric disclosed. "You're last name sounds familiar to me," the inspector said.

"You might have heard of my older brother, Count Vladimir Gruel"

"Unfortunately, all of Europe has heard of the famous Count Vladimir Gruel. So you're his younger brother."

"I am one of his brothers." Fredric said. "Is it true that he drinks the blood of the dead?" Annoyed, Fredric told him that rumors spread very fast, even all the way to London.

The inspector asked Fredric why he came to the Doctor's house. "To ask Dr. Stroud for his daughter's hand in marriage," he stated. "What was the Doctors answer?"

"He said yes and was congratulating me when he collapsed into his chair.

"Where do you live now?"

"I live in a house a few kilometers away."

The Inspector advised Fredric to come to the police station the next day. "That would be impossible because I sleep during the day. You see, I have a rare blood disease that affects me when I walk into the sunlight. That is what my research is all about," he informed the inspector. "Alright then, I will see you tomorrow evening." Fredric agreed, then stood up and began walking towards the front door when the Inspector called out to him, "By the way, what type of research do you do?" I do research in the study of blood," Fredric answered, "Good night inspector," then turned and left.

Fredric was very troubled when he reached his coach. He stepped in and told the coachman to take him home.

When the coach arrived in front of Fredric's house, he let himself out and walked slowly towards the front door. He stopped on the first step and looked up at the moon until it disappeared behind the clouds, then continued walking up the stairs. He opened the front door and went directly to the wine cellar where he retrieved two bottles of his special wine before going to bed.

All this additional pressure was beginning to take its toll on him. He wanted to just lie down and fall asleep but he could not. His mind was racing with thoughts of loving Leona then killing her father, and the police making inquiries. The thought that it might be found out that he is a vampire would be devastating.

Only after he drank the wine and allowed it to flow through his veins was he able to fall asleep.

FREDRIC'S TRIP TO THE POLICE STATION

The next evening, as promised, Fredric arrived at the police station.

He encountered a policeman sitting at a very high desk looking down at him. In a very thick English accent he asked, "Could I be of some service to you?" Fredric told him he was looking for Chief Inspector Michaels. "Wait here and I'll try to find him," he replied.

Fredric was very nervous when the Inspector walked into the room. Inspector Michaels noticed that he was nervous and asked him if there is anything wrong. "I am not accustomed to being in a police station," Fredric said. The inspector told Fredric in a very soft tone, "You have nothing to be concerned about, this is just routine questioning. Why don't you follow me into my office where you will be more comfortable?"

Fredric followed the inspector down a dark corridor to his office where he told Fredric to sit down. The office was very dark and dingy with only two lamps lit on the walls and one lamp lit on the Inspector's cluttered desk.

Fredric, looking around the tiny room, saw that there were no windows. He was beginning to feel very uncomfortable as the inspector began his questioning. "What country do you come from?"

"I come from Transylvania," Fredric replied. "Oh, I forgot, what do you do there again?" the inspector asked. "My home and laboratory are there. That is where I do my research."

"Why are you here?" the inspector inquired. "I am also one of the largest exporters of wine in Europe and I came here on business."

The inspector's voice was becoming louder, "How did you meet Miss Leona?" I met her at a ball given by Count Lexer several months ago."

"You know Count Lexer?" the Inspector asked. "I know him very well, he is a business associate of mine and we have become good friends."

"I did not know that," the inspector said in amazement.

"How long have you been engaged to Miss Leona?" Fredric replied, "I had gone to Dr. Stroud's house to ask him for Leona's hand in marriage."

"Have you known Miss Leona long," The inspector asked again. Fredric repeated, "I met her for the first time at Count Lexer's ball and fell in love with her right away."

"Please explain to me again exactly what happened last evening," the inspector requested. "I arrived at Dr. Stroud's home just after sunset and was allowed in by their servant who took me into Dr. Stroud's study. The doctor was sitting facing the fireplace when I was announced. The doctor stood up facing me when I told him that I was here to ask for Miss Leona's hand in marriage. The good doctor looked startled for a moment then as he put out his hand to shake mine, he collapsed back into his chair holding onto his left shoulder. I felt for a pulse, but there was none so I called out to the servant to get help. That is all there was. It happened so fast," Fredric recounted.

"Are you still planning to stay here and marry Miss Leona?" the inspector inquired. "Maybe I will bring her back with me to Transylvania in a couple of weeks," Fredric replied.

"That will be all doctor, thank you for your time," the inspector said.

Fredric stood up and began walking towards the door when the inspector called out to him, "I need you to stay in town until after the inquest. It would probably be best if you would restrict your self to your home for the next several days."

Fredric left the police station and walked to his coach that was waiting for him just outside. When he entered his coach, he sat there thinking of what had just occurred and worked himself into a state of rage. He sat there for a few moments trying to calm down. He then called to the coachman to take him home.

When the coach pulled up in front of his house, Fredric let himself out and began to walk towards the front steps; he stopped, looked up at the moon and just stood there confused not knowing if he should go to Leona's house or abide by what the inspector said and stay at home. He then turned and began to walk back to the coach that was still standing there. Changing his mind once again, he turned and walked fast up the steps to the front door.

He opened the door and went directly to his wine cellar letting the front door close behind him. Fredric then took several bottles of his special wine, placed them under his arms and carried them upstairs to his bedroom.

When he reached the bedroom, he immediately pulled the cork from one of the bottles and began drinking directly from the bottle. Fredric continued to drink while pacing back and forth, and was well aware of the fact that he could not stay in London much longer. He wanted to take Leona back with him to Transylvania and he also wanted to finally do away with his older brother, Count Gruel.

As the night dragged on, Fredric began to formulate a plan.

Several days past and Fredric did not hear from the inspector or Leona. Then one evening Fredric heard someone banging hard on the front door. He ran out of his bedroom and in his excitement jumped from the second floor balcony to the first floor. The banging became louder and louder. He opened the door and much to his surprise there stood Captain Ulrich who exclaimed, "I heard of your problem with the police and maybe I can be of some assistance to you." Fredric just stood there for a moment looking directly at the captain not saying a word, when the captain asked if he could come in. "Please do," Fredric answered.

The captain followed Fredric into the foyer and when he asked the captain if he wanted a glass of his special wine, Captain Ulrich replied, without any hesitation, "Why of course." Fredric told him it was the same wine he brought from Transylvania, but it was not. The captain drank the wine as fast as Fredric could pour it. He did not even give Fredric a chance to make his special toast.

The more the captain drank, the more talkative he became. Fredric finally told the captain, "I will not pour you any more wine unless you tell me what you heard on the street." The captain then told him, "Certain people are saying that you murdered your fiancé's father, and they want you to hang for the crime. They're also saying that you are now under house arrest."

As Fredric kept pouring wine in the captain's glass, the captain began to relay a plan of escape that would take Fredric and Leona out of London. Fredric asked him how long it would take to assemble a seaworthy ship and crew. The captain told him it would take at least five days.

"You must do it in three, before I am arrested," Fredric replied.

The captain hesitated, and then said, "I'll see you in three days." Fredric poured the remainder of the wine in the captain's glass and walked him to the front door, "I expect to see you in three days."

Fredric closed the door behind him and slowly walked back upstairs to his bedroom. At this point he was feeling trapped as he paced the floor searching for answers.

Another two days had past without hearing from anyone and he was getting quite nervous. Fredric decided to send a note to Leona.

He wrote, *I must leave for Transylvania tomorrow evening and I want you to come with me. Please say you will. Yours forever, Fredric.*

He summoned his coachman to take the letter to Leona's house and wait for an answer.

The coachman arrived at Leona's house and knocked on the front door several times before the servant asked who was there. "I am Dr. Gruel's coachman with a letter for Miss Leona." The servant opened the door cautiously and the coachman handed him the letter. He told him he had been instructed by Dr. Gruel to wait for an answer. "Wait here and I'll give the letter to Miss Leona."

The servant knocked lightly on Leona's door until she answered, "Who is it?"

"I have a letter for you from Dr. Gruel and his coachman was instructed to wait for a reply," he told her. Leona put her hand outside of the door to reach for the letter. "Wait downstairs with the coachman; I'll call you when I am ready with my reply."

Leona closed the door and anxiously opened Fredric's letter. After reading it, she felt so lonely; there was no one to talk to and no one to help her decide what to do.

Leona wrote her answer to Fredric, *Even though I love you very much I am very confused as to what to do. Please help me.*

Leona called the servant to her room and gave him her reply. She told him to give her letter to the coachman and that she will be waiting for his reply.

The coachman did exactly as he was told and drove back to Fredric's house and gave him Leona's reply.

After reading it, Fredric decided to go against the inspectors orders. He went directly to Leona's house and tried to convince her to go with him to Transylvania.

He did not know when the autopsy report would come back, but he was sure that it would show that Dr. Stroud's neck had been broken causing his death.

Fredric told his servant that he would be going on a long business trip and that he should pack all his clothing and necessary personal items that he would need for the trip.

Fredric then ran down the stairs, telling the coachman that there would not be a written reply to Miss Leona, "I will deliver it myself."

Turning himself into a bat, Fredric flew off to Leona's house.

Upon reaching Leona's house, Fredric immediately turned himself back, ran up the front steps, and banged on the front door until the servant answered. "Who is it?" the servant asked? "It is Dr. Gruel." As the servant opened the door, Fredric pushed his way in and asked the frightened servant, "Where is Miss Leona?" I believe she is asleep upstairs," he told Fredric. "I must see her at once." Fredric said. "She is resting, you cannot disturb her now," the servant shot back.

Leona, hearing the shouting down stairs, opened her bedroom door and saw that it was Fredric. She put on her robe, walked into the hall, and called out, "Fredric, Fredric, please come up." Fredric ran up the stairs to Leona and hugged her. "We must leave at once if we are to be together," he told her.

Leona began to tremble as Fredric told her that they must leave no later than tomorrow evening. "You must come back with me to Transylvania," he pleaded.

She was still shaking and had tears in her eyes as she reassured Fredric of her love for him and said, "There has been no one else but you Fredric, and I want to spend the rest of my life with you no matter what you are or where we go, as long as we are together."

Fredric, elated, gave Leona a reassuring hug then stepped back and looked directly into her eyes, "Be ready for my coachman. He will come by tomorrow evening to pick you up."

When Fredric arrived back at his house, he found Captain Ulrich waiting for him. As Fredric reappeared, the captain walked over to him and began to give him details of what he had arranged. "Not here you fool, come with me inside," Fredric said angrily.

The captain followed him through the front door and into the study. "I did not expect you until tomorrow evening," Fredric said. "I have completed all your travel arrangements, but you must act fast," the captain told him. "I heard on the street that the chief inspector plans to have you arrested tomorrow evening for the murder of Dr. Stroud."

Fredric told the captain that he will have a lady friend joining him on the voyage and he must have a separate cabin ready for her. "There is not much room for a female passenger," the Captain said, "but I will do the best I can."

"The front door will be unlocked while I sleep tomorrow, during the day. Have your men come in and get my belongings, and make sure that they do not drink the wine. Tomorrow evening I will take the young lady with me to the ship and we can leave immediately," Fredric explained. "Do you have any questions, captain?"

"I do not," the captain answered. "Very good, then take this bottle of wine with you and I will see you on the ship tomorrow evening and I hope this crew is more trust worthy than the last."

After the captain left, Fredric finished packing his belongings and made a mental list of things he had to do. "I must not forget to pack the box of earth that Joseph gave me, I must take several bottles of my special wine with me on board, and I must leave a note for the captain telling him to take the barrels of wine that are in the study."

Fredric was beginning to feel the stress of what he was about to undertake. He lay down, trying to sleep, while holding the small box of earth from Transylvania against his chest.

As the sun set the next evening, Fredric rose from his bed, went downstairs to the study, and was pleased to see that the captain's crew had taken out all his belongings and the barrels of wine.

He summoned his coachman to get ready, and then took one final walk around the house, knowing that he would never return.

LEONA'S TRIP TO TRANSYLVANIA

When Fredric left his house he found himself in a very dense fog. He could barely see the coach from the front steps. "This fog would make it very difficult for the coachman to drive," he thought.

He entered the coach and told the coachman to drive to Dr. Stroud's house, very slowly.

As the coach began to move, it came very close to being hit by another coach that was going very fast in the opposite direction.

What Fredric did not know, was that Inspector Michaels was in that coach going to his house to have him arrested.

When the inspector's coach pulled up in front of Fredric's house, the inspector jumped from the coach and went to the front door with several policemen behind him. He knocked on the door but soon realized that there was no one home or Fredric was hiding somewhere in the house. He ordered his men to break in the front door. They did so and began running throughout the house looking for Fredric, but he was no where to be found.

The inspector knew that if Fredric was not home, the only other place he could be was Dr. Stroud's house.

He ordered his men to get back into the police wagon, and then called out to his driver, "Go to Miss Leona Stroud's house, fast." The driver yelled back, "This fog is too thick, I cannot drive fast."

"Just get us there as fast as you can," the inspector retorted.

At the same time, Fredric was at Leona's house waiting for her to come down stairs while her servant and Fredric's coachman strapped her belongings onto the top of the coach.

When Leona came downstairs, Fredric gave her a hug and a kiss for reassurance as he told her, "This will be the beginning of a beautiful new life for us."

They walked to the coach together as Fredric helped Leona in, then told the coachman, "Take us to the pier where there is a ship waiting."

The fog was excessive, so the coachman had to be extremely careful. Leona held on to Fredric's arm as the coach slowly drove off.

Some time later, Inspector Michaels pulled up in front of Leona's house where the inspector and his policemen rushed out of the police wagon and began running towards the front door.

The inspector knocked hard on the door until the servant opened it and asked, "Can I help you?" The inspector was quick to answer, "Where are Miss Leona, and Dr. Gruel?" The servant told him that they all left a short time ago. "Do you know where they were going?" the inspector inquired. "Yes, they were going to the pier where there is a ship waiting for them."

The inspector turned to his men and yelled, "Drive to the pier."

The fog was still very heavy as Fredric's coachman drove ever so slowly through the narrow streets leading to the pier.

As they drove closer to the water's edge, they were able to see the ship and Captain Ulrich standing in front of the ship's plank with a few crewmen holding lanterns, anxiously awaiting their arrival.

Fredric helped Leona out of the coach when they arrived and they quickly followed the captain up the plank to the ship's deck. A few of the crew unloaded Leona's luggage and brought it aboard the ship.

Fredric told the captain that he believed they were being followed. "How long will it take for us to leave?" he asked. "I will make the ship ready at once," the captain said reassuringly.

The captain turned to the crew and shouted, "Pull up the plank and make ready the sails." Then he called out to his first mate, "Release the lines and hoist the sails."

A light breeze caught the sails and moved the ship slowly away from the dock.

Fredric and the captain could see Inspector Michaels and the police wagon rapidly approaching the pier, but they knew that it was too late for anyone to stop them now.

It was getting late in the evening and Leona was anxious to get some rest from all the excitement. "I will take you to your cabins. Be careful walking, just follow me," the captain told them.

Leona was holding tightly to Fredric's arm as they followed the captain down the rickety stairs to where they would be living for the next few weeks. As they approached their cabins, the captain stopped and said, "I suggest we make this Miss Leona's cabin, it is slightly larger."

The captain opened the cabin door and walked in followed by Fredric then Leona. "I am sure this will do until we reach port. I will be right next door if you need me," Fredric told her. Leona gave Fredric a hug and said, "I am very nervous about everything happening so fast. Maybe I will feel better about what we are doing if I get a good night sleep." As he was leaving, Fredric reminded Leona, "I cannot go outside while there is daylight, so I will not see you until the sun goes down tomorrow evening. If there is something that you need, just ask the captain.

"Good night, my love," he whispered.

Leona felt all alone and she was still nervous and upset. She could not fully comprehend what had happened over the last few days and began to weep thinking of her father's death and her uncertain future with Fredric.

Leona tried to compose herself as she looked around her cabin. There were no closets where she could hang up her dresses and no mirror. There was very little light, only a lit candle in a gold holder on a small table in the center of the room with a chair next to it. Her bed was in a far corner and had a small porthole above it. Two small sconces with an unlit candle in each, hung on the back wall giving off a strong smell of cheap wax. There was a small basin and pitcher on top of a broken dresser with three lopsided drawers.

"Oh my, how will I ever be comfortable here?" she thought as she lay down on the bed crying uncontrollably.

Fredric entered his cabin also exhausted by the events of the day, only to see a much smaller cabin than Leona's but with the same amount of furniture.

Before closing the cabin door, Fredric told the captain, "I guess this will have to do, but my main concern is that Miss Leona be made as comfortable as possible. The captain replied, with a smirk on his face, "I will personally take good care of your lady friend."

Fredric stared directly into the captain's eyes, "She is very close to me, so be careful of your actions." He then reminded the captain to place four bottles of his wine outside his cabin door each night after sunset.

Fredric took a step closer to the captain and placed one hand on his shoulder looked directly into his eyes and said, in a very authoritative voice, "But most important, keep your men away from Miss Leona and my wine." The captain nodded as he left the cabin and closed the door.

Fredric lay down but had difficulty falling asleep. He was very concerned about Leona's safety, knowing that he could not be there during the day, if she needed him. Also, thoughts of what Joseph had told him before leaving for Transylvania haunted him. The knowledge that Count Vladimir Gruel was actually his father was agonizing. He knew he would have to face the Count when he returned home.

LEONA HAS A BAD EXPERIENCE

The next morning, upon awakening, Leona just lay in her bed still depressed about everything. She looked around the cabin. It all seemed so strange.

She had no idea what time it was so she thought she had better get dressed and go up to the deck. Just as she was about to leave her cabin, there was a knock at the door. "Who is it?" she asked. She heard a voice with a thick Irish brogue tell her, "I am one of the crew, miss. The captain thought you might be hungry, so I brought you down something to eat." Leona thanked him and told him to leave it outside the door. The crewman responded, "The captain told me to bring the food into your cabin. "Very well," she replied and opened the door.

When he entered, Leona took a step back and looked at him with disgust. This unshaven wretched looking man was wearing torn pants with a dirty striped shirt and knit hat.

After placing the tray of food on the table he turned to Leona, "Your room smells nice and you are very pretty missy." The seaman kept staring at Leona's cleavage that was visible above her low cut dress. "You may leave now," Leona told him. She was beginning to get uneasy as he backed up towards the door, not taking his eyes off of her. "If you should need me for anything, just ask for Cat, that's what they call me, Cat, because I'm quiet as a cat," he said as he left.

After he was gone, Leona sat down at the table and ate the cold scrambled eggs but could only stare at the moldy cheese that shared the same plate with the eggs. There was also a slice of bread and a hot cup of tea that was not very satisfying, but she had it anyway.

When Leona finished eating, she went up on deck. The sun was shining with very few clouds in the sky.

Captain Ulrich was on the top deck holding the wheel and calling out orders to his crew. Leona then heard the captain call out to her, "Miss Leona, Miss Leona, come up here, and be careful walking up the stairs."

When Leona reached the top deck, the captain asked her if she slept well. "Not really, this is all new to me, being on a ship and all." she answered. "Well, you had better get used to this for a while. The seas are calm now and the weather is good, but it could change very quickly. Miss Leona, may I take the liberty of making a suggestion? Do not wear such revealing clothing in front of the crew," he advised, "who knows what goes through their minds."

Leona just stood there looking at the captain. Offended, she hurried down the stairway back to her cabin where she lay down on her bed and thankfully fell asleep.

When she awoke she looked out of the window to see that the sun was setting and that meant she would soon be seeing Fredric.

Leona decided to take the captain's advice and change into something not so revealing, when she heard a knock at the door. Thinking that it must be Fredric, she ran to the door and opened it, only to find Cat, the crewman who brought her breakfast, standing there. "What do you want?" she asked. "I brought you your dinner. You should eat it while it is still hot." Leona took the tray from him and told him, "I will place it on the table myself, thank you." Then she closed the door as Cat still stood there gawking at her.

Leona sat down to eat, and then realized that the candles in her room were lit. Someone must have crept in while she was napping and lit them. This made her even more anxious than before. Nevertheless, she was hungry so she removed the napkin that lay on top of the food. A slice of salted beef with cold boiled potatoes, a slice of bread and a cup of tea with no sugar were what she found. She tried to eat, but it was terrible tasting. She spit out the first bite.

Leona, getting very impatient to see Fredric, left her cabin and knocked on his door. She stood there waiting for him to open it, but he did not, so she slowly opened it herself. The room was totally dark except for the little bit of light that came through the opened door. She was startled when Fredric appeared from a dark corner, fully dressed. Leona said in a quivering voice, "Fredric, I knocked and I did not hear you." Fredric told her in a firm voice, *"You are never to enter my room again, under any circumstance. Is that understood?"* He instantly felt sorry for the way he spoke to her and immediately placed his arms around her, "Leona, please forgive me for talking to you that way. I am not accustomed to having anyone in my room while I am asleep." Then, as if nothing had happened, he suggested, "Why don't we go on deck, it feels like the moon is full and the stars are out."

When they reached the deck, Leona blurted out, "Fredric, I am not accustomed to living like this, maybe you can talk to Captain Ulrich about the food, it is terrible. Also, this one crewman, Cat, keeps staring at me. It is very difficult to go on deck without you being with me." Fredric answered her in a reassuring voice, "I will talk to Captain Ulrich, I am sure he will make other arrangement regarding your food and I will also see what he can do about this crewman, Cat."

Changing the subject, Fredric revealed, "I have a surprise for you. I have arranged to have the furniture removed from your house in London and sent to Transylvania. We should receive it in several weeks."

"Thank you Fredric, you seem to think of everything," Leona replied unenthusiastically.

The moon was rising, so Fredric suggested, "Why don't we go to the bow of the ship where we would be able to enjoy the intensity and power of the moon."

As they stood staring at the moon, Fredric bowed his head in silent prayer. Just then, heavy gusts of wind began to blow across the ship causing the sails and mast to make strange howling sounds. Waves began to break over the bow and the stern. Suddenly there was a loud shriek coming from the stern when two of the crew began to shout, "Man overboard, man overboard." The captain and some of the crew ran on deck as Leona held tightly onto Fredric. Then the wind subsided as quickly as it began.

"I am very scared, maybe we should go below," Leona anguished. Fredric calmly told her, "Just keep holding on to me, there is nothing to be afraid of."

They heard the captain shouting as he ran over to them, "Did you see or hear anything? One of my crew is missing." Fredric inquired as to which one of the crew was missing. "Cat," the captain answered, "he must have been taken overboard by a sudden wave. There is nothing we can do now but pray for his soul."

Fredric suggested they now go below to their cabins. "Fredric, please do not leave me alone, this is all getting to be too much for me," Leona lamented. "I will go with you to your cabin and stay with you until you fall asleep," Fredric offered.

Leona felt relieved as they both went below to her cabin. She told Fredric to sit on the chair while she changed into something else, for-getting that there was no other room for her to change in, then politely asked Fredric to turn his head.

As she began to remove her dress, Fredric stood up and placed both of his arms around her pulling her towards him. He then began kissing her on her neck and her breast as she just stood there enjoying his atten-tion. He picked her up and very gently placed her on the small bed. He lay down next to her whispering into her ear, "I love you very much Leona, I will never leave you."

As they lay close in each others arms, Fredric felt her relaxing for the first time as she fell into a deep sleep.

Fredric knew that, eventually, he would have to tell Leona more of his background, but how could he make her understand that he was really a vampire? He then realized that he had no choice but to give Leona his wine and slowly change her into a vampire.

He left her a note before leaving to go to his own cabin.

THE CHANGING OF LEONA

The next morning, when Leona awoke, she saw a note that Fredric left for her on the table.

"My dearest, I am very sorry that I could not stay with you the entire night. I know you will understand. If you have any problem eating the food, you will find some bottles of my special wine on top of your dresser. It will help you get through the day. I will be dreaming of you. All my love, Fredric."

After reading the note, Leona began to feel a lot better, until she heard a knock on her door. "Who is it?" she asked. "I am one of the crew with your breakfast." Leona shouted back, "Leave it by the door, I will take it in when I am ready." She pressed her ear against the door listening for the crewman's foot steps, as he walked away.

She opened the door slowly, afraid that he might still be standing there, then brought in the tray and placed it on the table. She looked at it for a while then decided to open a bottle of the wine Fredric left for her. She began to drink it with her breakfast instead of the terrible tasting tea. After tasting the wine, she thought how sweet it was and began to pour herself more.

Leona stood up from the table, reached for Fredric's letter and read it for a second time. It made her feel secure.

Feeling much better than she had the day before, Leona decided to put on a dress, with a high neck this time, and take a walk on deck.

When she went on deck, she felt the crewmen staring at her, giving her a strange feeling. She walked partially around the deck when suddenly one of the crewmen came up from behind her, grabbed her by her waist and covered her mouth. Leona began to kick and pull at his hands as he dragged her down a flight of stairs then pushed her into a small room, while still holding on to her.

She tried to fight him off, screaming, "Let me go, Dr. Gruel will kill you, let me go."

"He will never find out who I am," he laughed as he continued to rip off her dress. Suddenly, Fredric appeared from behind and pulled him off her. Using one hand, he grabbed the dastardly crewman by the neck and held him up off the floor until he stopped kicking. Leona watched in horror as Fredric released him and he fell to the floor, dead.

Leona was crying hysterically as Fredric tried to soothe her. He apologized for leaving her alone and told her, "Leona, this will never happen again, I promise you." He picked her up, covered her with her torn dress and carried her underneath the upper deck to his cabin avoiding the sunlight and other crewmen.

When they entered Fredric's cabin, he placed Leona on his bed. She was still sobbing as he gave her some of his wine to drink which immediately began to calm her down. He stroked her forehead telling her, "Try to calm down you're with me now, you're with me."

Leona looked up at Fredric and asked, "How did you find me? You were in your room sleeping." Fredric, trying to find words to convince her, blurted out, "Even though I am sleeping, you are always in my thoughts and I felt you were in trouble."

As Leona tried to catch her breath, Fredric poured her more wine telling her to drink slowly, knowing what would eventually happen if she continued drinking the wine. He sat on the chair next to the bed and watched her as she fell asleep.

Several hours passed and the sun was beginning to set when Leona opened her eyes and saw Fredric sitting there. "How did I get here? Please tell me what happened," she asked of Fredric. It was obvious that she did not remember anything. "You remember nothing?" Fredric asked. "I just remember walking on the deck," she replied.

"Captain Ulrich found you on the lower deck. You must have fallen down and hit your head. He carried you here and I have been with you ever since."

Leona tried to sit up but was having some difficulty. Fredric leaned over to help her, and then gave her a little more wine. "This will help you," he advised. Leona took the glass of wine using both hands. She drank the whole glass all at once then asked for more.

Fredric was afraid of the consequences of Leona drinking too much of his wine as he told her, "Let me bring you something to eat." Leona grabbed Fredric's hand before he could stand up and pleaded, "Do not leave me alone, I am not hungry now." Fredric leaned over her and told her, "I will never leave you, ever."

Leona seemed to be feeling better so Fredric suggested they take a walk on deck to get some fresh air. Fredric stood up and helped Leona off the bed holding on to her gently and at the same time giving her one more kiss on the lips. He took off his cape and wrapped it around her shoulders, then held her arm as they left the cabin.

When they reached the top deck, they both felt a slight chill in the air as the wind began to get stronger. Fredric held Leona by her arm as they walked towards the bow of the ship.

The sails were thrashing about in the howling wind and the moon was beginning to rise. Fredric turned to Leona, "Let us enjoy this moment together," he said as he faced the moon and bowed his head. He then turned slightly and noticed that Leona also had her head bowed as if in prayer. This was a sign that she was slowly turning into a vampire.

As the wind continued to howl and waves started to break over the side of the ship, Fredric thought it would be best for them to return to his cabin.

They could hardly walk across the deck when they heard Captain Ulrich calling out to them, "Get below you fools, get below." Before leaving the deck Fredric yelled back to the captain, "Take one of my barrels of wine and share it with the crew."

They carefully walked down the stairs to Fredric's cabin as the waves continued to toss the ship around. Fredric could see the fright in Leona's eyes as they entered his cabin. He sat her on his bed then took out a bottle of wine, poured it into two glasses and made a toast, "To life, and to the future of our lives together." Leona began to drink the wine with great delight.

Fredric placed their glasses on the table then gently pressed her shoulders against the bed and began to undress her. The room was dark except for one candle that was burning on the far side of the room. He leaned over Leona and began to kiss her on her soft lips and on her neck, while telling her, "Our new lives together will be eternal, we will live as one." Leona, placing both her arms around Fredric's neck, held him close to her, while kissing him. Pushing him up slightly she began to remove his jacket and unbutton his shirt only to start biting him on his chest and neck as she became more playful with him. Fredric sat up and removed Leona's dress. He kept staring down at her, as she lay naked on his bed. Her beauty as always captivated him. He leaned over her as they became deeply immersed in their passion.

The next sunset, Fredric awoke first and decided to get dressed while Leona continued to sleep. A few moments later, Leona opened her eyes, and suddenly realized that she was naked so she pulled the blankets up over her and shouted, "Where are my clothes? Get my clothes."

She kept the blanket pulled over her head with only her two feet sticking out from the other side. Fredric quickly responded by picking her dress up from the floor and placing it on top of the blanket. She called out from under the blanket, "Please turn around so I can get dressed." Fredric complied by telling her, "I am stepping outside the cabin for a moment, open the door when you are finished dressing."

Leona had no idea that Fredric can see through walls nor did she have any idea of the enormity of his powers.

Leona dressed then opened the cabin door to find Fredric leaning against the wall with his arms folded waiting impatiently. "I must go to my cabin and change my clothes, please give me a few more minutes," she said.

"Please hurry up, I do not want us to miss watching the moon rise, Fredric explained.

When Leona's cabin door finally opened, she stepped out wearing a light blue, low cut dress with white ruffles that partially covered her cleavage and ran down the center of the dress to the floor. Her hair, which usually hung below her shoulders, was braided and tied up on top of her head, exposing her shoulders.

Fredric just stood there looking at her, and exclaimed, "You look absolutely beautiful." Leona thanked him and explained, "I want to look worthy of you when we watch the moon rise this evening." Fredric then took Leona's arm as they walked, in silence, up to the main deck.

A DIFFERENT CREW

When Fredric and Leona reached the main deck, they noticed that the entire crew was facing the moon with their heads bowed. Fredric, remembering what happened on his first voyage to London, called out to Captain Ulrich, "What is going on here?" The captain called back, "It's your wine. It's your wine that caused this." Fredric approached the captain, "What do you mean it's my wine that caused this?"

"Don't you understand it was your wine? After you said I could give the crew a barrel of your wine, I sent several of the men to the hole to fetch one. When they brought it up on deck they all took out their metal cups and went into a drinking frenzy. They didn't even offer me one drop of your precious wine, so I went below to get some sleep. When I came up on deck this morning I found all the men lying there with their eyes closed and a second barrel of wine opened. I tried to wake them up, but I couldn't even get them to open their eyes and their skin looked like the color of ash. I have never seen anything like this before.

Then as the sun went down and the moon began to rise, they stood up, one by one, as if they were in a trance. Then they all walked over to the bow and just stared at the moon. This is where they've been until now when you and Miss Leona came on deck."

Fredric took Leona by the hand and began walking towards the crew. Then all at once the crew turned and began to walk slowly towards them. Fredric, not knowing what to expect, stepped in front of Leona and looked straight into the eyes of one of the crewmen. Leona, standing behind Fredric, held onto the back of his jacket as the crewmen began to form a straight line facing Fredric, bowing there heads, one by one, as they passed by.

Fredric took a few steps back and stood along side of Leona as each crewman, after bowing his head, kissed the back of Fredric's hand.

As Fredric looked into their eyes, he knew that they were slowly being transformed into partial vampires. He also knew that if the crew stayed in the sun for an extended period of time, ultimately, they would all die. The only thing he could do now was to sustain them on the wine until they reached port.

Fredric decided to tell Captain Ulrich what was happening to his crew so he asked the captain to join him in his cabin. When the captain arrived, Fredric told him to sit down, "Would you care to join me in a glass of my favorite wine?"

"No, no more wine, not now," the captain said firmly as he thought to himself, "as long as I've known Fredric, there was always something strange about him."

Fredric opened a new bottle of wine, poured some into a glass, then stood up facing the captain and made his toast, "To life and to the beauty of life." The captain held up an empty glass and clicked it against Fredric's. He then said cautiously, "I am not sure what's going on here, but I don't like what I see."

"Let me tell you what I have done," Fredric said calmly. "I have made a huge discovery. I have discovered the secret of immortality that could allow you to live forever." The captain, ignoring what Fredric had said, just sat there looking at him. "What did you do to my crew? What is wrong with them?"

"They will all become immortal. You can too if you drink my wine, stay out of the sunlight and follow my orders."

"How are we to get to port? We will all die at sea without someone manning the ship during the day," the captain advised.

"You will steer the ship during the day and the crew will work at night until we reach port which should be within three days. We will bring the ship into port at night. That is the only way it can be done."

The captain stood up, looked directly at Fredric and asked him, in his stern voice, "What about me? What will happen to me?" Fredric told the captain that since he did not drink as much wine as the rest of the crew, nothing will happen to him, as long as he does what he is told."

The captain sat back in his chair, not knowing whether to pour wine into his glass, but he could not take his eyes off the wine.

"Just follow my instructions and we will all arrive safely. It is time for us to go back on deck and check on the crew," Fredric ordered.

They both stood up to leave. The captain walked slowly behind Fredric with his head down until they reach the deck where they could see that the men were standing in the same place waiting for orders as to what to do next, either from Fredric or from the captain. Leona was also standing in the same spot staring at the crew and waiting for Fredric.

The captain approached the crew and advised them, "You must obey our orders for your own safety if we are to reach the port alive.

"You men, who have been drinking a lot of wine, stand over here. Those of you who have not been drinking too much wine, stand over there," the captain ordered.

One of the crew shouted, "What is happening to us, have we been poisoned?" The captain advised the men that there seems to be a slight problem with the wine. "Those of you who are on this line can continue to drink the wine but you are to man the ship only after the sunsets. You are not to go into the sunlight for your own protection. I tell you this and you must heed what I say or you will die. For the few men that claim they had little wine, you will work two daylight shifts no longer than three hours each. Is that understood?" Most of the men yelled back, "yes."

The captain then shouted to the men as he was leaving, "You men working the daylight shift go to your bunks and get some sleep, you'll need to be wide awake in the morning. The rest of you continue working."

The captain retreated to his cabin leaving Fredric and Leona on deck. Fredric told one of the crewmen to bring up several bottles of wine and pass them around to the men who will remain on deck. He told the other men, one more time, "Go down to your bunks before the sunrise. Do not stay in the sunlight."

As Fredric and Leona reached their cabins, Fredric suggested to Leona, "Drink some wine and try to sleep; my wine will help you sleep better. Make sure the curtains covering the windows are drawn tight so as not to allow any light to filter through and most important, as I just told the crew, you are not to step out into the sunlight."

He then put his arms around her giving her a big hug and a kiss as he told her, "I cannot explain all of this to you now, but I will be right next door if you should need me. Get a good nights rest, there is nothing to worry about."

She just stood there looking confused as Fredric left her room.

Leona still did not understand what was happening to her. "I have no desire for food, all I want is wine," she thought as she opened a bottle and began to drink.

Remembering what Fredric had told her about the sunlight, she took one of her dresses and draped it over the window to make sure that no sunlight would filter into the cabin. She then drank the wine until she was able to fall asleep.

The next sunset Leona was awakened by a loud knock at the door. She yelled, "Who's there?"

"It's me, Fredric, can I come in?" She jumped out of bed then opened the door.

Fredric entered giving her a hug and eagerly told her, "Even though it has only been one night since I saw you last, I miss you as if it were a month."

Leona was glad to see Fredric. Perhaps he can explain what is going on. "Fredric, I am beginning to feel very strange. I have lost my appetite and I have an insatiable craving for your wine. Why is this happening to me?" she asked.

Fredric was reluctant to tell her, but realized that he must.

"I want you to sit here," he told Leona as he sat down across from her at the small table. He reached out and held her hands as he began to speak. "Leona, I will explain everything to you. As you know, my older brother is Count Vladimir Gruel. He has large armies of men who raid and pillage all the townships surrounding Transylvania. He has done this for the past two hundred years. I also have a younger brother, Ludvig Von Gruel, and he is just as bad as the Count. He presides over the northern part of Europe, but no one talks about him.

Confused, Leona said in a sharp voice, "Are you telling me that your brothers are several hundred years old?"

"Yes, and I am over 100 years old," Fredric admitted.

Leona was shocked to hear this. She stood up from the table, pulled her dress off the window, then turned to Fredric and yelled out hysterically, "What are you trying to tell me, what are you, what are you doing to me?"

Fredric, trying to calm her down said, "I fell in love with you the very first time my eyes fell upon you. I knew I had to be with you for eternity.

"Leona, please believe me, I meant you no harm." Leona interrupted, "I still have no idea what you are and what you are doing to me." Fredric, trying to make her understand said, "I beg of you to understand, I just want to spend the rest of my life with you and in order for this to happen you must be like me, a vampire. Leona, I am giving you immortality. You will live with me forever."

Leona screamed at Fredric, "Don't I have a choice in what you are doing to me and don't I have any say in how I wish to live the rest of my life?"

"Leona, please think about this, immortality will make your life blissful forever, you will never grow old."

Leona could not believe what she was hearing. She began to bang on the table and screamed, "Go away, leave me alone, your sick."

"Please try to understand," he pleaded. "I thought you would understand what I am going through."

Fredric stood up and told Leona that he will be on deck if she needed him.

He was tormented by the thought of losing her.

Leona reached for another bottle of wine and began pouring it into a glass and without hesitation drank one glass after another as Fredric pleaded with her to stop.

Fredric then left to go up on deck and immediately heard the captain yelling at the crew, "What's wrong with you men? Why can't you just listen to me? We've lost two men because they didn't listen."

"What's going on," Fredric asked the captain. "Dr. Gruel, talk to them or we will never make port." Fredric asked one of the crew to explain what happened. "We began to take our turn and go on deck not realizing that the sun did not completely set. Suddenly, the first two men in front of me began to scream. We all watched in horror as their bodies began to burn and then disintegrate. I then pushed the other men back down the stairs so they wouldn't walk into the sunlight."

Fredric looked straight into the eyes of each of the remaining crewmen. Then the whites of his eyes turned a deep red as he grit his teeth, clenched his fist and yelled, "From now on you will follow every command that I or Captain Ulrich gives you. Do you understand? DO... YOU....UNDERSTAND?"

The remaining crew just stood there riveted.

Fredric then asked the captain to explain what he saw. "They didn't heed what I said. It was terrible. I saw two of the men walk onto the deck while the sun was still up and right in front of my eyes they began to burn. All we could do was watch as they ran screaming across the deck and fall down in a heap of ash. May they rest in peace?"

Fredric addressed the crew and Captain Ulrich, in his thick Baltic accent, "If the rest of you wish to live, you must believe what I am telling you or you will all die too."

Frustrated by their actions he quickly walked towards the stairway to get away from them and return to his cabin.

He was shocked when he walked into his cabin and found Leona, holding a bottle of wine in her hand, naked on the bed.

"What are you doing?" he asked. "If you want me to be a vampire then I will become a vampire. How does a vampire act, or am I called a vampiress?"

Fredric grabbed the bottle from her hand, "You do not have to behave like this, you can still be like the lovely gentle young woman I first met, and you can still have a long life ahead of you."

Leona looked up at Fredric and gave him a big smile as she fell backwards on the bed with her eyes wide open and a look of excitement on her face.

Fredric could not take his eyes off Leona as she lay there looking up at him. He took off his cape and jacket, leaned over her, and began to kiss her passionately.

They remained in each other's arms for a long while before Leona whispered, "Fredric, I will follow you anywhere and be whatever you want me to be, as long as we are together."

Fredric told her, "We will have a long and beautiful life together." Leona, still locked in his embrace responded, "Let us go on deck and look at the moon."

THE SHIP ARRIVES IN PORT

Two days later the ship arrived in port during one of the darkest nights of the year. There was a slight drizzle and the clouds were so thick that you could not see even a glimpse of the moon.

Fredric had already given the captain instructions to send all of his belongings, along with his wine, to his castle and keep three barrels on board for the crew. He also sent a telepathic message to Pulaski, his driver, telling him when to meet him and Leona at the pier.

Fredric wanted to leave the ship as quickly as possible so he took Leona by the hand and walked down the plank to wait for his coach to arrive.

Four black horses leading a coach with the Gruel family crest on the door approached just as they descended the plank. When the coach came to a stop the driver immediately jumped down and greeted Fredric, "It is good to see you again master, I received your message and came as fast as I could."

Fredric hurriedly made an introduction, "Pulaski, this is Miss Leona. She will soon be my wife. Leona, this is Pulaski. He has been my coachman for as long as I can remember."

"Pulaski, we want to get to the castle as fast as possible so we had better get started."

The coach went slowly through the city but once they were on the outskirts, Pulaski cracked his whip and the horses began to go faster and faster.

Leona, holding on to Fredric, sat in silence then blurted out, "How did the coachman know when and where to meet us?" Fredric hesitated for a moment then tried to explain, "I have a way of sending messages through the air by thought concentration."

Leona looked puzzled as she asked him to explain what he had just said. "This is how I knew you were in trouble aboard the ship and was able to find you," he explained. "I still do not understand," she said as she rested her head against his shoulder and fell asleep.

Fredric took out a blanket from beneath the seat and covered her. He was overjoyed knowing that they will be together throughout eternity.

The trip to the castle was very long, unpleasant and bumpy but it gave Fredric time to think of how he might make it easier for Leona to adapt to life in the castle, but foremost on his mind was how he could dispose of Count Gruel, once and for all.

"We must get to the castle before sunrise," Fredric thought. Many times he called out to Pulaski, "Make the horses go faster."

After a few hours more, the coach approached a clearing and Fredric was able to see a glimpse of his castle. Because of the thick mist and fog that was rising up from the swampy ground, Pulaski had to slow down the horses and guide them up the winding road that led to the castle where the air became thicker and the sound of life was still.

The coach crossed over the small bridge that led up to the castle and stopped in front of two large doors.

Pulaski jumped off the coach and opened the door allowing Fredric to step down while carrying the sleeping Leona.

When they entered the castle, his servant, Joseph, greeted Fredric. "Welcome home master." Fredric, still carrying Leona, put her down as he introduced her, "Leona, this is my oldest friend and teacher, Joseph, Fredric continued, "Joseph, Leona is the young lady that I told you about. She is the reason that I went back to London and she has agreed to marry me." Joseph, happy to hear the good news exclaimed, "Congratulations master. I am sure you will both live a very long and happy life together."

Joseph had been warned that Fredric and Leona would be arriving and had already prepared the master bedroom.

Fredric and Leona began the long walk up the stone steps that led to Fredric's bedroom that would now be the master bedroom.

"Fredric, this is a very cold looking castle. Why does it look this way?" Leona criticized. "We had a very long trip and the sun will be rising soon. What I think we should do now is go up to bed and tomorrow evening I will answer all your questions," Leona agreed, and asked, "Do you promise to tell me everything?"

"Yes," Fredric replied, "everything."

When they reached the bedroom, Leona lay down on the bed as Fredric walked over to the window to make sure the draperies were closed.

Looking around, Leona, with a little smirk on her face, asked Fredric, "What would you like to do now?" Fredric replied indifferently, "I am extremely tired from the trip and I would like to get into bed with you and go to sleep." Leona said coyly, "Is that all you wish to do?" Looking directly into Leona's eyes, Fredric said, "Change into your night clothes, get under the covers and go to sleep and do not go near the window until the next sunset, do you understand?"

Leona, who still appeared confused, did just that.

LEONA'S FIRST EVENING IN THE CASTLE

Fredric awoke and sat on the edge of the bed just watching Leona sleep with her long hair falling softly across the side of her face. He was overwhelmed with emotion, just seeing her in his bed and having her so close to him. For now, everything was as he had imagined it would be.

He then got up, walked to the window and pulled back the burgundy draperies revealing the black sky and the heavy mist that was rising from the nearby swamps. As he stood there, he thought back to when he was a child, all the vegetation around the castle was green and the trees changed with the seasons.

Fredric then walked back to the bed, leaned over Leona and gave her a gentle kiss on the lips. She awakened with a smile on her face. "Did the sun set already?"

"Yes it did," Fredric replied. "Do you have an appetite for some food or would you prefer to drink some wine with me?" Leona, who appeared unusually happy, replied, "Let's drink wine all night; we can celebrate my becoming a vampiress." Fredric losing patience scolded her, "What we are is real; this is not a game, as you will find out. Your body will go through a transition and you will be able to do things you never would have thought possible. You will never grow old, you will have sacred powers and you will live forever."

Leona began speaking as if she had not heard a word Fredric said, "You promised to take me around the castle and answer all my questions. Am I to meet your famous brother, Count Gruel?"

"Yes you will, I have already sent him a message telling him that I am back in Transylvania."

"Why don't you get dressed now and I will show you around the castle," Fredric suggested as he left the room.

Leona trying to decide which dress to wear held one up and began looking for a mirror. She walked into a dressing room adjoining the bedroom and saw that all the mirrors were covered. "That's strange," she thought as she pulled the cover off one. As she looked into the mirror she was only able to see a partial reflection of herself and it suddenly disappeared into the mirror. Frantic, she pulled the cover off another mirror and then another until they were all uncovered. She saw a fading reflection of herself in each one.

Leona cried as she smacked her hands against each of the mirrors trying to find her reflection. She did not know that she would never see her likeness ever again.

Upon hearing her cries, Fredric ran to the dressing room and found Leona sitting on the floor in front of one of the mirrors weeping. He knelt over her and tried to calm her down but, in her anguish, she began to hit him and screamed, "Look what you have done to me, I cannot see myself in the mirror, I am vanishing."

"Please calm down and let me explain this to you," he said as he picked her up and carried her back to the bedroom.

She continued to cry uncontrollably as Fredric poured her a glass of wine that she drank with delight only to ask for another, then another, "I do not want to stop drinking," she cried.

"Why don't you lie down? I will sit beside you while you rest," He said in a calm voice.

Fredric kept asking himself if he did the right thing by bringing Leona back with him to Transylvania, and try to turn her into a vampire. He decided that he would avoid telling her everything about being a vampire, for now.

She must have something to keep her mind occupied.

Fredric thought that he would tell Leona that she is now the mistress of the castle and that she is to bring the castle back to life the way it was when he was a young boy.

Fredric's mind began to fill with all sorts of ideas. We will have a grand ball in Leona's honor and invite all the dignitaries and their wives from the surrounding towns and of course, my good friends, but first, we must marry. We will say our vows to each other, privately, with only Joseph as a witness.

When Leona opened her eyes, Fredric immediately told her, "I have a wonderful idea. I wish to have a ball in your honor and invite all the dignitaries and their wives." Leona looked up at Fredric and pulled him down onto the bed. She placed her arms around his neck as she said, "Fredric that's a wonderful idea. I would love to meet all your friends and their wives. We will have to get musicians that can play waltzes and I will have to have a fancy new gown made. It all sounds so exciting. I hope my furniture from London will be here in time. When do you want to do this?"

"As soon as you can fix up the castle," he answered.

Leona jumped off the bed and began to dance around the room, forgetting what had happened earlier.

As Fredric watched Leona dance and frolic, he reminded himself of how young she really was and that she had not experienced much of anything before meeting him.

Leona began smothering Fredric with hugs and kisses, "Let's get married right away," she said. Fredric was so happy to hear this, "I want to make love to you right now," he exclaimed. He lay down along side of Leona, held her in his arms, and told her, "You will never regret coming with me.

LEONA BEGINS TO ASK QUESTIONS

Fredric covered up all the mirrors in the dressing room while Leona dressed. She did not seem to be bothered by the unpleasant mirror incident any longer.

"Fredric, you promised to answer all my questions," Leona said as they went down to the main room, which would eventually become the ballroom. "I did, and what would you like to know?" he replied. "I would first like to know how old you really are."

"I am almost one hundred and fifty years old."

"Are you really, and how did you manage to stay alive all these years?" He decided that he did not wish to tell her everything so he simply said, "I would rather not answer that question right now, if you don't mind?"

"You promised to tell me everything, she begged.

"I cannot answer that question now, Leona, but I will tell you in time."

Looking around the main hall, Leona asked, "Why do you have all those banners and flags hanging on the wall?"

"They all represent various battles that my family fought and won," he said.

"Was every one in your family a vampire?" she asked. "No, at one time we were a very loving and prosperous family. Tragedy struck when my father came back from the wars. He was very ill and my mother did not find out what was wrong with him until it was too late. He was sleeping in a cave one evening and a diseased vampire bat bit him. As time went on, he lost his appetite for all foods. All he required was blood to sustain him. It was very difficult for my mother. She tried to attend to him but she became very ill and died during a Small Pox epidemic that swept through our village. Joseph raised me practically by himself. He has been a father and educator to me all these years."

Leona, who was becoming even more inquisitive, asked, "Did you also kill people and drink their blood like vampires do?" Avoiding the question, Fredric said, "Let's move on, this is a very big castle and there are many things that I want to show you."

Leona was confused and troubled. "Why won't Fredric answer all my questions?" she wondered.

"Let me show you the Library," Fredric said as he opened the door that led into a room filled with hundreds of books neatly lined up on shelves that covered every wall. There was a large crystal chandelier hanging from the center of the room with at least a hundred lit candles. It brightened the room to allow anyone sitting at the oak table beneath it to see the small print in any book. Leona asked in amazement as she looked around the room, "Have you read them all?"

"At least twice, he said, and then suggested, "Let's continue this way."

He took Leona's hand and then led her down a long hallway. She spotted a door at the far end. "What's in there?" she inquired. "Nothing, it's empty," he said as she ran down the hall and opened the door to reveal a large empty kitchen. "Fredric, why didn't you tell me about this room?"

"Because this room has not been used in over one hundred years," he answered. "Fredric, have you not eaten food in all that time?"

"That's correct, except for certain foods on special occasions," he admitted. "What about your servant Joseph and your coachman Pulaski, what about them." Fredric placed his hands on Leona's arms, "They are exactly like me, vampires."

Leona backed away from Fredric with a worried look on her face and asked, "Are you going to drink my blood?"

"I no longer have to do that," he explained. "That is all behind me."

"When I left you and returned to Transylvania it was to complete my experiments. That is why I drink this wine. This special wine sustains us. That is why we can live together for eternity. We are immortals, and I intend to make more people immortal by having them drink my wine. They will follow me and do whatever I ask of them."

Leona did not have any more questions to ask of Fredric. She merely said, "I would like to go back up stairs now, if it is okay with you?" She turned away from Fredric and walked up the steep stairs to the bedroom. When she entered, she noticed several bottles of wine in a corner wine rack and one bottle already opened on the table along side of the bed. She changed into a night robe, sat on the edge of the bed, and started to drink the wine. She waited for Fredric to return. The longer she waited the more wine she drank.

It was then that she was suddenly overwhelmed with the realization that she had become a Vampire and had completely lost her appetite for food.

When Fredric returned some time later, he found Leona lying across the bed with two empty bottles of wine next to her. He was afraid that she drank too much. At the very least, this might cause a serious aging problem or even death if she were to continue drinking the wine uncontrollably.

He tried to wake her up, but there was no response. Fredric called out to Joseph for help, "Joseph, come up here, come help me at once."

"What happened master?" Joseph asked as he entered their bedroom. "I need your help; she drank to much wine. We must get her to walk or she will die."

"Why do you say that master?" Joseph asked. "If too much of my blood that is in this wine, mixes with her blood too fast and circulates throughout her system her veins will freeze causing her heart to stop. We must get her on her feet at once and keep her moving," Fredric explained.

After several minutes of trying to get Leona to walk, she opened her eyes and started to moan, "What happened, where am I?" Leona said half conscious. Then she closed her eyes again.

"Joseph, we must keep her walking, she cannot sleep yet," Fredric said as he opened the window to let some fresh air in.

Fredric noticed that the sun was beginning to rise so he left the window partially open and closed the draperies. He then told Joseph to leave as he continued to walk Leona around the room.

Fredric knew that if Leona fell asleep again she might not wake up. He began to panic, "Leona, please wake up, Leona please, the sun is beginning to rise.

Fredric, now using his telepathic powers, looked down at Leona and pleaded with her to wake up. Suddenly she began to regain consciousness. "Open your eyes, Leona, you had too much wine."

As Leona opened her eyes she began to speak incoherently, "What happened, what have I done? I am sorry Fredric, I am sorry for everything. I should not be here. I feel so weak."

Fredric walked her around for a few more minutes then picked her up and carried her to the bed. He lay her down and told her she would feel better tomorrow, then kissed her gently on the forehead and told her he would be lying next to her as she rested.

A SURPRISE VISIT

Early the next evening Joseph heard a loud knock at the front door. "Who is it?" He asked. "It is Dr. Ludin. Is Dr. Gruel home?" I will call him, wait in the library," Joseph said as he opened the door to let him in.

Fredric was just getting up when Joseph walked into the bedroom. "I am sorry master; I forgot Miss Leona was here."

"Well what is it Joseph?"

"Dr. Ludin is waiting for you in the library master, what should I tell him?"

"Tell him I will be right down and that I have a surprise for him."

As Joseph walked out of the room, Fredric leaned over Leona and gave her a light kiss on her lips telling her that she must wake up because he has a surprise for her. "What is it Fredric," she asked, "I still do not feel well from last night?"

"Get dressed; my best friend is waiting for us in the library. I want you to meet him. Please get dressed and come down now."

Fredric was anxious to see his old friend Rolf. "It has been too long," he said as he entered the library and hugged his friend. "Rolf, my good friend how did you know I was here?"

"Word spreads very fast in our village, especially when your name is Dr. Gruel," he replied.

"Rolf, I have a great surprise for you."

"What is it or should I say who it is?" Rolf said.

"Wait one moment and you will see for yourself." Just then, Leona entered the library. "Rolf, this is my wife to be, Leona," Fredric proudly announced. Rolf gazed upon this lovely young woman dressed in an elegant pale green dress with her hair flowing over her shoulders and thought that he had never seen anyone so beautiful in all his life. Her beauty mesmerized him.

"Leona, this is my dearest friend, Rolf." Leona, staring at this handsome gentleman, was captivated by him as well, "It is very nice to meet you, Rolf."

"The pleasure is all mine," he assured her as he kissed the back of her hand. She awkwardly pulled her hand away and gave Fredric a kiss on his cheek then took hold of his arm.

"Fredric," Leona asked, "do we have anything that we can serve Rolf? I am sure Joseph can find something."

"You do not have to bother; I have no appetite this evening. I just wanted to stop by to see my old friend," Rolf interrupted.

Leona turned to Fredric and whispered in his ear, "Is Rolf like us?" Fredric began to laugh. "Rolf is my oldest mortal friend. I know Rolf since he was a child, for at least thirty-five years. There is nothing I would keep from him or not trust him with, not even you." Leona and Rolf began to blush as Fredric continued to laugh.

"Rolf, why don't you sit down, we have a lot to talk about? Leona, why don't you join us?" Fredric suggested. "May I be excused I would like to walk around the castle." Both men stood up as Leona extended her hand to Rolf. "It has been a pleasure," he said as he kissed the back of her hand again.

Leona gave Fredric a gentle kiss on the cheek and walked out of the library.

Fredric, glad to be able to give his full attention to Rolf, asked, "So how are our grapes doing?"

"You will have a wonderful harvest Fredric, and make a lot of money."

"No," Fredric replied, "We will make a lot of money." Rolf just smiled and said, "From what I can see, you had a very successful trip, my friend."

"Rolf, I am very concerned about Leona," Fredric confided.

"You are a very lucky man, Leona is a beautiful woman. What more could you ask for?" Rolf responded.

"I do not know if she can survive in this environment. Rolf, I would kill myself if I lost her," Fredric lamented.

Rolf, trying to be helpful said, "Fredric, put everything in its right perspective. You both just returned from a long, arduous trip. She is hundreds of miles away from her friends and family. You must give her time to adjust, be gentle with her."

"Rolf, I am so glad you came here this evening," Fredric began, "I have not told Leona as yet, but I am planning a two week trip to France to meet with some of my distributors. I would not feel comfortable leaving her here by herself. Would you, my dear friend, be able to stay with her while I am away?"

"I would need a little time to make arrangements, but I would be happy to oblige," Rolf assured Fredric.

While Fredric and Rolf continued their conversation, Leona walked around the castle. She was amazed at all the different banners hanging on the walls and all the swords and battle armor hanging along side of them.

Then she noticed a room at the far end of the hall. It had a wooden door with crossed steel bars nailed on it. Curious, Leona opened the door and stepped inside the dark room.

Once inside, the entire room suddenly illuminated in a deep red glow.

Leona was beginning to attain certain powers that she was not aware of and one of them was being able see in the dark.

She started to walk when she tripped over something and landed on the floor. She tried to move the object that she tripped over only to realize that it was a skeleton wearing full body armor.

Leona tried to stand up but she felt herself being pulled to the floor again.

She soon realized that she was sitting in the middle of a room filled with skeletons, including one that was holding onto her leg. Leona was terrified; she tried to stand up again but could not. Noticing that all the skeletons were slowly walking towards her, the only thing she could do was scream.

When they heard Leona's screams, Fredric along with Rolf and Joseph ran down the hall.

Fredric entered the room alone and saw what was happening. He grabbed Leona away from the skeletons then picked her up and carried her out into the hall. He tried to calm her down but she was too hysterical.

"Joseph," Fredric shouted, "Why was Miss Leona allowed to enter that room? It was supposed to be locked."

"Master, I do not know what happened, I never unlocked that door."

"Something is terribly wrong. That room was never opened," Fredric said as he angrily looked at Joseph. "Master, it will never happen again," assured Joseph.

Leona tried to calm herself while Rolf held her hand. Fredric walked back to that room and slammed the door shut.

"Fredric, this is a bad time, maybe I should leave," Rolf said. "Nonsense," Fredric answered, "in a short time Leona will be fine and we will all go into the study and have some wine."

"Joseph, please bring some of my vintage wine for Rolf and my special wine for Miss Leona and me to the study."

"Rolf, everything will be just fine. Why don't you go into the study now, Leona and I will join you shortly."

As Rolf walked away, Fredric leaned on one knee and held Leona's hand. "Are you feeling better?" he asked. Leona, who was still trembling from the frightening experience asked, "What happened in that room Fredric, what were those skeletons doing there and why did one of them try to attack me?" Fredric, avoiding her question merely said, "We have a guest waiting for us in the study, let us join him and drink some wine. That should make you feel better."

They walked arm in arm into the study where Rolf was comfortably sitting across from the lit fireplace.

"Fredric, this looks so familiar, just like the study I had at home," Leona shared. "Yes it does my dear, but this is your home now," Fredric replied.

"How was your trip to London," Rolf asked. "Just being able to come back with Leona made the trip worthwhile," he answered. "Are you planning on staying?" I hope so, Rolf"

Just then Joseph walked in with several bottles of wine. "This is a special vintage for you Rolf, and these are for Leona and me," Fredric said. He then poured the wine and made a toast, "To life and to the beauty of life."

As they clicked their glasses, Rolf asked Leona, "Do you miss London?"

"Yes I do, very much, but I am sure as time goes on, my mind will be on other things."

"Well said, Leona, well said," Fredric thought to himself.

"It is getting late, I must be going now," Rolf said.

"It is early for me but I will see you to the door," Fredric replied.

"Good night Leona, I am sure we will be seeing more of each other," Rolf said, as he walked towards the front door.

Joseph brought Rolf his cape and hat and Fredric held the door open for him. "Get home safely," he said to his old friend as he closed the door.

Fredric walked back to the study where Leona was still standing by the fireplace. "Fredric, please tell me again what happened in my father's study the night he died. I would like you to tell me again."

Fredric knew that what he had told Leona before were all lies. He did not want to go over the details again, but felt he should before she becomes too suspicious. Hoping that he retells the story exactly the same way as before, he began to stoke the fire, giving him time to think of how to start.

Then he began, "When I came into your father's study he was sitting across from the fire. As he stood up he turned to me and asked why I had come there so late. I told him that I came to ask for your hand in marriage. He took a step towards me as if to shake my hand when he suddenly grabbed his shoulder and fell into his chair."

"Did he say yes? I want to know if he said yes," she pressed. "He said yes Leona. Then he went to raise his hand as if he was going to congratulate me and he fell back into his chair and died."

"I had to hear it again, Fredric, I had to know," she said as she walked out of the study.

A few minutes later Fredric followed her upstairs to the bedroom. They were both in a dismal mood as they lay down on the bed next to each other not saying a word.

The next evening they awakened at the same time staring at the darkened ceiling without acknowledging each other at all.

LEONA BEGINS TO CHANGE

As days, then weeks went by, Fredric noticed a change in Leona's attitude. She was not as out going as she had been when she arrived from London. She would walk around the castle with a sad look on her face.

The only person Fredric could reach out to would be his good friend Rolf.

When Fredric summoned Rolf to the castle, he arrived a few days later.

"Rolf, I am so glad you were able to come," Fredric said excitedly. "You are my closest friend, Fredric, if you need my help you know I am here for you. What is wrong now?" Rolf asked as Joseph helped him remove his hat and cape. "I think we should go into my study," Fredric said as he put his arm around Rolf and led him down the hall into the study at the same time telling Joseph to bring them some wine.

There was a chill in the air so they both moved their chairs closer to the lit fireplace. Joseph walked in carrying a tray with two bottles of wine and two glasses. As Fredric poured wine into Rolf's glass, he grabbed the bottle to make sure he would be drinking the vintage wine and not Fredric's special wine. Fredric stood up and made his toast, "To life and to the beauty of life."

"What is wrong, Fredric? I have never seen you like this," Rolf asked. Looking directly at him he answered, "The problem is not me, the problem is Leona."

"What do you mean?" Rolf inquired. "I have decided to put off my business trip for the time being."

"Why?" Rolf asked. "As you know, Leona has been drinking my wine and has completely turned into a vampire. I offered her immortality but I had not considered her soul. She is having a difficult time accepting her new life. She wakes up at night and just walks around the castle not seeming to care about anything. While in London, she was the life of the party. What have I done to her?" he asked of his friend.

"You told me you would like to have a grand ball in Leona's honor, so have it."

Fredric, excitedly asked Rolf, "Can you get all the dignitaries and their wives who live in the surrounding villages together? I had promised Leona I would."

"I know every important person for one hundred miles around. I will make sure they all come," Rolf promised.

"I could never repay you for the friendship you have shown me throughout the years," Fredric told Rolf. "Where is Leona now? Rolf inquired. "Maybe I can get her to smile."

"Let me tell her you are here. I am sure she will be very happy to see you," Fredric replied.

"Why don't you plan your two week business trip while I stay here? Leona and I can plan the ball together and she can help me decorate the castle while I take care of all the other arrangements," Rolf said eagerly. "That is a wonderful idea, I'm sure Leona would like that very much," Fredric said as he left to find her.

When Fredric left the study, Rolf decided to try Fredric's special wine again to see what would happen. He poured one glass and then another and another as he waited for Fredric to return.

When Fredric walked into the study with Leona holding onto his arm, Rolf stood up, walked over to Leona and gently kissed the back of her hand.

"Isn't this a wonderful surprise, Leona?" Fredric asked. "Yes it is," she replied.

"What made you come here Rolf?" she then asked.

"I have missed the both of you so I thought I would take a ride into the country and see how you are doing," Rolf said. "How kind of you, you were dearly missed. I wish you would come more often," Leona said.

"Rolf came up with a wonderful idea! He wants to help us plan the grand ball in your honor that we spoke about weeks ago. How would you like that Leona?" asked Fredric. "We could invite all the dignitaries and their wives from the surrounding villages just to meet you."

Leona turned to Fredric and asked, "Does Rolf really mean this, or is he just saying this to make me feel better?"

Looking at Leona, Fredric answered her with a big smile on his face, "Yes Leona we are going to have our first ball."

Leona gave Fredric a hug then walked over to Rolf and gave him a kiss on the cheek.

Rolf, taken by surprise, looked at Fredric who shrugged his shoulders as if to say, "It worked."

Fredric called out to Joseph to bring more wine.

When he appeared with two more bottles, Rolf took them from him and began to pour the special wine into Leona's glass, then Fredric's and then his own. Leona quickly looked up at Fredric, "Rolf do you realize what you just did?" Fredric asked. "Yes I do, while you were upstairs I poured some of your wine into my glass and drank it. How many glasses of this wine did you have?" Fredric inquired. "About four glasses, he confessed.

"Why did you do this?"

Rolf decisively replied, "Because I wanted to feel like you. I have waited years for the chance to see what it would be like to become a vampire. I have always wanted to have the strength you have in your body and in your mind."

Rolf then sat back in his chair and looked straight into the fire as Fredric walked over to him saying, "I had no idea that you felt like this, but you must understand that being a vampire is not necessarily the best thing in the world. It has its consequences."

"I think it might be a good idea for you to sleep in the castle tonight. I do not want you on the road while it is dark," Fredric told him.

Rolf just sat there looking down with his head in his hands. He then looked up at Fredric, "I came here to make Leona smile, look at me."

Fredric and Leona could only sit there in silence.

Fredric called Joseph to get a room ready for Rolf, "I need a comfortable room for my best friend; he is going to sleep in the castle tonight. Just make sure the drapes are drawn tight, thank you Joseph."

"This has been a very long day for you, Rolf, why don't you go upstairs now and get some rest. Leona and I will stay down here and talk about the ball. Remember, when you wake up in the morning, do not walk out into the sunlight."

Rolf then stood up and just said, "Good night," as he followed Joseph upstairs to his room.

Fredric, still stunned by what Rolf had told him, said, "I have known Rolf all of his life and I never had any idea what was going through his mind. I now feel bad for him."

"Fredric, do you think he had enough wine to be turned into one of us?" Leona asked. "I hope not. I think he will just feel ill in the morning but I hope he heeds what I said about staying out of the direct sunlight."

ROLF HAS A BAD DAY

Rolf awakened early the next morning and suddenly remembered what took place the night before. He felt embarrassed about what he had done. He knew Fredric well enough to know that he would forgive him, but would Leona?

He went downstairs to Fredric's study. He peeked through the drapes and noticed that the sun had not set yet which meant that Fredric and Leona would not awaken for a few more hours.

Rolf sat in front of the fireplace thinking of how he met Fredric.

His parents had died when he was ten years old and he was placed in an orphanage. Life in the orphanage was hard and depressing, especially for such a precocious child as Rolf. One day, while playing out side, he came upon a hole in the fence that surrounded the orphanage. It was then that he decided to wait for the right moment, climb through the hole, and make his escape. One afternoon two of the orphan boys began to fight and the other orphans and the matrons ran to see what was happening. This was Rolf's chance, so he climbed through the hole and started to run until he could not run one more step. Joseph found him wondering in the woods and took him into the castle to care for him.

As young boys, Fredric and Rolf would run around making believe they were soldiers defending the castle. They were inseparable. When he was very young, he was turned into a vampire and he aged in stages. When Fredric was forty years old, he looked and acted like a ten year old.

Joseph educated Rolf together with Fredric but noticed early on that Rolf was an exceptionally intelligent child. He sent him to a boarding school and then to the university where he studied medicine.

As years past Rolf became well known throughout Transylvania as a brilliant physician. Fredric also went to the university to study medicine, but he only wanted to attain knowledge about the human body, the circulatory system and blood so he would be prepared to do his research.

Rolf was also an incredible negotiator and he was able to help Fredric complete many of his business transactions throughout Europe.

As Rolf sat in the study, an overpowering urge, not unlike when he was a child, overtook him. He thought that this would be a good time to explore parts of the castle that he was not allowed to when he lived there as a child. He decided to go to the lower level that was off limits. This was where the dungeons were located.

Rolf tried to make as little noise as possible. He knew that Fredric had the power to hear any noise, any where in the castle, "If he knew what I was about to do he would be very upset with me," he thought.

Rolf cautiously made his way down a stone stairway that led to a hallway beneath the castle. As he walked further down into the dungeon, it became darker and darker. Then suddenly a deep red glow appeared allowing Rolf to see his way.

As Rolf continued to walk deeper down into the dungeons, he heard a strange banging noise. He followed what sounded like metal hitting metal when all of a sudden he encountered a skeleton standing right in front of him, dressed in full body armor with a sword raised ready to strike.

"Stop, stop," Rolf yelled. "What are you and what do you want?"

"I am my master's general, why are you here?" answered the skeleton as he raised his sword high above his head ready to strike. Rolf then raised his hand as if to defend himself and stepped back falling over another skeleton. Terrified, Rolf yelled out, "I am a friend of Dr. Fredric Gruel, please do not hurt me."

All Rolf could do was just stay on the floor, petrified.

Unexpectedly, the skeleton put down his sword, bowed his head and muttered, "Master."

Rolf then looked up and much to his surprise and relief, he saw Fredric standing over him. "Why are you down here, Rolf" asked Fredric in a calm voice. "You are beginning to disappoint me."

"Why?" asked Rolf. "I awoke early and decided to walk through the castle where we played as boys. I found myself going deeper into the castle when I heard strange noises. Then I noticed the dungeons, then this, this skeleton or person or what ever it is tried to attack me."

"Is this true?" Fredric asked facing the skeleton who answered in a deep, gruff voice, "Yes master, it is true."

"What shall we do with him," asked the skeleton. "Nothing," Fredric replied. "But he knows our secret location, master."

"Yes he does, but he will never say anything to anyone, he is my closest and most trusted friend. Isn't that right, Rolf?"

Looking up at Fredric, "Yes, I will never say anything to anyone," Rolf repeated in a shaky voice.

"No one would believe Rolf anyway," Fredric thought to himself.

Fredric helped his friend stand up, "Let me show you around. Oh, this skeleton is the general in charge of all my soldiers."

Rolf, not believing any of this said, "Where are your soldiers?"

"Look around you Rolf, they are in dungeons like this one throughout the castle, just waiting for a command from me."

Fredric continued to explain that these were once men that were the best soldiers in all of Europe until they were captured and their families tortured by his older brother, Count Vladimir Gruel. These men vowed to avenge their families and not rest until they have killed Count Gruel.

"Rolf, what you have seen today, no one has ever seen and no one will until the time is right. The only way I can let you walk out of here tonight is with your pledge of secrecy, you will never talk about what you have seen to anyone, is that understood?"

"I give you my pledge," Rolf replied.

Fredric placed his arm around Rolf, "Let us go upstairs before the sun rises and get some rest. This must have been a very exhausting experience for you."

ROLF'S ENCOUNTER WITH LEONA

Soon after the next sunset, Rolf went down to the study to wait for Fredric and Leona to come down stairs.

A short time later Leona walked into the study. She was wearing a provocative black dress that accentuated her beautiful figure. Rolf, who was not expecting to see Leona by herself, immediately stood up, walked over to her, and gently kissed the back of her hand.

"Please accept my apologies for last evening," he asked of Leona. "All is forgiven," she replied.

"You must be hungry. Can I have Joseph prepare something for you?" Leona asked. "For some reason, I seem to have lost my appetite. I do not know why."

"Then I will have Joseph bring in something for you to drink," Leona suggested. "That's a good idea, thank you."

Then all at once, reality overtook him and he asked Leona, "What will I do if I turn into a vampire?" She moved closer To Rolf, "That is something you will have to give great thought to," she said with a flirtatious look on her face.

"Do you always dress this way for guests?" Rolf asked. "Only when there is a special guest in the castle that I care for," Leona answered. "Then I should consider myself honored," Rolf said as he stepped even closer to her.

Leona just stood there waiting to see what Rolf would do next. Rolf, not able to resist Leona's beauty, placed his hands on her arms and pulled her towards him tenderly kissing her on her lips.

As he went to kiss her again, Leona stepped back and told him, "Remember Rolf, even though Fredric is not standing here he can read your mind and knows exactly what you are thinking."

Rolf immediately put his hands down and took several steps back as Leona laughed.

"By the way, where is Fredric?" Rolf asked. "He is in his laboratory working," she replied. "Is there something I could help him with?" Rolf asked. "Yes," Leona replied, "You can stay with me."

Rolf, who appeared confused by her answer sat down across from the fireplace, then turned to Leona, "I think we should discuss the ball." Leona answered with a big smile on her face, "I think that is a grand idea."

"Leave everything up to me, this will be my gift to you and Fredric," Rolf offered. "How sweet of you," Leona replied.

"I have never been as excited as this before, a grand ball in my honor," she exclaimed as she walked over to Rolf in a provocative way and gave him a fast kiss on the lips. Just then, Fredric walked into the room. "What did Rolf do to deserve that?" he asked. They were both taken by surprise as they both just stood there not knowing what to say.

Leona finally said, "Guess what? Rolf will make all the arrangements for my grand ball and this will be his gift to us. Isn't that wonderful, Fredric?" Fredric shook Rolf's hand saying, "This is a very generous gift. I can see why Leona is so excited."

"Fredric, I must talk to you privately. Can we go into the library?" Rolf asked.

When they entered the library, Fredric asked him what was wrong. "I am scared Fredric, very scared about the amount of wine I drank. I was out of my head when I spoke last night, I really do not want to be a vampire," he admitted. Fredric answered Rolf with a smile on his face, "That should not be too much of a problem. I believe I can reverse your situation by cleansing your blood."

"Can you do this right away?" Rolf pleaded. "As soon as you wish," Fredric replied then added, "I will have to give you a transfusion."

"Has this ever been done before?" Rolf asked. "Only on mice, but the procedure will be the same. If you want this to be done now, I must go down to my laboratory and prepare everything."

Leona walked in and asked if everything was all right. "Everything is fine, Rolf will explain," Fredric told her as he left the study to go to his laboratory.

ROLF RETURNS TO MORTALITY

The transfusion took longer than expected, but Fredric was able to restore Rolf to mortality with few side effects.

What Fredric did not realize at the time was that Rolf, being a doctor himself, would now be able to restore Leona back to mortality using the same process, if he chose.

Rolf was now able to function as he did before drinking Fredric's special wine. However, he wanted to stay in the castle several more days and wait to see if there would be any after effects from the transfusion. At least that is what he told Fredric.

Rolf was apparently falling in love with Leona and wanted to continue to see her and talk to her even if it was for a short time each day while Fredric worked in his laboratory.

After several more days of recovering, Fredric thought it was time for Rolf to go home. Before leaving, Rolf reminded Fredric that he promised to stay in the castle with Leona, "I will be back next week so make your travel arrangements and do not forget to tell Leona," Rolf told Fredric as he left the castle.

Fredric went upstairs to tell Leona of his plans. Leona was pleasantly surprised that he would leave her alone for two weeks with Rolf. "I think that is a very good idea Fredric, you have not been on a business trip for a long while. I think this trip will be good for you."

Leona seemed very anxious for Fredric to go on this business trip, and Fredric could not understand why.

One week had gone by when Rolf's coach pulled up in front of the castle. It was early evening and the sun had already set. Rolf had brought his personal belongings and plenty of food to last for the two weeks he would be staying there.

Rolf was extremely excited about being alone with Leona for the next two weeks.

He walked to the front door and knocked while his coachman took down his belongings.

Joseph opened the door and told Rolf to come in. "They are expecting you," he said.

Rolf walked inside while Joseph summoned Fredric and Leona.

They both came from the library to greet him. "We were getting worried, we thought you might have forgotten," Leona said. Rolf looked directly at Leona and replied, "I could not forget my promise."

Rolf's coachman carried his belongings inside and then left as Rolf told him, "Do not forget to come back and pick me up two weeks from today at the same time."

Fredric, noticing that Rolf brought bags of food, told Joseph to take his luggage upstairs and the food to the kitchen.

"I cannot thank you enough for all you are doing," Fredric said.

Leona agreed, and then gave Rolf a kiss on the cheek.

Rolf replied by saying, "This stay will be my pleasure."

TWO WEEKS ALONE WITH LEONA

Early the next evening Fredric was ready to leave for his trip. Before he left, he walked over to Leona, gave her a long kiss, and whispered in her ear, "I will miss you very much my love. You will be safe here with Rolf." He shook Rolf's hand and said good-bye.

Joseph held the door open as Fredric left the castle to enter a coach that would take him to the railway station.

Rolf asked Joseph to bring some wine into the study. He turned towards Leona and said with a smirk on his face, "Since I will be the master of this castle for the next two weeks, I expect you both to do as I say."

Rolf took Leona by her hand and they walked into the study towards the warmth of the fireplace.

The minute they walked in the room, Rolf turned Leona around, embraced, and kissed her before telling her, "You must know by now that I have fallen in love with you." Leona, not surprised by Rolf's confession, said coyly, "I think love is not the word, Rolf." He gave her another kiss, but they parted quickly as Joseph came into the study carrying a tray with two bottles of wine and two glasses.

The vintage wine was for Rolf and the other, special wine, for Leona.

Rolf poured the wine from each bottle into the glasses. He then made a toast holding his glass up, "To the future of our love for each other." He then clicked his glass against Leona's and they both began to drink.

"Why don't we go upstairs, Leona?"

"I think that is a very good idea," she replied.

They then walked up the stairs together and as soon as they reached Leona's bedroom, Rolf took her in his arms and kissed her passionately. He then lay her down on the bed as he whispered, "I have dreamed of this day. I have wanted to make love to you since the first moment I saw you."

Rolf could not believe that this beautiful woman was willing to give herself to him freely.

She lay there, in anticipation, awaiting his next move. Rolf gazed upon her loveliness and then made ardent love to her.

As the evening went on they were not aware of how much time had passed and the sun was about to rise. Rolf jumped from the bed and closed the draperies, as Leona lay there ready to fall asleep. He picked his clothes up from the floor and slipped into his own room.

As the days passed, it seemed that Rolf and Leona got themselves into a routine of drinking wine and making love every evening.

Near the end of the second week, after making love, Leona whispered to Rolf, "What are we to do about Fredric finding out?"

"There is little we can do, but I do know that we have to make preparations for the ball, it is rapidly approaching."

"We should send out the invitations and hire musicians. We must show Fredric that we have been working together on this," he continued, "so, tomorrow I will go to the village and arrange for all the food to be assembled in one place so Joseph and Pulaski can pick it up. I will hire help to polish the silver and all the armor and others to serve the guests.

When I return, Joseph and I will rearrange the furniture and I will organize the seating. Everything will be fine."

Rolf and Leona did not have to worry. Fredric would never suspect that Leona and his closest friend would ever betray him.

What Fredric was not suspicious of to begin with, he would not focus on while he was away.

Two weeks had gone by when Fredric returned home from his tiresome trip.

Upon entering the castle, he heard voices coming from the study. He walked down the hall and entered to see Rolf and Leona, sitting across from each other talking about which guests will be coming to the ball.

Leona stood up when she saw him and ran over and gave him a kiss on the cheek. "We did not hear you come in, let me call Joseph to take your cape and luggage," she said. Rolf also stood up and shook Fredric's hand as he said, "It is good to see you my friend. Leona and I were beginning to get bored with each other. Let me pour you some wine. I hope you had a successful trip."

Rolf was clearly nervous as he relayed one thought after the other to Fredric. "I had a very successful trip, thank you," Fredric replied as he sat down next to Leona.

"How did you two get along while I was away?" Fredric inquired in a sort of doubtful manor. "All the arrangements have been made for Leona's grand ball and Leona is quite excited. Isn't that so?" Rolf asked, as he turned and looked at Leona, making sure that she was in agreement with him, knowing very well that he had not answered Fredric's question.

"You must be exhausted from your long trip, why don't we go upstairs and spend some time together and you can rest," Leona suggested.

Fredric and Leona left the study while Rolf sat in front of the fireplace feeling very envious.

The next evening Rolf's coachman knocked on the door. When Joseph answered, the coachman simply said, "Please tell Dr. Ludin that I am here and I'll be waiting for him."

Joseph walked into the study where the three were discussing the upcoming ball.

"Dr. Rolf's coachman is waiting outside," Joseph informed them.

All three stood up at the same time. Leona gave Rolf a kiss on the cheek as Fredric watched, then put his hand on Rolf's shoulder and walked him to the front door.

"Thank you for everything, and I'm sure Leona appreciates all you have done as well. We'll see you at the ball," Fredric said as Rolf climbed in his coach and drove off.

THE GRAND BALL

Rolf had arranged for the main hall to be turned into a magnificent ballroom. There were brightly lit crystal chandeliers. All the sconces and armor were polished. The Couches and chairs covered in burgundy and gold velvet and all the draperies in the entranceways matched. The servers wore white wigs, ruffled shirts and silk jackets that had gold buttons running down the sides.

At approximately six-thirty that evening, just as the sun went down, the guests began to arrive. Servants greeted them as they stepped out from their coaches. As each guest walked into the main ballroom he was announced. Then Rolf greeted them personally.

Musicians played traditional music as servants walked around offering guests champagne and hors d'oeuvres.

After Rolf was assured that all the guests had arrived, he announced that everyone should look up towards the top of the stairs.

"Let me introduce you to Dr. Fredric Gruel and his fiancée, Miss Leona Stroud of London," Rolf called out, as they made their grand entrance.

Leona and Fredric stood at the top of the staircase. Leona looked down at the crowded ballroom and whispered to Fredric, "They are all here for me," as they started to walk down the stairs arm in arm.

The guests began to applaud as Fredric and Leona reached the last step.

Then the couple walked to the center of the dance floor. The musicians started to play a waltz and they began to dance.

They each looked into the other's eyes as they moved effortlessly around the dance floor. Everyone applauded them again as they turned gracefully around to the music. One could see by the expressions on their faces that they were very happy.

The men could not help but talk among themselves about Leona's beauty and how lucky Fredric was to be engaged to such a woman.

The women, on the other hand, although acknowledging her beauty, could not stop talking about her off the shoulder, low cut burgundy gown, the diamond pins holding up her curls that fell over one shoulder and a diamond teardrop necklace that rested above her cleavage. "She is magnificent and she is so young. Are they really vampires?" the guests whispered to each other, with no one knowing the answer.

For many years there were rumors going around about the Gruel family being vampires but Fredric was so well respected for his friendship and generosity to the villagers that no one truly believed this.

After awhile the men came up to Leona and one by one asked her to dance. This made Fredric very proud. As a gentleman would ask Leona to dance, Fredric would then walk up to the gentleman's wife and ask her to dance.

The women were intrigued by Fredric. One woman said, as they began to dance, "You are a very handsome man. Are you a real vampire?"

"Yes I am," Fredric replied looking into her eyes. She then asked, "Do you get pleasure out of biting women on their necks?" He then smiled at her as they continued to dance. "Only women with beautiful necks like yours." She giggled as they continued to dance. The music ended and Fredric bowed and thanked her for the dance.

Fredric then walked up to where the musicians were playing and called out to his guests, "May I have your attention, please." Everyone looked at Fredric as he began to speak. "I would like to thank you all for coming here this evening. You have made my beautiful Leona welcome, but this ball would not have been possible without the help of my closest friend, who you all know as Dr. Rolf Ludin. He was the one who arranged everything in our honor. If everyone would please raise their glass, I would like to propose a toast to my beautiful fiancée Leona and my best friend Rolf, and to the future and beauty of life."

As soon as everyone took a sip from their glass, the musicians began to play again. Rolf walked over to Leona and asked, "May I have this dance, Leona?" She turned towards him and raised her arms allowing him to place his arms around her. He began to whisk her around the dance floor while all the guests looked on.

As they danced, Rolf held her close and said, "You are the most beautiful woman in all of Europe this evening."

"Thank you Rolf, and thank you for this ball and for being such a good friend." All Rolf could do was to stare at her as they danced around the floor without saying another word.

THE BALL HITS A LOW NOTE

The time was getting late but no one was leaving. Everyone was having such a good time.

It was nearing midnight when suddenly a heavy gust of cold air blew into the ballroom blowing out candles and creating a cold draft.

The musicians stopped playing and the guests turned towards the front doors to see a tall, slim man enter wearing a black tuxedo with a black cape over his shoulders. His graying hair was long, parted in the center and slickly pulled back. As he raised his hand to remove his cape, one could see the strange rings that were on three of his fingers.

He walked slowly towards the center of the ballroom as the guests began to whisper among themselves, "It is Count Gruel. Why is he here? Was he invited?"

Count Gruel, a rather distinguished looking man with a profound look of death in his eyes, looked around at all the guests that were now, standing around him.

Fredric and Leona walked out onto the center of the ballroom floor to meet him. Fredric introduced Leona. "Leona, this is my oldest brother, Count Vladimir Gruel that I have spoken so much about."

"Only good things I hope," Count Gruel said as he kissed Leona's hand. "It is good to finally meet you Count Gruel, can I have one of the servants bring you something to drink?"

"No thank you," the count replied, "it is very kind of you to ask, maybe a little later."

The count, in a gruff voice, turned to face Fredric and told him "I had heard about your ball, but I guess the invitation to me must have gotten lost."

Fredric could not answer the Count as they both stared into each other's eyes with extreme dislike, trying to read each other's mind.

The count, looking at Leona, said, "Now that you have such a beautiful fiancée, life can only get better, Fredric, wouldn't you agree?"

Unexpectedly, one of the servants pulled a sword off the wall and ran onto the ballroom floor towards Count Gruel yelling, "You killed my father, you killed my brothers."

As he came closer to the Count swinging his sword, the count stared at him and two piercing beams of red lights shot out of his eyes causing the servant to scream out in pain, then burn and disintegrate before every ones eyes.

Fredric and Leona could do nothing but watch as the guests began to panic and run out of the castle. The women screamed in horror and the men pushed their way out.

Count Gruel then turned to Leona and said, "Please accept my apology for this intrusion."

He kissed Leona's hand and fled the castle disappearing into the cold night.

After everyone had gone, Leona began to cry, "The ball was so wonderful and then it ended so horribly."

Fredric and Rolf tried unsuccessfully to console Leona.

Then Fredric, with anger welling up inside of him, exclaimed, "I am going to kill Count Vladimir Gruel. The fact that he is my brother does not matter."

Fredric, in his rage, began using his telepathic powers to hurl objects around the ballroom, upsetting Leona even more. Rolf stepped in and yelled, "Fredric, calm down."

Fredric sat down and then Leona began to stroke his head, very gently, trying to soothe him.

Fredric was incensed, as he stood up and exclaimed, "I have never been as humiliated in my whole life as I was this evening. I will never allow this to happen to me again."

Without saying another word, Fredric walked out of the ballroom and went upstairs leaving Leona and Rolf behind.

"I feel terrible about what had happened this evening, but there was little that anyone could have done to avoid this terrible intrusion," Rolf said as he tried to console Leona by placing his hand on her arm and gently kissing her. She stepped back and told him, "Rolf, I care for you very much but this must stop. If Fredric finds out he will kill us both."

Rolf watched as Leona walked up the stairs and disappeared behind her bedroom door. He was left standing in the middle of the ballroom, alone and brokenhearted.

FREDRIC HAS A PLAN

Fredric was having difficulty sleeping. As he lay in bed next to Leona he came up with a very simplistic plan that would allow Rolf to continue maintaining his vineyards, while he made arrangements for him and Leona to leave Transylvania for good, but most important, he would kill Count Gruel before they go.

It would be the latter that would be most difficult, but Fredric knew it could only be done by his own hand.

Fredric spent most of his time in his study planning his and Leona's future.

Days then weeks passed and he still had no idea where they would go, but he knew that if he was to leave Transylvania it must be to a country that had soil compatible with that of Transylvania so he could continue to grow the same type of wine grapes that would sustain them for eternity.

Rolf would come to the castle on a regular basis to visit. During these visits he would see that Fredric was always preoccupied with his planning.

One evening, Fredric told Rolf, "I have completed my plans for our future. It is most important that I share my thoughts with you."

"Is Leona aware of your intentions?" Rolf asked. "No, not yet, but she will know shortly,"

"Rolf," Fredric said, as he placed his hand on his friend's shoulder, "Leona and I must leave Transylvania for good and never return. But first I must do away with Count Gruel. He must be gone for good."

"How do you intend to do that," Rolf asked. "I intend to travel to the city of Walachia and gain access to the count's castle and kill him while he sleeps."

"How can you travel in daylight with out dying?" Rolf asked.

Fredric reached into his pocket, "This is how," he said as he handed a colored glass object to Rolf. "What is this?" Rolf questioned, "How will this colored glass allow you to kill the count, it is only a piece of glass."

Fredric took the glass from Rolf's hand. "This is more than just a piece of glass, Rolf, this has my blood baked into it. When this glass covers my eyes, it will work as protection against the sunlight. As long as sunlight does not directly enter my eyes, I will be all right. There is no way for me to approach the castle, except in daylight when the count and his men are asleep."

Rolf just looked at Fredric knowing that his friend was totally obsessed with this idea.

THE END OF A FRIENDSHIP

Several more weeks past while Fredric prepared for his big day. He decided that he must tell Leona what he had in mind for them and what he was about to do regarding his brother.

Leona was extremely disturbed when Fredric told her of his plans. "I will follow you anywhere, Fredric, but I do not want you to die. Please do not do this, I am pleading with you," she said.

Holding Leona in his arms he told her, "This is something that should have been taken care of over a hundred years ago."

Leona, still in Fredric's arms said, "I have something very important to tell you."

"What is so important," he asked.

Leona looked straight at him and said, "Fredric, I am with child." Fredric was stunned as he sat down on the edge of the bed, "How long have you known this?" he asked.

Leona, not wanting to discuss why she had not told him before, said, "Only a short while. That is why Rolf had been coming here so often. He wants to make sure that I am all right."

"Who will deliver the baby, and when will it be born?" Fredric asked.

"Rolf has already made arrangements for me and is expecting me to give birth sometime in early spring."

As Leona was explaining, Fredric stood up, "I am so happy for you, you will be so happy when the baby arrives. This is wonderful," he said without emotion.

Not having any more to say, he gave Leona a kiss and walked out of the bedroom.

Fredric knew he could not leave Transylvania until the child was born. This news gave Fredric little choice; he still had to continue with his plans.

Several days later there was a knock on the castle door. Joseph went to see who it was. At the same time, Fredric was coming up from the laboratory and heard Joseph ask who was there. "It is Rolf."

"Come in, the weather looks terrible; let me take your hat and cape. Go sit by the fire while I make you some soup and find Fredric?" Joseph suggested. "I will, thank you," answered Rolf.

Fredric walked into the study looking upset. Without greeting Rolf, he asked him, "Why didn't you tell me about Leona? You are supposed to be my friend, Rolf."

"I am your friend Fredric which is why I did not say anything to you. Besides, would you have changed your plans?" Rolf asked, "Perhaps not," Fredric answered as he stared into the fireplace, "but there was still no reason not to tell me."

"You have so much on your mind. Planning this move and the problem regarding your brother," Rolf answered, then cheerfully told him, "Leona is going to have a healthy baby in early spring."

"Will the baby be mortal?" Fredric asked.

"We will have to wait until the child is born to know the answer," Rolf replied.

"What is done is done, I must move on now," Fredric continued, "there are a lot of things that I have to discuss with you, but you must be hungry. Joseph made some hot soup for a vagrant who worked on the castle grounds today. I will have him bring you some, it will warm you up."

"I assume you are here to see Leona?" Fredric asked. "Yes I am," he answered.

"Rolf, why don't you have your soup first, then go upstairs to examine Leona. I will go down to the laboratory to do some work."

Rolf walked upstairs and saw Leona sitting by her dressing table brushing her hair. He just stood there watching her and realized that he still had very strong feelings for her.

Leona heard Rolf and turned around. She still had strong feelings for him too. "Where is Fredric," she asked.

"He is in his laboratory," he answered, then told her, "I am still in love with you, Leona," as he put his arms around her. "I will never forget the love we shared. If there was only some way we could be together."

"Yes, I know my love, perhaps some day we can be together."

They continued to talk unaware that Fredric was outside the room and overheard everything they said.

Suddenly Fredric appeared. He walked over to Rolf and threw him to the floor as the whites of his eyes turned to blood red. He picked Rolf up with one hand and flung him against the wall then he grabbed him and held him up in the air as Rolf pleaded for forgiveness.

Leona jumped on top of Fredric, screaming, "You're killing him, let him go." With that, Fredric dropped Rolf and he landed on the floor with a thud.

Rolf looked up at Fredric and kept repeating, "I'm sorry, I'm sorry. I don't know what came over me."

Fredric picked Rolf up from the floor and held onto his shirt with both hands as he told him, "I considered you my best friend, but I never want to look at you again. Do you hear me Rolf? Never come to this castle again or I will kill you."

Rolf gave Leona a quick glance as he walked out of the room. Leona stayed on the bed wrapped in a blanket while Fredric walked into the hall to watch Rolf leave.

Leona yelled to Fredric, "It was my fault. Rolf was in love with me and I did not try to discourage him. When he walked into the room I was so surprised. I was not expecting him. He started talking about us being together, which of course was silly, Fredric, because I love you. I will never leave you," she rambled on. "Think of our baby and our future together."

Fredric felt lost for the first time in his long life. "What should I do?" he thought. I know why I lost my closest friend and confidante, but I still love Leona."

Fredric paced around the bedroom, "If I had not brought Leona here this would not have happened," he thought.

Leona, feeling helpless, watched him in silence.

After making up his mind, Fredric sat down on the bed next to Leona, took her hands in his and told her, "There are only three people that I care about, you, me and our baby and that will never change."

Feeling justified in his actions, Fredric went down to the laboratory to continue his work. All of a sudden thoughts of Rolf overwhelmed him, *"He knows all my secrets. What will he do with this information and will he ever use it against me?"*

FREDRIC COMPLETES HIS PROJECT

Several months had past since the incident with Rolf.

Fredric had not been spending much time with Leona because he knew that if he were to stop working on his experiments now, he would not be able to kill Count Gruel and leave Transylvania in a timely manor after Leona gives birth.

Another several weeks past and it was spring. Leona tried to keep herself busy during this time but all she could think about was giving birth to a healthy baby.

Then one evening near the end of March, Fredric and Joseph heard a loud shriek that echoed throughout the castle.

Fredric ran up from the laboratory to find Leona sitting on the side of her bed, "Fredric, the baby will be here soon. Send Pulaski to get the midwife."

Joseph summoned Pulaski to go to the village to bring back Hanna, the midwife.

Fredric sat with Leona and comforted her as best as he could. With each pain she would scream out, and then gradually quiet down.

Finally, a woman of about fifty with rosy cheeks and grey streaked hair twisted on top of her head entered the castle and asked Joseph, "Where is she?"

"Follow me," he said as he led Hanna up the stairs to the master bedroom.

"Okay, Dr. Gruel, you can leave the room now. You," she said as she pointed to Joseph, "bring me some towels and a basin of hot water."

After the tasks were done, both men just stood outside of the bedroom and waited.

After many hours of hearing Leona scream, they finally heard the cry of a baby.

The two men did not have the courage to open the door, so they waited. When the door opened, Hanna beckoned them to come in. "It is a boy, a beautiful boy," she told them.

Fredric was beaming as he gazed upon Leona holding his son. "Isn't he beautiful, Fredric?" she asked as she held the baby's tiny fingers. Fredric was so overwhelmed with joy he could not speak.

As Hanna was cleaning up, Fredric inconspicuously wrapped the umbilical cord in a towel and told Leona he would be right back. He then brought it down to the laboratory to check the blood. After diluting his newborn son's blood samples he was able to see that it came up positive, which meant that his son was born a mortal.

Fredric sat back in his chair not knowing what to think, "Could this be Rolf's baby and not mine." Anger began to well up inside of him. For a split second he considered killing the baby but knew that would destroy Leona.

He went back upstairs to tell Leona of his findings. When he entered the bedroom, Leona was holding the crying baby. He sat along side of her and then she held the baby up and handed him to Fredric, "Here, hold your son he needs your strength." Fredric took the baby in his arms and all of a sudden the baby stopped crying. Fredric was delighted as he held him up high and walked around the room. He was truly captivated by this child.

"Did you find out, is he a mortal?" Leona asked. "Yes Leona, he is a mortal," Fredric replied. "What should we do?" she asked. "When he gets older I will give him a transfusion that will make him immortal like us, then I will teach him how to use his powers in a good way."

THE ATTACK ON COUNT GRUEL

The year was now 1810, nearly two years since Fredric and Leona had left London for Transylvania. Their son was now four months old.

Leona wanted to have their son baptized in a church, but Fredric said it would be impossible because he could not cross the threshold of a church without dire consequences. Leona was also determined to name the child Seth Elton, after her father. Fredric reluctantly agreed.

Fredric knew the day was coming closer to when he would attack Count Gruel's castle. He had decided on one more experiment. He would assemble several of the village men and offer them money to stay in his castle for several days.

When they arrived, he offered them his special wine and told them, "Eat and drink all you want, you are my guests."

After several days of waiting and watching, Fredric began to notice that their appetite for food was diminishing and they had difficulty seeing when a bright light would enter their eyes.

He decided to take one of the men outside into the sunlight. Within fifteen minutes his body turned an ash color. He began to scream for help as he burned and disintegrated. This proved that the villagers were turning into vampires.

Fredric made the remaining villagers cover their eyes with the special protective colored glass that he developed. He cut the special glass into strips and made two slits on each side of a towel. He cut out two circles in the towel, inserted the glass into the slits on either side of the circle, and then placed the glass over each villager's eyes. He then tied the towel tightly in the back..

Fredric sent the villagers into the garden and told them to walk around in the sunlight as he stayed in the castle and watched to see what would happen.

The experiment was going well until a towel slid off the face of one of the men and uncovered his eyes. He could not put it back over his eyes fast enough. In just a few seconds, his face turned an ash color and then his body burned and disintegrated, just like the other villager.

Fredric now knew that his experiment with the protective glass worked, but his design with the towel did not. He knew he had to have special eyeglass frames made with his protective glass inserted in them by an eyeglass maker, so Joseph went to the next village to have the local spectacle maker make a number of eyeglasses. Joseph brought along enough protective glass to make eyeglasses for everyone during the long journey they will soon be taking.

Fredric, not wanting the villagers to tell anyone what they had witnessed, decided to keep them at the castle until he, Leona and the baby were gone.

Fredric sent for Pulaski and told him to drive to the village and locate Captain Ulrich and bring him back to the castle.

Fredric was very excited as he ran up the stairs to where Leona was playing with young Seth. He picked the baby up, held him high in the air, and repeated, "Soon, soon." Then handed him back to his mother and said with a huge smile on his face, "We will be taking a very long voyage shortly and we will have to take all of our possessions so we can start our new life together in a new land."

Two days later Joseph heard knocking on the front door and opened it to see Captain Ulrich standing there. "Come in captain, you can wait in the study while I get Dr. Gruel."

A few minutes later Fredric entered the study with Leona by his side. The captain shook Fredric's hand as he said, "It has been a long time since we have seen each other, hasn't it?"

"Yes, too long, but I am glad to see you. I am sure you remember Leona."

"Yes," the captain replied as he kissed the back of Leona's hand, "how could I forget her?"

"Can I get you some food or wine?" Fredric asked of the captain. "Yes you can, some of your wine, you know the good one," he answered.

Fredric looked at Leona, puzzled as he called for Joseph to bring them his special wine and three glasses.

"Do you have anything new to tell me," asked the captain. "Yes I do, Leona and I have a son, he is four months old," Fredric proudly told him. "That's wonderful, said the captain, as he continued, "I assume you brought me all the way here because you need a ship?"

"That is right," Fredric answered. "I need a ship that can take me and my family across the Atlantic Ocean."

"There must be enough room for me to take many barrels of my wine, several of my grape plants and all our belongings."

"This sounds like a permanent move. Where across the Atlantic do you want to go?" the captain inquired. "I need a place that has similar soil as here, a place where I can grow my grapes. Do you know of such a place?"

"The only land like that would be in the Northeastern part of America. I do know that there is plenty of land to be had, but I also heard that there are plenty of hostile Indians. How would you protect your family?" Fredric said in a confident voice, "I am not worried, I can take care of the Indians myself."

"How long would it take to make such a crossing?" Fredric asked. "I have never made this trip, but I would think, if the weather holds up, we could do it in less than four weeks," the captain, repeating himself while scratching his chin, "only if the weather holds up."

"I would also need an extra room for my servant, and my coach driver, oh and also, I would like you to find the same crew, if possible, that brought us here from England. Do you think you can do that?"

"I will see what I can do," The captain said and then asked, "When are you looking to take this voyage?"

"I would hope within the next three weeks."

"Now, let me pour you some of your favorite wine and let us make a toast, "To life and to the beauty of life."

Fredric told the captain that it would be best if he slept in the castle that evening. He reminded him of what happened to the crew during the last voyage when they drank the wine and then went into sunlight. "I do not want a repeat of that, do you understand?"

"Yes I do," muttered the captain as he continued to drink the wine with a great deal of delight.

The next morning the captain awoke, dressed and walked around the castle after realizing that every one else was still asleep.

He ventured out into Joseph's vegetable garden without taking heed as to what Fredric warned him about the previous evening.

As he walked around he started to feel very weak and then he fell to the ground. His hands were turning an ash color and he was feeling pain throughout his body. Frightened, he began to scream for help.

When Fredric heard him screaming, he appeared in the garden holding the protective colored glass over his eyes. He put the glass over the captain's eyes then carried him down to the laboratory.

"You are too important a person for me to lose," Fredric told the captain as he prepared to give him a blood transfusion.

The captain just lay there not saying a word; he just followed Fredric with his eyes.

Fredric did not want to leave him alone for fear that he might pull out the tube that was pumping pure blood into his veins, so he sat by his side until he fell asleep.

The next evening Fredric saw that the captain was just lying there with his eyes wide open staring at the ceiling, "How are you feeling?" Fredric asked.

"Did I have too much to drink last night?"

"You had too much of my wine to drink last night and you will not be allowed to drink anymore of it until we reach the other side of the ocean. Is that understood?"

"Yes," said the captain as Fredric helped him off the bed.

"I had Joseph prepare something for you to eat. It will make you feel better," Fredric told him as they walked up the stairs to the kitchen.

He watched the captain gulp down his food and told him, "I want you to arrange for a ship that could take us across the ocean to the place you call America."

"Do you remember what we spoke about?"

"Yes I do," the captain said with certainty.

"Pulaski will drive you back to the village this evening so you can make all the arrangements. I will wait to hear from you. In the mean time we will prepare for the voyage."

Fredric walked the captain to the front door, "You and your crew will be well rewarded when we arrive in our new homeland," he promised.

THE FINAL PREPARATIONS

Fredric knew that without the help of his former friend, Rolf, he would have to undertake all the responsibilities and preparations for this final voyage by himself.

The most important preparation was the attack on Count Gruel's castle, which would involve detailed planning.

First, he had to get enough wine ready for the voyage. The grapes had gone through all the processes of fermentation and aging and was now wine. He utilized the townsmen that he had turned into vampires to make the wine barrels that would hold all this wine to be stored in the hull of the ship and had them bottle much of the wine so bottles could be stored in his cabin aboard the ship.

One week had past when there was a loud knock at the door. Joseph opened it to find Captain Ulrich standing there, "Is Dr. Gruel home?" he asked.

"Come in, I will get him for you," Joseph replied.

As the captain stood there, he could not take his eyes off all the armor and banners that were hanging in the hallway. Just then, Fredric walked in, "I hope you have good news for me captain."

"Yes I do," he replied. "But first, do you intend to take all these banners and armor that are on the wall?"

"Yes, captain, I intend to take the banners and armor and the chandeliers as well."

"When do we sail?"

"Three weeks from tomorrow evening."

"I will arrange to have all your belongings picked up and brought on board the afternoon before we set sail."

Fredric was elated to know when they would be leaving. He placed his arm around the captain's shoulders and asked, "Why don't you stay for some dinner and have some wine?"

"I will take you up on something to drink, but I must be getting back to the village."

Fredric then called out to Joseph, "Bring several bottles of our regular vintage wine for the captain."

"I hope this is not your special wine?" the captain asked when Joseph brought in the bottles.

"No, you have nothing to fear, this is not that wine, you will not taste my special wine again until we arrive in America."

Joseph put the bottles of wine in the back of the captain's wagon before he drove away shouting, "See you in three weeks."

Fredric ran up the stairs to tell Leona about his meeting with the captain.

"Leona, it is time for you to start packing and preparing for the voyage. It could take as long as four weeks and I want you and Seth to be as comfortable as possible."

"I intend to give Seth a transfusion, within the next few days, to make him like us."

Leona wished that Fredric would have a change of heart and reconsider doing this, but she knew that it was hopeless.

Fredric went down to the laboratory to complete his planning.

The first thing he had to do was make more of the protective glass to take with him to America. He was sure that the eyeglasses he had made in the village would not be enough for all the disciples he intended to recruit.

Fredric took blood from his arm, put it into a vile, and mixed it with his special wine grapes. He then placed this mixture over a flame until his blood and the grapes blended.

The next step was to spread the mixture over glass and bake it until it tinted to a dark burgundy color.

After packing all the furniture and important belongings that they would needed, Fredric decided it was time to give Seth his transfusion.

This was very difficult for Leona to accept. She knew from this day forward, Seth would be different from all other children.

Fredric prepared the laboratory for the last time and then went upstairs to get Seth.

Leona tried hard to hold onto Seth as Fredric took him from her arms.

Seth began to cry as Leona screamed at Fredric, "Seth is not your son, he is Rolf's son, and you cannot do this. Do you hear me? That is why he was born a mortal."

Fredric hesitated for a moment and said, "Why are you telling this to me now?"

He continued to carry Seth to the laboratory when Leona yelled out, "I don't love you, Fredric. Look at what you have done to me and I know that you murdered my father."

Fredric stopped at the bottom of the stairs and looked up at Leona, "Who told you that?" Leona answered sobbing, "You told me, you told me when I asked you to tell me again what happened to my father in the study. Did you forget that when you turned me into a vampire you also gave me telepathic powers? I am able to read into your mind just as you can read into mine."

Fredric just looked up at Leona trying hard to absorb what she had just said. He then retreated into his laboratory with Seth in his arms, closed, and locked the door behind him.

In Fredric's state of mind, it was very difficult to strap the young boy to the cot and give him the transfusion.

When it was all over, Fredric carried Seth back up stairs and handed him to Leona.

She took the child in her arms and then told Fredric, "We will never make love again. Do you hear me, never?"

Fredric looked at Leona with contempt and then left the room.

He went down to his study to complete the plans on how he would kill Count Gruel, but first, there was something he had to take care of.

Fredric summoned Joseph and Pulaski to the study and told them, "Both of you have been like family to me and I have arranged to have you come with Miss Leona and me on our voyage to a new land called America."

Very pleased to hear this, both men thanked Fredric and left him to plan his mission.

THE DAY OF THE ATTACK

Three weeks had gone by and Fredric's castle stood empty of its furnishings.

On the morning of the attack on Count Gruel's castle, Fredric called Joseph into his study.

"Joseph, Captain Ulrich will be here soon to take all our belongings and you, Miss Leona and Seth to the ship that is waiting in the harbor. Pulaski will take me to Walachia where I intend to engage Count Gruel for the last time. When my mission is done we will all go to America and start our new life. I am giving you a list of all the articles that captain Ulrich should be taking with him and I am counting on you to see that everything on this list is on board."

"Joseph," Fredric said in a somber voice, "Right now, you are the only one I can trust. I thank you for all your loyalty and the knowledge that you have passed on to me throughout the years."

Fredric gave Joseph a big hug and handshake and then bolted up the stairs and told Leona, "I will see you and Seth on the ship."

He gave Seth a kiss on his cheek and did not say anything more to Leona.

Fredric turned his attentions towards the dungeons underneath the castle where he went to inform the skeleton general of his plans.

It was very overcast on the morning of the attack. Fredric and Pulaski left the castle with both of them wearing their special glasses.

Pulaski was to drive Fredric to the town of Walachia where he would finally end the life of Count Gruel.

As he sat in the back of the coach, all Fredric could think about was Leona's scathing words and how his best friend had betrayed him, but he knew that his concentration must be on what lay ahead of him today if he was to complete his mission.

The coach continued down a winding road that appeared to be getting more hazardous. Trees were falling down on both sides of the road and a large number of black ravens were flying extremely low over Pulaski's head almost hitting him and another flew into the side of the coach almost hitting Fredric. These were all early signs that made Fredric aware of the fact that they were approaching Count Gruel's castle.

"Pulaski, pull off to the side of the road; I will go the rest of the way on foot."

Pulaski stopped the coach, jumped from his seat, and opened the door for Fredric, "Is there anything else I can do for you, master?"

"No thank you," Fredric answered with a slight quiver in his voice. I want you to wait here for me."

Fredric proceeded to walk into the forest. He soon realized that a storm was approaching. The sky darkened and the wind began to howl as it blew between the branches of the trees. A light rain started then became very heavy with deafening sounds of thunder and bolts of lightening striking all around Fredric as he continued to walk deeper into the forest.

Fredric then noticed a small clearing up ahead. He stopped for a moment then realized, "There it is."

Above the heavy mist and fog stood Count Gruel's castle on top of a rocky mountain surrounded by thousands of wooden stakes. These stakes appeared to be growing up from the ground with remnants of clothing and bones hanging from each one.

Fredric never anticipated seeing such a spectacle.

He walked along a narrow road, always keeping the castle in his sight, as heavy dark clouds formed over the castle and lightening strikes became more intense.

Every so often, a bolt of lightening would strike causing a tree to burst into flames.

Fredric was being extremely cautious as he continued to walk up the narrow road when hundreds of black ravens flew out from behind the castle and hovered above his head. He crouched behind one of the nearby stakes mistakenly thinking they would not notice him. Instead, they landed around him blocking his path to the castle.

Fredric now sensed that Count Gruel was aware that he was approaching and was trying to prevent him from entering.

Fredric stood up from the wet ground and noticed something strange taking place.

The stakes appeared to be shifting from side to side and the bones beneath the wooden stakes started to take on the form of human figures.

Fredric continued to walk up the path to get closer to the castle. He turned and saw the bones turn into full bodies and begin to walk up the path towards him at a very slow pace. They made strange sounds as hundreds of them began to follow him up the path.

Fredric, trying to destroy as many of these undead creatures as possible before they could reach him, shot bolts of fire from each of his eyes.

Just then, as these creatures were closing in around Fredric, thousands of skeletons led by Fredric's general came out from the forest and charged up the mountain ready for battle.

As the creatures turned to fight and protect the castle, the general and his army charged up the mountain chanting, "Kill the count, kill the count."

Both groups engaged in hand-to-hand combat cutting off each other's heads and limbs.

The skeleton army continued its charge up the side of the mountain giving Fredric time to find his way into the castle through a side door.

Once in side he came close to reaching the main hall when several of the count's vampire bodyguards jumped out and tried to attack him.

They took Fredric by surprise but he put his own telekinesis powers to use. He released wooden spears attached to each side of the wall and transported them in the direction of the oncoming vampires. Each spear struck its mark and pierced the heart of a vampire.

They began to fall to the floor with blood splattering from their mouths and ears.

As each vampire fell, the body disintegrated and their bloodstained clothing lay in a heap on the floor.

When Fredric reached the main hall, he stood against a wall that was directly under a balcony where he was able to see the signs of death and destruction caused by the hand of Count Gruel and his armies everywhere. Also hanging on the walls were hundreds of battle flags and captured armor pieces that the count had pillaged or murdered for over hundreds of years in Europe.

Then suddenly, Fredric heard a very deep piercing voice echo throughout the castle. "Why do you want to harm me Fredric, I am your father, you are my son. Why don't you step out into the open where we can see each other?"

Just then a bolt of fire came shooting from above and landed near Fredric's feet.

"If I wanted to kill you, I could have done that many years ago. Instead, I turned you into a vampire hoping you would follow in my foot steps."

Then it must be true, this evil creature is really my father, Fredric lamented.

Fredric stayed under the balcony trying to think of a way to get within reach of the count.

Then the count spoke again, "Fredric you have a beautiful wife and son. Why don't you just leave here and go to them?"

Fredric wondered how the count attained all this information.

Knowing that he would have to make the next move, Fredric stepped out from under the balcony just as a spear was thrust at him. Acting fast and using his powers, he was able to turn the spear around and send it crashing into a stone wall.

The count stepped out from the balcony wearing his old tuxedo and ruffled shirt, "I think there are other people here who do not care for you Fredric."

Just then Rolf stepped out from the shadows and stood next to Count Gruel. He said, sarcastically, "You are a very lucky man Fredric; you have everything a man could want. You have Leona and you have my son. What more could you ask for?"

Fredric could not speak. Rage welled up inside of him as he turned away.

"Look at me Fredric," Rolf yelled, "I have always looked up to you my entire life and then I drank your wine. That was when I knew what real power felt like. I want to have that power and immortality. Now I stand here along side of your archenemy, your father, wanting to see you dead. Leona and I love each other; we want to be together with our son for eternity," Rolf continued.

Rolf then pulled a wooden spear from the wall and threw it, aiming at Fredric's heart.

Fredric reacted fast and redirected the spear.

Just then, Count Gruel pulled a sword off the wall and thrust it through Rolf's heart. "I gave Fredric life and I will be the one to take it," the count said as Rolf's dead body fell over the balcony.

The count shot a number of laser beams from his eyes but Fredric was able to deflect the beams using his own powers.

The count then ranted as he jumped from the balcony to the main floor where Fredric was standing, "My blood is the life line to all that is evil, but I will give you one last chance to go back to your family."

"I have no family, father. I have no home," Fredric shouted as he unleashed a group of spears towards the count. The count just stood there as the spears flew by narrowly missing him.

"Fredric," the count shouted back, "end this foolishness now or I will have to kill you." Fredric laughed at him, "You killed me when you turned me into a vampire."

Just as the battle outside the castle raged on, the front doors of the castle burst open and Fredric's general and his skeleton army entered.

Count Gruel, for the first time ever, was feeling a sense of failure and defeat. He leaped onto one of the balconies trying to flee, sensing that his end was near.

He unleashed all his telekinesis powers towards Fredric and the skeleton soldiers.

First, he sent an intense barrage of spears from the wall flying through the air hitting many of the general's soldiers breaking their bones and cutting off their heads. Then he unleashed large projectiles of fire that flew out from the torches hanging along the castle walls.

In his final attempt, the count shot laser beams from his eyes which caused massive destruction to the castle.

As the fight went on, more of the general's soldiers entered the castle screaming at the count, "You murdered our children and our wives and you will die."

As the soldier's came closer to reaching the count, he jumped back onto the balcony, dislodged a large wooden beam from the ceiling and hurled it in Fredric's direction, in one final effort to destroy him. Fredric then sent the beam crashing through several of the side windows allowing daylight to enter. The castle was then bathed in sunlight trapping the count on his balcony.

Fredric covered his eyes with his protective glasses and stayed only to watch as his evil father, Count Vladimir Gruel screamed in agony as he burned and his remains disintegrated.

Relieved, Fredric told the general, "You and your men fought well. Now you can all rest in peace."

Fredric, wearing his protective glasses, walked out of the castle into the sunlight.

All of his soldiers stood at attention and bowed their heads as Fredric passed by and walked down the mountain.

Fredric, triumphant, walked back to where Pulaski was waiting with his coach.

He took one last look towards the battlefield and noticed that all the skeleton soldiers had disappeared and the sun was now shining brightly.

Fredric climbed into the rear of the coach telling Pulaski, "Take me to the harbor; we can now go to our new home."

As they drove off, Fredric could see smoke rising from the top of the mountain as the castle burned to the ground.

THEIR NEW LIFE BEGINS

By the time Fredric and Pulaski reached the pier the sun had set.

Captain Ulrich, Joseph and Leona with Seth in her arms, were standing on the upper deck patiently waiting for them.

As Fredric walked up the ship's plank, he noticed the full moon glowing as if it was just hanging there above the three tall masts waiting for him. Then Fredric turned to take one final look at his homeland. "I will never return," he thought, as he boarded the ship.

The day that started out overcast with lots of wind, rain and turbulence, had turned into a beautiful evening.

Captain Ulrich urged the passengers to follow him to the cabins they will be living in for the next few weeks.

Leona carrying Seth, followed the captain as Joseph, Pulaski and Fredric walked closely behind. They went down to the hull of the ship where the captain stopped at the first door, "Joseph, Pulaski, this is the room you will be sharing." The two men hesitated before entering. The room was dreadful, but they had no choice.

Leading Fredric and Leona to the rear of the ship, the Captain opened a door at the end of the corridor, "This will be for the young family."

The room was quite large with a medium size bed alongside the rear wall. A night table was located on one side of the bed with a burning lantern on top. There was also a single bed that was large enough to fit Fredric, if need be. A large table stood in the center of the cabin with another lantern hanging from a cross beam above it. Along the far wall were some closets where Leona could hang her dresses and one window which the captain had boarded up so as not to allow any light to filter in.

Leona, who was sticking to her promise of not talking or making love to Fredric, just stood there looking around the room while holding Seth.

"You must stop this foolishness," We are going to be living in this room together for the next few weeks. Why don't you try to make the situation bearable and as pleasant as possible?" Fredric pleaded.

Leona, holding Seth, walked over to the large bed and lay down with Seth next to her. She just looked up at the ceiling saying nothing.

Fredric decided to go back on deck to gaze at the moon once more, but before leaving the cabin, he said, "I hope you have a change of heart before we get to America." He then left not noticing the tears that began to run down Leona's face.

Fredric walked onto the deck and saw Captain Ulrich standing by the steering wheel calling out orders to his first mate, Carl Rummel, "Man the mast, have the men set the sails, release all lines and pull the anchor."

The first mate called out to the crew repeating the Captain's orders.

Fredric watched all the activity that was going on and decided to stand on the side of the deck, out of the way, bowing his head towards the full moon.

As the ship began to move away from the pier, Fredric approached the captain, "I see you are a very busy man."

"Yes I am," the captain replied as he held on to the wheel carefully directing the ship out of the harbor. "How many crewmen do you have?" Fredric asked. "Twenty-three," the captain replied.

"Did you have much trouble bringing all my goods on board?"

"No not at all," the captain answered with a slight smirk on his face, "All your barrels of wine have been stowed away in a very safe place in the lower hull, only I and my first mate have access to it."

Fredric, a little bit embarrassed, began walking to his cabin when he past the first mate who stopped to introduce himself, "Dr. Gruel, I am Carl Rummel, the first mate."

Fredric stared at the young man who was wearing a navy knit cap that hung over one side of his face and practically covered his right eye, a heavy knit sweater and a pair of striped pants that came down to his ankles. He seemed pleasant enough as he continued to speak in his thick Eastern European accent, "If there is anything me or my crew could do to make you and your family more comfortable, please ask."

Fredric thanked him and started to walk away when the first mate called out to him, "By the way Doctor, all those barrels of wine we carried down to the hull, I hope you intend to share some of it with the crew." Fredric thought for a moment and then said, "Why don't you wait until we get into open waters, then we will see what can be done for you and the crew. I must return to my family now. I am sure they miss me," Fredric said. He then started to go below stopping only for a moment to take one last look at the full moon.

When Fredric entered the cabin Leona was still lying on the bed holding on to Seth with her eyes closed as the ship rocked from side to side.

Before doing anything else, he opened one of his suitcases and took out the burgundy and gold box that contained Transylvanian earth that Joseph had given him long ago. He then walked over to Leona and stared at her until she opened her eyes and looked up at him. "We must talk now," he told her. Leona, without saying a word, got up from the bed, walked over to the table, and sat down.

Fredric took two bottles of wine and two glasses from the closet and poured the wine. "Leona, you must keep drinking the wine in order to keep up your strength." Leona looked at him with contempt.

He then told her, "Rolf is dead and Count Gruel will never walk this earth again. Do you understand what I just said?" Leona, looking straight ahead, began to drink the wine then answered, "Yes master, what ever you want from me I will give you master. If you want to make love, I will, but I will never forgive you for what you have done to my father, Seth and me. Do you understand?"

Fredric, without defending himself, replied, "Yes I do."

Fredric finished his wine and went to lie down on the single bed as Leona continued to drink her wine.

Two weeks went by and the voyage was going well.

Every evening Leona would take Seth up on deck to see the stars. Occasionally a shooting star would fly by and Leona would say, "That's your grandfather looking down at you making sure you are safe."

She would go back to the cabin and Fredric would then take his strange eyeglasses and go on deck so he could watch the sunrise.

Late one morning while Fredric and the captain were on deck, they heard one of the crew call out from the crow's nest, "French war ship approaching off the starboard side." The crewman yelled again, "French war ship approaching on the starboard side closing in fast."

The captain looked through his telescope while Fredric and the first mate ran to the bow of the ship to see just how far away the French ship was.

The first mate exclaimed, "Captain, we have no cannons to protect ourselves, what should we do?" The captain replied in a stern voice, "Let's see if we can out run her," and began giving orders to Carl Rummel, "Keep the ship with the wind to our backs and make sure all sails are up. I'll take over the wheel."

The first mate followed the captain's orders immediately as the crew scrambled around the ship finding something to do.

Fredric called out to the captain, "The ship is gaining on us what should we do?" The captain yelled out to the first mate, "Hoist our flags. Maybe they will see that we are neutral and leave us alone."

Fredric called out again, "They are still gaining on us."

Just then, a loud noise came from the French ship, followed by a large puff of smoke and a crash a few seconds later hitting the center mast of the ship. The first mate called out to the captain, "What should we do now, we can't defend ourselves?"

Then another cannon shot was fired hitting another mast.

Fredric was still standing on the bow of the ship facing towards the French ship. He held up both of his hands in the direction of the sky and suddenly the sky turned very dark and the wind began to howl. Thick black clouds moved in over the two ships and from beneath the clouds heavy rains began to pound the sea. Then lightening struck the French war vessel. The winds blew in the direction of the French ship causing it to turn and lose control. Then, from behind Captain Ulrich's ship, a large sixty-foot wave rose up and lifted it above the wave. The ship miraculously rode the wave and then it came down to rest on the water as the wave came crashing down on top of the French ship breaking it in half, causing it to sink.

As the rough weather settled, the triumphant crew gathered on deck to watch the French war ship sink into the dark sea. Afterwards, the crew began to repair the damages created by the French ship.

The next morning, the first mate approached Fredric, "Dr. Gruel, how has this voyage been so far for you and your family?"

"Much more exciting than I expected," he replied.

"What ever happened to that wine you were going to share with the crew?" the first mate asked. "Why don't you go down to the hull after the sun sets and bring up a barrel for you and the crew to share?"

"Why after sunset?" he asked.

"It will taste better," Fredric answered.

That evening Leona was on deck with Seth when she saw some of the crew go below and bring up a barrel of Fredric's wine. One of them took an ax and smashed open the top of the barrel and they all began to drink the sweet tasting wine. They did not know what it was made of or what it would ultimately do to them.

The level of wine in the barrel became lower and lower and many of the crew started to sing and dance around the barrel while Leona, holding on to Seth, just stood on the side watching with a smile on her face.

Two of the intoxicated men noticed Leona and walked over to her, "You're such a pretty lady. Why don't you come and dance with us?" they asked. She told them, "Perhaps some other time, I have my son with me now."

As Leona began to walk away, one of them grabbed her by the arm and tried to pull Seth away from her. Leona was starting to panic as she pulled back from him. Then she remembered the powers she was given when she was turned into a vampire. She had never used them to hurt anyone, but she must use them now to protect herself and Seth. She threw the two men back. They looked at each other for a moment and decided to rush her. Again, Leona, using her powers, released a gaffing hook that was leaning against the railing towards one of the men striking him on the leg then released an ax at the other, hitting him in the arm.

When the other crewmen heard the screams, they stopped dancing and went to see what was happening. Noticing their injured fellow crewmen on the ground, they surrounded Leona and taunted her.

Then from behind, all sorts of objects were being hurled in their direction. They turned around to see Fredric standing there.

The men motioned to each other to rush Fredric.

Being as powerful as he was, Fredric picked up two of the men, held one in each hand, and tossed them overboard. They screamed as they plunged into the rough sea with the other crewmen looking on in disbelief.

Fredric started to walk towards the other men when one of them picked up an ax and hurled it in Fredric's direction.

Using his powers, Fredric stopped the ax in mid air and threw it back piercing the stomach of the crewman who threw it, causing his death.

Fredric, showing off more of his powers, stared at a wooden water barrel and using laser beams shooting from his eyes, caused the barrel to burst open.

He then said in a loud voice, "Did you see enough, or shall we continue this?" The men backing away from Fredric were told, "Why don't you finish the wine and I will have another barrel brought up for you tomorrow evening."

The crewmen looked bewildered at what they had just witnessed. After a few moments, they all walked back to the wine barrel and drink again as if nothing had happened.

Leona was leaning against the railing of the ship holding onto Seth as she watched all that had transpired. She began to think that Fredric only acted out when he was provoked. She was sure that he was not evil like his father or brother, *He was always kind and loving and he even said that he would teach Seth to use his powers for good, not evil, she reflected. I am being too hard on him.*

She then ran over to Fredric and hugged him as she whispered in his ear, "Forgive me, Fredric. Please forgive me. I am sorry for not believing in you, but I do now."

Fredric took Seth from Leona's arms and held him as the three of them went to their cabin.

The next morning, wearing his protective glasses, Fredric went on deck to speak to the captain.

It was very bright and sunny but Fredric did not fear being outside.

When the captain saw Fredric he was incensed; "I see you did it again and this time you killed three of my men."

"I had little choice; they tried to attack Leona and Seth while they were on deck alone last evening. That must not happen again or there will be more deaths, I promise you," Fredric shot back.

"I will make sure that it does not happen again," the captain reassured him and then asked, "What do I tell the men who drank your wine last night?"

"Tell them the truth; otherwise they will die if they go into direct sunlight.

You can give them a choice, they can be like me, a vampire and be immortal or I can give them a transfusion that will turn them back to being a mortal."

"Speak to your men this evening and if you can stay away from my wine until we make land, I can also make you immortal and you can become one of my lieutenants. I will buy this ship and keep it for my business. What do you think?"

The captain thought for a moment then replied, "Let me think about this. I will give you my decision before we speak to the crew."

The captain, who had no family of his own, pondered living forever and it baffled him. He was still confused when he met with Fredric again later that afternoon.

"Fredric," the captain asked, "I would like to talk with you in my cabin, if it's okay with you?"

"Let's talk now," Fredric answered and the two men walked below to the captain's cabin.

As Fredric entered the cabin he looked around, "I see you keep everything in an orderly manner, captain. That is very important and would be commendable if you were to work for me."

There was a narrow bed along the far wall with a small hot stove next to it so the captain could cook for himself and keep the cabin warm as well. In the center of the room sat a table with four chairs and a burning lantern in the middle.

Across the room, under a small porthole, was a desk with another lantern on it with maps and a variety of charts that the captain used to navigate across the ocean.

"Why don't you sit down and let me pour you some of my wine, if that's okay with you?" the captain asked. Fredric smiled and said, "Pour away."

"I am sure what I told you this afternoon stirred some interest in you."

"Yes, yes it did," replied the captain. Please tell me more before I say yes to this crazy scheme of yours."

Leaning over the table and looking directly at the captain, Fredric told him, "What I can do for you is not crazy. It is very simple, captain, I am indestructible and you can be too. You will have unbelievable strength and powers and you will live forever."

"What guarantees do you give me if I should decide to go along with this?" he asked of Fredric.

"As long as you continue to drink my special wine you can live forever," he answered. There are only three things that can kill you," First, direct sunlight, but I have developed a protective glass that covers the eyes and would prevent any sunlight from entering your eyes. Second, a wooden stake or any pure wooden object that pierces your heart, and three, holy water from the church thrown upon you. Any one of these could cause instant death. Otherwise, you can remain immortal for hundreds of years to come.

The captain looked straight into Fredric's eyes and asked, "How soon can we start this process?"

"As soon as we set foot on dry land, I will make you my first Lieutenant." Pleased, the captain said, "You now have a first lieutenant officer for your army or navy or whichever and we will both talk to the crew later."

"Good," Fredric said, "but I must talk to Miss Leona now, I will meet you on deck later."

When Fredric walked into his cabin, Leona was sitting on top of the bed playing with Seth. He just stood there watching them.

This was the first time in several weeks that he saw Leona laugh.

"Why don't you join us Fredric, Seth is so much fun," Leona said when she noticed him watching them.

Fredric walked over to the bed, sat down next to Leona, and gave her a kiss.

Leona appeared to be very responsive as she pulled Fredric closer and gave him a kiss on the lips. "Please forgive me for my childish behavior, we are going to a new land and we will start all over again."

Fredric felt a happiness that he had not felt for a very long time.

Later that evening Fredric met with Captain Ulrich on the ship's deck and called the crew together.

It was a clear evening with a multitude of stars brightening the sky. The captain stood on a water barrel by the mast and began to speak.

"I brought you all together for a very important reason that could change the lives and future of everyone on this ship. As you are all aware of by now, we are taking several passengers across the ocean to America. Standing besides me is Dr. Fredric Gruel. Those of you who were on deck last evening and those of you who were able to witness the sinking of the French war ship earlier, know first hand what powers Dr. Gruel and his wife posses. I would like the doctor to explain these powers to you and what they can do for you."

The captain stepped off the barrel allowing Fredric to get on to further address the crewmen.

"All of you know me as Dr. Gruel, but what you do not know is that I am the son of Count Vladimir Gruel, the vampire who died in a fire three and a half weeks ago. My wife, my son and I are also vampires, but we are not vampires like my father. We do not have to bite you on the neck and drink your blood. I have developed a wine that sustains us and we do not crave blood. This wine also has another purpose. If a mortal drinks an excessive amount of my wine, it will circulate through his veins and slowly turn him into a vampire. Within a few days he will lose the desire for food then he will find that he cannot stay in the sun without wearing my special eyeglasses. He will sleep during the day and arise as the sun sets. He will become immortal and live for hundreds of years as one of my disciples without contracting any diseases. He will have special powers like I have; strength like you could never imagine and telekinetic powers that will allow him to read into anyone's mind.

If you decide to join us, tell Captain Ulrich. I will take care of the rest. For those of you who do not want eternal life, you will get a return trip to Europe.

Do you have any questions?"

One crewman stepped forward asking, "How are we going to survive?"

"I will take care of you; I will make sure that you have plenty of my wine to drink," Fredric answered.

Another crewman asked, "What are you expecting of us in return?"

"Loyalty is what I expect."

"Are we expected to work or just hang around and drink wine?"

Fredric explained, "You will work. You will work hard. I will teach you how to plant and cultivate grapes and you will learn how to make wine in the winery that you will build. We will then be able to sell this wine throughout the world. My intentions are for us to be the start of a new race of people. You will be known as my disciples. Does that answer your questions?"

Fredric spoke with a great deal of conviction and hoped that he would be successful in recruiting these men. He watched as they gathered to contemplate their future.

Captain Ulrich stood up on the barrel again and told the men, "I intend to become a disciple of Dr. Gruel. I do not wish to go back to the life I had. If I could live without disease or growing old or being concerned with dying, why should I not do this? All I have is a ship and no more."

The crew began talking amongst themselves when the first mate stepped forward and spoke, "What about god? Who do I pray to or will there be no god?"

The captain looked at Fredric for the answer. "I will be your god; I will give you sustenance, I will become your leader. Now go back and talk this out among yourselves then let us know what your decision is."

Two more days passed when one of the crew yelled out, "Land, I see land." The first mate then gave the wheel to one of his men, ran down to the captain's quarters, and began knocking on his door. The captain called out, "What is it, come in?"

The captain and Fredric were sitting at the table drinking wine together when the first mate exclaimed, "Land sir, we spotted land off the starboard bow."

Both the captain and Fredric stood up at the same time and rushed out of the cabin to see for themselves.

Fredric, after acknowledging the sighting, went down to his cabin to tell Leona. She was sitting on the bed with Seth and stood up as soon as she saw the expression on Fredric's face, "What happened?" she asked. Fredric picked her up and began to swing her around, "We made it, put the protective glasses on both of you and come on deck. We found land, see for yourself." He then went to tell Joseph and Pulaski the good news.

Everyone went on deck and watched from the bow of the ship as it approached this land called America.

As the captain took over the wheel, Fredric stood next to him and called out to the crew, "Tonight we will all celebrate. For those of you, who wish to join me and the Captain, we will open my special wine and we will drink together."

THE NEW LAND

Fredric and the captain were extremely excited about the land sighting but the captain was not sure exactly where they were in relation to the map. Both men took the charts and maps off the captain's wall and spread them out over the table.

The captain pointed to an area on the map, "If my charts are correct this is where we should be, not to far from a river called the Hudson which is an inlet to an area that should be good for settling. I was told that this land should be fertile for your grapes and we would not be far from the ocean."

"We must find out if this land is for sale so we can establish a new homeland," Fredric said.

"I think it would be best if we lowered our sails and dropped anchor here and stayed on the ship for the night. We can get an early start in the morning," advised the captain.

Fredric and the captain went back on deck to get ready to celebrate.

As the sun was setting in the west, a full moon was rising in the east. The winds were still and the sky was full of stars.

Fredric called out to the first mate, "Go down to the hull and bring up a barrel of my wine."

Now each of the crew was standing on deck holding his metal cup and patiently waiting for the wine.

When the keg arrived, Fredric opened it. He filled his cup, held it up high and made a toast, "To life and to the beauty and future of life. Everybody drink up and enjoy."

The men surrounded the barrel, dunked their cups in and began to drink.

One of the men played a concertina and they started to sing and dance as they began to feel the effects of the wine.

Fredric was bowing his head to the moon when Leona came on deck. She wanted to surprise him so she had Joseph and Pulaski watch Seth.

All of a sudden, the music stopped and everyone turned his head to look at Leona. She was wearing a very low cut dark green dress, which was quite revealing.

As she walked towards Fredric he turned around and was surprised to see her without Seth and looking so radiant.

The crew, who had not seen Leona for a few days, stopped and stared at her. The first mate walked up to her and said, "You look very pretty tonight Miss Leona. May I have this dance?" Leona looked in Fredric's direction to see if he was watching. Fredric decided it would be best for everyone if Leona danced with the first mate so he nodded his head in approval.

The music began to play and Leona and the first mate began to dance. They twirled around the deck until another of the crew decided to cut in and tapped the first mate on his shoulder. He stopped dancing and turned to the crewman and said, "Can't you see that I am dancing with the lady?" This crewman, who obviously had too much to drink, took hold of the first mate and punched him on the chin as the other men gathered around.

The first mate and the crewman continued to fight as the other men called out to Leona, "Aren't we good enough for you?"

Fredric watched until some of the men began to pull at Leona's dress causing it to tear.

As the fight became more intense, Fredric pulled Leona away and told her to go below to their cabin.

The captain then stood up on top of a barrel and began to shout, "Stop this fighting, you idiots, stop at once."

The crewmen were becoming very loud and drunk and refused to stop fighting until Fredric used his powers and flung two water barrels in their direction causing the barrels to break and splash over them.

He then picked up one of the crewmen and threw him against the mast knocking him out.

When the rest of the crew realized what was happening they stopped fighting.

"I think you all had enough to drink tonight. Get some rest because we have a long day ahead of us tomorrow," Fredric advised.

The crew then disbursed and Fredric told the captain that he was going to his cabin and he would see him in the morning.

When Fredric entered his cabin, Leona was sitting next to the table wearing a sheer negligee while Seth slept in the small bed.

She looked up at him, "I thought I was doing the right thing by wearing that dress and dancing with the crew, I guess I was wrong."

Fredric told her not to worry about what happened as he walked over to her. "We have not made love in a very long time Fredric, and I have been waiting for you.

Leona stood up and Fredric put his arms around her with a feeling of immense excitement. Then, stepping back, he looked at the silhouette of her young body as it showed through her negligee causing him to want her even more.

Leona seemed to have a magical glow about her that made her even more beautiful.

Falling on top of the bed, they made passionate love until they fell asleep in each other's arms.

Seth woke up the next morning hungry for his mother's milk.

As Leona drank the wine, it mixed with her breast milk, giving Seth the needed sustenance to help him grow as well as allowing him to remain a vampire.

After sharing several glasses of wine with Leona, Fredric put on his special glasses and went on deck to meet with the captain and his first mate.

"Good morning," said the captain. "It looks like we have ourselves a very nice day."

"Yes we do and have you been able to find us an inlet that we can sail into?"

"Yes," The captain replied, "it's called the Hudson and it runs all the way north."

"How difficult is it to find?" inquired Fredric.

"According to this map, we should be here," the captain said, pointing to a spot on the map, "about fifteen miles south. If we follow the coastline north we should be able to come right into the mouth of the river, if we are lucky."

"Have you spoken to the men about our plans?"

"Yes," the captain replied, "I had a meeting with them this morning and they are all willing to join us as long as you are willing to continue sharing the wine with them."

"Then I suggest that you give each one of them a pair of my protective glasses and explain that they must wear them at all times during the sunlight hours," Fredric said.

Then the captain added, "They also want you to promise that they can remain immortal plus they want you to allow them certain freedoms."

Fredric, looking the captain straight in the eye, told him, "This is what I will promise, no more. Once our first planting of grapes begin to ferment and the wine is complete, I will make them immortal, not before. For now, I will give them food and a small amount of wine, but not enough to turn them into full disciples. Right now there is only enough wine left for my family, Joseph, Pulaski and you, if you want to join us now. Once I turn the crew into immortals, they must follow my commands or I will have them killed. Is that understood?"

"Yes, I understand perfectly," answered the captain.

The captain yelled to the first mate, "Strike the sails, starboard we go. Don't get too close to the shore until we find the inlet."

"Aye, Aye, captain," he answered as the sails went up and the ship began to move swiftly through the water.

It was a beautiful clear day with only a few clouds in the sky. A mild wind pushed the ship north as the sails arched and took flight.

The crew was wearing their protective glasses and they acted as one when the first mate called out his commands. They were ready to follow his orders.

Leona and Seth came on deck wearing their special glasses. Fredric called out to Leona, "Be careful, watch your step." Just then Leona tripped over a heavy rope causing her to lose her balance and drop Seth overboard into the choppy waters. Leona, frantic, called out for help as Seth began to slip under the water.

Fredric leaped from the bow of the ship and by using his power of thought transference, stared into the choppy water where Seth had fallen.

Suddenly a large Dolphin appeared from under the sea holding Seth in his mouth and leaped out of the water along side of the ship allowing Fredric to grab hold of the crying baby.

The Dolphin then dove back into the water and disappeared.

As the captain and the rest of the crew looked on in disbelief, Fredric handed Seth back to Leona telling her, "You must watch where you walking, Leona. You were very lucky this time."

Now fearful, Leona held on to Seth very tightly and just sat on a barrel while the crew went about their business.

The first mate steered the ship up the coast going north while Fredric and the captain reviewed their charts, double-checking for the Hudson River inlet passage, when suddenly they heard a loud scream from the crewman in the crow's nest, "I see the inlet, I see the inlet. It's straight ahead."

Captain Ulrich took out his telescope to see for himself.

The inlet that they were all waiting to find was clearly in sight.

Fredric called out to Leona, "Join me on the bow of the ship; we are almost at the Hudson inlet."

It was already midday when they approached the mouth of the river. The captain told Fredric that he had never seen an inlet like this. Then the first mate called out, "Captain, I think you should take charge of the wheel."

The captain walked hastily to the stern of the ship as Fredric and Leona, holding Seth with both arms, watched from the bow as the ship turned into the choppy waters of the Hudson.

The captain told Fredric that he had never seen currents like this. The ship kept turning from side to side as they moved further north.

Captain Ulrich, who was now steering, tried to keep the ship steady with some difficulty.

As the swirling currents began to take hold of the ship, the captain called out to the first mate, "Cut back on the sails. I'm having trouble holding the ship."

Meanwhile, Fredric and Leona were still on the bow of the ship as the winds picked up spraying water from the Hudson on them.

Leona called out, "Look there Fredric, I can see houses on the tip of that land. Where are we?"

"I don't know," Fredric answered, "There are some houses scattered along the other side also."

It was late afternoon as the ship continued cautiously on a northern course. The further north they traveled, the fewer homes they would see.

The captain called out to Fredric, "I think we should drop anchor here. It will be getting dark soon and I'm not familiar with these waters."

Fredric agreed as the captain called out to the first mate to prepare to drop the anchor and lower the sails.

The crew knew exactly what to do as they climbed the rope ladders to pull in and tie down the sails. They dropped anchor as the strong currents began to turn the ship around. That's when Captain Ulrich called out to Fredric, "While there is still some light, if you would like, we can take a row boat with some of the men to that land butting out on the west bank."

"Let's leave at once," Fredric anxiously shouted to the captain.

The captain called to the crew to get a boat ready to go ashore. Several minutes later the first mate called out, "The boat is ready."

The captain, Fredric and a few of the crew climbed into the boat and began rowing towards the land.

The currents were making it difficult to row causing the boat to drift south. Just as they were about to dock, one of the crewmen yelled out, "I've been hit."

Then moments later, another of the crew screamed as he stood up and fell into the water with an arrow sticking out of his chest.

The captain called out for everyone to get down.

The boat continued to drift down the river by itself until it hit some logs. They were all huddled together in the boat when Fredric heard ruffling sounds coming from the nearby trees. He picked his head up fast and spotted some Indians.

He shot infrared laser beams from his eyes, killing two of them instantly.

Fredric decided to climb over the side of the boat and told everyone to keep their heads down. "I'll be back in a little while," he told them as he jumped over the side into the water, which he soon realized came up to his waist. He was wearing his black velvet jacket, which made it difficult to wade through the water.

Fredric was trying to track the sounds that were coming from behind the trees.

When he came on shore, three more Indians came running at him with spears and knives. As they threw their weapons, Fredric redirected them and then attacked the Indians. He twisted the head off of one then took the other two warriors and threw them high into the trees.

Fredric stood still, listening for other sounds, but he did not hear any.

He walked back to the waters edge watching as the small rowboat was drifting by itself towards the middle of the river.

Fredric then concentrated on the boat and used his powers; he was able to draw it back to the rivers edge to where he was standing.

Wading into the water, Fredric was able to help the other crewmen and the captain get out of the boat.

As the sun began to set, Fredric had to make a decision as to whether or not to remain on shore for the night or row back to the ship in the dark. That's when the captain said, "It would be in our best interest to stay on shore tonight. The currents are too strong and I don't want us to be taken down river."

Fredric agreed and told the men to make a small fire alerting the crew on the ship of their location and that they are safe. He also sent a message to Leona by way of thought transference telling her what was happening.

Fredric took the night watch so the men could get some rest. He then told the men, "In the morning we will all go inland."

The men lay down near the fire and Fredric sat leaning against a tree paying attention to the strange sounds that were coming from the woods.

Early the next morning, when the men awoke, they noticed that Fredric had kept the fire burning all night. He wanted those aboard the ship to know they were still safe. He also sent another message to Leona.

"What should we do for food?" the hungry crew asked Fredric.

"I will go into the woods and see what I can find," Fredric answered as he left the campsite.

By using his powers, he killed a rabbit as it ran out from behind a tree and then a few minutes later, a wild boar came out from behind some bushes charging Fredric at full speed. Fredric quickly fired two laser beams, killing the boar instantly.

Fredric then slung the boar over his shoulder, picked up the rabbit and walked back to the crew. When they saw Fredric approaching with his catch, they were very relieved.

The captain rushed over, took the animals, prepared them, and put them on the fire.

They all had a hearty breakfast except, of course, for Fredric.

While the men were eating, Fredric walked into the woods, took out a flask from his jacket, and began to drink his wine. This would replenish his strength before he decided on his next move.

Fredric strolled around the area picking up earth to see if it would be compatible to the land in Transylvania and enable him to start planting his grape vines. As he studied the earth, he was very disappointed. The ground was too sandy for his special grapes that needed a variety of minerals in order to grow.

Fredric walked back to the camp while the crew was finishing their breakfast. He suggested that it would be best for all if they went back to the ship and not go farther north up the river. The captain asked, "Why?"

"I would like to establish a base camp. Since we are near the river we would be able to ship our wine up and down the coast, and I can travel further west to try and find suitable land where I can grow my grapes," Fredric explained.

Fredric, looking across the water, could see Leona and the first mate standing on the bow of the ship.

Suddenly Leona let out a loud scream. The first mate asked, "What's wrong?" Leona pointing towards the water said, "There is a dead man's body floating in the water below the bow with an arrow sticking out of his chest."

In the mean time the captain told Fredric, "It sounds like we should get back to the ship right away."

Just as the captain and the three remaining crewmen were climbing into the rowboat, an arrow shot across the boat, narrowly missing Fredric. Rather than look for the Indian who shot the arrow, Fredric transformed himself into a raven, flew to the ship and landed on the deck, while the rest of the crew rapidly rowed back to the ship.

Once aboard the ship Leona ran to Fredric, "I was so worried about you when you did not come back to the ship last night. I received your message and we saw your fire," she said, "but I was still worried and today I stood on the deck with the first mate when the body of a crewman floated past with an arrow through his heart. I was so scared."

"There is nothing to be scared of; I will keep you safe," Fredric promised, "We are here for good. This land will be our home and this is where we will make our future."

Leona gave Fredric a reassuring look and took him by the hand. They retreated to their cabin so Fredric could have some wine and some needed rest.

DEVELOPING THE NEW LAND

Several hours later, Fredric woke up and telepathically called his servant Joseph who was in the cabin he shared with Pulaski.

Joseph and Pulaski had managed to keep out of everyone's way during the voyage, but now Fredric needed to speak to Joseph.

When Joseph entered the cabin, Fredric offered him a glass of wine then explained, "I will be leaving tomorrow to look for suitable land so we can start planting our grape vines. Joseph, it will be extremely important for you to look after Seth and Leona while I am gone and the only way you can reach me is by using your mind. Promise me you will contact me and let me know how they are doing."

"I promise, master," Joseph answered.

Fredric left the cabin leaving Leona and Seth with Joseph.

The next day Fredric met with the captain and the crew that would accompany them. The captain advised Fredric, "My intentions are to take three row boats and a crew of twelve men and enough rations for two weeks. I have also prepared to take tools and as you requested two barrels of wine, one with your special wine and the other with regular wine. I have also packed guns, just in case we have to fight some Indians."

"That's a good idea but my intentions are to find the Indian village and see if I can make peace with them."

"We can't afford to lose you," the captain advised.

Fredric replied in a very positive way, "You will not lose me; you can be assured of that."

Fredric stood on the deck with Leona and Seth watching as the crew loaded the rowboats with supplies.

"Good bye my love, I will see you in two weeks," Fredric told Leona as he kissed her and Seth good-bye.

Captain Ulrich gave the first mate some last minute orders and both men climbed into one of the boats with four crewmen. The remaining crew climbed into the other two boats.

As they rowed closer to shore, Fredric made sure that his boat stayed in the lead so he could watch for hostile Indians.

When they reached the shore, he told the captain to stay with the boats while he went on land to see if it was safe.

As soon as Fredric walked towards the woods, two Indians came out from behind the trees with their knives out.

Fredric was able to sidestep them. Then both Indians holding up their knives, tried to jump him, but Fredric was able to grab both of them by their necks and hold them up until they were unconscious.

He carried them back to the boats where the crew tied them up.

When the Indians opened their eyes Fredric was standing over them using his telepathic powers to find out where their village was located. The Indians appeared dazed and it was easy for him to retrieve the needed information.

"Captain, I want you to stay here with eight of the men and I will take the others with me along with the two Indians and go to their village. If I am not back in two days, leave me a boat and go back to the ship and wait until I return, is that understood?"

"I understand," the captain replied.

In the mean time, Fredric took two barrels of wine and some guns and told the men to take the Indians and follow him.

Fredric walked back into the woods with the Indians and crew walking behind him.

As the day went on he knew they were getting closer to the village because he continued to read into one of the captive Indian's mind.

As they came to the end of the woods, they saw a clearing with tee-pees and wooden shacks.

Taken by surprise Fredric found himself and his men surrounded by Indians with their faces painted and trinkets hanging around their necks. They were all chanting as they held their weapons against them.

Fredric turned towards his men and told them not to resist as he let the two captured Indians go.

Once the Indians were let go, several of the tribesmen grabbed Fredric and his men by their arms and pulled them towards the center of the village where there were more Indians including a large well built Indian who stood out from all the rest. He was also wearing colored paint on his face and had protective gear on his chest that looked like bones.

As the Indians held their spears against Fredric and his men, the larger Indian, who appeared to be the chief, stepped forward and began to talk to Fredric in his native tongue.

The crewmen felt uneasy as several of the Indians held their spears against them with a look of hostility on their faces.

The chief began to scream at Fredric pulling at his arm. Then he took a spear from one of the Indians and pointed it against Fredric's chest.

Fredric then closed his eyes while facing the chief, and without warning, all the spears went flying from the Indian's hands towards the center of the village creating a circle.

The chief could not understand what had just happened. He stepped back and began screaming at the other Indians.

Fredric then stared at one of the teepees causing it to catch on fire. Then staring at another teepee he caused that one to catch on fire too.

The chief looked frightened. He stepped away from Fredric as the other Indians released the crewmen.

Fredric then told the crew to place the barrel with the regular wine in front of the chief. He then broke open the top of the barrel and pointing to the wine, motioned to the chief to drink.

The chief appeared apprehensive about drinking the wine, so Fredric took a metal cup from the supply bag, filled it with wine from the barrel and began to drink his wine. He then handed the cup to the chief and gestured for him to drink.

The chief, with the cup in his hand looked around at the other Indians. He then placed the cup in the barrel showing the other Indians his satisfaction with the wine as Fredric too placed a cup in the barrel and drank wine along with the chief.

It was quite apparent that the chief never drank wine before. He would fill his cup, drink, and then fill it repeatedly. After a few more cups, the chief called upon several of the Indians to drink with him.

Pointing to himself, Fredric said, "My name is Fredric." He repeated it again, "My name is Fredric." Then the chief pointed to himself saying, "Secorda, Secorda." Fredric pointed to the chief and repeated, "Secorda."

The chief appeared to be a little light headed from drinking the wine as he pointed to the teepee that Fredric just burnt down, and then pointed to a tree near the edge of the woods.

Fredric knew what the chief wanted to see, so he turned his attention to the tree and let out two beams of light making the tree burst into flames.

The chief and the other Indians were delighted and frightened at the same time as they all backed away from Fredric and the crew.

Fredric turned towards the chief and pointed west looking into the woods. The chief seemed to understand his gestures as he took one of the Indians by the arm and pushed him in Fredric's direction. Then, in his own language, he told the Indian to guide Fredric wherever he wanted to go. In return, Fredric decided to leave the rest of the wine with the chief.

Walking with his new guide leading him and his men back into the woods they walked at a fast pace going west when suddenly a large black bear came out of nowhere and attacked one of the crew.

Hearing his cries, Fredric ran and grabbed the bear and pulled him off the bleeding crewman.

The bear broke free and turned towards Fredric, charging at him. Fredric wrestled with the bear until he was able to grab the huge animal around its neck and choke it until it fell dead.

The Indian guide and the crew never witnessed a feat of strength such as that.

Fredric then stood up and pointed towards the woods for the Indian guide to continue leading them again.

They walked through the woods for several more miles until the sun went down.

Fredric suggested that his men stay where they were for the night and start early the next morning. The Indian guide, who feared Fredric, left the camp to rest somewhere else.

Fredric told his men to take out some food from the storage bags for their dinner. He then took out a bottle of his wine and sat under a large oak tree so he could rest and look up at the moon as it passed overhead.

Early the next morning the men awakened to see the Indian guide, squatting not to far away from them, starting a fire for their breakfast.

Fredric was already up walking around the damp campsite looking for any signs of fertile soil that would be good for planting.

The woods were thick with trees and underbrush, adding to a heavy morning mist that was rising from the damp ground with little sun shining through.

When the men finished eating, the Indian picked up a hand full of wet leaves and threw it on the fire. The men packed their things and began following the guide.

Every so often Fredric would stop to test the soil with poor results each time.

After a few hours of walking, Fredric decided that the men needed to rest. "You men stay here; the Indian and I will go a little further west and be back in a few hours. You should be safe here," he told them.

As they walked away, Fredric heard them complaining to each other, "Why are we here?"

"What are we going to get from all this?"

"I thought we were seamen not Bushmen."

The two continued walking, when the Indian ran ahead, stopped, then ran back to Fredric and excitedly pointed in a westerly direction. Fredric followed him to a large clearing with a stream running along side. He smiled at the Indian as he walked into the middle of the clearing, knelt down to pick up some soil, and let it slip through his fingers. He walked several yards more and repeated the process.

Elated, Fredric grabbed the Indian's arm shaking it and talking to him even though the Indian did not understand a word he was saying, "This is the place. This is where we will plant our grapes and build our home."

Fredric claimed this land by putting a wooden marker in the ground. He then pointed to his new Indian friend, indicating that he wanted to go back.

Fredric turned around to take one last look at the plot of land where he and Leona will spend eternity.

"I have claimed this land on behalf of the Gruel family and it is now mine," Fredric shouted with delight.

When they approached the area where they left the men, Fredric knew that something was wrong. The men were not there but most of their belongings were.

The Indian guide walked around, searched the ground, then pointed and showed Fredric footprints that lead through the woods. Fredric sensed that hostile Indians made them.

They both followed the footprints and after awhile, the Indian put his hand up indicating to Fredric that he should not make any sounds as he listened for noises coming from an area not too far ahead of them.

They approached a campsite where Indians were sitting around a fire and then saw the crewmen tied to trees.

Catching the Indians by surprise, Fredric concentrated his powers on a large tree, lifted it out of the ground, and made it fall across their fire, terrifying them.

Fredric then picked up three of the Indians and hurled them towards the woods.

The five remaining Indians decided to fight. Two of them picked up their bows shooting arrows at Fredric who was able to catch one arrow in each hand while the others lunged at him. Fredric continued to shoot laser beams from his eyes into the ground, creating a ditch. He then pushed the Indians in.

The crewmen, still tied to the trees, began to yell, "Go get 'em Fredric, beat 'em, kill 'em." Fredric did not want to kill them. He wanted the Indians to go back to their village and tell their chief what they had witnessed.

Fredric then walked over to the ditch, looked down at the frightened Indians and watched as they placed their hands over their heads as a sign of surrender.

The Indian guide, speaking to them in their own language, put out his hand and helped them climb out.

When they were all out he pointed to the woods, and they all ran off.

"Hopefully, this will not happen again," Fredric told his men as he untied them.

First, the men went back to the camp where their belongings were and then they followed the guide and Fredric towards the river.

When they reached the river, they saw the captain and the remaining crew waiting for them by the rowboats.

As they approached, everyone shook hands and hugged.

The captain shook Fredric's hand saying, "I was getting worried about you."

Fredric excitedly told the captain, "I found the land that we were searching for. I will tell you about it aboard the ship. Oh, I brought back an Indian guide; he helped us find this land."

The captain faced his men and said, "I want everyone in their boats, we're going back to the ship."

When the men arrived back at the ship, Leona, who had been waiting patiently, ran over to Fredric and hugged him.

Leona, "I found the land we were looking for. The earth is fertile and it's near a stream. We can build a big house. You and Seth will love it," he eagerly told her.

"That is wonderful, Fredric, I am so happy."

"Is Seth alright? Where is he?" Fredric asked.

"He is fine." Leona replied, "Joseph is watching him in his cabin."

Fredric suggested to Leona, "Why don't you go to the cabin, I will be down in a few minutes, I need to talk to the captain."

Just as Leona left, Captain Ulrich called out to Fredric, "Tell me what happened. I heard you ran into some hostile Indians."

"Yes we did but I believe they will help us. The land we found is perfect for growing our grapes and there is a stream running along side of it."

"Captain, you must excuse me, I must go to my cabin, Leona is waiting for me."

The captain said with a smile on his face, "Go, Go, I understand."

When Fredric entered the cabin, Leona was sitting up in bed and there was a bottle of wine and two glasses on the table beside her.

Fredric walked over to Leona and looked down at her, "You are just as beautiful now as you were when I saw you for the first time."

Leona then placed her arms around Fredric as he leaned over her, kissing her on her neck, then her lips and once again, they were lost in their passion.

Afterwards, Fredric poured wine into a glass for Leona as she sat up and began talking about the virtues of being a vampire.

Fredric sat on the bed alongside of her and explained, "You should consider it an honor to be selected as one of the few vampires in the world. You will remain as you are for eternity and as you know you will always have your special powers. You will understand the true meaning of life and we shall be together for eternity."

Leona placed her glass on the table and looked at Fredric as he whispered, "I love you very much, but I must go on deck now and talk to the captain." He dressed and left the cabin, quietly closing the door behind him.

Fredric walked back on deck as the sun was starting to set.

He spotted Captain Ulrich who was checking the center mast that split during the big storm. As he approached him, he called out, "Captain, I would like to discuss my plans for planting my vines and building a winery. I think it is rather important and we should get started as soon as possible."

The captain asked, "Where are your plans?"

Fredric advised the captain that he did not have them written down, but he knew exactly what must be done. "I would like to leave in the morning with some men, if that is alright with you?" he asked.

The captain replied, "I will have supplies ready for you in the morning, this way you can get an early start. How many men do you feel you will need?"

"I could start with eight good men plus a carpenter," Fredric replied.

"I will have everything ready for you by morning."

Fredric went back to the cabin where Leona was still in bed drinking her wine.

"I did not expect to see you so soon, are you here to stay, or are you just passing through?" she asked.

"I will be leaving in the morning to go to our new land," he told her.

"Why, you just came back?" she questioned.

"I will be taking several men including the first mate and my new Indian guide to survey our new property. Right now, I must work up plans for planting the vines and building the winery. This will take a while.

Joseph is aware that I will be going," Fredric said, as he sat down at the table with paper, a pen and a glass of wine.

Fredric began to draft his plans for the winery knowing that winter would be approaching and they should plant the sibling vines before the first frost.

Early the next morning Fredric walked on deck to find the Indian guide, the men and the supplies waiting for him.

Fredric walked over to the Indian guide and pointed to himself, "My name is Fredric." Then he pointed to the Indian, "Your name is now Goodluck." The Indian pointed at Fredric and said, "You Fredric. Then pointing to himself said, "Goodluck." The crew began to laugh as Fredric placed both hands on Goodluck's shoulders showing a sign of approval.

"I do not expect any problems with the Indians," Fredric said to his men as they climbed into the boats to go ashore.

After rowing and then securing the boats on land, Goodluck and two of the crew began cutting branches off trees to create a narrow path that they could follow to the clearing and back.

Goodluck walked ahead with the two crewmen as Fredric and the others followed.

As the sun was beginning to set, Goodluck motioned for everyone to stop. Then he ran ahead, only to return several minutes later, motioning for everyone to follow him, and they all walked to the clearing together.

After a short rest, Fredric decided that they should unpack the tools needed to start the planting and make camp for the night in the woods, just outside the clearing.

Early the next morning Fredric told his men, "Go collect as many thick branches as you can carry, and put them in the center of the clearing."

As they left, he told the first mate, "Wait, I need you here. I want you to count off one hundred and fifty steps in that direction and then place a wooden stake into the ground. I will do the same going in this direction."

When the men came back to the clearing, with their arms full of branches, a group of Indians surrounded them. Then, stepping out from behind them was Secorda, their chief. Goodluck then spoke to Secorda in their native tongue.

Fredric approached the chief and extended his hand. Secorda, avoiding Fredric's request to shake hands, pointed to a tree. Fredric understood what he wanted, so he shot two laser beams from his eyes towards the tree. Secorda watched in amazement as the tree burst into flames. Then grabbing Fredric's hand, he began shaking it hard in his excitement.

Fredric decided to open a barrel of wine and let the Indians drink. It did not take long for them to feel its effects.

Fredric showed Goodluck what he was going to do with the grape vines. Goodluck explained the process to Secorda.

Secorda then ordered the other Indians to help Fredric and his men with the planting. The crew was very glad to see that the Indians were friendly towards them as they worked together, side-by-side, planting grape vines and building wooden huts for the men and Fredric's family to live in.

As months past and winter was coming upon them, Fredric, along with his family and the crew, moved back on the ship.

The winter turned out to be extremely harsh. Parts of the river froze over but the men were able to walk on the ice to the mainland to retrieve wood to make fires for cooking and warmth. When they began to run low on food the Indians would bring food to the ship.

As the weather became exceptionally cold, Fredric, Leona and Seth would huddle together in bed and Fredric would tell them stories of when he was a boy.

Occasionally, Fredric would walk on deck alone at night just to feel the comfort of the moon.

FREDRIC MEETS HIS MATCH

Several months had gone by and the heavy snows were beginning to melt. Fredric, becoming extremely impatient, decided to take a few men and Goodluck with him to look at the vineyards and make sure the grape vines were still standing.

As they approached the clearing, Fredric was able to see the tops of the vines through the melting snow but because of the extreme frost, he could not see any new growth. This worried him because he knew that if he could not grow the grapes to make his wine he would turn back into a blood-sucking vampire.

Fredric suddenly came up with an idea. He told the men to get large rocks and follow him as he walked to the end of the field. He had the men pile up the rocks, one on top of the other; then standing on top of the rocks facing the vines, Fredric blew large billows of flames from his mouth across the field causing the snow to melt. Within a few minutes all the snow that was covering the stakes and the vines had melted to a point where Fredric could see the ground once more. He was ecstatic.

Fredric turned to his first mate and asked, "How many barrels of wine do we have left?"

The first mate replied, "Twenty-eight barrels, master."

"Could you repeat that?"

"Twenty-eight barrels," he said again.

Fredric, concerned, asked, "Has someone been drinking my wine?"

The first mate answered, "Yes, I have."

"Who told you that you could have this wine without my permission?"

"No one told me."

"Then why did you do it?" Fredric asked.

"I want to be like you, a man with power, a vampire. I witnessed what you did during the storm, and when you set the trees and the teepee on fire in the Indian village I knew with that kind of power I could be of help to you."

Staring into the eyes of the first mate, Fredric said, "I think we should all go back to the ship and discuss this matter with the captain."

Fredric, wearing his black velvet suit with an outer cape and high button boots, walked in the high snow with the men and Goodluck following behind as they headed back towards the ship.

The sky was still grey with the color of winter cold when Fredric and his men boarded the ship. Captain Ulrich was waiting for him, "What did you find?" He asked.

"All the plantings were there and in a few more weeks we should start to see the first signs of growth. But now I have a more serious problem to contend with, and I think we should go to your cabin to discuss this."

When Fredric entered the captain's cabin, he felt the warmth of the fire coming from the stove. The captain brewed some tea and offered Fredric a cup. When they both sat down the captain asked him what was the problem.

"Have you noticed anything different about your first mate, Carl Rummel?"

"He has been acting a little strange lately. Why, what's wrong?"

"He has been drinking my wine for a while and he does not realize it yet but he has turned himself into a partial vampire. That could be dangerous for everyone aboard the ship if he discovers how to use these powers," Fredric advised.

"What can we do?" the captain asked.

"We must prevent him from getting access to the hull. He must not be allowed to drink any more of my wine."

"How do we stop him?" asked the captain.

"I don't believe that he knows his own strength and the powers he has attained. I suggest we bolt the door that leads to the room with the wine. I would also keep two crewmen in front of the door and if he tries to get in he should be stopped or killed."

"I will bolt the door at once and place two men on guard," said the captain.

Fredric then went on deck as the moon began to rise.

Two hours later, when the moon was high in the sky, all seemed to be quiet. Suddenly Fredric heard loud screams coming from the direction of the hull. He ran down to find the two guards unconscious with the door open. As Fredric approached the fallen guards, the first mate ran past him and leaped up the stairs holding bottles of wine in his arms. As Fredric tried to catch him, the first mate leaped over the side of the ship, landed on the ice and disappeared into the woods. Fredric called out to him, "You will die out there, come back, no one will hurt you. Come back."

Fredric stayed on deck for a while using his telepathic powers to see or hear if there was anything unusual coming from the woods, but there was nothing.

Fredric went to the captain's cabin and woke him up, "The room where you posted the two guards was broken into. I found the two guards unconscious and your first mate, Rummel, escaping, taking several bottles of wine with him. You must post two more guards on deck at all times, until we find him. Once he has no more wine, his body will break down creating a thirst for blood and this will make him extremely dangerous."

After hearing this, the captain promised that he would post two more men immediately. "The only way the first mate can be killed is by thrusting a sharp wooden object into his heart or by staying in the sunlight for a period of time without his protective glasses. It is imperative that he be stopped," Fredric told the captain before he went back on deck.

Several days had gone by without any signs of the first mate. Fredric decided to tell the captain that it would be in the best interest of everyone on this ship if he were to go on land, alone, and try to track Rummel's foot steps."

The captain thought for a while then said, "If you think he could be that dangerous perhaps you should go and I will keep extra men on the deck at all times."

Fredric shook the captain's hand and went to tell Leona of his next move. He knew that if he were to catch the first mate he would have to start thinking again like a bloodthirsty vampire.

Suddenly, the weather became warmer and the ice around the ship began melting so Fredric had the crew lower one the rowboats into the still frigid water. He climbed in and rowed towards the shore. Once he reached the shore, he secured the boat and began walking into the woods. It did not take him long before he spotted some recently made tracks in the melting snow.

As Fredric followed the tracks, he came across the partially decomposed body of a raccoon drained of its blood. As he walked further into the woods, he came across other small animals that had met the same fate. He soon realized that the trail he was following lead to Secorda's village. Thinking fast, Fredric turned himself into a Black Raven and flew towards the village where he came across the body of a dead squaw lying in the snow with her eyes wide open and her body drained of blood. Fredric then turned himself back and walked into the village where he saw Secorda and several warriors. Secorda led him to a teepee where they found two more squaws with their necks torn open and their blood drained.

Secorda took Fredric outside the teepee and pointed towards the woods. He and the other Indians thought a bear did these killings, but Fredric knew otherwise. "Stay in the village with your men and I will go and kill the bear," he told Secorda.

Secorda handed Fredric a spear but he refused it, saying he does not need one. He then walked out of the village and back into the woods, calmly trying not to show the Indians any fear. As he retraced his steps, he was able to pick up the first mates trail. This time it led him back to his rowboat. As Fredric approached the shoreline, he saw that the boat was gone. "The first mate probably took the boat back to the ship," he thought.

Fredric, again thinking like a vampire, turned himself into a raven and flew to the ship landing on the upper deck. The first thing that he noticed was that the guards who were supposed to be topside, were not there.

Fredric then changed back and walked down towards the hull where the wine was stored when he heard a noise. As Fredric approached, the first mate lunged at him with his mouth wide open and his eyeteeth protruding downward.

The first mate, in fact, had turned into a bloodthirsty vampire.

Fredric tried to stop him from running on deck but the first mate grabbed Fredric, threw him to the floor, and then tried to bite him on the neck. Fredric, using all his strength, was able to push him off and throw him against the far wall. Then the first mate stood up, grabbed Fredric by his jacket, and threw him down the hallway.

Fredric just lay there, noticing that the eyes of the first mate had turned to a blood red as he shot two laser beams at Fredric, narrowly missing him.

Fredric realized what he was up against for the first time. He shot two of his own laser beams at the first mate just missing him as he bolted up the stairs to the upper deck. Fredric was right behind him using his telekinetic powers to throw heavy water barrels at the first mate, but he was so strong that he was able to push them aside as if they were empty.

Rummel then charged at Fredric and managed to turn him around by grabbing a rope that was hanging from the mast and wrap it around Fredric's neck. Fredric then found himself hoisted up the mast. Struggling to get free, he kicked and tried desperately to grab on to the mast. Then he suddenly fell down to the deck and the rope tied around his neck broke.

As Fredric struggled to stand up, he could see the first mate fall to one knee with a long wooden grappling hook protruding through his chest. Rummel's hands were holding one end of the hook as he tried desperately to remove it from his body. He then fell to the ground and howled as he looked up at Fredric as if asking for forgiveness.

Then the first mate's body burst into flames and disintegrated in the cold air.

Fredric was shocked when he saw who was holding the other end of the wooden pole that struck the first mate. It was Leona. She dropped it and ran to Fredric telling him, "I never want this to happen to us ever again."

When the excitement was over the captain and most of the crew began to come back on deck to see what had happened. The captain turned to the crew and yelled out to them, "This is an example of what happens if you do not obey. I forbid you to drink any of the doctor's wine unless permission is given, that is an order. Now all of you get back to work and clean up this mess."

The crew looked very nervous as they did exactly as the captain ordered.

Fredric and Leona held onto each other as they walked back to their cabin.

FREDRIC STARTS TO BUILD

Several more weeks past and it was now early April.

Fredric summoned the captain and the crew together and told them that it was time to go ashore and start to build the winery.

"Bring all your tools and take as many men as you can spare, but leave at least two behind to look after my family. I would like to leave tomorrow morning if possible," Fredric advised.

Captain Ulrich replied, "Everything you need will be ready for you tomorrow morning."

Fredric decided to have Leona and Seth stay on deck with him to watch the men prepare for the morning departure. Since that horrible incident with the first mate, Fredric and Leona had a great need to be together as much as possible. They have found a new love and trust for each other.

The next morning every member of the crew that was going ashore seemed anxious to get started. They began to load their supplies on each of the rowboats taking enough food for several weeks and enough wine for Fredric.

The sun was rising, the air was beginning to warm up, and Fredric had already put on his protective glasses.

Fredric felt confident that Leona and Seth would be safe with Joseph, Pulaski and two crewmen. After saying good-bye them, Fredric and Captain Ulrich climbed into their boat and began rowing towards the shore with the other men rowing behind them.

Once the men arrived, they brought their supplies ashore and walked into the woods together with Goodluck leading them down the previously cleared path.

After walking through the woods most of the day, they finally reached the clearing where Fredric had staked his claim.

Fredric was so excited that he told the men to break open a barrel of regular wine for them and another barrel of special wine for him and they all drank with gusto.

Fredric knew it would take at least two months to build the winery if the weather remained good.

He would watch his grapes grow on their vines every day. Using his telepathic powers, he would stare at the grapes and make them mature faster.

As the winery came closer to completion, the grapes came closer to being ripe. They would soon be ready for picking. This was just in time because the reserves aboard the ship were getting extremely low.

Even though his family was still living on the ship with Joseph and Pulaski, Fredric thought it would be a good idea to have everyone, including Secorda and his people, get together in the vineyards for a celebration.

Leona was excited when Fredric telepathically sent her a message about the celebration.

A few days later Secorda and the Indians arrived. They brought specialty foods to share with the crewmembers.

Finally, Leona, Seth, Joseph and Pulaski arrived after Goodluck led them through the woods.

Secorda pointed to Leona and motioned to Fredric that he likes her. Fredric tried to explain to him, using Goodluck as the interpreter that Leona is his squaw and Seth is his son. Secorda smiled at Fredric then pointed to his squaw. She was a short, stout woman with long braids holding a baby girl he called Lotada.

Fredric poured Secorda a cup of the regular wine and then poured himself his special wine. He raised his cup and made a toast, "To life and to the beauty of life."

When one of the crew began to play the concertina and another played the fiddle, almost everyone started to dance.

Leona, holding Seth, walked over to Fredric and asked, "May I have the next dance?" Fredric, beginning to regain his sense of humor, said to Leona, "I am afraid you will have to wait. As you can see there is a long line of women waiting to dance with me," he said as he pointed to the Indian squaws sitting on a log. Leona gave him a huge smile as she handed Seth to Joseph. She removed her cape and all the men just stared at her as Fredric put his arms around her and they began to dance.

FREDRIC'S WINE BUSINESS GROWS

As the years went by, Fredric's wine business began to prosper. He had a good reputation for producing wine of a very high quality. As his business grew so did his wealth and popularity considering that no one knew that Fredric, Leona and Seth were vampires. The only people that knew were Secorda and his people.

As promised, Fredric offered his men a chance to become vampire disciples after the first harvest, but Captain Ulrich was the only one to accept the offer. The other men declined due to their religious beliefs. They continued to work for Fredric but as the years went by; they grew old and died while Captain Ulrich, Fredric and Leona stayed the same.

Seth had grown into a fine young man and demonstrated to Fredric that he was capable of running the business so Fredric gave him more of the day-to-day responsibilities to handle.

Fredric wanted to expand his business so he spent more of his time buying up land. He built a house and an underground laboratory on one of the parcels located on the Jersey side of the Hudson River.

SETH MATURES

The year was now 1830 and Seth had just turned twenty. Being a vampire, Seth felt very limited as to what he could do with his future and the people he could associate with. He would spend most of his time with his father, learning the business and his spare time with his Indian friends. He especially liked being with Secorda's daughter, Lotada.

Lotada, which meant Sweet Flower, was a bit of a tease. This lovely, tan skinned, young woman was not at all like her name. Since they were small children, Seth always felt that he had to protect her from other boys.

Lotada grew into a beautiful young woman and the other young men were always trying to get close to her.

As time went on, Seth and Lotada began to have very strong feelings for each other and no one else mattered, but Seth knew that Secorda would never allow his daughter to marry him.

One evening when Seth and Lotada were alone near the river, Lotada told him, "I want you to turn me into a vampire." Seth, very surprised, told her, "My mother and father would never allow that no matter how much I love you."

Lotada pleaded, "Seth, we grew up together and we are like one person and I want to spend the rest of eternity with you."

Seth smiled at her as she leaned towards him and kissed him. She then took his hand and placed it on her breast. Seth had never experienced anything like this before and he quickly pulled his hand away, "We should go now. I don't think this is right," he told her.

Lotada just looked into Seth's eyes and said, "I don't think you know what love is or how it can make you feel."

"I think we should go home now. I will walk you back to your village," Seth said ignoring what she just said.

Lotada started to run back to the Village and then stopped, turned, looked at Seth and broke into laughter. Seth then began to chase after her, laughing as well.

THE BUSINESS KEEPS GROWING

Three more winters had passed and in that time Fredric and Seth built two more wineries to keep up with sales. Fredric purchased more land to expand their business while Seth continued to spend his time in the vineyards as Captain Ulrich delivered cargos of wine up and down the river.

One day, Fredric and Leona asked Seth to sit with them in the parlor to discuss his future.

"Seth, your mother and I thought that it was time for you to understand exactly what you are and the powers you hold."

Seth looking upset, asked, "Did I do something wrong?"

"No Seth, you did nothing wrong," Leona answered. "It's just that you are one of a kind in many ways. You cannot eat food for any length of time. You must drink a special wine every day and you have the power to destroy, if you choose to do so. These powers must be contained if you wish to remain successful. Also your father and I know you spend a lot of time with Lotada and we understand the love you have for her."

"Mother," Seth replied, "Our love for each other runs very deep, she even told me that she wants to marry me."

"Once I was a mortal like Lotada," Leona said, "I am very concerned for both of you. I would like to explain to her what it is like to be a vampire and what being the wife of a vampire is like."

Fredric then explained to Seth, "I would like to teach you how to use your powers the same way Joseph taught me."

"I would like you to teach me everything father."

Fredric continued to explain, "Since our wine business has expanded throughout the east and up to Canada, your mother and I thought it would be a good idea for you to go with me on my next trip. I will be traveling west. This will give you more time to learn the business and more time to think about Lotada."

"I think that would be a very good idea," Seth said, then joked, "Maybe we will see some wild Indians."

"I must first plan the route we will take with Captain Ulrich," Fredric advised his son, then looked at Leona and told her, "If all goes well we could leave in two weeks."

Leona looked at Fredric with a very long face. She did not want him to leave again, especially with Seth.

THEIR FIRST BUSINESS TRIP TOGETHER

Over the next two weeks, Fredric prepared for the trip with Seth. This would allow him to continue to teach him more about running the business and the making of his special wine. Fredric felt that being alone with Seth would also give him a chance to explain how he became a vampire and about his father, Count Gruel and his life growing up in Transylvania. He would also tell him how he met and fell in love with his mother.

After two weeks of preparations, Fredric sat down with Leona and Seth and took out a map. He began to explain to both of them where they would be going on this trip.

"Leona, this is a map that you can follow, it will show you the trails we will be taking and where we should be on certain days, and you know you will be able to communicate with us where ever we are. Joseph and Captain Ulrich will stay here to help you."

This would be the first time that Leona would be separated from Fredric and Seth for such a long time and she felt nervous about it. "When do you expect to return?" Leona asked.

"If all goes as planned we should be back within four weeks."

Seth decided that he would go to the Indian village to say good-bye to Lotada and profess his love for her.

Fredric saw how upset Leona was after Seth left the house. He picked her up and carried her into their bedroom. He lay her down on the bed and sat next to her as he kissed her and whispered in her ear, "I cannot begin to tell you how much I love you and how much I will miss you."

"You look as beautiful today as you did the first time I met you. Do you remember the first time we danced together at Count Lexer's ball? All those young men were upset with me, and jealous."

"It seems as if it was yesterday," Leona nodded in agreement.

Seth arrived at the Indian village and quietly snuck into the teepee where Lotada was sleeping and placed his hand over her mouth. She jumped up frightened and was relieved to see that it was Seth. Like little children, they quietly ran out into the woods together.

When Seth stopped to kiss her, Lotada placed both her arms around his neck and gave him a passionate kiss in return.

Seth then began to tell her, "I am leaving in the morning to go on a business trip with my father and I will be gone for about four weeks. When I return I will speak to your father and ask him for your hand in marriage."

Lotada was so excited to hear Seth say this. She started kissing him and then wispered, "I cannot wait for your return."

"I will walk you back to your village before you are missed," he told her. When they reached the camp, Lotada gave Seth one more kiss.

Seth then walked back to his house with only thoughts of Lotada in his mind.

The following morning, Pulaski with Goodluck next to him, led a horse drawn covered buckboard around to the front of the house. In the back of the buckboard, along with their supplies, were large cases of Fredric's special wine underneath a large canvas covering. Painted on both sides of the canvas was, "Fredric Gruel and Son, Vintage Wines".

Fredric and Seth mounted their horses and Fredric leaned over to kiss Leona good-bye one more time.

The two men, both wearing their protective glasses, with Fredric in his usual black suit and boots, rode side by side behind the wagon. As Pulaski picked up the reins, the four horses moved slowly down the road while Leona stood in front of their house waving. She then sat on the porch watching as they slowly disappeared from view.

Seth began to ask Fredric questions about the trip. Questions he already knew the answers to. "Father, how far west are you intending to go?"

"We will go past the Ohio Valley to the Mississippi River and come back east through Virginia, Maryland and the Delaware Valley," Fredric replied. "Seth, this is a very important trip for us. Not only do I want to expand the number of distributors we have, but my intentions are to change them into vampire disciples."

Seth, with a very inquisitive expression on his face asked, "How do you intend to do that?"

"We will stay in a town for several days selling our wines, then we will engage the new distributor in a conversation about immortality and for those distributors that are interested, we will let them drink my special wine.

We will explain the advantages of their becoming one of our disciples, but we must stay in town and give them support as they change over. Hopefully, they will want to become one of us."

As the group rode west into Pennsylvania, they stopped in a small town called Scranton. As they rode down the main street of this bustling town, they noticed a number of small stores lining both sides of the street. On the right side of the street, they spotted an overhead sign that read Spirits. Fredric told Pulaski to pull up in front.

Seth and Fredric, still wearing their glasses, entered the saloon. This was the first time that Seth was ever in a Saloon and he was surprised to see women standing by the bar talking to the men and drinking.

Noticing Fredric and Seth, two women sitting at a nearby table, stood up and approached them. One of them asked Seth, "Are you blind?" While the other said, "Can we help you two good looking men?"

Surprised, Seth did not know what to say, he just took off his glasses and stared at them. Fredric answered for Seth, "My son and I are here on business. Maybe you can direct us to the owner of this establishment."

"That's him sitting over there," she answered as she pointed to a plump, unshaven, middle-aged man puffing a cigar.

Fredric and Seth went over to the owner. Fredric extended his hand first and tried to introduce himself. The man just sat there looking at them, and then asked in a harsh voice, "What can I do for you?"

Fredric replied, extending his hand again, "My name is Dr. Fredric Gruel and this is my son Seth. We just arrived in town with a wagon full of special wine that we make and bottle ourselves."

The owner, still not shaking Fredric's hand, said, "They call me Scotty. Are you looking to sell your wine?"

Fredric replied, "Not just wine but a whole lot more."

"What do you mean by a whole lot more?" Scotty asked.

"What do you think of immortality?" Fredric asked.

"Are you trying to make a fool out of me? There is no such thing as immortality." Scotty answered.

"There is," Fredric said, "and I can offer it to you with my wine. You can sell this wine to your best customers making them immortal too."

Scotty stood up and looked directly at Fredric, "You must think I'm crazy or something. I think you should take your son and your wine and leave."

"I don't think you're crazy at all. I am just offering you a chance to live for ever." Scotty became so enraged that he picked up the chair he was sitting on, raised it over his head, and flung it towards Fredric. Fredric responded fast by using his powers to make the chair fly in the direction of the bar, breaking bottles of whiskey.

Scotty pulled out a knife from his belt and threw it at Seth. Seth used his powers, deflected the knife, and made it stick in a beam in the center of the ceiling.

All Scotty could do was just stare at them. Finally, he said, "What kind of tricks are these?"

"These are not tricks. I could give you these powers, if you wish."

Scotty, intrigued by what he heard, thought for a moment then said, "Why don't you and your son sit down so we can talk." Scotty then pulled over another chair and the three men sat down.

"If you become a distributor of my wine I will give you wealth and eternal life and eventually turn you into one of our disciples," Fredric explained.

Scotty began to speak in a very low voice not wanting any one around to hear him ask, "How much money will this cost me and how long must I wait for this to happen?"

Fredric told him, "All you have to do is drink four bottles of my special wine each day for three days. The wine will flow through your veins and you will begin to lose your appetite for food. That will be the beginning."

"Then how do I get to learn those tricks you just did?" he asked.

"It will take time for me to teach you," said Fredric.

"But you are leaving town. Something does not sound right. Once you leave how do I get your special wine?"

Fredric told Scotty to follow him out side and introduced him to Pulaski. "This is my driver, Pulaski, he will bring you the wine every three weeks. In the mean time I will stay here with you if you decide to go ahead with this."

Scotty walked around the wagon and looked in the back to make sure there was wine there. He seemed to be willing to do this, but he did not trust Fredric. He then asked him, "Do you see that wagon across the street? I want you to set it on fire."

Fredric told him, "The powers I will give you are not to be misused to hurt people in any way. You must be able to follow my instructions at all times so that we will all benefit from this, is that understood?"

Fredric then nodded to Seth and he shot two laser beams from his eyes at the wagon causing it to burst into flames.

Scotty stared at the burning wagon and said, "Let's go back in side. I need a drink."

Once inside the bar Scotty began firing questions at Fredric, "What if I don't like this disciple stuff? How do I change back? How many years could I live? Could I have a family?"

"If you follow Seth and me you can have it all. You could live for hundreds of years, you could become wealthy, you could have a family, but you could die if you do not listen to us. Most important to us is your loyalty."

Scotty made up his mind and asked, "When can we get started?

"We can start whenever you want. All you have to do is drink my wine. It is that simple."

"How much money is this going to cost me?" Scotty asked. "No money, just loyalty and obedience to Seth and me, is that understood?"

Looking into Fredric's eyes, Scotty said, "Bring in four cases of your special wine and let's have a drink together. Bartender, bring over three glasses."

Seth left the table, went to the wagon, and told Pulaski to bring in four cases of their special wine.

Pulaski brought in the cases and set them down near the rear of the bar. Fredric opened one of the cases, took out a bottle, and poured wine into each of the three glasses. He then raised his glass and made his toast, "To life and to the beauty of life." Scotty and Seth raised their glasses and then they all drank.

After they finished the first bottle, Scotty said, "This is a very tasty wine, but it is very sweet and it almost has the taste of blood. Let's open another bottle and see how fast I can turn into a vampire."

Seth and Fredric looked at each other then Fredric told Scotty, "You should drink this wine in moderation to enjoy the full effect. If you drink too much, too fast, you will get very sick and perhaps die. Once you start to turn, I will give you a special pair of darkened glasses that must be worn at all times when you go into the sunlight. They are like the ones Seth and I are wearing. If you do not wear them, your body will absorb the sunlight and you will burn and disintegrate. That is only one of a few ways that you can die. Remember, it is not just becoming a disciple. You must learn how to be a disciple."

"No more talk about death now. Is it possible that you have an empty room that Seth, my driver and I could have for the evening?"

"That would not be a problem," Scotty replied, then asked, "Is there anything else you need?"

"That would be all for now. My driver will bring the wagon around to the back of your saloon where my Indian friend will rest for the night."

Scotty led Fredric and Seth up a wooden staircase to their room, then suggested, "It is still early, you might want to join me this evening."

"We will see," Fredric told Scotty as he closed the door behind him.

It was extremely important to Fredric that he spends as much time as possible alone with Seth so he could teach him the secrets of making his special wine. He had already taught him how to make their regular wine but he wanted to explain the secrets and the process by which the special wine is made and most important, that it contains his blood. Fredric was very apprehensive about telling Seth that part.

Fredric started by explaining the secrets of his powers, when to use them and how to use them properly. Seth was exceptionally bright and absorbed all of the information his father told him.

"Are you going to teach Scotty your secrets too?" Seth asked.

"No," Fredric answered. "I will tell him just enough. I am a little afraid of him abusing the powers."

Later that evening both men heard music coming from down stairs. "Why don't we go down stairs, father, and see what is happening?"

Fredric agreed.

The bar was crowded with men and women dancing together. They seemed to be having a good time.

As Fredric and Seth approached the dance floor, Scotty came over and invited them to sit with him at his table, as his special guests.

They followed him through the crowded dance floor to his table. When the three men sat down together, Scotty said, "This crowd is having a great time. I am selling your wine at ninety cents a bottle and they love it. Especially when I tell them that this wine will make them all immortal. Just look at them."

Fredric looked at Seth, "Pulaski carried in forty eight bottles, go see how many bottles are left." Seth walked to the back of the bar. All he could find was one opened case with eight bottles in it.

He returned to the table, and Sat down next to Fredric and whispered, "Father I think we have a serious problem. We are missing forty-two bottles." Fredric just stared at Seth for a moment trying to absorb what his son had just told him.

Fredric then turned to Scotty and asked, "What happened to all the bottles of wine that we gave you this afternoon?"

Scotty timidly told him, "I gave some of the bottles to my best customers and I sold the rest."

"Why would you do that? This is special wine that is not for sale," Fredric scolded.

"You wanted disciples. I will give you disciples, a whole room full of them," he shot back.

Scotty stood up and began walking towards the bar when he suddenly jumped up on top of the bar and began to speak in a loud voice, "Everyone! Everyone stop. I want everyone to stop dancing and talking. I have an announcement to make. Listen to me. The wine you have been drinking all evening is a special wine brought here by my good friend Dr. Fredric Gruel."

"What's so special about this wine?" One of the patrons shouted. "This wine will make all of us immortal. We won't die, we'll live forever and ever, how's that?," he shouted back.

As everyone began to laugh, Fredric stood up on a chair and began to speak, "You must all stop drinking this wine at once or you will become sick and possibly die. Do you understand me? Stop drinking the wine now."

Then one of the patrons stepped forward and told Fredric, "We want to live forever." Then the whole crowd began to yell, "We want to live forever." Then someone else screamed out, "The wagon with the rest of the wine is tied up behind the saloon. Let's go get it."

Fredric and Seth immediately realized the problem they had created so Fredric screamed out again, "Stop, everyone, stop where you are."

As the men rushed towards the doors, Fredric had no choice but to use his powers and lock all the windows and doors.

The crowd grew very wild. They began to turn over tables while at the same time yelling, "We want to become immortal. We want to live forever."

Their chants became louder and louder as they continued throwing empty bottles at Scotty who was still standing on the bar. Scotty watched, helplessly as they broke the mirror and bottles of whiskey that were behind him. Then the patrons tried to pull him off of the bar.

Fredric, thinking fast, told Seth, "Go to the wagon with Pulaski and bring back two cases of our regular sweet wine. Hurry up, go."

Fredric turned to Scotty, "Look what you started. I hope for your sake my idea works." A few minutes later Seth and Pulaski carried in the two cases of regular wine and began handing out the bottles to the patrons.

"I am hoping they all get drunk and fall asleep before the sun rises. I do not think anyone had enough wine in their system to hurt them."

Scotty was very nervous and kept apologizing to Fredric. "What have I done? What have I done? Please forgive me," Scotty said repeatedly.

Fredric told him, "I hope you have learned a great lesson from this."

All Scotty could do was look around his wrecked saloon and hope everyone would get drunk and fall asleep like Fredric said.

Fredric and Seth sat down and watched Scotty pour the customers his regular wine at no charge. The patrons thought they were all drinking Fredric's special wine that would make them immortal so they all calmed down and drank with delight.

Then many of the patrons began to fall asleep on chairs, under tables, on top of tables, or anywhere they could rest their heads.

When the last barmaid left the saloon, Scotty walked over to Fredric and asked, "Do I still qualify to become a disciple after all this?"

Fredric, looking directly into Scotty's eyes said, "Scotty after what you caused tonight, you probably will make the best disciple of all. I believe you have learned something from this mess."

Scotty then sat down and asked Fredric and Seth, "Would you like a glass of wine?" The two just looked at each other and began to laugh.

Fredric and Seth went to their room, but not before they told Scotty to keep the doors locked until the next evening. "Do you understand?" Fredric asked him. "Yes, master," Scotty replied. Seth and Fredric just looked again at each other thinking, "Could he have turned so fast?"

The next evening Fredric woke up to sounds coming from the saloon. He decided to go downstairs to see what was going on. As he approached the top of the staircase he looked down to see a number of people that seemed to be having a good time talking about the previous evening.

Fredric went back to his room to get Seth and they both went down stairs to the bar together.

The saloon doors were still locked so Fredric went over to Scotty who was behind the bar serving some of his customers. "Good evening Scotty."

"Good evening, master," he replied.

Seth then asked him, "How are you feeling this evening?"

"Like a new man, very strange and alert," he replied.

Fredric asked him, "Have you had any problems with your customers?"

"Just one, he is sitting over there."

Fredric went over to talk to the man Scotty pointed to, "My name is Dr. Gruel," he said as he extended his hand to him. "My name is Dr. Langer, master," the man said as he shook Fredric's hand.

"Why do you call me master?" Fredric asked. "I call you master because you are my master."

Fredric was puzzled and he asked the man again, "Why are you calling me master?"

"I drank a lot of your wine last night and when I woke up a short time ago I felt very different. I was a little dazed then I felt very strong as if I had the power do things that I had never done before. When you introduced yourself, I was compelled to call you master. These powers are being transmitted through you, isn't that right Dr. Gruel?"

Fredric told him, "That could be correct. I see you are an educated man. What is your specialty?"

"I specialize in the new field of Psychiatry, which is the study of human behavior. What about you Dr. Gruel?"

"I do not practice any longer, but my specialty was Hematology, the study of blood."

"Why do I have this feeling that you have a strange power over me?" Dr. Langer asked.

"In your studies did you ever read about or hear of vampires?" Fredric asked.

"Yes I have, it is some kind of myth that was supposed to have come from a small town in Romania called Transylvania, I believe."

"Yes," Fredric answered, you know your European history."

Dr. Langer then said, "It had something to do with people drinking the blood of other human beings and they could only come alive at night and cannot go out when there is sunlight. Am I right, Dr. Gruel?"

"Yes you are, and whatever you have heard about vampires is mostly true. I know because I come from Transylvania and my son standing over there talking to Scotty, my wife and a few others are vampires," Fredric explained.

"Are you telling me that it is not a myth? There is such a thing?"

"Yes, it is true but we do not walk around at night taking the blood of humans. I made a discovery while experimenting in my laboratory in Transylvania. I developed a blood substitute that takes away the desire to kill people for their blood, but I am still immortal and have all the powers that I have always had".

"Dr. Langer, would you be interested in becoming one of us? I can offer you immortality; your life can go on forever. You can have whatever you want by joining us."

Dr. Langer answered, "I don't know. I am travelling out west to start a new practice."

"You drank a lot of my wine yesterday and without realizing it you have partially changed over already. My blood is mixing with yours as we speak and if you continue to drink my wine, within a day or so, you will turn into a vampire like me."

"I need people like you and I would like you to come with us. Our plans are to travel to Ohio to sell our wine and take on more disciples. Then we will go back to our home in the east."

Dr. Langer thought for a moment, and then said, "You're telling me I can become immortal? What will happen to me if I refuse?"

Fredric explained, "One of three things will happen; you could go into the sunlight without protective glasses and your body will disintegrate or you could walk the streets at night until you develop a thirst for blood and you will kill for it or I can give you a transfusion and turn you back to being a mere mortal. It is you choice."

The two men stared into each other's eyes as if they were playing a game of cards. Each man was waiting to see who will make the next move when Dr. Langer said, "I will only consider joining you if I could work by your side and continue my work as well."

Fredric replied without giving any thought to the request, "Agreed. We will be leaving within the hour. If you have a carriage you can ride along with us, otherwise you can stay here and look after Scotty."

"I would prefer to ride along."

"Very good, get your belongings together and we well meet you in front of the saloon in one hour. Oh, yes, do not let me forget to give you a pair of my special glasses."

Fredric then walked over to the bar where Seth and Scotty were talking. "We will be leaving within the hour. Do you see that man sitting over there? He has agreed to join us and he will be leaving with us."

"Scotty, do you have any last minute questions for me or Seth?"

"Yes I do. How do I get the wine? Can I share it with anyone if I think they are right for us?"

"Only if you think they are right for us and they could help our cause," Fredric replied. "What is our cause?" Scotty inquired. Fredric boldly told him, "To develop a secret army of disciples to work for the good of mankind and to keep law and order throughout the country."

"What about the wine?" Scotty asked again. "I will go out back and have Pulaski bring you a couple of cases. You are not to drink more than four bottles a day, is that understood? Pulaski will bring you more wine in a few weeks."

When Pulaski brought the wagon to the front of the saloon, Fredric and Seth began to count the number of cases. When they went to the rear of the wagon where the special wine was located, they saw that someone had taken several cases. Fredric became enraged, thinking that someone could actually take his wine without permission.

Fredric walked back into the saloon and approached Scotty who was still standing behind the bar serving. "Someone took several cases of wine from the back of our wagon. Do you have any idea who could have done this?" Fredric then demanded in a loud voice, "I want every one in this saloon to step outside now." Scotty appeared nervous as he rounded up his patrons and bar girls telling them all to stand outside.

Fredric, facing all the patrons from the saloon, said in a stern voice, "Someone took cases of wine from the back of my wagon and I want to know who did this." As everyone began to look at each other, Fredric said, "Watch this." He then went to the back of the wagon, took out a bottle of wine, and placed it, facing the sun, in the center of the street. Within moments, the bottle exploded then totally disintegrated.

Someone yelled out, "That's a magic trick."

Fredric then turned his attention towards an empty building across the street and told everyone to keep his or her eyes on that building. He then let out two laser beams from his eyes and shot them directly at the building causing it to burst into flames. Everyone watched in disbelief and horror.

Fredric, looking directly at Scotty, shouted out again, "Now who took my wine?"

Scotty stepped forward, looked at the crowd then at Fredric and said, "I took it by accident."

"What do you mean, by accident?" Worried, Scotty said, "Last night while they were carrying in the cases of wine I slipped a few extra cases off the back of the wagon. I did not really know if you would come back to bring me more wine. Forgive me master, please forgive me."

Fredric faced Scotty, "All these people standing here have witnessed just some of my powers. You will never lie to me again or you will find out what other powers I possess, is that understood?"

"Yes master," he replied.

"Go back inside and drink some of my wine, it will relax you. Just remember you are not to drink more than four bottles a day and do not forget your glasses when you go out into the sunlight."

The crowd disbursed as Seth and Fredric climbed on their horses while Pulaski and Good luck sat on the buckboard with Dr. Langer following behind in his wagon.

When they left Scranton, Fredric decided to review his inventory. Realizing that they had lost a lot of their wine supply, he decided that it would be best for them to return home and replenish their supply before continuing on their trip.

Even though Fredric found two new disciples, he was disappointed that they had to return so soon. Then he came up with an idea. "We should head to Philadelphia where there is a large population that we could service and then go home.

We certainly have enough wine for one more town. We will travel until sunset then make camp so we can get an early start in the morning.

"It's a good thing we brought Goodluck with us to navigate these new trails," Fredric told everyone.

"How long will it take us to reach Philadelphia?" Seth asked.

"We should have a better idea in the morning," Fredric told him.

Fredric, even with his special powers, did not want to admit to Seth and the others that he was lost.

As they pushed on, they followed a river that flowed south. When the sun began to set, they decided to stop and make camp.

Seth and Good Luck found firewood and Fredric, using his powers, started a fire.

A short time later, Seth told everyone that he was going to take a walk in the woods. Fredric asked him if he would like him to walk with him. "That's okay father, I will not be gone long," Seth said as he stood up and took a bottle of wine and walked into the woods.

About twenty minutes later Seth returned and told everyone, "I have a treat for you."

As everyone looked at Seth, Dr. Langer asked, "What do you have for us?"

Seth then held up the same bottle saying, "I brought back a full bottle of fresh blood."

Fredric jumped up, grabbed the bottle away from Seth, and threw it against a tree. "You are never to do that again, never, is that understood?" he yelled.

Fredric walked away as the rest of the group just sat in silence. They never saw Fredric act this way before.

The next morning the men traveled in a southeasterly direction along the Delaware River when they came across a group of Lenape Indians. As the wagons pulled into the Indian village a few young warriors, some holding spears and others holding bows and arrows, formed a circle around the two wagons.

Seth and Fredric were sitting on their horses when a very tall, well built Indian dressed in war gear, along with two other chiefs walked up to Pulaski's wagon and held up, what appeared to be, a Spiritual spear with colorful feathers on top.

Pulaski and Dr. Langer looked at each other, not knowing what to do. Then Goodluck jumped off the wagon and walked towards the chief. He raised his hand making the sign of peace. The head chief turned towards the other chiefs and they began talking.

Goodluck told Fredric, in his poor English, "Give them gift as sign of friendship."

Dr. Langer looked at the chiefs and asked, "Does anyone here speak English?"

The chiefs continued to talk among themselves when a young Indian brave came forward and said, "I speak little English. What you want?"

"We are on our way to a place called Philadelphia. Maybe we can give the chiefs something to show friendship," Dr Langer told the young boy.

"What?" the young brave asked.

"We have a special drink called wine that will make them feel good."

The young brave told that to the chiefs.

Fredric then jumped from his horse, retrieved a bottle of wine from the wagon and offered it to one of the chiefs. The chief opened the bottle and took a drink, then passed it on to the other chiefs. They all appeared to like the taste of it.

The chiefs then followed Fredric to the back of the wagon where they saw the rest of the cases. Fredric did not like what the chiefs were thinking, so he told Pulaski to take one case and offer it to them.

The chief did not want just one case as he motioned to his braves to remove all the cases from the back of the wagon.

Good luck and Fredric tried to reason with the braves telling them to tell the chiefs, "The wine will make you all sick," as Fredric pointed to his stomach and shook his head.

The chiefs did not understand.

Dr. Langer and Good luck stepped in front of the braves and tried to stop them by holding up their hands.

Seth and Fredric tried to stop the other Indians from taking more cases off the wagon, when one them shot a wooden faced arrow from behind, piercing Fredric's shoulder.

Fredric grabbed onto the arrow and tried to pull it out but he could not.

As he fell to the ground, he looked at Seth and told him, "Tell your mother I love her."

Together, Dr. Langer and Seth pulled the arrow out from Fredric's shoulder knowing that if the arrow was any closer to his heart it would have meant Fredric's demise.

There was little that Seth could do to help his father.

Seething with anger, Seth let out a loud howl. He then stood up, opened his eyes wide and shot laser beams hitting the chiefs as they stood together cutting their bodies in half.

The other Indian warriors were petrified and began to run away.

Seth and Pulaski shot laser beams from their eyes killing more Indians. Seth then charged into the rest of them and began to hurl them, one by one, above the trees. He watched as the high branches pierced their bodies as they fell on them.

Dr. Langer, Pulaski and Goodluck just looked on with fright and amazement.

Seth was beside himself as he continued to cry and howl so loud he was heard throughout the forest.

Placing Fredric gently in the back of the wagon, Seth sat next to him for the ride home.

Seth realized that he would have to assume the responsibilities that his father had been teaching him, and he would now be the leader of the disciples until his father recovered, but all he wanted to do was go back home to be with his mother and Lotada.

As Seth sat in the wagon with his wounded father, he looked around and saw all the bodies of the young warriors. "This did not have to happen," he thought.

As they drove off, Seth noticed a small torn piece of his father's jacket lying in the dirt. He jumped out of the wagon, retrieved it, and then jumped back in.

Pulaski and Good luck drove the wagon. Dr. Langer following in his wagon with Fredric and Seth's horses tied to the rear.

The group rode in silence the entire trip home.

As the travelers approached Fredric's house Leona saw Fredric's horse without a rider and began to cry.

Seth jumped out of the wagon, gave his mother a hug and told her,

"Mother, father has been wounded. He is in the wagon. Leona holding on to Seth said, "I know, I felt the arrow pierce his body as if it had also pierced mine."

Leona then ran to her wounded beloved, crying, "Fredric, Fredric, you will be alright. I know you will."

"Let's take your father into the house where he can rest."

Pulaski and Good luck carried Fredric upstairs to his bedroom with Dr. Langer following.

Leona then placed her arm around her son as they walked into the house.

Leona and Seth sat in the parlor for a long time with neither of them speaking. Without Fredric sitting in his favorite chair next to them, there was an emptiness that that they could feel.

Leona stood up and went to the pantry in the kitchen where she kept several bottles of wine. Taking one bottle off the shelf, she poured the wine into two special glasses.

As she handed Seth a glass she told him, "Your father and I would drink from these glasses all the time. Then your father would raise his glass and always make the same toast, "To life and to the beauty of life." I think of these words and I am reminded of how much your father loves life."

Leona and Seth continued to sit in silence just thinking of Fredric and of their future.

SETH'S OPPORTUNITY

"Mother, before we discuss anything regarding our future I must go to the Indian village to see Lotada and tell her what has happened. Before I left I promised her that I would ask her father for her hand in marriage. Now things have changed and I must talk to her."

"You should go at once and explain to her that you now have new responsibilities as a leader. I am sure she will understand."

As Seth walked through the woods in the direction of the Indian village, the sun was already going down. The birds and animals that he usually heard were strangely quiet.

When he reached the village, he noticed that many of the male Indians were dancing and chanting as they moved in a circle around a fire that was located in the middle of the village. Many of the squaws were crying outside their teepees.

Seth walked to Lotada's teepee and saw spiritual burial poles standing outside.

He paused before walking in, scared of what he might find inside.

Lying on the floor in the center of the teepee was the outline of a woman covered with a blanket. There were several elderly women, including Lotada's mother, sitting on the floor next to the body chanting. Seth gasped for air and his eyes filled with tears. He slowly approached the body and bent down to pull back the blanket when he heard Lotada's voice asking, "Seth, what are you doing here?"

Seth turned and saw Lotada standing in front of him. He grabbed her and hugged her while the elderly women continued to chant.

"What happened? Who is lying here?" Seth asked.

Lotada began to cry as she told him that her mother's sister had died,

"She was one of the elders of our tribe and I was very close to her," Lotada explained and then asked Seth, "I thought you were away. What made you come back so soon?"

Seth, visibly upset, explained, "We were attacked by a group of Lenape Indians along the Delaware and father was badly wounded by one of them."

Seth took Lotada by her hand and led her outside. They walked hand in hand to their favorite spot in the woods and sat down.

Lotada, "I love you very much and I want to spend the rest of my life with you, but with my father hurt, now is not the right time for us to get married. I am now the leader of the disciples and I have new responsibilities.

"Seth, I want you to turn me into a vampire. I want to be like you and live forever with you, when you say the time is right."

"I cannot offer you such a life. Look what happened to my father. The same thing could happen to me, and then what would you do?" Seth asked.

Lotada answered with tears in her eyes, "I would take a wooden stake and thrust it through my heart so I could be with you."

"Don't be foolish. I want you to talk to my mother and let her explain what being a vampire is like."

"Okay, then take me to your mother right now," she demanded.

Lotada stood up, grabbed Seth by the hand, and pulled him until he stood up. Then they ran to his house.

As they approached the house, they could see Leona sitting on the front porch looking up at the moon.

She was wearing a dress that was Fredric's favorite and she was crying. I am just sitting here looking up at the moon the same way your father and I would always do."

Seth, trying to cheer her up said, "Mother, you look so beautiful and so young."

"I am young. I am only eighteen. That is how old I was when your father turned me into a vampire. I look and feel exactly the same".

"Mother we have to talk to you. Lotada wants to marry me and become a vampire like you. I have tried to explain to her what it would be like, but she will not listen to me. You must tell her the truth."

"Please sit next to me Lotada and I will tell you."

"It is a beautiful thing to be a vampire. I am forty-three years old and I look and feel like eighteen. I have great strength and powers like no other woman and I fear no one. I can walk through the woods and hear the birds singing from miles away."

"You are very strong willed, my dear, just like I was when I was your age. You are very lucky to have Seth to love the same way I love his father. Seth needs you."

"So what is the answer?"

"I would consider it an honor to have you as my daughter, despite what Seth thinks. Only a few people know what I am and if you decide to become one of us, you do not have to tell anyone."

Lotada gave Leona a hug and thanked her, then told Seth, "Your mother is a very wise and brave woman."

Seth stood up, walked over to his mother, and kissed her cheek then he told Lotada, "I will walk you home now. I have a lot to think about."

SETH TAKES CHARGE

As the days went on word began to spread about Fredric's tragedy.

Seth decided to have his closest disciples come to his house and discuss their future.

One by one they came into the parlor and sat down. Joseph, Captain Ulrich along with Pulaski and Dr. Langer sat in front.

Leona took out several bottles of wine and began pouring it into each glass. Seth then stood up and raised his glass to make a toast, "This is for my father, to life and to the beauty of life."

They all stood up, raised their glasses, and then began to drink.

Seth looked around the room and said, "We will be without our leader until he is well. I must take my father's place but it will be difficult. My intentions are to continue my father's work, with your help. We will spread the word of our beliefs and recruit new disciples wherever we can. We will grow in number and become more involved in the politics of our young country. We must defend the rights of all people, not just our disciples and I will need all of your help to do this."

They all shook their heads in agreement.

As everyone was leaving, Seth called out to Dr. Langer, "Can I speak with you for a moment?"

"Yes," the doctor said as he came back into the parlor.

Seth began, "I need your help. Even though I know you for a very short time I can see that you are well educated, and I feel you could be trusted with what I have to say."

"Thank you for your trust. I will try to help you in any way I can," Dr. Langer replied.

The doctor paused for a moment then continued, "I have grown fond of you and your father in the short time before this tragedy but I would not know what to do or how to help you."

Seth explained, "I will teach you all that I know, but I must have one hundred percent of your loyalty. That must be understood right from the beginning."

Dr. Langer, pleased by Seth's show of confidence said, "I promise you my loyalty, master."

"I do not want you to call me master any longer, just Seth."

"Then why don't you just call me Doc?"

They stood up and shook hands. Seth, for the first time, felt that he had made his first real alliance. He also knew that his future was in the balance. He must get his disciples to organize and begin to recruit.

The first thing he wanted to do was to go to the winery to show Doc how they made the wine.

As they walked through the vineyards, Doc was full of questions. "How much growing land do you have?"

Seth explained, "When my father first staked his claim on this land he walked off one hundred and fifty feet in one direction and one hundred and fifty feet in another. We now grow our grapes on over five hundred acres. We can purchase more land, if we needed it. Let's walk over to the winery."

As they walked into the winery, Doc was surprised to see how many workers there were. As they walked through, Doc continued to ask questions.

Seth answered all his questions without hesitation. "This is how we pulverize the grapes and extract the juice from the skin. This is done all in one process."

"All the wood that was used to build this winery came from the forest around us. As we expand our business we are preparing to build a much larger winery."

Doc was very impressed with what he saw as he followed Seth around, and then he asked, "How do you formulate the wine?"

Seth said, "Come with me." Then they both walked into a narrow building attached to the back of the winery.

"I have never seen anything like this before," Doc exclaimed. In front of him he saw fifty beds with men and some women lying on them. The beds were lined up next to each other with twenty five on each side of the long narrow room. Rubber tubing ran along the back of each bed into individual glass flasks that stood on a table with each donor's name on it.

In the far corner of the room, sitting on top of a platform, sat three musicians, two men playing the violin and a woman playing a harp.

The music played softly as the occupant of each bed lay there with their eyes closed and their blood running from their veins through the narrow tubes into the flasks.

"Aren't you afraid of them dying?" Doc asked.

"Absolutely not, they are all vampires and the blood they give was my father's blood and my father's blood was pure from his father."

Doc then asked, "How much blood can they give?"

"Each vampire must fill two flasks a day three times a week. We play the music to relax them and help them get through this process."

"Now you understand why we need more disciples. We need them so we can have more blood and make more of our special wine."

"This is remarkable but how do you make a large enough profit to sustain your selves and your workers?" Doc asked.

Seth told Doc to come back with him to the winery. "As you can see we have different vats of wines that we will sell on the open market. These grapes will go into those three vats where we crush them manually. We age the wine by using our telepathic powers. All our workers are vampires and they require very little pay plus we sustain them with our special wine."

My father has taught me the business. He has also taught me to understand and appreciate the magnificence of being a vampire."

"Until he gets well I will be guided by his wisdom."

Doc, realizing the strain Seth was under, tried to give him encouragement and commented, "Seth, this all seems very complicated to me but you seem to know what you are doing. Just let me know how I can help you. Would it be alright if I walk around so I can get a better understanding of your processes?"

Seth said it would not be a problem.

He left Doc in the winery and went back to the house to see his father. He knew that if he was to grow his business the first thing he would have to do is entrust other people with the knowledge of how the winery worked.

He was also aware that his father trusted him to do the right thing.

When Seth entered the house, Leona was sitting in the parlor. "How is father feeling?" he asked.

"He should be up and about soon. Why don't you go up stairs and talk to him. I am sure he would like to see you."

Seth entered the bedroom to see Fredric sitting in a rocking chair wearing his special glasses and looking out of the window. He was happy to see Seth and told him, "I heard what you did at the Indian camp after I was struck down by an arrow and what you are doing here. I am very proud of you."

"Thank you father but I never expected you to get struck by an arrow," Seth told him. "I never expected it either. I just can't understand how I didn't see it coming. Maybe this is a sign of my getting old," Fredric said joking.

"Nonsense, the Indian shot the arrow from a far distance. He was just lucky," Seth said.

"No, the Indian is dead, I was lucky. The arrow missed my heart by inches. This was the closest I have ever come to death."

"I just came up to see how you are doing Father, and to let you know that everything is under control in the winery."

"Thank you, Seth, why don't you go down stairs now and spend some time with your mother, she seems so lost these days. I will be alright."

Leona was still sitting in the parlor when Seth came down stairs. "How is your father feeling?" she asked.

"I have never seen him scared before," Seth replied. "This was a dose of reality for him. I don't think he has ever thought of his own death."

"He is a very brave man and I have a very deep love for him and for you to, my son."

"We talk about how we cannot die, but in reality we can die, just like any mortal, but only it is more painful."

Seth sat with Leona for a while and listened to her talk about her life with Fredric.

Suddenly, Seth interrupted, "I'm going to see Lotada." As he stood up, Leona said to him, "Please be careful, Seth."

Seth kissed his mother good-bye and walked into the woods towards Lotada's village. When he arrived he went directly to her teepee and stood outside pacing for a few minutes trying to get up enough courage to go in.

When he did enter, he saw Lotada sitting next to her mother. She immediately stood up, looked at him with a coy expression on her face and said, "What can I do for you?"

Seth blurted out, "I made up my mind. I want to marry you. Let's do it before I change my mind."

Lotada jumped on Seth, hugged, and kissed him.

Seth just stood there not knowing what to say to Lotada's mother, so he just smiled at her and told Lotada, "We must talk outside."

Lotada was so excited she grabbed Seth's hand and pulled at him to go outside.

They walked to their favorite spot in the woods to be alone. "Sit over here," Seth told her.

Obediently, she sat down and sheepishly looked up at Seth with her big brown eyes as Seth told her, "We must talk about you becoming a vampire. If you decide not to turn, you will grow old and die and I will stay young forever, aging only slightly. So I would like to marry you as soon as possible before I change my mind and you get any older."

Lotada was thrilled, "I must tell my father at once."

As she stood up Seth said, "Wait," and he grabbed her hand. "You cannot tell your parents that you are going to be turned into a vampire."

"Why not, they will find out sooner or later?"

"Better later than sooner," Seth told her.

Lotada reluctantly agreed and they walked back to the village.

When they reached the village, Secorda was standing outside of Lotada's teepee with a grim look on his face.

As Lotada approached him she said, "Father, Seth and I want to get married."

Secorda, trying not to let his anger show, said, "I know Seth since he little boy, I love him like son, but he is vampire and you not marry vampire."

"I don't see why that should make a difference, I love him and I know he will be good to me and make me happy," she pleaded.

Secorda looked at Seth and repeated, "You are vampire, you not marry daughter. Go now; I talk with Lotada in teepee with her mother."

Lotada walked into the teepee with Secorda, and Seth started walking home.

As he walked deeper into the woods he became aware that it was exceptionally quiet, almost eerily quiet as if something unheard of was about to happen.

Suddenly, from behind a tree, a vicious grey wolf with saliva dripping from his mouth, jumped out, tore into Seth's neck, and would not let go. They fell to the ground and wrestled until Seth was able to grab hold of the wolf and throw it high above the trees.

Seth, bleeding profusely from his neck, managed to pull himself up and head toward home. With blood still gushing from his neck he climbed the stairs to his father's room where he collapsed on the floor.

Fredric hearing a thud looked down to see Seth laying there.

Leona also heard the thud and ran up to the bedroom in a panic.

They both gasped when they saw Seth holding on to his neck with blood pouring through his fingers.

Fredric and Leona tried to stop the bleeding as Seth explained what had happened, "I was attacked by a wolf in the woods but I killed it."

"Let me put my hand on your neck, I will close up the wound and stop the bleeding," Fredric said as he placed his hand on Seth's neck and closed his eyes. The open wound began to close and the bleeding stopped.

"Take two bottles of wine and go to your room and rest, you should feel fine by tomorrow," Fredric advised.

When Seth left the room Leona became hysterical and sat down next to Fredric, "Why is this happening to us? What have we done to deserve this?" she asked.

Fredric reached over, placed his hand gently on the back of her head, and held Leona against him assuring her that everything will get better.

The next day Fredric seemed to feel a lot stronger and was able to walk down stairs to join Leona and Seth in the parlor.

The two men sat there comparing their scares with death, when Leona stood up and yelled at them, "What are you both talking about? Do you realize what this has done to me? Do you realize that I live every day with the fear of losing both of you? Do you have any understanding of the way we live and what we are?"

"Do not talk of death in front of me, is that understood?"

They all sat in silence until Seth suddenly said, "I have something else we can talk about. Lotada and I want to get married."

"That is wonderful," Leona said. "But what does Secorda have to say about it?"

"I think her father will try to stop us," replied Seth.

"If you and Lotada are very sure of your feelings you can always stay with us until you build your own house."

Seth stood up, kissed Leona and thanked her. "I would like to stay in and rest today with you and father and tomorrow I will go to the village and tell Lotada.

That afternoon Doc Langer came to the house to see how everyone was.

Fredric and Leona were downstairs while Seth rested in his bedroom.

Doc asked Fredric, "When will you be ready to get back to work?"

"I am hoping that within the next three weeks, then we can arrange another trip, but in the meantime I would like to send you and Pulaski to Scotty's place to deliver some wine like I promised, this way you can see how he is doing."

"That's a good idea," Doc replied.

"I will make arrangements for you to leave within the week," Fredric said.

"That will be fine; in the mean time I will spend time with my new plant manager, Bob Stillwell and see if he is ready to be turned into a disciple.

When Doc left, Fredric told Leona, "I think Doc is going to work out very well for Seth."

After recovering from a time of turmoil, things seemed to be getting back to normal. Fredric started going to the winery again and Seth was trying hard to figure out a way to marry Lotada without upsetting Secorda.

A few days later doc pulled up in front of Fredric's house with Pulaski, Goodluck, and a wagon filled with wine for Scotty.

Fredric and Seth walked out to meet them when Fredric turned to Seth, "You're in charge now. You tell them what they have to do."

Seth, surprised by what his father said, told the men, "Before you give Scotty any more wine, you must find out what he did with the extra wine we left him and make sure that you do not leave the wagon unattended while you are there."

Seth and Fredric walked over to Doc, shook his hand, and wished him a safe trip.

After the wagon left, Fredric went to his study and Seth decided to talk to Lotada to see what he could do to help the situation between him and her parents.

When Seth arrived at the Indian village the first person he encountered was Secorda who said, "Why are you here? I not want you marry Lotada. I not want Lotada be vampire like you and your family. Go now, forget Lotada. She will marry Indian, real man."

All Seth could do was listen as Secorda degraded him.

Seth tried to control his anger so he turned around as if he were leaving the village.

Then he snuck around the back to Lotada's teepee so he could talk to her. Using his Laser vision, he burnt a hole in the back of the teepee where he saw Lotada naked as she changed her clothes. Seth stood there transfixed, never having seen a naked woman before. A squaw spotted him and she began to scream.

Seth did not know what to do when warriors came running towards him shooting their arrows. Not wanting to hurt any of them, he deflected their arrows into different directions.

Then he quickly made a large slit in the back of Lotada's teepee, allowing him to enter.

When Lotada saw him, she screamed, "What are you doing here?" she said as she tried to cover herself.

"There is no time to explain," Seth said. "You must come with me now."

Lotada quickly dressed and Seth took her hand as they ran out the front of the teepee.

Secorda and his warriors chased after them.

Lotada was having difficulty keeping up with Seth so he picked her up and carried her until they reached his house.

Fredric and Leona sensed that Seth was in some kind of trouble.

When they walked out on the front porch, they saw Seth running towards them carrying Lotada. "What did you do?" Leona asked.

Seth put Lotada down and explained, "All I did was go to the village and when Secorda saw me he told me I was not welcome in his village any more and I am not a real man, just a vampire, so I took Lotada back with me."

"Does Secorda know what you have done?" Fredric asked.

"He has been following us and should be here shortly with the rest of his warriors."

Just then, Secorda with his warriors following came out of the woods and walked slowly up to Fredric's house where Fredric and Leona were waiting for him.

Secorda spoke, "Fredric, I no want Lotada marry Seth. I no want her be vampire like you. You must give Lotada back to me or we will fight."

"Why don't you ask Lotada what she wants to do?"

"She loves Seth and they want to be married and have plenty of children together. That would be very good for both of us," Fredric said, pointing to Secorda then himself.

Secorda then shouted, "Lotada will not be vampire."

Secorda raised his hand as a signal for a warrior to shoot an arrow.

As the arrow headed directly for Fredric, he deflected it into the ground, and then stared at the arrow until it caught on fire.

Secorda then raised both his hands and all the warriors began to shoot arrows at Fredric. This time Fredric, Seth and Leona all stared at the arrows in flight and they began to catch on fire before doing any damage.

Lotada then surprised everyone. She raised her hand to Secorda and angrily said, "I am not going back with you. I intend to marry Seth and you cannot stop me. Take your warriors and go back to the village before someone gets killed. I will come back to the village later. Now go."

Secorda, realized he could lose his daughter forever if he continued in this quest to prevent the two from marrying, so he told his warriors to go back to the village and they peacefully followed him into the woods.

Lotada gave Seth a hug and then Fredric and Leona joined in and they all hugged and laughed at their victory.

"Lotada will sleep here tonight and we will all try to see how we can convince Secorda to change his mind. In the mean time let us all go into the house and have some wine,"

Fredric knew that if Lotada wanted to become a true vampire she would need a transfusion, otherwise she could just drink the wine and feel some of the effects before deciding if this was what she really wanted to do.

Early the next morning Lotada decided to go back to the Indian village and see if she could convince her father to change his mind.

When she went into his teepee, Secorda greeted her with a very angry look.

"Father, I do not want you to be angry with me. Please forgive me but I love Seth and I love you and mother too."

"I do not want you become vampire. If you do, you not welcome in village any more." Lotada, trying to hold back tears told her father, "Then I am leaving. If you change your mind about Seth, I will be living in his house."

Without another word, Lotada kissed her mother good bye and walked into the woods towards Seth's house.

When Lotada reached the house, Leona was sitting on the porch. She stood up, gave Lotada a hug, and told her, "I am so happy you will be marrying Seth.

I will now have the daughter I always wanted."

SCOTTY'S DEMISE

While everyone was trying to make peace at home, Doc, Pulaski and Good luck rode into Scranton with their delivery of wine.

As they rode into town, they noticed that the streets were empty. "Something is very wrong here. Where are all the people?" Doc asked, not expecting an answer.

When they reached Scotty's Saloon, Doc told Pulaski and Good luck to stay in the wagon while he goes inside to look around.

Doc then went into the saloon and saw Scotty standing behind the bar with a couple of his barmaids standing on the opposite side.

As Doc approached the bar, he asked Scotty, "Where is everyone? Is today a holiday?" Scotty nervously answered, "What happened here is not my fault. I could not control anybody from drinking the wine; they kept coming back for more. I could not control them they were giving the wine to their wives and then their children," he continued. "Everyone wanted to live forever but instead they were dying. They would come here at night and drink the wine and then they would go home. They would walk into the sunlight the next day. I would hear screams coming from the streets then I would go outside wearing my glasses only to see the town's people burn up and disintegrate right in front of my eyes. It was horrible."

"How many people do you think died here?"

Without hesitating, Scotty answered, "One hundred or more. Now everybody is afraid to go outside."

"I want you to call a town meeting for this evening. Let me talk to the people and explain why this happened," Doc suggested.

Scotty said, "I will go out now and knock on every door. Hopefully I can get them all to come."

"You do that, and we will talk when you get back," said Doc.

After Scotty left, Doc went out front where Pulaski was waiting and explained what happened inside the saloon. He told Pulaski to stay with the wagon until he finishes dealing with Scotty.

About an hour later, Scotty came back to the Saloon. As he entered Doc asked, "Well, what happened?"

"I knocked on every door, but many people were just too afraid to answer and those that I talked to are afraid to step outside. We will have to wait and see how many people will show up this evening," he answered.

"How many bottles of wine do you have left, Scotty," Doc asked.

"About eight bottles," he replied.

"We left you with over one hundred bottles and you are telling me that you only have eight bottles left?

We do not want to do business this way. We offered you something special. We offered you immortality and you abused the privilege for your own personal greed. You are the one who is responsible for killing over one hundred people. We cannot continue with you Scotty and you must pay for this mishandling of power."

Scotty slowly inched his way behind the bar where he kept a loaded shotgun. As he reached for it, Doc Langer, using his telepathic powers, caused Scotty to point the gun at himself and shoot.

Doc went out to Pulaski and told him what happened to Scotty and then explained, "Let's take the wine off the wagon and bring it into the Saloon.

Tonight when we have our meeting I will see if there is anyone who would be willing to take charge."

As the afternoon turned into evening, the remaining town's people began to come into the saloon.

As families entered, Doc Langer stood there greeting them by the door.

When the room was full, Doc Langer stood up on top of the bar and started to speak, "I would like to apologize, on behalf of the Gruel family, for what took place here over the past few weeks. We hold ourselves responsible for the many deaths that took place here. I know I cannot replace your loved ones, but I assure you that this will never happen again."

"For those of you who do not know me, my name is Doc Langer. I was in town when Scotty got the wine. Scotty, by the way, is no longer with us. We gave Scotty the wine as a test that would have made him and his disciples immortal. Instead he abused the opportunity by selling this wine to you".

"I was like you, a mortal, and no different; until Dr. Gruel explained to me what it is like to be immortal and how beautiful life can be when you never grow old, never contract diseases and also have special powers. For the rest of your lives you can build your companies, prosper and watch your families grow and stay exactly as you are now, forever and ever, if you wish. All we ask for in return is your loyalty."

If Scotty did not sell you the wine and would have explained the affects to you, we would not be here this evening. If you had followed a few simple rules and had a better understanding of what took place over the last few weeks, this would never have happened.

If I had not come here now, this tragedy would have continued until you were all dead."

Then one of the men standing in the back raised his hand and said, "Scotty never told us of any rules. All he said was we should buy this wine and enjoy life."

Then another man began to speak, "We are all god fearing people here and we really don't know what happened to us. What you are asking sounds sacrilegious. We were raised to love and fear God. What will happen to us if we denounce god?"

Doc explained to the people, "You do not have to denounce your god. You just have to follow us and recognize Dr. Gruel as your leader and follow his teachings of loyalty. And when he needs you, you must respond to him."

"Those of you who can accept this way of life will be turned into disciples over a period of time and taught how to use your special powers for the good."

"Those of you, who do not wish to follow us, must stay out of the sunlight for the next several days until your own blood circulates through your veins again."

"In the mean time, I will stay here for the next several days for those who wish to talk to me about becoming a disciple."

"You are all welcome to join me and my other disciples, but I will repeat this again, if you go into the sunlight without wearing your special glasses, you will self-destruct and it will be very painful."

"Thank you all for coming here this evening."

After everyone left, one young man stayed behind and walked up to Doc Langer and said, "I was standing in the back of the room while you were speaking and I am very interested in what you had to say."

"Why don't you join me over here," Doc Langer said as he led him to a table near the bar.

"You look very young," Doc surmised.

"I am thirty four, my name is John Saber and I do not have any family to worry about."

John was about five feet nine inches tall, well build with sandy hair and a fair complexion and he did have some formal education.

Doc then asked him, "What do you do for a living?"

"I am a production manager down at the lumber yard," he answered. "I have worked there for five years and I need a change," he continued.

Doc then asked, "Why would you like to join us?"

John eagerly replied, "I don't believe in God, I have no family and I do believe in the future."

Doc, listened carefully, then said, "That was well said. I believe you are what we are looking for. Would you like a glass of wine?"

SETH AND LOTADA 'S WEDDING

Fredric had just finished hanging decorative candles around the front lawn. It was a beautiful evening, the stars were out and there was a full moon, almost as if Fredric planned it that way.

Fredric and Seth were waiting for Lotada and Leona to come downstairs as guests began to arrive. Friends from the surrounding villages we in attendance to see the young couple marry.

After all the guests had arrived, Leona walked out of the house wearing the same dress that she wore when she met Fredric for the first time so many years before.

She looked young and beautiful. Fredric walked over to her and told her, "You look radiant this evening. Will you save the first dance for me?"

Leona answered with a puzzled look on her face, "But Fredric, there is no music."

"We will make our own music," he answered.

Just then, Lotada came out of the house wearing one of Leona's gowns. Her long dark brown hair rested over one shoulder and Leona's diamond necklace sparkled from around her neck.

Seth never experienced a celebration like this before and he could not take his eyes off Lotada who beamed as guests came up to her to tell her how beautiful she looked.

As Fredric began to gather his guests together for the brief ceremony, several of his disciple employees sat on chairs on the front lawn.

As soon as the ceremony began, Joseph, wearing his dark burgundy jacket with gold buttons and tails, walked out of the house holding a black book under his arm. He walked down a narrow path, stopped in front of a large oak tree then turned around. Fredric and Leona who walked proudly, arm in arm, down the narrow path to where Joseph was now standing, followed him.

Then Seth and Lotada walked out of the house together with big smiles on their faces as they walked slowly down the isle together holding hands.

Joseph motioned for everyone to be seated.

He then faced Seth and Lotada and began to speak in a very soft voice, "On behalf of the Gruel family I would like to thank everyone for coming here today to witness the bonding of these two special people, Seth and Lotada. I have known Seth's father Fredric Gruel for a great many years and I have watched Seth grow up to be the responsible young man he is today. When we moved to this new land over twenty years ago I remember meeting a young Indian girl who would play with Seth. He was always there to protect her as they grew up together. Before I pronounce them man and wife, I would like everyone here to look up at the moon and feel the power of the moon as we say a prayer for Seth and Lotada."

As the guests were looking up at the moon, Seth held on to Lotada's hand. Then Seth began to perspire heavily and his body began to shake. He was still holding on to Lotada's hand when he fell to the ground. Lotada let out a loud scream.

Fredric and Leona immediately leaned over Seth to see what was wrong. As Seth turned over on his back, everyone gasped as they watched his face become distorted and he began to take on the features of a wolf.

First, the hair on his head started growing; covering his eyes and ears, then his clothing began to tear apart exposing his shoulders and back. Then his body began to expand as his arms and fingers grew bigger and longer.

All Fredric and Leona could do was look on as their terrified guests began to run.

Fredric tried holding Seth down on the ground, but Seth, now having super strength, was able to fight his way out of Fredric's grip. Seth then stood up, looked at his terrified guests, made harrowing sounds, and then bolted into the woods with Fredric in close pursuit.

Not only did Fredric have Seth's own strength to contend with, but the fact that he had turned into a werewolf made him even stronger and faster.

Fredric followed Seth to the Indian village when he suddenly heard screams. Fearful, he ran towards Secorda's teepee only to see warriors running towards the other side of the village. As he approached Secorda's teepee, he saw a group of Indian squaws, including Lotada's mother, crying.

Fredric then ran to the center of the village. He was horrified to see Secorda's body lying on the ground, along side of another warrior, torn apart.

He then ran into the woods and continued to search for Seth.

Several hours had past and the moon was going down when Fredric heard moaning coming from the underbrush. He followed the sound and saw Seth's body lying there.

Fredric then picked Seth up and ran several miles towards his winery.

He carried Seth into the building where the transfusions took place and gently placed him on a bed.

Fredric then gave Seth a transfusion using his own blood. Fredric worked fast as he inserted a needle that extended from a narrow tube into his vein and then inserted the needle at the other end into Seth's vein, allowing his blood to flow freely into Seth.

About twenty minutes later Seth opened his eyes. He realized what was happening to him now, but he could not remember why he would be getting a transfusion.

The very last thing he could remember was standing alongside Lotada and they were about to marry.

When Seth turned his head, he saw his father giving him blood. "Why am I here? What happened to me?" he asked.

"It's a long story. Do you remember anything?" Fredric asked.

"No, not a thing," Seth said, "Where is Lotada, and mother?"

"I want you to rest now we will talk about what happened later," Fredric said as Seth closed his eyes and fell asleep.

Meanwhile, Lotada was so distraught that Leona and Joseph carried her to an upstairs bedroom, applied a cold compress to her far head, and tried to calm her down.

A short while later, Lotada calmed down enough to asked Leona, "What happened to me? Where is Seth?"

"I want you to rest here for a while, and then we will talk. In the meantime, I will sit next to you. Now try to close your eyes and get some rest."

Lotada took hold of Leona's hand, "I must have had a bad dream."

Leona continued to hold onto Lotada's hand until she fell asleep.

As the night turned into morning Fredric sent a telepathic message to Leona, "Seth is alright and I will be home with him later."

Leona just sat there holding Lotada's hand as tears rolled down her cheeks.

Back in Scranton, Doc Langer and John Saber became fast friends.

"When would you like me to become a disciple and what would my duties be?" John asked.

Doc replied, "You would eventually be working under me but first you must drink the wine for several days until you feel the affects of change. Then you must, and most important, follow my instructions. If you can prove to us that you are capable, we will make you one of our disciples. You will then become immortal and have special powers."

"What powers?" he asked.

"Sit here and watch me," Doc said. Then he shot two laser beams from his eyes hitting several of the liquor bottles that were sitting on top of the bar causing them to explode.

"Amazed by what he saw, John asked, "Will I be able to have this power?"

"If you follow our rules in the future you will be given these powers and more. Most important, if this is what you choose, while your body changes over, you cannot walk into the sunlight or you will burn up and die a painful death the same way the other towns people did. Why don't you think about this and let me know what you want to do."

Without any hesitation, John said, "I thought about it while you were speaking and I am willing if you are."

"Good," Doc said. "Let me pour you a glass of my special wine, you'll enjoy drinking this, it has a sweet taste."

Seth slept for several hours at the winery. When he opened his eyes, much to his surprise, he saw Fredric sitting on a chair next to him.

Seth tried to sit up only to fall back on the bed from weakness. After a few minutes, with Fredric's help, Seth was able to sit up and then walk around.

Fredric then told Seth everything that happened the day he was supposed to marry Lotada.

Seth looked at his father in disbelief, "How do I explain to Lotada that I killed her father?"

"Did you tell Lotada that you were attached and bitten by a wolf a few weeks ago?

No, I did not," Seth answered; I did not want her to worry about me."

"You could never have expected something like this to happen," said Fredric.

"Does Lotada know about her father's death?"

"No," Fredric answered.

"I think we should go home now," Seth said anxiously.

As Fredric and Seth left the winery to go back home, Lotada was just waking up.

When Lotada opened her eyes she saw Leona sitting on a chair next to her holding her hand wearing the same gown she had on the night before.

"I just had a terrible dream. Why are you sitting here?" Lotada asked.

"Don't you remember anything?" Leona asked, as she leaned over giving Lotada a kiss on her far head.

Not answering, she asked, "What happened to me? Where is Seth?"

As Leona helped Lotada off the bed she told her, "Fredric and Seth will be here soon and we will all sit down and talk."

In the mean time, Leona and Lotada went down stairs to the parlor to wait for Fredric and Seth to come home.

Leona then offered Lotada something to eat. "I thought vampires do not ear food?"

"They eat food on special occasions, but you should have something to eat in the meantime, you are not a vampire yet," Leona told her.

While Joseph prepared something light for Lotada to eat she asked Leona, "What happened to Seth? I know what I saw, so what would cause him to change like that?" Leona began, "I guess Seth did not tell you."

"Tell me what?" Lotada asked.

"Several weeks ago, while Seth was walking home from your village, he was attacked and bitten by a wolf. Seth killed the wolf, but Fredric and I believe that the wolf carried a disease that he gave to Seth. We were not sure until the other night. We should not have had your wedding during the full moon."

Just then, Fredric and Seth came walking through the front door.

When Seth saw Lotada sitting in the parlor he put his head down saying, "I am very sorry for what happened but I do not remember what I did or why I did it. I do know that I ruined our wedding and embarrassed you and my family, but I have something to tell you, Lotada that is a lot worse."

Lotada, with a puzzled look on her face, walked over to Seth and held his hand, "What is it that you have to tell me?" she asked.

Seth appeared ashamed as he tried to explain. "Lotada, a very serious thing happened to me. A wolf bit me a few weeks ago and I changed into a werewolf during the full moon. Then a very horrifying thing happened. I have no memory of this, but my father told me what I did."

"What are you trying to tell me?" she asked.

"My father told me that I entered your village and killed your father and one of his warriors."

"What do you mean? You are not a murderer; you could not do anything like that." Seth, fearing that he will lose Lotada for good said, "I do not know how you will feel towards me after knowing this, but this was not me, the person you love, this was someone else, a werewolf, a monster, but you must believe that this cannot arise in me again."

"My father found me outside the village and carried me to the winery where he gave me a transfusion using his own blood."

"Please Lotada, you know me all my life, I love you. Say you still love me," he pleaded. "Everyone in the village believes your father was killed by a wolf, not by me."

Lotada, sad and angry, told Seth she wanted to go to her village to be with her mother. Seth reluctantly agreed as they walked together in total silence.

When they neared the village Seth told Lotada, "Go the rest of the way by yourself. I can only hope that you will feel differently towards me in time. If you do, all you have to do is think deeply about me and I will hear you."

Seth stood there watching as Lotada reached her village, then sadly walked back home.

Doc Langer and Pulaski returned home from their trip two weeks after that horrible incident. Knowing what happened, he was glad to see Seth with Fredric in front of the house as they arrived.

Doc was also excited to tell Fredric about their new disciple, John Saber.

"I see you are coming back with an empty wagon, Scotty must have been pleasantly surprised to see you," Fredric said.

"He was very surprised and he is also dead."

A troubled look appeared on Fredric's face as Doc explained what happened.

"We found ourselves a new disciple. He goes by the name of John Sabor and I observed him for a week. I believe he will be very loyal to us. He has no responsibilities except to us. I am sure he will be the perfect man to help build the territory."

"You are doing a very good job for us Doc."

Pleased by Fredric's comment, Doc thanked him then climbed back onto the wagon and rode off to the winery.

Seth, who spent most of his time feeling depressed and staying at home, asked Fredric, "Father, can I go with Captain Ulrich on his next trip?"

"That sounds like a good idea," he replied.

He knew that time and distance would help Seth get over the incident.

Three days later Fredric received a message from Bob Stillwell, his plant manager, saying that their next shipment of regular wine was ready.

Fredric thought that it would be a good idea to have Seth go with Captain Ulrich to the coast of Virginia to find new disciples where they could deliver this shipment.

After the wine was loaded onto the ship they were ready to sail.

Fredric and Leona gave Seth a hug and told him, "By the time you get back every thing will be all right."

They waved to Seth as they stood on the dock watching as Captain Ulrich took charge as the ship moved slowly towards the mouth of the Hudson.

After several days of sailing down the Atlantic Coast, they finally landed at their destination. It was a small town on the tip of a peninsular called Cape Charles, which was located off the coast of mainland Virginia.

After docking, Captain Ulrich and Seth decided to venture ashore.

They were looking for the nearest saloon, which they found in the center of this busy town. The saloon was filled with plenty of smoke and noisy patrons. Most of the men were wearing grey uniforms, some were dancing with young women and others were sitting at the bar or at tables drinking.

Seth and the captain were then approached by a waitress who asked them, in her thick southern drawl, "Do you gentlemen need a table?"

The captain nodded and she sat them at a small table near the center of the room, "What can I get for you?" she asked.

"Bring me a bottle of your best bourbon and bring my young friend a bottle of your best red wine," the captain replied.

As the two sat with their drinks, Seth observed the patrons hoping to find a future disciple.

After sitting there for an hour or so, the place became very crowded when Seth and the captain noticed a very well dressed young man looking for a place to sit.

After passing by Seth and the captain's table several times, he stopped and stood near them. Seth got up and asked, "Sir, you can join us if you like."

"Well that's mighty nice of you. I'll be happy to join you," he replied. He extended his hand to Seth and introduced himself, "My name is Henry Radcliff, nice to meet you and you are?"

"Seth, Seth Gruel and this is Captain Ulrich. We are from New Jersey."

"What brings you way down here?" Henry asked.

"We are in the wine business and are looking for more customers," Seth told him.

"This must be your lucky day. I have a wholesale food business that supplies saloons, restaurants and some small general stores throughout the entire South. Maybe we can do some business together." Henry suggested.

Seth, excited to think that he might be attaining a new customer and possibly a new disciple all by himself replied, "Maybe today is a lucky day for both of us."

Seth called over the waitress and told her, "Give this gentleman anything he wants to drink."

The waitress told Seth, "You mean Henry? He'll drink anything you put in front of him."

"Then bring a bottle of anything," Seth said, making them all laugh.

"Where do you make your wines?' Henry inquired.

"We have our own vineyards and winery in New Jersey," Seth answered then continued, "My father brought the original grape vines from Transylvania to America many years ago. We make a variety of wines that have been proven to be very successful. Then we make a special, sweet red wine for those people who want to become immortal and live forever."

Not believing what he heard, Henry asked, "What did you just say?"

Seth repeated, "We make a special, sweet red wine for those people who want to become immortal and live forever."

"That sounds like a very good vintage," Henry said, still not quite believing what he heard, as the three men laughed.

"Immortal, doesn't that mean forever, for eternity?"

"That's right," Seth said just as the waitress returned with a bottle of red wine for Henry.

Seth then poured the wine into Henry's glass and they raised their glasses as Seth proposed a toast, "To life and to the beauty of life."

"That was a beautiful toast," Henry said as he raised his glass also making a toast, "To new friends and future business."

The three men sat at the table talking until Henry finished his wine and stood up, "Some of us have to go to work tomorrow. Here is my card, why don't you stop by my office in the morning so we can continue this conversation."

After Henry left, Seth and the captain, feeling a sense of accomplishment, walked back to the ship.

Early the next morning Seth and the captain decided to pay Henry a visit. They walked into his office that was located in front of his warehouse and were greeted by a worker,

"How can I help you gentlemen?"

"We are looking for Henry Radcliff."

The worker instructed them to follow him into the warehouse.

Once inside the warehouse Seth and the captain could see at least three dozen black men loading and unloading wagons of produce, meat and other general goods.

Just then a wagon pulled up alongside the warehouse and Henry stepped down and walked directly over to Seth and the captain and extended his hand, "Good morning gentlemen, I see you found me."

"You have a very impressive warehouse," Seth said as Henry offered to show them around.

Henry then began to explain his operation, "Just about all of our merchandise comes in either by way of the ocean or the river. All our tobacco products and cotton come to us overland and our produce is delivered by ship. Only our whiskey is imported from Europe. Our general merchandise comes from the north and fabrics from the south."

"So what can I do for you?" Seth asked.

"Let's go to my office," Henry said.

Once inside Henry's office he asked, "Gentlemen, I know it is early, but would either of you care to join me in a drink?"

Seth said no, but the captain asked for bourbon.

"I knew you were a drinking man," he said as he poured a glass for the captain.

"You used the word immortal last evening and I just want to make sure you were not joking. I am an educated man so I believe I know the meaning of the word immortality but what does it mean to you?"

Seth replied that he was not joking. "I can give you the power to live forever if you decide you want this. You will become one of my father's disciples, and then possibly a vampire."

"I did hear about vampires when I was in Europe last year. They suck the blood from people then they return from the dead," Henry said with uncertainty.

"Not quite, that was the old fashioned way," Seth answered. "My father, Dr. Fredric Gruel is the son of Count Von Gruel who was not only a blood sucking vampire but also a ruthless killer of thousands. He killed just for the love of it. He was the last of the blood-sucking vampires. My father destroyed him and he developed a wine that enables us to drink and be a vampire without the need for human blood. I drink a minimum of four bottles a day and do not have any desire for fresh blood."

"We lead our lives just like any other mortal."

"And what makes you think that I would want to be immortal?" asked Henry.

"Because you are a successful businessman who could watch his business grow throughout eternity," Seth replied.

"You are talking about life, what about death? You use the word eternity, and if I understand you correctly, I cannot die or ever be killed?"

"I did not say that," Seth said. "I am saying that if you follow our rules you could live for eternity with special powers."

Henry asked, in a pessimistic manner, "And what kind of special powers will I have?"

"Follow me," said Seth, and the three men went outside to the back of the warehouse. Seth told Henry to keep his eyes on an old broken wagon. Shooting two laser beams from his eyes across a narrow road, Seth hit the wagon causing it to burst into flames.

Henry, not believing any of this said, "What kind of a fool do you take me for? That was just a trick."

"You pick the target, any target," Seth said.

"Okay, do you see that old warehouse across the road?" Henry asked.

"Okay, keep your eye on it," Seth told him. Then two red laser rays shot out from Seth's eyes hitting the warehouse as they all watched it burst into flames.

"Thank you that was my competitor's warehouse you just burnt down. Now you are making a believer out of me."

Just then, Henry's competitor came running down the street with another man and each was carrying a loaded musket. They both aimed and fired their guns at Henry. Just as the musket balls were about to hit Henry, Seth stepped in front of him catching the bullets in his hand and handed them to Henry. Then the two men reloaded and were about to shoot again but Seth shot two lasers, hitting each gun before they could fire again.

"How did you know they were coming at us with loaded guns?" Henry asked.

"When you told me that it was your competitor's warehouse, I thought, "Someone is going to come after you, so I focused my mind on your competitor."

Henry appeared very impressed with what Seth showed him, "Why don't we all go back to my office and discuss your proposition."

The three men sat down in Henry's office. "Captain," Henry said, "After what I just saw, I'm going to pour myself some bourbon, how about you?"

"You just keep pouring, I'll tell you when to stop," answered the captain.

Two bottles of Bourbon later, Henry asked the captain, "How much of this Bourbon can you drink?"

"Henry, as much as you can pour, you see, I am also a vampire. You cannot get me drunk."

Annoyed, Henry told the captain, "You should have told me this before I took out a second bottle of the good stuff."

"Now let's get down to business. If you join us I will make you one of our territorial lieutenants, which will allow you to convert men and women into vampires or what we call disciples. Once they are converted, they will follow your commands and you will follow my father's or my commands," Seth explained.

"What if I disapprove of what you request of me?" Henry asked.

"One of your powers will be telepathy and we could talk through each other's mind. If we are constantly in disagreement or if you do not follow our orders, you will be removed."

"On the other hand, you could become a very wealthy man, well beyond your greatest visions. As our expansion takes on greater meaning so would your importance to us. You can become governor of Virginia and live for hundreds of years like my father."

"All we ask is for your loyalty. We will supply you with our regular wines which you can sell and our special wine which is only for our disciples."

"If you say yes to this proposition I will stay with you for a week while you go through the transition of becoming immortal, but if you abuse or misuse the powers we give you, it's simple, you will die."

After thinking about what Seth just told him, Henry surmised," This is like selling your soul to the devil."

"Not exactly, you can become a true southern leader and your life will go on as usual. No one would have to know what you have become."

Looking into Seth's eyes, Henry asked, "What will kill me, there has to be something that could kill a vampire?"

"Any wooden object going straight through your heart could kill you. I am sure you noticed by now that Captain Ulrich and I wear colored glasses when we go outside. Our eyes must be protected when we go out into sunlight. If we do not wear them, we will burn and die a painful death. If someone threw holy water on me, I would disintegrate. You cannot die from disease or old age."

"What else would you like to know?"

"That will be all for now, Henry said, "Why don't we meet for dinner this evening in the saloon and I will give you my answer. Let's say eight o'clock?"

"We'll be there," Seth said.

"By the way, are you going to talk to anyone else about this?" Henry asked as Seth and the captain were about to leave.

"That depends on your answer, see you tonight."

When Seth and the captain reached the ship, several of the crewmen were lying on the deck wearing their protective glasses waiting for orders.

As Seth climbed onto the deck he noticed a crowd of towns' people coming towards the ship bearing muskets and shouting, "This is Satan's ship."

Then the crowd began to shoot their muskets at the crewmen hitting one of them causing him to fall over the side of the ship and land in front of the mob. His protective glasses fell off, and then his body disintegrated.

The crowd watched in horror and disbelief then ran away.

Seth kept a few men on deck to keep watch while he went below to his cabin.

He grabbed a bottle of wine and held his head as he began to receive a telepathic message from Lotada, "Seth, I miss you. Please come back to me as soon as you can. I understand what happened and I forgive you."

Seth lay down on his bed, closed his eyes and sent a message to Lotada, "I'm very glad to hear that you miss me, I miss you too and I am very sorry for everything that has happened. I love you."

Lotada messaged back, "I understand."

Seth then closed his eyes and fell asleep.

HENRY RADCLIFF'S CONVICTION

Later that evening Seth decided to meet with Henry by himself and leave the captain behind incase there was trouble.

Henry was already at the saloon when Seth arrived. Seth walked over to him holding a bottle of his special wine. "What do you have there?" Henry inquired.

"This is for you if you decide to join us."

"I heard there was an incident by your ship, is it true?" Henry asked.

"My crew was not expecting anyone to attack them, "Seth replied.

"Could this happen to me?" Henry asked.

"Not with the additional powers you will have, Seth began, "I have already spoken to my father about you. He was very pleased."

Perplexed, Henry said, "I thought he was five hundred miles away."

"He is but we speak to each other through our telepathic minds. You would also have the same powers."

Henry, now excited said, "Let's drink before I change my mind," as he opened Seth's bottle of special wine and poured it into Seth's glass, then his.

Henry raised his glass and made a toast, "To life and to the beauty of life." Seth gave Henry a big smile as they clicked their glasses together.

"When do I get started," Henry asked.

"We will make this your first bottle of wine."

"Let me know how you feel in the morning, and then I will bring more bottles to your warehouse. In the mean time let's see if this bottle has any affect on you."

"I would like to get back to my ship now. After the incident this afternoon, one can never tell what people will try to do. See you in the morning."

Seth stood up to shake Henry's hand and left the saloon.

He soon felt that he was being followed as he walked back to the ship.

When he was near the edge of town, he ducked in between two buildings. That is when he saw a large group of men carrying muskets and bats and heading towards his ship. Seth decided to let them pass until they reached an open field where he called out to them, taking them by surprise, "Can I help you gentlemen?" Seth called out again, "Is there any way I can help you?"

One of them shouted, "You're the devil."

"What if I am?" Seth shouted back. Another raised his musket to shoot. Seth, using his powers, made all their muskets fly out of their hands and land across the field.

The entire mob tried to rush Seth and he just stared at them and shouted, "Stop, stop before someone gets hurt."

The mob kept coming. That's when Seth shot two laser beams in front of them causing high flames to erupt, encircling the mob preventing them from fleeing.

Seth just watched as the men screamed for help inside the wall of flames. He soon decided that the men had enough. He put out the fire and the men scattered in all directions.

Seth continued to walk back to the ship as if nothing had happened.

Early the next morning Seth and some of his crew unloaded several cases of his special wine and several cases of his regular wine from the ship onto the back of Henry's buckboard. On the assumption that Henry will become a future disciple, Seth went along with the driver.

As they approached Henry's warehouse the sound of a shot rang out from behind a building across the street and the driver fell off the buckboard.

Henry ran outside when he heard the shot and was hit in the arm by another shot.

Seth was able to see where the gunmen were shooting from so he shot laser beams from his eyes and hit and killed the two gunmen.

Seth picked Henry up and carried him into his office where he tore off his jacket and shirtsleeve to see where he was wounded.

The musket ball had pierced through Henry's right arm causing a lot of bleeding.

Seth, who was not accustomed to seeing real human blood, just stared at the bleeding arm. During the excitement, Seth placed his finger on the open wound and brought it up to his mouth to taste.

Henry, in agonizing pain, opened his eyes, looked up at Seth begging him for help.

By now, Seth had put his mouth over the open wound and continued to enjoy the taste of the blood while looking down at Henry.

One of Henry's workers came over to Seth and said, "Let me help you, I'll hold his arm."

Seth suddenly realized what he was doing and quickly placed his hand over the wound as it began to heal, in front of everyone's eyes.

After Henry was feeling better, he told Seth, "I was getting nervous. I thought for a minute that you were going to drink all my blood."

"I was," Seth replied.

He then helped Henry to a chair and brought him a bottle of the special wine to drink.

As Henry drank from the bottle, he asked, "What happened to my powers?"

"Give it a few weeks, next time you will see the musket shot coming," Seth told him as he handed him a pair of his special glasses.

"For my sake I hope you're right," Henry said as he put the glasses on.

Seth suggested they start unloading the wine from the buckboard, "If you keep this wine in the sun for any length of time it will disintegrate."

"I'm glad you told me, there is nothing worse than losing good wine," Henry said. He then called out to a few of his workers to help unload the wine.

Seth spent the next several days with Henry to teach him as much as possible.

Seth was very anxious to go home but Henry insisted that the three men have a drink together at the saloon the night before Seth and the captain were to sail home.

That evening they met at the saloon. They sat down at a table and Henry, with a funny look on his face said, I seem to have lost my appetite."

Seth and the captain looked at each other and then Seth said to Henry, "Welcome, you are now a disciple of a select group of vampires."

Seth took out a bottle of his special wine from under his jacket and poured a glass for each of them. Henry then made the toast, "To life and to the beauty of life."

"Seth," Henry said, "I never thanked you for saving my life."

"I am glad I did and you will never have this problem again," Seth assured him.

Seth and the captain felt comfortable about leaving Henry by himself.

They were now confident that they found a good man that would help their cause grow in the south.

His parting words to Henry, before boarding the ship was, "If you have anything to discuss with me or my father, all you have to do is think of either of us and we will respond to you. You will do fine."

SETH RETURNS TO EDGEWATER

By the time Seth and the crew arrived back in Edgewater, the problems that he had before he left were far behind him.

As Seth descended from the ship, he was delighted to see Fredric, Leona and Lotada waiting for him on the pier. As Seth approached, Lotada ran up to him and gave him a hug. It was then that Leona noticed physical changes in Seth's appearance. When Lotada let go of Seth she also notice changes, the sides of his hair had turned grey and he looked as if he aged slightly.

"I missed all of you," Seth said.

Leona stepped back and looked at Seth, "You look different and your voice has changed, did anything happened to you while you were away?" "Only good things mother, only good things."

Seth put his arm around Lotada and they began walking towards their house with Fredric and Leona following.

By the time they reached the house Doc Langer was there waiting for them. They all walked into the parlor, Fredric brought in several bottles of wine, and poured it into everyone's glass including Lotada's.

Before drinking, Fredric raised his glass making his toast, "To life and to the beauty of life."

After drinking the wine Seth looked directly at Lotada, "Do you realize what you are drinking?" Lotada looked at Seth and gave him a big smile, "I know exactly what I am drinking."

THE CIVIL WAR ERUPTS

Several years past and Fredric purchased more land on the New York and New Jersey sides of the Hudson River.

As his wealth and business increased substantially so did his number of disciples. It was most important to Fredric that his growth would be throughout the United States not just the northeast. This was due to the hard work of Doc Langer, Henry Radcliff and John Saber who proved to be very loyal disciples.

The year was now 1861 and there were a lot of problems brewing between the Northern and Southern states and it was threatening to destroy the Republic of the United States.

After the southern forces of the Confederate Army attacked Fort Sumter in April of 1862, it was obvious that the Confederate Army was a lot stronger than previously thought.

This army, led by the newly elected Jefferson Davis, wanted the south to have their own confederacy and break away from the union.

President Lincoln was becoming increasingly worried about the loss of men and battles caused by the strong southern forces. He was under a great deal of pressure to crush the south and show his leadership as commander and chief of the Union armies, plus he had to show many of his colleagues in Washington that the northern states were capable of defeating the confederacy before the war would get out of control.

Back in New Jersey, Fredric and Seth continued to build their business.

Seth and Lotada were married and built their own home several acres away from Fredric and Leona.

As time went on Seth gradually began to handle more of the business end of the wineries, guiding its growth.

During the early part of July 1862, Seth received a disturbing message from Henry Radcliff advising him that there had been naval blockades set up by the north that could affect their wine business and the acquisition of more disciples.

Seth sent a return message to Henry stating that he would make the next run himself with Captain Ulrich and he would let him know when he was leaving.

After a few days of receiving Henry's frantic telepathic messages telling him what was going on in the south, Captain Ulrich and Seth had the ship loaded with wine and other dry goods and was ready to try and run the northern blockade.

Not only was the northern blockade preventing Seth's wine from getting through, it was hindering the south from receiving goods from Europe and additional slaves from being brought over from Africa.

The ship that Seth and Captain Ulrich traveled on was the same ship that Fredric used when he came to America. It had no guns and no means of protection, except for Seth, Captain Ulrich and the crew's powers.

Seth knew he must get the wine through if he was going to sustain Henry and his disciples before he ran out of wine, and also to prevent Henry and his men from turning into full fledged vampires.

As they continued to sail south, Seth received a message from Henry telling him that he was beginning to run low on their wine reserve.

Captain Ulrich tried desperately to keep the wind to his back in order to keep up a fast pace to reach Henry in a timely manner.

As they sailed closer to Cape Charles the lookout from the high mast called out, "Ships ahead, ships ahead."

Captain Ulrich went to the bow, looked through his telescope, and saw three war ships flying the union flag coming towards them. The captain immediately called out to Seth, "What should we do?"

Seth called back to the captain, "Keep sailing, fly the colors of the Union with a white flag but keep the sails up and the wind to your back."

As the three Union war ships came closer, Seth and the captain could hear the sound of cannon fire. They realized that they were being fired upon, when the shells landed across the bow of their ship.

Captain Ulrich called out to Seth, "They will sink us if we don't stop and let them board."

Seth, not wanting to take any action towards the Union ships, yelled back to the Captain, "Try to sail closer to shore, maybe we can out run them."

As the captain steered closer to the shore, a second cannon shot rang out landing in front of their ship.

"We're to close to the shore line we must move away," the captain shouted.

Seth then raised his hands and caused large waves to appear from behind the union ships. They grew higher and higher until the waves overtook the three ships causing one to turn on its side.

The other two tried to move forward to reach the sinking ship that was now taking on water fast, when two laser beams shot from Seth's eyes hit one of the ships in the bow.

Leaving the distressed ships behind, Captain Ulrich continued to sail towards Cape Charles.

Keeping in close contact with Henry Radcliff, Seth sent him a message saying he would be arriving that night and he should bring several wagons to meet him.

By the time the ship arrived, Henry was already waiting on the dock with his men. When the ship pulled along side the dock the crew immediately lowered the plank.

Henry, who was very glad to see Seth and the captain, ran up the plank to greet them, "I don't usually get nervous but this time I was. How did you get through the blockade?"

"It was not easy, but we managed to out run it," Seth replied and then asked, "How bad is it in the south?"

"Because of the blockades by the north it is creating shortages on most merchandise and day to day living is getting more difficult for the average person, especially if you're in the liquor business. It has created shortages of good wine," Henry advised.

"What about bourbon?" the captain asked quizzically. Henry looked at the captain and said, "For you captain, I will always have bourbon. Let's go to my office."

After the three men walked down the plank towards the buckboard, Henry's men began to cheer as they unloaded the cargo of wine.

It was a very overcast evening with a heavy fog blowing across the bay and a mist coming off the surrounding swamps, and you could still hear the sound of cannon fire from across the bay.

The men continued to unload the cargo as Seth, Henry and the captain rode away.

When they reached the warehouse, the first thing Henry did was take Seth and the captain into the warehouse.

"This will give you some idea of how bad things are getting," Henry said, looking at his nearly empty shelves. The confederate army is beginning to run out of goods. This makes life down here very difficult."

"How many disciples do you have now?" Seth asked.

"About nine hundred and growing," Henry proudly answered.

"Splendid," Seth said.

"There will be a problem if you are not able to keep up with the delivery of your wine," Henry explained.

"It is getting more difficult with the on going blockade, but I have an idea that might work," Seth continued, "do not add anymore disciples until I can break the blockade, which could be soon."

"On our way here we were attacked by three northern blockade ships. When we refused to back down, they fired on us. I used my powers to sink one of them and disable the other two. Then we were able to out run them."

"That calls for a celebration," Henry said as he took out a bottle of wine and filled three glasses, then raised his glass and made a toast, "To the breaking of the blockade." Seth then added, "To life and to the beauty of life."

After drinking the wine, Henry told the captain, "I didn't forget you, how about some bourbon?"

The captain looked at Henry with a big smile on his face and then said, "I heard the war has not been going well for the south even though they have achieved a few victories. It seems that your northern General McDowell has not proven himself and he might be replaced by General McClellan."

Seth interrupted, "I also heard that the south has some secretive commando force fighting for them that no one wants to talk about. Do you know anything about them?"

Henry said he heard the same thing, "They're supposed to be a small secretive army of paid rebel soldiers brought over from Europe just to fight the north. I also heard they have no honor and they kill just for the love of it. Even our soldiers were told to stay away from them. Nobody knows or talks about where their camp is located. They just keep moving around at night and surprise the enemy when it gets dark, leaving no survivors."

Seth told Henry that he will increase his shipping to him but repeated to him that he must not recruit any more disciples for the time being.

"How are your disciples working for you?" Seth asked.

"They are all working very well for me and I don't foresee any problems as long as the wine keeps coming."

"The captain and I will be leaving this evening when the tide goes out, but I will look into this secretive army and continue to communicate with you."

"Henry," Seth said, "we are very pleased with the work you are doing, but if you notice any change in the behavior of your disciples, it is extremely important that you notify me at once."

Henry stood up and shook hands with Seth and the captain as they both were leaving. Henry noticed that the captain was holding on to a bottle of bourbon, so he shouted out to him, "Captain, why don't you keep the bottle."

As the captain and Seth were driving back to the ship, Seth told the captain, "I am very concerned about this army that only fights at night."

"I can understand your concern; we must discuss this matter with your father."

THE BEGINNING OF THE FIGHT

After boarding the ship, Captain Ulrich wasted no time in calling out to his crew and first mate, "Raise the sails we leave as soon as the tide goes out."

There were strong gusts of wind still blowing off the cape and the air was still and thick with mist and fog which were hovering over the water, but it was crucial that they leave with the first tide.

Seth stood at the bow of the ship as the moon took hold from behind fast moving, dark clouds.

Then from the stern, Seth heard the captain call out, "Raise the anchor we will sail north by northeast, be careful of the shoreline and look out for reefs until we reach deep water."

The crew knew exactly what to do as they headed towards deep water.

Seth stayed on the bow of the ship with his head bowed to the moon which was directly above him.

When the cloud cover thickened and Seth could no longer see the moon he went to his cabin to send his father a message about the commandos that were only attacking Union troops at night.

A SURPRISE FOR FREDRIC

That evening, as Fredric was sitting in his parlor, he began to receive a telepathic message from Seth telling him about the commandos that came over from Europe to fight for the south.

He messaged back, "Find out what part of Europe they came from, and how they fight."

Seth then contacted Henry," Where in Europe do these commandos come from and how do they kill? Also try and get their leaders name."

"This may take a few days but I will find out what I can," replied Henry.

As Captain Ulrich sailed the ship out of the bay into open waters, the crewman on the mast called out, "Several ships ahead flying the Union flags."

The captain sent for Seth to come topside.

"What's the matter?" he asked.

"We spotted several Union war ships sailing in our direction."

"Have they spotted us yet? Can we sail around them," Seth asked.

"I think they were waiting for us to come out of the bay. It looks like they are trying to encircle us, what should we do?" the captain asked.

"This looks like it is turning into a game of chess. I need to give this some thought," Seth said as he went back to his cabin to send a message to his father explaining the situation.

"Seth, you must go topside and concentrate on what you have to do in order to stop those ships. Think it out and use logic," Fredric told him.

Seth walked up to the bow of the ship just as cannon shots zipped across the bow and landed in the water near by. A second hail of shots fired from another ship hit the front mast causing it to fall.

As the Captain steered his ship into open waters, he realized that there were many more war ships than they thought.

Seth knew he was surrounded. He also knew that he did not have the experience and knowledge to use his powers to fight off so many ships.

Without thoroughly thinking this through, he raised his hands towards the sky, faced the moon with his head raised and began to say, "Help me grandfather I am the son of Fredric. I need your help. Do not leave me here to die. I am asking for your help and forgiveness for my father and myself. Please hear me. You are the demon of all demons and I am asking for your strength. Show me your powers."

After a few moments, the waters around the Union ships slowly began to swirl and continued to swirl faster and faster.

The Union ships fired their cannons as thick dark clouds formed over them creating high winds and bolts of lightening that shot down from the dark clouds hitting one of the ships in its mast.

The mast fell on a keg of gunpowder that exploded on impact. Then high waves began to rise and break over the other Union ships as funnels of swirling water spouted up reaching high up into the sky.

As the waves continued to rise from the center of the ocean, the Union ships were tossed around like toys. Then gale force winds lifted the Union ships up from the turbulent sea creating large funnels of water then crashed them down into a large sinkhole that sucked the Union ships to the bottom of the sea, one by one.

Seth stood on the bow of the ship watching as the Union ships were being swallowed up by the sea.

Then the skies cleared and the ocean became calm as if nothing had happened. Seth bowed his head, "Thank you grandfather."

The captain was still holding the steering wheel trying to control the ship.

When Seth walked towards him, while assessing the damage caused by the cannon fire, he told the captain, "It seems we're having a rough evening. How are you holding up?"

"I'm glad this does not happen to often," the captain replied.

Looking towards the horizon, the captain advised, "There are several more war ships out there but we should be able to sail around them."

Seth left the captain to do his job and went to his cabin.

He lay down, closed his eyes, and began to send a message to Fredric telling him what took place. When Seth told his father that he prayed to Count Gruel for help, Fredric became extremely upset, "Why would you pray to the man that I hated and killed? How could you do such a thing?"

Seth explained that he was scared and did not know what to do. "I needed someone from the dark side to help me."

Fredric, feeling betrayed by his own son avoided any more conversation, "You should be home within three days, and we will talk then."

Three days later Seth sailed up the Hudson River and noticed Fredric and Leona waiting patiently on the pier.

As the ship approached, Seth waved to his father and mother but did not get a response from either of them.

After the ship docked, Captain Ulrich ordered the plank to be lowered.

Leona and Fredric went aboard the ship before any of the crew was able to leave. They walked directly to Seth, "We must talk in your cabin."

When they entered the cabin Fredric asked Seth, "Where do you keep the wine?"

Seth walked over to a closed cabinet and took out a bottle of wine and three grasses. Seth poured the wine into their glasses as Fredric immediately began to drink without making his usual toast.

Seth sat quietly not saying a word, waiting for his father to speak.

Fredric kept looking straight at him then said, "How could you do this to me? How could you be so stupid as to pray and ask for help from my father's soul? He was evil, I hated him and I killed him. Tell me what you were thinking." Seth did not reply to his father.

Fredric yelled out, "Say something."

Seth then began to talk to Fredric for the first time with anger in his voice. "I had no choice, and there were nine Union war ships to our one, firing on us. I had no choice," he answered.

"You had plenty of choices and you had me," Fredric said.

"You told me to do what was necessary and I did that, father."

Fredric answered in a harsh voice, "You don't understand. I thought I taught you better. We are talking about your leadership and our lives. Get that through your head."

Confused, Seth said, "Father, please explain to me what I did that was so wrong."

Leona, walking over to Fredric, placed her hands on his shoulders, trying to calm him down, "Seth is our son, explain to him the consequences of what he has done."

Fredric began to explain, "Even though I killed Count Gruel, his spirit still lives. I found out that his spirit is controlling my older brother, Ludwig who is leading the commando forces and fighting with the Confederate troops now."

Meekly Seth said, "Father I had no idea."

Fredric stood up and paced around the cabin, "That's right, you had no idea. Well, we must put our heads together and think of how we are going to approach and solve this problem."

Seth then said, "I have an idea father. We have over two thousand disciples that we can call upon,"

"Yes, but do they know how to fight real vampires? We must communicate with Henry Radcliff and Doc Langer at once and explain the situation. We must all be able to combine our powers in order to stop my brother."

"I understand perfectly, father, and I deeply apologize for what I have done."

Leona went over to Seth and placed her arms around him, "I am very proud of what you and your father are doing. Now I think you should go home to Lotada. Tell her you missed her and tell her how much you love her. I know everything will be all right."

Seth stood up, kissed his mother on the cheek and then left.

Fredric then called upon Doc Langer to come to the main house to discuss the problems they faced.

Seth quietly walked up behind Lotada, who was on her knees plant-ing vegetable seeds for the people in her village, placed both hands over her breasts, startling her, causing her to jump up and turn around quickly. Not realizing who it was, she punched Seth in the face causing him to fall down. As Seth lay on the ground, Lotada stood over him, embarrassed, with her hands covering her face.

Seth just lay there looking up at her said, "That's some way to greet your husband." Then he began to laugh.

Lotada, looking down at Seth with a very serious look on her face said, "That's some way to greet your wife." Then they both began to laugh.

"Help me up," Seth said as he extended his hand to her.

Lotada extended her hand to help Seth. He then grabbed her hand, pulling her down on top of him and began to kiss her. "I needed that kiss," he said and he kissed her again as they rolled all through the veg-etable garden.

Just then, Seth began to receive a message from Fredric to return to his house immediately.

Seth, knowing that he was already in hot water with his father, decided he had better go to him at once.

On the way to Fredric's house, he told Lotada what happened on the ship and what he did. She took Seth by the arm, stepped in front of him giving him a playful kiss, "I am very proud of you. You did the best you could and I'm glad you are home."

They walked into the house where Fredric, Leona, Captain Ulrich and Doc Langer were all sitting and discussing the situation.

THE MEETING

As Seth entered the parlor, he looked around the room noticing grim expressions on everyone's face.

Fredric stood up and began to speak, "As you know, since we have been in this country, our wine business has grown tenfold and so has the number of disciples that we have recruited. We have had only one death among us in the last twenty-five years and that was Scotty who broke our rules. As promised, I have managed to protect all of you. I have watched our company grow and all of us prosper, but for the first time I feel that we are threatened."

"As you all know I am the son of Count Vlad Gruel, but what you do not know is that I have an older brother, Ludwig Von Gruel who had a large army of vampires in the Baltic's. I do not believe he knew about my experiments or that I came to America, until now. The problem is that they are real vampires that kill and drink the blood of mortals and I believe they are the secret commandos who are now fighting with the Confederate forces. It will be up to us to outsmart my brother and his army. Also, my brother and his army are the only power that could totally annihilate us."

"Doc Langer, what do you think?"

"I think we should fight blood with blood," he replied.

"What do you mean, blood with blood?"

"Just that, blood with blood. Why can't we take one hundred of our best disciples and turn them into real vampires? All we would need is one hundred of them to be willing to be turned. Between Henry, you, Seth and myself, I am sure we could put a raiding party together and attack them. They will never expect us. What do you think of that idea?"

Fredric, trying to wrap his head around Doc's idea said, "It is something that can be done. At least we can turn ourselves back when we are finished. Let me think about it and I will let you know."

After Doc Langer left, Fredric sat down with Seth and Leona to discuss the situation.

A few hours later they decided that Fredric should contact Henry Radcliff.

Fredric stood up and went into another room where he was able to send his thoughts to Henry.

"Henry, you now know our position with regard to the commando situation. Do you think you are in a position to do what Doc Langer suggested? Could you get one hundred of your best disciples that would be willing to turn themselves into full vampires and fight the Confederate secret commandos? I believe these secret commandos are vampires brought over from Europe."

Henry said that he would need some time to talk with these men, "Fredric, this will not be easy."

"I know," Fredric answered, "but I do not believe there is any other way to fight them. If we lose, the north will lose. If we win, our disciples will have nothing but a long life ahead of them. We can turn all our men back into disciples when this is over. Talk to your disciples and get back to me as soon as possible."

"You will be hearing from me shortly," Henry replied.

A few days later Fredric received a message from Henry telling him that he has one hundred disciples who are willing to turn themselves into full vampires for our cause.

Fredric was very pleased and told Henry he would get in touch with him soon.

Using some of the powers that he had not used in many years, Fredric turned himself into a bat and flew to Cape Charles so he could meet with Henry Radcliff in person.

Shortly after they communicated, Fredric appeared in the warehouse and startled Henry. "I am Dr. Fredric Gruel, Seth's father. I hope I am not intruding, but I believe our problem is important enough for me to meet with you in person."

"You took me by surprise," Henry said. "Can I offer you a glass of your wine?"

"Thank you," Fredric said and then complimented him on his warehouse.

"Thank you," Henry replied, "this is all your wine," he said pointing to the stocked shelves.

"Seth has told me great things about you and I am pleased to finally meet you," Fredric said.

"You have a very devoted and dedicated son," Henry remarked. "Yes he is, thank you, but he still has a lot to learn."

Henry then told Fredric that he has the one hundred disciples ready for action.

"That's wonderful and we will need every one of them, Fredric replied while continuing to drink more of his wine, "You must understand the extreme importance of my visit; these secret commandos we are up against are real vampires. They kill at night; anywhere, any time and any one they please. They are vicious and have no respect for the law, but what is worse; they are led by my older brother, who would kill me the first chance he gets."

Fredric, suddenly having the need to tell Henry about his past continued, "I killed my father, Count Vladimir Gruel, who was a ruthless fiend. He and his armies wiped out towns and villages, killing and raping."

"When I was young I decided I would be different than my father and brother. I would study and go to the university and do some good. I studied about human blood and did research for many years until I was able to discover my blood substitute. I have not been in touch with my brother in over one hundred years and he has no idea that I have settled here and what I have been doing and that will be the big surprise."

I am here talking to you because I trust you. I must destroy my brother and his army in one night if the North is going to survive," he explained and then asked Henry, "Do you think you can find out where his army is located so we can plan our attack? This must be done without our being exposed; do you think that is possible?"

"Yes, Henry replied, and I think his camp is located in South Carolina, but I will find out exactly where as soon as I can and let you know."

"Now, let's make a toast to our success together," Fredric said as he raised his glass and then toasted to the beauty of life.

With that said, Fredric walked out of the warehouse. Henry then called out, "Wait Fredric, I'll be right there." By the time Henry went outside, Fredric was gone.

When Henry went back inside, he notified several of his lieutenants to be on the lookout for Ludwig Von Gruel's army.

Several days went by when one of Henry's Lieutenants notified him that Ludwig Von Gruel's camp was located high up in the Smokey Mountains away from any towns or cities.

Henry then reached out to Fredric to give him the information he had been waiting for.

Fredric was glad to hear from Henry so soon and he immediately arranged for a meeting between Seth, Doc Langer, Captain Ulrich and Henry at Henry's warehouse.

A serious problem arose when Doc asked Fredric, "How are we going to get to Henry's warehouse if we are only your disciples and do not have all your secretive powers?"

"I will turn you all into vampires until we wipe out my brother's army. When this is over I will turn you back, is that agreed?" he replied.

They all looked at each other and shook their heads. Doc Langer spoke for all of them, "If we do not stop your brother and his army now, he will have us all killed, so it is agreed. When do you want us to turn?" Fredric said he must tell Leona of his plans then he will start the process.

Seth stood up, "Let's drink some wine and raise our glasses to my father, Dr. Fredric Gruel, "To life and to the beauty of life." Fredric then added, "We have been together for a good many years and I intend for us to be together for hundreds, if not thousands more."

Fredric put his glass down and discussed his plan of attack.

"Once you all become full vampires we will join Henry and his volunteer army. We will then attack my brother and his army and put an end to their merciless crimes.

After agreeing how they would accomplish this, Fredric went up stairs to explain his plans to Leona.

"You do not have to explain anything to me," Leona said as she looked up at Fredric, "I understand." He kissed her and returned to the parlor.

"The first thing you must do is stop drinking my wine," Fredric said as he entered the parlor, "then we must wait several days until the wine has passed through your blood stream. Remember, you must continue to wear your protective glasses or you will die immediately if you go out into sunlight without them."

"Let's meet back here in three days. I will notify Henry and tell him what we are doing."

After the men left, Fredric told Seth, "I am very proud of you, son. This will be a great undertaking for you."

Seth was feeling uneasy about this mission and was beginning to feel that there was no future for him.

Fredric then placed his hand on Seth's shoulder and said, "Now, I would like you to spend the next few days, before we leave, with Lotada. Tell her how much you love her. We will all meet back here in three days."

Seth unenthusiastically went back to Lotada to tell her of Fredric's plans to annihilate his uncle and his army and that he would be leaving soon.

Seth seemed to be sinking into a profound depression since he came back from his trip to Cape Charles and he was becoming increasingly more suspicious of Lotada. For a long time he had been feeling that she was hiding something from him but he could not read into her mind. She was too clever for that to happen.

Lotada began to see changes in Seth. He was not showing any affection or displaying any of his usual playfulness. His attitude had changed for the worse. His hair was unruly and his demeanor was different.

On the third day, when he was about to leave for the raid, Seth found it very difficult to say good-bye to Lotada. He merely ignored her and left the house without saying a word. Lotada was terribly hurt and angry. "What has happened to Seth? Will he ever be the same again?" she wondered, "and did she even care?"

All the men met, one last time, in Fredric's parlor. Fredric, dressed in the black tuxedo that he always wore in Europe, asked, "Is every one ready?"

"Yes we are," they all answered.

"This will be a great undertaking for all of you," he said, "you will feel like you have never felt before. You will also have the powers of a full vampire and these powers are much greater than anything you could have imagined. You must use them well and not abuse them. You must think before you act. It is not difficult, just think from within."

Fredric and his men went outside. The night was still and the moon was full. He told the men to follow his thoughts. Then they all turned into Black Raven like figures and flew past the full moon. In a short time they flew from New Jersey to Henry Radcliff's warehouse in Cape Charles, Virginia.

When they arrived, Fredric looked at the men. They could not believe what they had just done, "I see you all made it," he said.

Henry was working in his office when the men walked in together. He looked up with a surprised look on his face, "I see you didn't waste any time getting here."

My men are here and my plan is ready. I want everyone to understand the importance of this surprise attack.

You must follow my rules:

1. There will be no communicating between us for fear of my brother intercepting our thoughts.
2. You must make sure that your men do not have wine to drink for at least three days.
3. The key to the success of this attack is total surprise.
4. Your men must have their colored glasses with them at all times.
5. Each man will carry five wooden stakes. These stakes will be thrust through the hearts of our enemy. That is the only way they will die.

6. No man shall attack until I give the signal
7. There will be no prisoners taken. They must all be killed, right down to the very last one.
8. My brother will be left for me to kill.

I want every one of your disciples ready by tomorrow afternoon.

THE BEGINNING OF THE END

Just then, there was a knock at the warehouse door. Henry stood up and opened the door slowly. There stood a well-dressed Union Army officer. "Who are you?" Henry asked.

"I am Lieutenant Colonel Jefferies of the Union Army sent here by General Grant to speak with Dr. Fredric Gruel."

"Who told you he was here?" Henry asked.

"I cannot reveal my source, but I know Dr. Gruel is inside your office and I must speak with him at once."

Henry, looking suspiciously at the officer said, "Stay here I will be right back."

Henry closed the door, went into the back office, and told Fredric, "An Officer Jeffries is waiting to speak to you with a message from General Grant."

Puzzled, Fredric said, "No one knows where we are except my wife, and Seth's wife, Lotada. Let him in, I will speak to him."

Henry let the officer in. He was dressed in the uniform of a Union Lieutenant Colonel and he walked right over to Fredric, "You must be Dr. Gruel?" he asked.

"Yes I am. How do you know about me and how did you find my location?"

The Lieutenant answered with a slight hesitation, "Why, everyone knows about the famous Count Gruel. Fredric looking directly at the officer said, "Count Von Gruel is dead. He was my father. I am Dr. Fredric Gruel. Who told you of my location?"

"General Grant sent me here to give you this message," the lieutenant replied.

"Why don't you wait here while I read the message?"

"Seth, Henry, Doc, come with me."

When the four men entered the back office, Fredric faced them saying, "Something is very wrong. Nobody knew were I was going and nobody knew when we were going to attack, not even General Grant. I think we found ourselves an imposter. I would like to move the attack date back, if he is an imposter and working with my brother, he would be looking for more time."

"What does the message from Grant say?' Doc asked.

"From General Grant to Dr. Fredric Gruel; I am aware of your impending attack. Please do not attack until Thursday evening of this week."

"I think I will agree to that request and keep Jeffries here with us," Fredric decided. "Why would you do something like that?" Seth asked.

"I do not think General Grant ever heard of a Lieutenant Colonel Jeffries," Fredric reasoned and then said, "I have an idea. Let's go back to the office and you must pay attention to what I say."

Back in the office Fredric talked to the Lieutenant, "You must be very tired from your long trip. When must you return?"

"At once sir," the young officer answered.

"Why don't you stay here through tomorrow? It will be morning soon and you can rest in the meantime," Fredric suggested.

"I really must be getting back, sir," the office replied.

"I agree to what Grant is asking but you can sleep for a couple of hours then leave in the morning, how's that?"

Jeffries replied, "I will stay the night as long as you agree that I can leave by tomorrow evening."

"A very wise decision, Fredric said, "Oh, by the way have you seen Lotada lately?" He asked.

Jeffries, caught off guard, said, "Why yes, I have."

"When was that?" Fredric asked. "Just the other day," the lieutenant replied.

When Jeffries realized that Fredric was probing his mind, he asked, "Do you also know that Indian girl from Washington?"

Seth then realized what Fredric was doing and said, "She's that Indian squaw that's dark and is very pretty and likes to fool around with Union soldiers?"

"Yes," the officer replied, "she's a real whore."

Seth, swallowing hard said, "Yes, she must be."

At this point Fredric said to Jeffries, "You can rest in there as he pointed to a small office, we will talk again later."

After Jeffries left the room Fredric said, "I think he's a vampire, and I'm sure he will be notifying my brother of our plans."

Fredric turned to Seth and told him to send a message to Lotada telling her of their change of plans and to sound very calm. "Instead of attacking in three days we will attack in four."

"What if you are wrong?" Doc asked.

"I do not think I am but we will find out tomorrow," Fredric said.

The next day the sun was shining brightly when Fredric walked into the Lieutenant's room, "Good morning Lieutenant. Since you are a high rank, would you like to inspect my troops?"

Jeffries looked at Fredric in a strange way, and then said, "I am not feeling well. It must be the trip yesterday. Perhaps I can inspect them in the evening before I leave?"

Fredric said that would be fine, knowing why he did not want to go outside.

A few hours later Seth walked into the warehouse, "I heard there was new movement by Southern troops. I wonder if the Lieutenant knows anything about this."

"Why don't you go in and find out?" Fredric suggested. "Okay, I will."

When Seth walked into the room, the Lieutenant was putting on his uniform. Seth asked, "Have you heard about any Southern troop movement?"

The officer answered that he had not and asked where this was happening. "About ten miles north of here and I would like you to take a ride with me, maybe we can see something," Seth advised.

Jeffries appeared very nervous about going with Seth, "You know Seth, I have a tendency of getting a bad burn from the sunlight if I stay in it too long."

"We won't be that long and I have special glasses that will protect you from the sun. Let's go, I'll get the buckboard ready."

When Seth left the room the Lieutenant continued to dress and then walked into Henry's office, "That sleep really helped but I don't feel that I should be going outside."

Seth walked back in saying, "Well Lieutenant, the buckboard is ready, let's go."

"What about the special glasses you told me about?" he asked.

"Oh, yes I almost forgot." The Lieutenant put on the glasses before going outside and told Seth, "This is a brilliant idea. Who thought of this?"

"Well, as you know we are vampires and cannot go out in sunlight. In order to survive during the day we wear these glasses. If Ludwig ever found out about this he could rule the world," Seth professed.

Jeffries then slipped and said, "I know what you mean, he'd jump right on this."

Seth then asked him to tell him more about the Indian Lotada.

"She's beautiful and what a bite she has when making love. Once she bit my neck, so hard I started to bleed. I was told that she has a hold on a number of high-ranking Union officers. Sometimes when I am by myself I can feel her in my mind as if she was talking to me, then I answer her."

"When are you going back to Washington?" Seth asked.

"Tonight, Jeffries answered, "It's strange, I could swear that I heard her voice asking me about the attack, so I told her in four days.

"That's great," Seth said as he pulled the protective glasses off the Lieutenant's eyes and pushed him off the wagon. When he landed along side of the wagon, he screamed out to Seth, "What are you doing?"

Seth then stood on top of the wagon and watched as Jeffries body began to burn and he shouted for the last time, "What have you done to me?"

Seth said with a grin, "That Indian, Lotada, she's my wife," as he continued to watch Jeffries body slowly disintegrate.

Seth, feeling betrayed by Lotada, drove the wagon back to Henry's warehouse with a heavy heart. When he entered, Fredric, Henry, and Doc Langer were waiting. No one spoke; they just looked at Seth, waiting for him to say something.

Finally Seth spoke, "Father, you were right about Jeffries, he was a vampire, but what should I do about Lotada?"

"Nothing," Fredric said, "not until this is over. I am positive that my brother thinks we will now attack in four days, instead we will attack in three."

"Henry, did your men finish making the wooden stakes?" Fredric asked. "Yes," he replied. "Good, we will distribute them to your men tonight and I will have your men turn themselves into Ravens and fly to the bottom of the Smokey Mountain trails which will lead to Ludwig's camp and then we will wait."

That evening Fredric and Seth stood outside the warehouse with Henry, Doc and Captain Ulrich and watched his men assemble.

Seth told Fredric, "I heard that all of Ludwig's men were back in their camp. Now is the time to attack."

Fredric turned to his men and began to speak, "Men, the situation we are in is critical. We are all here for a common cause, our survival. I promised you eternal life, but this is what it has come down to, them or us. The armies of the south have brought armies of true fighting vampires from Eastern Europe led by my older brother, Ludwig. His greatest pleasure would be to see us all dead. It is up to us to stop this plague of barbarianism before they take over our country. I made arrangements with top northern generals that we will not be disturbed or prosecuted for what we are about to do today or for what we are. We are all fighting for a common cause and we must win. We cannot afford to lose. Now let's go."

Fredric then turned himself into a Raven and started to fly. All of his men followed, flying together making a high-pitched sound that only they could hear. They flew past the full moon to the lower paths of the Smokey Mountains and upon their landing turned back into vampires.

As the sun began to rise, Fredric had his men secure their protective sunglasses and gather in a small clearing.

He showed them how to kill using the wooden stakes. Before embarking on their task, Fredric made sure that each man had a stake with him and his protective glasses were secure over their eyes.

He explained that the success of this mission was based on total surprise. "I do not know exactly where or how they are sleeping, but the element of surprise is the key."

Then Fredric waved them on and they all marched up the side of the mountain.

It took longer than expected to reach the caves where Ludwig's army was sleeping and Fredric was afraid that the sun would set before he could accomplish his task.

When they arrived at the top of the mountain, they noticed that this army of vampires was divided into three separate caves that kept them out of the sun's rays.

Fredric decided to break up his men into three groups with guards standing on the outside of each cave to prevent any of Ludwig's men from escaping.

Fredric's men were very cautious when entering each cave.

Taking one third of his men with him, Fredric entered the first cave, as Seth entered the second and Henry and Doc silently entered the third with their men.

Fredric's men were the first to come upon the vampires lying in their coffins with the lids open. The men took their positions as they waited for Fredric's signal to plunge their wooden stakes into the hearts of the sleeping vampires.

Fredric took a moment to look around, hoping to find his brother's coffin. When he could not find it he decided to go ahead with staking the other vampires before it was too late.

Fredric took a stake and plunged it into the heart of a vampire as his men watched in silence. He then took another stake and plunged it through the heart of another. This vampire immediately grabbed hold of the stake. His eyes opened and he tried to sit up as a strange substance began to flow from his mouth, eyes and ears. He made moaning sounds until Fredric pulled out the stake only to plunge it in a second time and hold it in until the vampire stopped moving.

Then Fredric's men, following his lead, took their stake and plunged it through the hearts of the other vampires as they lay in their coffins. Some of them tried to escape but Fredric's men were able to subdue them.

Once there was no more movement in each coffin, Fredric ordered his men to drag them out into the sunlight.

The men watched in horror as the vampires burnt and disintegrated right before their eyes.

With the vampires from the first cave all dead, Fredric went back in to search again for his brother until he was convinced he was not in there.

Seth, along with his men, found more vampires lying in their coffins wearing Confederate uniforms. Then he gave the order to plunge the stakes through their hearts.

The sleeping vampires reacted by trying to pull the stakes out of their quivering bodies, to no avail. Then Seth motioned to his men to drag the coffins, with the dead vampires lying in them, into the sunlight to burn and disintegrate.

Fredric ordered the men to wait outside the second cave while he went in to search for his brother's body. After a short while he emerged with a look of disappointment on his face. "He must be in there," he said.

"Doc and Henry are in that cave, why don't you wait for them to come out," suggested Seth. "It might be too late, I must go in now," Fredric said as he reentered the second cave.

He could hear the grunts and moans coming from the vampires as his men continued to thrust stakes through their hearts.

As Fredric walked further into the cave, he heard the sound of a bat fluttering around in the back end of the cave. He was extra cautious as he continued to walk. He called out, "I know it's you Ludwig, I can smell you and feel your evil."

The sound stopped and a voice came from the back of the cave, "Turn back brother, I do not wish to harm you. Go now and I will leave you and your armies alone."

With anger in his voice, Fredric called back, "I have come here to kill you the same way I killed our father. You will not scour the earth any longer murdering innocent people. Then there was silence as Fredric sensed two objects coming towards him. The first one missed but the second one pierced through Fredric's heart. He screamed so loud that it echoed throughout the entire mountainside.

Everyone outside turned towards the entrance of the second cave.

Fredric walked out into the sunlight, holding his hands against his chest. He fell to the ground and looked up at Seth, "Take my ring; you will make a great leader, my son." His body then burned and disintegrated.

Seth, overwhelmed with grief, knew he had to kill Ludwig. He rushed into the cave and walked deeper and deeper into its bowels until he heard a voice, "Seth, I am distraught that we are meeting under these circumstances and I am sorry about the demise of your father, but he gave me no choice. I would like you to join forces with me, and we can rule the world together, what do you think?"

Seth, trying to sound as enthusiastic as possible, said, "Now that my father is gone, uncle, that sounds like a good idea."

"Let me show myself to you so we can talk some more."

"Yes, make yourself visible uncle; I would like to meet you."

Ludwig walked out from the darkness of the back of the cave and put his arms out to embrace Seth, when Seth totally surprised Ludwig and thrust a wooden stake through his heart. He watched him as he screamed in pain and tried to pull the stake out. Seth picked up another stake from the ground and plunged that stake through Ludwig's heart as well, causing an excessive amount of blood to shoot from Ludwig's mouth, eyes and ears as he fell to his knees looking up at Seth.

Seth grabbed him by his hair, dragged him outside the cave into the sunlight as everyone watched him burn, and slowly disintegrate.

After witnessing Ludwig's death, something strange happened; all the men from Fredric's army lined up with Captain Ulrich, Doc Langer and Henry Radcliff and one after the other formed a single line, took Seth's hand, knelt before him and kissed his ring as the sun set and the moon began to rise.

After the last disciple kissed Seth's ring, Seth looked up, "I am your leader now but I do not want anyone to forget my father; he was a good and brave man. Before you go back to your homes, I want you all to start drinking my father's wine again so you can continue to live your eternal lives. When you make your toast, please do not forget to say, "To life and to the beauty of life," because from here on, it will be just that."

Everything that had just happened seemed so surreal as the captain, Doc and Seth transformed themselves back into ravens and headed towards their homes in Edgewater.

When Seth arrived home, he immediately went to see his mother. He knew that she felt his father's death as sure as if she was with him in the cave. He wanted to tell her of the love he had for his father. "Mother, I would like to apologize for all the wrong I did, but my intentions were only to make you and father proud of me."

Leona grievingly said, "I will never forget your father, he will always be in my heart and mind. Seth, be assured that your father and I were always proud of you and I know your father will be looking after us as we move on to the future."

Seth then gave Leona a kiss on her far head, "I will always be here to protect you, mother as long as I have breath in my body."

DENISE FINISHES HER STORY

Seth left Leona's house to go home to face Lotada. He entered the house but could not find her on the first floor. He quietly jumped to the second floor and found her sitting by a window. Surprised to see Seth alive, she asked, "How did you manage to escape your uncle and his armies?" Repulsed by the site of her, he said "Maybe you should explain to me everything you told Lieutenant Jeffries and all the other Union officers that you have been spending your time with. Just tell me, how could you have done this to my family, and why would you do this to me?"

Lotada looked at Seth with hatred, "That was for my father's death. I have not loved you since you murdered him. I now have my revenge and I want you to stay away from me."

Seth, seething with anger told her, "I will make you pay for this for as many years as you breathe, do you understand?"

Seth, in his madness, pulled the door off its hinges as he left the bedroom and his house for the last time.

As the years went by and the century past, Seth continued to keep an eye on Lotada, just to make sure that she did not do anything foolish. Her beauty never changed and there was still a small part of him that did still love her.

BACK IN THE PRESENT

"I find this story very hard to believe," I told her.

"Ron, I know that it's true because I was there," Denise said.

"What do you mean, you were there?"

"You see, I am Lotada and Heidi is Seth's mother, Leona. We were both there. After the massacre of the five hundred vampires, everyone involved was sworn to secrecy by the President of the United States, Abraham Lincoln and then again by President Grant. As the years went by, the incumbent Presidents and the Secret Service only knew our secrets. Our existence has never been divulged."

"The reason you were brought here is because Seth found out that you are single and have a background working in a laboratory, but most important, you will not be missed. In addition, Seth was looking for a new, independent leader for our East Coast disciples. He interviewed hundred of men before you were selected."

"Ron, you should consider yourself honored," Denise continued, "Seth recently found out that one of our disciples went rogue and is creating a new group of true vampires. I know he does not know who it is. I also know that Seth has purchased two wineries in Northern California and he has already begun planting wine grapes for his expansion."

"Do you have any idea who this person might be?" I asked.

"Yes I do, but I cannot say now. I do know that the winery in Edgewater has been tampered with. That is why there is so much panic in the building."

I stood up and grabbed Denise's arms, "What does Seth want from me?"

"You are being turned into a vampire, as we speak," she said as she pulled away from my grip.

333

"I don't believe you."

"Go look in the mirror, tell me what you see," Denise said, "and then walk out onto the terrace and tell me how you feel."

I ran to the bathroom to look at myself in the mirror, and I only saw a partial reflection. I then ran onto the terrace and as soon as the sun hit my body I felt myself burning and I ran back inside.

"Do you believe me now?" Denise asked. "You are practically turned and you cannot fight it. Join me and you will have immortality forever."

"You are the one causing all of this to happen," I said.

"Yes I am, Ron, Join with me now and I will see that you have everything you ever wanted, plus me. We can be together and rule the world."

Revolted by her offer I told her, "I don't want to rule the world. I like things the way they were two weeks ago. I enjoyed my freedom. This is not what I came here for. I want out."

"The only way out is death, is that what you want? Think of what I am offering you."

I walked around the room for a while then concluded that I had no choice. Reluctantly I said, "Okay, I will go with you."

Denise walked over to me and gave me a kiss, "We must hurry before Seth finds us. Here, put these glasses on, let's go."

The elevator door opened and we both stepped in and waited for it to arrive at the lobby, but instead, when the door opened, Seth, Doc Langer and a few of their disciples entered the elevator and grabbed us.

Seth told Denise, "You hurt me a long time ago and I let you get away with it, but this time you won't."

As the elevator went further down to the basement, the door opened and we all began walking towards the laboratory.

"It is most unfortunate, Ron, that you became involved in this, Seth said looking directly at me, but I knew all along what Denise was up to." Seth then told Doc Langer, "Take her to the laboratory, I will be right there."

I watched as the disciples held tightly on to Denise's arms as they brought her into the laboratory. Just then, using her strength, she broke away throwing two of the disciples holding her, across the laboratory, breaking many of the Petri dishes and blood contamination jars. Then turning herself into a bat she flew out through the back door into the tunnels underneath the apartment house.

By the time the disciples notified Seth, it was too late. Denise had already escaped.

Seth was visibly upset. Only he knew what could happen if Denise was able to start her own cult of vampires.

Seth called out, "Pauly, Doc, Captain, take a few disciples with you and bring her back. I want to destroy her myself. I am taking Ron upstairs to talk to him."

As Doc Langer and the rest of the disciples left to look for Denise, Seth took me back to the penthouse where he offered me more wine. I declined, then Seth said, "If you do not drink the wine the chances are very good that you will turn into a full vampire, at which time I would be forced to kill you. Now what will it be?"

"Are there any other alternatives?" I asked.

"None," Seth said, "this is the only time I will ask you to reconsider, and the choice is yours. If you decide to be one of us, you will be working directly with Doc Langer and Heidi."

"You mean your mother?" I asked.

"I see Denise told you. What else did she tell you about me?"

"She told me how your father wanted to do some good in this world and he wanted you to do the same. She also told me how you killed her father and she has never forgiven you for that."

I could see the concern on Seth's face as he continued to pace around the living room. Then he turned to me, "Ron, tell me, have you made up your mind yet?"

"Yes, I will join you."

Seth, putting out his hand, said, "Let's make a toast together."

I raised my glass to Seth's as he said, "To life and to the beauty of life," then added, "and to the future of life." We then clicked our glasses.

I could feel the power of Seth's mind trying to reach into mine as my thoughts went blank and I must have passed out.

I awoke a few hours later when Doc Langer arrived back at the penthouse and told Seth, "We were unable to find Denise. She must still be hiding somewhere in the building,"

"Get as many disciples together as you can, and notify the outer guards," Seth ordered. "Denise must be prevented from leaving."

Several more hours past, the sun was starting to set and the moon was beginning to rise. Doc Langer and Pauly came back to the penthouse, "I think she might have escaped, the body of a man was found not to far from here, he was drained of all his blood."

Seth turned to me and asked, "Ron, tell me the truth, did she give you any hint as to what her intentions were? You did spend time alone with her, didn't you?"

"I am as surprised as you, she said nothing," I told him, "I had no idea what she was doing to me and if you could turn me back to being a mortal, I will not tell a sole about you and your disciples. Just leave me on a street somewhere, anywhere."

Seth, ignoring what I was saying told Pauly, "You stay here with Ron and give him more wine to drink. I do not want another full vampire on my hands. Is that understood?"

"Yes master," Pauly answered.

Seth and Doc Langer went to the lobby and asked Sal, "Have you seen Denise?"

"No, but I did see Ellen go out towards the pool several hours ago and she has not come back yet."

"If you see either of them, let me know at once."

Seth then went back down to the laboratory. When the door slid open, Seth and Doc Langer were startled to hear what they thought was the sound of a bat deep inside the tunnel.

"Stay here until I return." Seth then turned himself into a bat and flew down the tunnel in the direction of the sound that he had heard. He knew that if Denise turned herself into a full vampire she would have the same powers as him. Seth moved through the tunnel cautiously. Then suddenly he saw the red eyes of a bat staring at him. He immediately sent two laser beams from his eyes hitting the bat. He heard a loud screech as it fell to the ground. He then turned himself back and ran over to what he thought would be Denise. Instead, it was a real bat. Denise, in fact, had escaped.

Seth went back to the elevator where Doc Langer was waiting for him. Pauly and Ron and then the captain joined them. "We just found another body of a young woman with her blood drained. What do you want us to do?" The captain asked.

Seth thought for a moment then told Pauly to bring the limo around the front. "We are going to the winery," he said.

When Pauly left, Seth told Doc Langer and me, "We now have a second full vampire to deal with." I asked who he meant. "Ellen, she has joined with Denise. Let's go to her apartment and see if she left anything behind."

When we entered Ellen's apartment we saw the wine cabinet open and all the bottles of wine missing. The picture of Seth was now leaning against the couch, slit from end to end.

We then went back up to the penthouse and found all the bottles of Seth's wine missing from his wine cabinets also.

Seth told Doc, "They had been planning this for a long time and will probably use the wine to create their own disciples. We must go to the plant at once and notify Bob Stillwell that Denise and Ellen must be stopped because they know too much. They will multiply until the United States and then the world could possibly be taken over."

When the limo pulled up in front of the lobby, Pauly held the door open as Doc Langer, Seth and I sat in the back.

Pauly slowly walked around to the front driver's side, slid in, and began to drive away.

I turned my head to look through the rear window only to see two vampire bats sitting in a tree across from the lobby.

I watched, in disbelief, as they turned themselves back into the bodies of Denise and Ellen.

They smirked at me, and then looked up at the full moon.

WARNING
BEWARE!

The next bottle of red wine you drink may
be Fredric's *Special* wine.

So let us make a toast...

"To life and to the beauty of life"

THE BEGINNING

www.ingramcontent.com/pod-product-compliance
Lightning Source LLC
Chambersburg PA
CBHW062017170626
46813CB00001B/195